Red Clay, Blue Cadillac

Stories of Twelve Southern Women

by
Michael Malone

SOURCEBOOKS LANDMARK™
AN IMPRINT OF SOURCEBOOKS, INC.®
NAPERVILLE, ILLINOIS

Published by Sourcebooks, Inc.
P.O. Box 4410, Naperville, Illinois 60567-4410
(630) 961-3900
FAX: (630) 961-2168
www.sourcebooks.com

Library of Congress Cataloging-in-Publication Data
Malone, Michael.
  Red clay, blue Cadillac : twelve Southern women / by Michael Malone.
      p. cm.
  ISBN 1-57071-824-5 (alk. paper)
  1. Southern States—Social life and customs—Fiction. 2.Women—Southern States—Fiction. I. Title.
  PS3563.A43244 R43 2002
  813'.54—dc21

                                    2001054287

Printed and bound in the United States of America
        LB 10 9 8 7 6 5 4 3 2 1

For
Otto Penzler

The Rising of the South and Flonnie Rogers first appeared in *Viva*; the character of Flonnie Rogers later appeared in the novel *Handling Sin*.

Fast Love appeared in *Mademoiselle* and in *O. Henry Prize Stories*.

Blue Cadillac first appeared in *Playboy*.

Winners and Losers appeared in a different version titled "High School Losers" in *Partisan Review*.

Red Clay first appeared in *Murder for Love*, published by Delacorte. It won the 1997 Edgar Allan Poe Award from the Mystery Writers of America. It appeared in *Best American Mystery Stories*, Houghton Mifflin, 1998; in *Best American Mystery Stories of the Century*, Houghton Mifflin, 2000, and in *Best Suspense Stories of the Century*, Berkeley, 2001.

Love and Other Crimes first appeared in *Criminal Records*, Orion, 2000.

Invitation to the Ball first appeared in *Murder and Obsession*, Delacorte, 1998.

Maniac Loose first appeared in *A Confederacy of Crime*, NAL, 2000.

The Power first appeared in *Murderers Row*, Millennium Press, 2001.

CONTENTS

Red Clay, Blue Cadillac

Stella

Red Clay

Up on its short slope, the columned front of our courthouse was waxy in the August sun, like a courthouse in lake water. The leaves hung from maples, and the flag of North Carolina wilted flat against its metal pole. Heat sat sodden over the county week by relentless week; they called the weather "dog days" after the star, Sirius, but none of us knew that. We thought they meant no dog would leave shade for the street on such days—no dog except a mad one. I was ten that late August in 1959; I remembered the summer because of the long heat wave, and because of Stella Doyle.

We waited a long time. When finally they pushed open the doors, the policemen and lawyers hurrying out of them flung their arms up to their faces to block the sun and stopped there in the doorway as if the hot light were shoving them back inside. Stella Doyle came out last, a deputy on either side to walk her down to where the patrol car, orange as Halloween candles, waited to take her away until the jury could make up its mind about what had happened two months earlier out at Red Hills. It was the only house in the county big enough to have a name. It was where Stella Doyle had, maybe, shot her husband Hugh Doyle to death.

Excitement over Doyle's murder had swarmed through the town and stung us alive. No thrill would replace it until the assassination of John Kennedy. Outside the courthouse, sidewalk heat steaming up through our shoes, we stood impatiently waiting to hear Mrs. Doyle found guilty. The news stood waiting too, for she was, after all, not merely the murderer of the wealthiest man we knew; she was Stella Doyle. She was the movie star.

Papa's hand squeezed down on my shoulder and there was a tight line to his mouth as he pulled me into the crowd and said, "Listen now, Buddy, if anybody ever asks you when you're grown, 'Did you ever see the most beautiful woman God made in your lifetime?' Son, you say, 'Yes, I had that luck and her name was Stella Dora Doyle.'" His voice got louder, right there in the crowd for everybody to hear. "You tell them how her beauty was so bright it burned back the shame they tried to heap on her head, burned it right on back to scorch their faces."

Papa spoke these strange words in a strange loud voice, looking up the steps at the woman in black that the deputies were holding. Papa's arms were folded over his seersucker vest, his fingers tight on the sleeves of his shirt. People around us had turned to stare and somebody snickered.

Embarrassed for him, I whispered, "Oh Papa, she's nothing but an old murderer. Everybody knows how she got drunk and killed Mr. Doyle. She shot him right through the head with a gun."

Papa frowned. "You don't know that."

I kept on. "Everybody says she was so bad and drunk all the time, she wouldn't let his folks even live in their own house with her. She made him throw out his mama and papa."

My father shook his head at me. "I don't like to hear ugly gossip coming out of your mouth, all right, Buddy?"

"Yes, sir."

"She didn't kill Hugh Doyle."

"Yes, sir."

His frown scared me; it was so rare. I stepped closer and took his hand, took his stand against the rest. I had no loyalty to this woman Papa thought so beautiful. I just could never bear to be cut loose from the safety of his good opinion. I suppose from that moment on, I felt toward Stella Doyle something of what my father felt, though in the end perhaps she meant less to me, and stood for more. Papa never had my habit of symbolizing.

The courthouse steps were wide, uneven stone slabs. As Mrs. Doyle came down them, the buzzing of the crowd hushed. All together, like trained dancers, people stepped back to clear a half-circle around the orange patrol car. Newsmen shoved their cameras to the front. She was rushed down so fast that her shoe caught in the crumbling stone and she fell against one of the deputies.

"She's drunk!" hooted a woman near me, a country woman in a flowered dress belted with a strip of painted rope. She and the child she jiggled against her shoulder were puffy with the fat of poverty. "Look'it her"—the woman pointed—"look at that dress. She thinks she's still out there in Hollywood." The woman beside her nodded, squinting out from under the visor of the kind of hat pier fishermen wear. "I went and killed my husband, wouldn't no rich lawyers come running to weasel me out of the law." She slapped at a fly's buzz.

Then they were quiet and everybody else was quiet and our circle of sun-stunned eyes fixed on the woman in black, stared at the wonder of one as high as Mrs. Doyle about to be brought so low.

Holding to the stiff, tan arm of the young deputy, Mrs. Doyle reached down to check the heel of her shoe. Black shoes, black suit and purse, wide black hat—they all sinned against us by their fashionableness, blazing wealth as well as death. She stood there, arrested a moment in the hot immobility of the air, then she hurried down, rushing the two big deputies down with her, to the open door of the orange patrol car. Papa stepped forward so quickly that the gap filled with people before I could follow him. I squeezed through, fighting with my elbows, and I saw that he was holding his white straw hat in one hand and offering the other hand out to the murderer. "Stella, how are you? Clayton Hayes."

As she turned, I saw the strawberry gold hair beneath the hat; her hand, bright with a big diamond, took away the dark glasses. I saw what Papa meant. She was beautiful. Her eyes were the color of lilacs, but darker than lilacs. And her skin held the light like the inside of a shell. She was not like other pretty women, because the difference was not one of degree. I have never seen anyone else of her kind.

"Why, Clayton! God Almighty, it's been years."

"Well, yes, a long time now, I guess," he said and shook her hand.

She took the hand in both of hers. "You look the same as ever. Is this your boy?" The violet eyes turned to me.

"Yes, this is Buddy. Ada and I have six so far, three of each."

"Six? Are we that old?" She smiled. "They said you'd married Ada Hackney."

A deputy cleared his throat. "Sorry, Clayton, we're going to have to get going."

"Just a minute, Lonnie. Listen, Stella, I just wanted you to know I'm sorry as I can be about your losing Hugh."

Tears welled in her eyes. "He did it himself, Clayton," she said.

"I know that. I know you didn't do this." Papa nodded slowly again and again, the way he did when he was listening. "I know that. Good luck to you."

She swatted tears away. "Thank you."

"I'm telling everybody I'm sure of that."

"Clayton, thank you."

Papa nodded again, then tilted his head back to give her his slow, peaceful smile. "You call Ada and me if there's ever something we can do to help you, you hear?" She kissed his cheek and he stepped back with me into the crowd of hostile, avid faces as she entered the police car. It moved slow as the sun through the sightseers. Cameras pushed against its windows.

A sallow man biting a pipe skipped down the steps to join some other reporters next to us. "Jury sent out for food," he told them. "No telling with these yokels. Could go either way." He pulled off his jacket and balled it under his arm. "Jesus, it's hot."

A younger reporter with thin, wet hair disagreed. "They all think Hollywood's Babylon and she's the whore. Hugh Doyle was the local prince, his daddy kept the mills open in the bad times, quote unquote half the rednecks in the county. They'll fry her. For that hat if nothing else."

"Could go either way," grinned the man with the pipe. "She was born in a shack six miles from here. Hat or no hat, that makes her one of them. So what if she did shoot the guy, he was dying of cancer anyhow, for Christ sake. Well, she never could act worth the price of a bag of popcorn, but Jesus damn she was something to look at!"

Now that Stella Doyle was gone, people felt the heat again and went back to where they could sit still in the shade until the evening breeze and wait for the jury's decision. Papa and I walked back down Main Street to our furniture store. Papa owned a butcher shop too, but he didn't like the meat business and wasn't very good at it, so my oldest brother ran it while Papa sat among the mahogany bedroom suites and red maple dining room sets in a big rocking chair and read, or talked to friends who dropped by. The rocker was actually for sale, but he had sat in it for so long now that it was just Papa's chair. Three ceiling fans stirred against the quiet shady air while he answered my questions about Stella Doyle.

He said that she grew up Stella Dora Hibble on Route 19, in a three-room, tin-roofed little house propped above the red clay by concrete blocks—the kind of saggy-porched pinewood house whose owners leave on display in their dirt yards, like sculptures, the broken artifacts of their aspirations and the debris of their unmendable lives: the doorless refrigerator and the rusting car, the pyre of metal and plastic that tells drivers along the highway, "Dreams don't last."

Stella's mother, Dora Hibble, believed in dreams anyhow. Dora had been a pretty girl who'd married a farmer and worked harder than she had the health for, because hard work was necessary just to keep from going under. But in the evenings Mrs.

Hibble had looked at movie magazines. She had believed that romance was out there and she wanted it, if not for her, for her children. At twenty-seven, she died during her fifth labor. Stella was eight when she watched from the door of the bedroom as they covered her mother's face with a thin blanket. When Stella was fourteen, her father died when a machine jammed at Doyle Mills. When Stella was sixteen, Hugh Doyle Jr., who was her age, my father's age, fell in love with her.

"Did you love her too, Papa?"

"Oh yes. All us boys in town were crazy about Stella Doyle, one time or another. I had my attack of it, same as the rest. We were sweethearts in seventh grade. I bought a big-size Whitman's Sampler on Valentine's. I remember it cost every cent I had."

"Why were y'all crazy about her?"

"I guess you'd have to worry you'd missed out on being alive if you didn't feel that way about Stella one time or another."

I was feeling a terrible emotion I later defined as jealousy. "But didn't you love Mama?"

"Well, now, this was before it was my luck to get to know your mama."

"And you met her coming to town along the railroad track and you told all your friends, 'That's the girl for me and I'm going to marry her,' didn't you?"

"Yes, sir, and I was right on both counts." Papa rocked back in the big chair, his hands peaceful on the armrests.

"Was Stella Dora still crazy about you after you met Mama?"

His face crinkled into the lines of his ready laughter. "No, sir, she wasn't. She loved Hugh Doyle minute she laid eyes on him. And he felt the same. But Stella had this notion about going off to get to be somebody in the movies. And Hugh couldn't hold her back, and I guess she couldn't get him to see what it was made her want to go off so bad either."

"What was it made her want to go?"

Papa smiled at me. "Well, I don't know, son. What makes you want to go off so bad? You're always saying you're going here and going there, 'cross the world, up to the moon. I reckon you're more like Stella than I am."

"Do you think she was wrong to want to go be in the movies?"

"No."

"You don't think she killed him?"

"No, sir, I don't."

"Somebody killed him."

"Well, Buddy, sometimes people lose hope and heart and feel like they can't go on living."

"Yeah, I know. Suicide."

Papa's shoes tapped the floor as the rocker creaked back and forth. "That's right. Now you tell me, why're you sitting in here? Why don't you ride your bike on over to the ballpark and see who's there?"

"I want to hear about Stella Doyle."

"You want to hear. Well. Let's go get us a Coca-Cola then. I don't guess somebody's planning to show up in this heat to buy a chest of drawers they got to haul home."

"You ought to sell air conditioners, Papa. People would buy air conditioners."

"Think so? Well, you're probably right."

So Papa told me his story. Or at least his version of it. He said Hugh and Stella were meant for each other. From the beginning it had seemed to the whole town a fact as natural as harvest that so much money and so much beauty belonged together. Only Hugh Doyle with his long, free, easy stride was rich enough to match the looks of Stella Dora. But even Hugh Doyle couldn't hold her. He was only halfway through the state university where his father had told him he'd have to go before he married Stella if he wanted a home to bring her to, when she quit her job at Coldstream's beauty parlor and took the bus to California. She was out there for six years before Hugh broke down and went after her.

By then every girl in the county was cutting Stella's pictures out of the movie magazines and reading how she got her lucky break, how she married a big director, and divorced him, and married a big star, and how that marriage broke up even quicker. Photographers traveled all the way to Thermopylae to take pictures of where she was born. People tried to tell them her house was gone, had fallen down and been used for firewood, but they just took photographs of Reverend Ballister's house instead and said Stella had grown up in it. Before long, even local girls would go stand in front of the Ballister house like a shrine, sometimes they'd steal flowers out of the yard. The year that *Fever*, her best movie, came to the Grand Theater on Main Street, Hugh Doyle flew out to Los Angeles and won her back. He took her down to Mexico to divorce the businessman she'd married after the big star. Then Hugh married her himself and put her on an ocean liner and took her all over the world. Afterwards, he came back with her to Hollywood and played tennis and poker while she made movies. Two years later, they came home to Thermopylae. Everybody in the county called it Hugh's two-year honeymoon. Hugh Sr. confessed to some friends that he was disgusted by his son's way of life.

When the couple did come home, Hugh walked right into the mills and turned a profit. His father told the same friends that he was flabbergasted Hugh had it in him. But after the father died, Hugh started drinking, and when she wasn't in Hollywood, Stella joined him. A few more years and she wasn't in Hollywood as much. The parties at Red Hills turned a little wild. The fights grew louder. People talked. They said he had other women, she had other men. They said Stella'd been locked up in a sanitarium for drinkers. They said the Doyles were breaking up.

And then one June day a maid at Red Hills, walking to work before the morning heat, fell over something that lay across a path to the stables. And it was Hugh in riding clothes with a bloody hole in the side of his head. Not far from his gloved hand, the police found Stella's pistol, already too hot from the sun to touch. The cook testified that the Doyles had been fighting like cats and dogs all night long the night before, and Hugh's mother testified that he wanted to divorce Stella, but Stella had said she'd kill him before she'd let him, and so Stella was arrested. She told the police she was innocent, but it was her gun, she was his heir, and she had no alibi. Her trial lasted almost as long as that August heat wave.

• • •

A neighbor strolled past our porch, where we sat out the evening heat, waiting for the air to lift. "Jury's still out," he said. Mama waved her hand at him. She pushed herself and me in the big green wood swing that hung from two chains to the porch roof as she answered my questions about Stella Doyle. "Oh yes, they all said Stella was 'specially pretty. I never knew her much to talk myself."

"But if Papa liked her so much, why didn't y'all get invited out to their house and everything?"

"Her and your papa just went to school together, that's all. That was a long time back. Rich folks like the Doyles wouldn't ask folks like us over to Red Hills."

"Why not? Papa's family used to have a whole lot of money. That's what you said. And Papa went right up to her at the courthouse today, right in front of everybody. He told her, 'You let us know if there's something we can do.'"

Mama chuckled the way she always did about Papa, a low ripple like a pigeon nesting, a little exasperated at having to sit still so long. "You know your papa'd try to help out anybody he figured be in trouble, white or black. That's just him, that's not any Stella Dora Doyle. Your papa's just a good man. You remember that, Buddy."

Goodness was Papa's stock in trade; it was what he had instead of money or ambition, and Mama often reminded us of it. In him she kept safe all the kindness she had never felt she could afford for herself. She, who could neither read nor write, who had stood all day in a cigarette factory from the age of eight until the morning Papa married her, was a fighter. She wanted her children to go farther than she and Papa had. Still, for years after he died, she would carry down from the attic the yellow, mildewed ledgers where his value was recorded in almost $100,000 of out-of-date bills he had been unwilling to force people in trouble to pay. Running her sun-spotted finger down the brittle wisps of names and the money they owed, she would sigh that proud, exasperated sigh and shake her head over foolish, generous Papa.

Through the front parlor windows that night I could hear two of my sisters practicing the theme from *The Apartment* on the piano. Someone across the street turned on a light. Then we heard the sound of Papa's shoes coming a little faster than usual down the sidewalk. He turned at the hedge carrying the package of shiny butcher's paper in which he brought meat home every evening. "Verdict just came in!" he called out happily. "Not guilty! Jury came back about forty minutes ago. They already took her home."

Mama put the package on a chair and sat Papa down in the swing next to her. "Well, well," she said. "They let her off."

"Never ought to have come up for trial in the first place, Ada, like I told everybody all along. It's like her lawyers showed. Hugh went down to Atlanta, saw that doctor, found out he had cancer, and he took his own life. Stella never even knew he was sick."

Mama patted his knee. "Not guilty. Well, well."

Papa made a noise of disgust. "Can you believe some folks out on Main tonight are all fired up because Stella got off? Adele Simpson acted downright indignant!"

Mama said, "And you're surprised?" And she shook her head with me at Papa's innocence.

Talking of the trial, my parents made one shadow along the wood floor of the porch, while inside my sisters played endless variations of "Chopsticks," the notes handed down by ghostly creators long passed away.

A few weeks after the verdict, Papa was invited to Red Hills and he let me come along. We brought jars of fruit jams Mama had made for Mrs. Doyle.

As soon as Papa drove past the wide white gate, I learned how money could change even weather. It was cooler at Red Hills, and the grass was the greenest grass in the county. A black man in a white suit let us into the house, then led us down a wide hallway of pale yellow wood into a big room shuttered against the heat. There were white shelves in the room, full of books. She was there in an armchair almost the color of her eyes. She wore loose-legged pants and a loose shirt soiled and rumpled over a waist she tried to hide. She was pouring whiskey from a bottle into a glass.

"Clayton, thanks for coming. Hello there, little Buddy. Look, I hope I didn't drag you away from business."

Papa laughed. "Stella, I could stay gone all day and never miss a customer." It embarrassed me to hear him admit such failure to her.

But she laughed too and then she said she could tell I liked books, so maybe I wouldn't mind if they left me there to read while she borrowed my daddy for a little bit. I said I didn't mind, but I did. I both wanted to stop her from taking him away and to keep on seeing her myself. Even with her face swollen from heat and drink and grief, she was something you wanted to look at as long as possible.

They left me alone. On the white piano were dozens of photographs of Stella Doyle in silver frames. From a big painting over the mantelpiece her remarkable eyes followed me around the room. I looked at that painting as sun deepened across it, until finally she and Papa came back. She had a tissue to her nose, a new drink in her hand. "I'm sorry, Buddy," she said. "Your daddy's been sweet letting me run on. I just needed somebody to talk to for a while about what happened to me." She kissed the top of my head and I could feel her warm lips at the part in my hair.

We followed her down the wide hall out onto the porch. "Clayton, you'll forgive a fat old souse talking your ear off and bawling like a jackass."

"No such thing, Stella."

"And you *never* thought I killed him, even when you first heard. My God, thank you."

Papa took her hand again. "You take care now," he said.

Then suddenly she was hugging herself, rocking from side to side. Words burst from her like a door flung open by wind. "I could kick his ass, that bastard! Why didn't he tell me? To quit, to *quit,* and use *my* gun, and just about get me strapped in the gas chamber, that goddamn bastard, and never say a word!" Her profanity must have shocked Papa as much as it did me. He never used it, much less heard it from Mama.

But he just nodded and said, "Well, good-bye, I guess, Stella. Probably won't be seeing each other again."

"Oh Lord, Clayton, I'll be back. The world's so goddamn small."

She stood at the top of her porch, tears wet in those violet eyes that the movie magazines had loved to talk about. On her cheek a mosquito bite flamed like a slap. Holding to the big white column, she waved as we drove off into the dusty heat. Ice flew from the glass in her hand like diamonds.

•   •   •

Papa was right; they never met again. He lost his legs from diabetes, but he'd never gone much of anywhere even before that. And afterward, he was one of two places—home or the store. He'd sit in his big wood wheelchair in the furniture store, with his hands peaceful on the armrests, talking with whoever came by.

I did see Stella Doyle again; the first time in Belgium, twelve years later. I went farther than Papa.

In Bruges, there are small restaurants that lean like elegant elbows on the canals and glance down at passing pleasure boats.

Stella Doyle was sitting, one evening, at a table in the crook of the elbow of one of them, against an iron railing that curved its reflection in the water. She was alone there when I saw her. She stood, leaned over the rail, and slipped the ice cubes from her glass into the canal. The gesture struck a memory. I was in a motor launch full of tourists passing below. She waved with a smile at us and we waved back. It had been a lot of years since her last picture, but probably she waved out of habit. For the tourists motoring past, Stella in white against the dark restaurant was another snapshot of Bruges. For me, she was home. I craned to look back as long as I could, and leapt from the boat at the next possible stop.

When I found the restaurant, she was yelling at a well-dressed young man who was leaning across their table, trying to soothe her in French. They appeared to be quarreling over his late arrival. All at once she hit him, her diamond flashing into his face. He filled the air with angry gestures, then turned and left, a white napkin to his cheek. I was made shy by what I'd seen—the young man was scarcely older than I was. There was no one else on the balcony and I stood unable to speak until her noticing my stare jarred me forward. I said, "Mrs. Doyle? I'm Buddy Hayes. I came out to see you at Red Hills with my father Clayton Hayes one time. You let me look at your books."

She sat back down and poured herself a glass of wine. "You're *that* little boy? God Almighty, how old am I? Am I a hundred yet?" Her laugh had been loosened by years of drink. "Well, you're a red clay rambler like me. How 'bout that. Sit down. What are *you* doing over here?"

I told her as nonchalantly as I could manage that I was leaving tomorrow for Paris to fly home. I'd been traveling on college prize money, a journalism award. I wrote a prize essay about a murder trial.

"Mine?" she asked and laughed.

A waiter, plump and flushed in his neat black suit, trotted to her side. He shook his head at the untouched plates of food.

"Madame, your friend has left then?"

Stella said, "Mister, I helped him along. And you know what? He was no friend."

The waiter then turned his eyes, sad and reproachful, to the trout on the plate. Stella patted his hand. "It's beautiful. How about another bottle of that wine and a great big bucket of ice out here?"

The waiter flapped his fat quick hands around his head, entreating us to come inside. "*Ici? Les moustiques, madame!*"

"I just let them bite," she said and he went away grieved.

She was slender now, and elegantly dressed. And while her hands and throat were older, the eyes hadn't changed, nor the red-gold hair. She was still the most beautiful woman God had made in my lifetime, the woman of whom my father had said that any man who had not desired her had missed out on being alive, the woman for whose honor my father had turned his back on the whole town of Thermopylae. Because of Papa, I had entered my adolescence daydreaming about fighting for Stella Doyle's honor; we had starred together in a dozen of her movies: I dazzled her jury; I cured Hugh Doyle while hiding my own noble love for his wife. And amazingly now here I sat drinking wine with her on a veranda in Bruges; me, the first Hayes ever to win a college prize to take me abroad. Here I sat with a movie star, drinking a bottle of wine.

She finished her cigarette, dropped it spinning down into the black canal. "I'm sorry about his diabetes. I'm not sure I could take being in a wheelchair. You look like him," she said. "Your dad."

"But I don't think like him," I told her.

She tipped the wine bottle upside down in the bucket. "You want the world. Go get it, honey."

"That's what my father doesn't understand."

"He's a good man," she told me. Slowly she stood up. "And I think Clayton would want me to get you to your hotel."

All the fenders of her Mercedes were crushed. She

explained, "When I've had a few drinks, I like a strong car between me and the rest of the cockeyed world."

The big sedan bounced over the moon-white street. "You know what, Buddy? It was Hugh Doyle gave me my first Mercedes and told me don't drive anything else. One morning in Paris. At breakfast. He held the keys out like a damn daffodil he'd picked in the yard. He gave me *this* goddamn thing." She waved her finger with its huge diamond. "This goddamn thing was tied to my big toe one Christmas morning!"

And she smiled up at the stars as if Hugh Doyle were up there tying diamonds on them. "He had a beautiful grin, Buddy, but he was a son of a bitch."

The car bumped to a stop on the curb outside my little hotel. "Listen to me," she said. "Don't go back home tomorrow. Go to Rome."

"I don't have time."

She looked at me. "*Take* time. Just take it. Don't get scared, honey."

Then she put her hand in my jacket pocket and the moon came around her hair and my heart panicked crazily, thudding against my shirt, thinking she might seduce me. But she kissed my forehead and her hand went away and all she said was, "Say hi to Clayton when you get home, all right? Even losing his legs and all, maybe your daddy's lucky, you know that?"

I said, "I don't see how."

"Oh I didn't either 'til I was a lot older than you. And had my damn in-laws trying to throw me in the gas chamber. Go to bed. So long, Red Clay."

Her silver car floated off into the watery streets. In my pocket I found a large wad of French money, enough for Rome, and a little ribboned box, clearly a gift she had decided not to give the angry young man in the beautiful suit who'd arrived too late. On the black velvet lay a man's wristwatch, reddish gold.

It's an extremely handsome watch, and it still tells me the time.

•　　•　　•

I only went home to Thermopylae for the funerals. It was the worst of the dog days when Papa died in the hospital bed they'd set up next to his and Mama's big four-poster in their bedroom. At his grave, the clots of red clay had already dried to a dusty dull color by the time we shoveled them down upon him, friend after friend taking a turn at the shovel. The petals that fell from roses fell limp to the red earth, wilted like the crowd who stood by the grave while Reverend Ballister told us that Clayton Hayes was "a good man." Behind the cluster of family, I saw a woman in black turn away and walk down the grassy incline to a car, a Mercedes.

After the reception, I went driving, but I couldn't outtravel Papa in Devereaux County. The man at the gas pump listed Papa's virtues as he cleaned my windshield. The woman who sold me the bottle of bourbon said she'd owed Papa $215.00 for thirty years and when she'd paid him back, he'd forgotten all about it.

I drove along the highway where the foundations of tin-roofed shacks were covered now by the parking lots of minimalls; beneath the asphalt somewhere was Stella's birthplace. Stella Dora Hibble. Papa's first love.

Past the white gates, the Red Hills lawn was as parched as the rest of the county. Paint blistered and peeled on the big white columns. I waited a long time before the elderly black man I'd met two decades ago opened the door irritably.

I heard her voice from the shadowy hall yelling, "Jonas! Let him in."

On the white shelves the books were the same. The photos on the piano looked as young as ever. She frowned when I came into the room and I thought she must have been expecting someone else and didn't recognize me.

"I'm Buddy Hayes, Clayton's—"

"I know who you are."

"I saw you leaving the cemetery."

"I know you did."

I held out the bottle.

Together we finished the bourbon in memory of Papa, while shutters beat back the sun, hid some of the dirty glasses scattered on the floor, hid Stella Doyle in her lilac armchair. Her hair was cropped short and gray. Cigarette burns scarred the armrests, left their marks on the oak floor. Behind her the big portrait showed Time up for the heartless bastard he is. Only the color of her eyes had stayed the same. They looked as remarkable as ever in the swollen face.

I said, "I came out here to bring you something."

She held up her glass and toasted me. "Thanks."

"No, something else." I gave her the thin, cheap, yellowed envelope I'd found in Papa's desk with his special letters and papers. It was addressed in neat cursive pencil to "Clayton." Inside was a silly Valentine card. Betty Boop popping bonbons in her pouty lips, exclaiming, "Ooooh, I'm sweet on you!" It was childish and lascivious at the same time, and it was signed with a lipstick blot, now brown with age. The name Stella was circled by a heart.

I said, "He kept this since the seventh grade."

She nodded. "Clayton was a good man." Her cigarette fell from her ashtray onto the floor. When I came over to pick it up, she said, "Goodness is luck; like money, like looks. Clayton was lucky that way. That's what I was trying to tell you." She had resumed our conversation in Bruges over twenty years ago.

"Yes, you were right, he was lucky," I said. "But you had all kinds of luck."

She went to the piano and took more ice from the bucket there; one piece she rubbed around the back of her neck, then dropped into her glass. She turned, the eyes wet, like lilac stars. "You know, in Hollywood, they said, '*Hibble?* What kind of hick name is that? We can't use that!' So I said, 'Doyle.' I mean, it popped right out of my mouth. I took Hugh's name six years before I ever saw him again. Because I knew he'd come. The day I left Thermopylae he kept yelling at me, 'You can't have both!' He kept yelling it while the bus was pulling out. 'You can't have it and me both.' He wanted to rip my heart out for leaving, for *wanting* to go."

I nodded. "But you could have both."

Stella moved along the curve of the white piano to a photograph of Hugh Doyle in a white open shirt, grinning straight out at the sun. She said, "Two things I had to have in this little world, and one was the lead in a movie called *Fever* and the other one was Hugh Doyle." She put his photograph down carefully. "I didn't know about the cancer 'til midway through the trial my lawyers found out he'd been to see that doctor in Atlanta. Then it was easy to get the jury to go for suicide." She looked at me for a long moment. "Well, not easy. But we turned them around. I think your father was the only man in town who *never* thought I was guilty."

It took me a while to take it in. Odd but I'd never suspected. I smiled. "Well, he sure convinced me."

She smiled back at me. "He convinced a lot of people. Everybody thought so much of Clayton."

I poured the last drink. "You killed your husband." We looked at each other and I shook my head. "Why?"

She glanced for a while around the room as if the answer was in it somewhere, then she shrugged. "We were drunk. We were fighting. He was sleeping with my fucking maid. I was crazy. Lots of reasons, no reason. I didn't plan it."

"You didn't confess it either."

She put out her cigarette. "What good would that have done? Hugh was dead. I wasn't about to let his snooty-ass mother shove me in the gas chamber and pocket the money."

"Jesus." I finished my drink. "And you've never felt a day's guilt."

Her head tilted back, smoothing her throat. The shuttered sun had fallen, down the room onto the floor, and evening light did a movie fade and turned Stella Doyle into the star in the painting behind her. She said quietly, "Ah baby, don't believe it."

The room stayed still. I stood up and dropped the empty bottle in the wastebasket. I said, "Papa told me how he was in love with you."

Her laugh came warmly through the shuttered dusk. "Yes and I guess I was sweet on him too, boop boop de doo."

"I was ten when Papa told me no man could say he'd been alive if he'd seen you and not been in love. I just wanted to tell you I know what he meant." I raised my hand at the door to say good-bye.

"Come over here," she said and I went to her chair and she reached up and brought my head down to her and kissed me full and long on the mouth. "So long, Buddy." Slowly her hand moved down my face, the huge diamond radiant.

• • •

News came over the wire at my paper. Then the tabloids played with it for a few days on back pages. They had some pictures. They dug up the Hugh Doyle trial photos to put beside the old studio glossies. The dramatic death of an old movie star was worth sending a news camera down to Thermopylae, North Carolina, to get a shot of the charred ruin that had once been Red Hills. A shot of the funeral parlor and the flowers on the casket.

One of my sisters phoned me that there was even a crowd at the coroner's inquest in the courthouse. The verdict was that Stella Doyle had died in her sleep after a cigarette accidentally dropped set fire to her bed. But rumors started that her body had been found at the foot of the stairs as if she had been trying to escape the fire but had fallen down the stairs. Some said she was drunk. Some said her dead husband's brother had killed her for the money. They buried her beside Hugh Doyle in the family plot, the fanciest tomb in the cemetery, far up the hill from where my parents were buried together.

Not long after Stella died, one of the cable networks did a night of her movies. I stayed up to watch *Fever* again.

My wife said, "Buddy, I'm sorry, but this is the biggest bunch of sentimental slop I ever saw. The whore'll sell her jewels and get the medicine and they'll beat the epidemic, but she'll die to pay for her past and then the town'll see she was really a saint. Am I right?"

"You're right."

She sat down to watch awhile for company's sake. "You know, I can't decide if she's a really lousy actress or a really good one. It's weird."

I said, "Actually, I think she was a much better actress than anyone gave her credit for."

My wife went to bed but I watched through the night. I sat in Papa's old rocking chair that I'd brought north with me after his death. Finally at dawn I turned off the set and Stella's face disappeared into a star and went out. The reception was awful and the screen too small. Besides, the last movie was in black and white. I couldn't see her eyes as well as I could remember the shock of their color, when she first turned toward me at the foot of the courthouse steps, that hot August day when I was ten, when my father stepped forward out of the crowd to take her hand, when her eyes were lilacs turned up to his face, and his straw hat in the summer sun was shining like a knight's helmet.

Marie

Blue Cadillac

West out of Nashville in a red and white Mustang, Braxton Cox swung too fast around a curve and his body remembered old times. All of a sudden he felt in a sweet slide. He felt the rush again, the gliding just above the asphalt, just free of friction. The Mustang bucking, he toed off his loafer and splayed his bare foot over the accelerator pedal. A sun like money and a moon from a song bounced ahead of him, both of them big in the sky together.

"Goddamn! This is goddamn beautiful!" he said aloud.

Braxton was a high-tech sales rep going home to Memphis for his mama's sake to eat Thanksgiving dinner. His wife had left him and married a Brazilian oilman who was, according to her, better in bed than Braxton. His wife had been a stewardess. That's how she'd met the Brazilian, less than a year back.

Braxton was scooting through the woodlands of the Natchez Trace where Interstate 40 cuts across the old Indian trail that pioneers and hunted men had cleared from Natchez to Tupelo and on to Nashville. He was near where Captain Meriweather Lewis of Lewis and Clark had shot himself to death at a place called Grinder's Inn, now a plaque in the wilderness. Pines covered the hills, undiminishable. This was God's country, home country.

A view like this had to have a soundtrack. Braxton's right hand scooped tapes onto the seat beside him, then shuffled among them for *Elvis's Worldwide Gold Award Hits, Volumes 1 and 2*, a twin pack he'd bought on sale in a spasm of nostalgia like the one that squeezed him now.

Elvis came on loud, moaning, *Anyway you want me, that's the way I'll be.*

Braxton one-handed another curve, a horseshoe, and, panicked, smashed down on the brakes, then swerved out and accelerated all the way to the floor, because he'd come up on a car almost standing still at about forty miles-per-hour, which was about half what he was doing.

Palm on horn, hard, he squealed past with his eyes bursting. The car beside him was just incredible! A baby blue Cadillac convertible with the endless fin fenders of the old profligate days. It was as if Elvis's voice itself, like Aladdin's, had summoned out of the air of the past a dream car to match Braxton's mood.

He was around the corner and hurling along the straight stretch before his brain could get his hand off the horn and his foot off the pedal. In his rear-view mirror the stupendous machine rolled over the hilltop and streamed toward him. He got his window down, back-twirling the handle like crazy.

Elvis yelled, *I'm in love! I'm all shook up!* out the open window.

Even louder, Braxton heard *Oogah! Oogah! Oogah!* Here the blue convertible came like a tidal wave. Sticking his head out, he opened his mouth to say, "Hi! Where'd you get that car?" But instead he just gasped and swallowed a hundred feet of air.

A blonde girl, just beautiful, her hair flying like fire, had one hand on the white steering wheel and with her other hand, just as her car skimmed past his, she *pulled down* her strapless blue halter. The elastic popped right down below her breasts, setting them loose, as if she'd all of a sudden decided to give them some air. Then she raised her bare arm and, like a Walt Disney flower, unfolded her middle finger at Braxton Cox! The blue Cadillac convertible varoomed away in a puff of exhaust that probably used up two gallons of gas.

Braxton was thirty-four. He'd been to college in the sixties, when even at Ole Miss the world had gone wild. He'd horsed around, flying helicopters for the Navy in Corpus Christi, and

Texas ports are not shy places. But *goddamn* he'd never seen anything like what he'd just seen going past him in Tennessee. A big
truck roaring up from the other direction almost blew his Mustang off the road, while the trucker had his head out the window,
staring in the sideview mirror. The trucker's mouth looked as if
he were blowing smoke rings.

Ten minutes later, Braxton saw the blue Cadillac in the
roadside parking lot of a silver train engine called the Casey
Jones Bar & Diner, after the famous local railroad man who'd
killed himself trying to bring old 382 in on time. Braxton cut
Elvis off in a gurgle, skidded into the lot, and, fishing for his
loafers, rolled out of his bucket seat. He leaned down into the
Cadillac like King Arthur looking for the lady of the lake. "I love
this car," he said and sighed and felt the white dash and white
upholstery with powder blue piping. There wasn't a speck on it
or a thing in it except…"Good Lawdy Miss Clawdy!" whispered
Braxton…except a pair of pink bikini underpants lying like an
orchid on the shiny white seat.

•   •   •

Braxton shook down his plaid trousers and smoothed down
his yellow V-neck sweater and patted his wallet and patted his
zipper. He was thinking he was about to jump backward through
his life, like a child in a home movie, sped up and reversed, who's
sucked out of the pool and returned to the diving board. He
walked into the diner and the girl from the blue Cadillac looked
up and saw him.

On the checkout counter, a stand-up picture of a little Puri-
tan boy praying said, THANKSGIVING DELUX FAMILY DINNER, $7.95.
Braxton ordered a double Wild Turkey and a Heineken; he
pulled a pack of Marlboro Lights from the cigarette machine.
The prices had gone up since he'd quit smoking and drinking last
year, after his best man had driven drunk right into an underpass
embankment. Bourbon and Winstons were cheaper when he'd

given them up thinking he might be able to get his wife back from the Brazilian if he never stank or stumbled.

Sitting down on the counter stool across from the blonde girl's booth, he could see that her eyes were the same color as her Cadillac, as if she were a part of a world where people had cars made to match their eyes. The blue halter was so skimpy she had goose bumps. Somehow he'd been sure she'd be in shorts but of course she wasn't, in late November. She had on a tight denim skirt and tight boots with thin gold chains around the backs of the heels. She was sucking the orange peel from a whiskey sour. Her other hand floated deep into a blue Eastern Airlines shoulder bag and brought out menthol Virginia Slims cigarettes.

Braxton leaned out from the counter. "Excuse me. Where'd you get that car?" He topped his glass with beer foam without looking; he'd worked on the act two years in Corpus Christi. "That's one of the prettiest cars I've ever seen."

On the outblow of her match she said, "Why don't you stop following me, all right?" She had a Tennessee voice, home country.

"I'm not. It's just luck. Anyhow," he tried a smile, "I thought you left me a message on your car seat."

"Like what?"

He let it go. He didn't want to offend her mentioning her underpants. "Did you buy that car?"

"My momma left it to me."

She'd finished the spikes of orange meat and was now eating the rind itself. "Why'd you keep blowing your horn at me back there?"

"You're eating the rind."

She finished it. "You almost killed me, passing me, blowing that horn."

Braxton smiled sweetly on one side of his mouth. "I'll let you in on a secret, you almost killed me ditto, what you did back there."

"Good!" she said. She giggled. "Sometimes I'll just act crazy. That's what my friends say. They never know what's next."

"I bet." What had she been doing in that car...with her panties off?

She lifted her bare arms to twist her hair into a ponytail. A rubber band was on her wrist. "I heard Elvis on your radio," she said, "but I couldn't pick it up."

"It was a tape." Braxton took his drink over to her booth. "Lots of people used to tell me I looked like Elvis."

"I don't know why."

He was defensive but tried not to show it. "Well, I guess they thought I did."

"I don't much."

"How about if I do this?" He curled part of his upper lip over his teeth, dropped his eyelids, and pulled a curl down over his forehead.

"Well, a little," she admitted.

"Well, how about this?" He jumped up, sawed his leg back and forth and thwacked the air with his arm. "How about this?" He spun in air, chopping space with karate hands, kicking as if he could knock off years with his feet. He couldn't believe he was doing it. Neither could the half-dozen other customers who hadn't stayed home or gone home or had homes for Thanksgiving dinner. Four were startled. Two were glazed.

Ears throbbing, out of breath, Braxton slid into the girl's booth while she was laughing. A waitress came, a railroad cap high on a blue-black wing-tip hairdo. Braxton was still breathing through his grin while she took their orders. Braxton wanted the special. The blonde girl wanted waffles for supper.

Her name was Marie. She was nineteen and had lived her whole life in Dayton, Tennessee. Braxton told her, "You live right where *Inherit the Wind* happened. I know somebody's mother was an extra in the movie. With Spencer Tracy?" She hadn't known about it. It was before her time and she'd never heard of Clarence Darrow and William Jennings Bryan fighting the famous monkey trial over teaching evolution.

She leaned toward him, blue eyes like postcard lagoons. "You like Elvis?"

Braxton held up his hand as if he were a witness. "He was the King."

The girl said, "My whole life is based on Elvis. Because of my momma. That's why she named me Marie. You know, '*Marie's the name of his latest flame.*'"

Braxton said, "Well, Marie, you smoke a lot for somebody so young."

"I only smoke menthol."

"You smoke a lot. I used to smoke two packs a day. But I quit." He noticed his burning cigarette in the ashtray. "I cut back. I had a cousin killed himself smoking four packs a day. Emphysema."

"What's that?"

"Your lungs clog up."

She filled hers with air. The elastic halter swelled.

Cranberry juice wet Braxton's turkey meat. The sight nagged at him, parent to child, relentless. He should drive home at once for Thanksgiving dinner; he could still get there by seven if he scrambled. His mother would still be in and out of the kitchen to check the oven, check the time. But her mouth would be thinning by the minute. She'd warned him, "Don't be late," as if she'd expected this betrayal. Sullen, he swatted off the guilt by waving his arm for drinks.

He said, "I guess your momma really liked Elvis."

Marie scooped another orange peel from her drink. "She'd laugh if she heard you say that. Liked! Back in school, she had an "E" tattooed over one breast and a "P" over the other one." She pointed. "Right across, like that."

"Goddamn!...Excuse me."

Marie looked deep into his eyes. "He was the only man she ever loved, that's all. She told me that when she was dying."

"Well, I'm sorry you lost her."

"Oh, that's all right."

"Was it a while back?" He put down his drink to show more interest.

"Five days ago today."

He was surprised. "That's terrible."

"It was diabetes. But she'd had it a long time."

"That's terrible. I'm sorry to hear that."

Braxton's voice was so sympathetic the girl's voice thickened. She coughed and leaned toward him. "So anyhow. Momma asked me to do something for her and that's what I'm doing. And that's why I'm sitting here right now, because otherwise I'd be going in the opposite direction. But the last thing she asked me was would I drive to Memphis and go to Graceland and let him know she was gone and give him her souvenirs and her hair that she never cut?" The girl rubbed her blue Eastern Airlines bag as she talked as if she consoled some creature inside.

"Let who know?"

"Elvis."

Braxton didn't know what to say and ate some mashed potatoes.

"He's buried there at his home because of the violence at the public cemetery. You know how it was." She took out of the bag a soft rumpled paper sack. From the sack she drew a thin shank of brownish gray hair in a ponytail several feet long. The humanness of the thing jolted Braxton so much he bit his tongue while he chewed.

Marie kept smoothing the hair. "This was my momma's hair. She made a vow to Elvis and never cut it. Isn't it long?"

Braxton nodded and moved her new drink closer.

Lagoon water splashed from the girl's blue eyes in tears. One, two, three in a row. The last hung there too full to drop. Braxton was moved to pat her hand. He could feel the dead hair underneath it.

Marie spoke solemnly. "That last night, she pulled me right down to her face in the hospital bed. 'He was all I had. He was everything. No one will ever understand,' is what she kept trying to whisper."

Braxton grew solemn too. "Marie. I'm just a stranger. But believe me in all sincerity, I am really sorry to hear about your loss. I mean, a mother is, well…"

Nodding, the girl started to take out dozens of articles from the blue vinyl bag. She picked through them—pins, buttons, charms, photos—pushing them about on the table like a vendor at Lourdes.

•   •   •

With an index finger Braxton looped wide circles that ringed his head and Marie's, as if to tell the waitress they were angels haloed, or insane. But the waitress understood and brought two more drinks. She had to clear away all the old ones because there was no room left on the table. Braxton decided it couldn't possibly be as late as the waitress's watch implied. He kept nodding at the objects Marie was explaining to him.

"This is the ticket. Overton Park Shell, Memphis, that was the first. She saw him there and at the fairgrounds and everywhere, way before he got famous. So that's what I mean, it proves it was sincere how she felt, not a fad. She had over twenty thousand pictures of him. All the albums. Everything. Look here, see." She shuffled out a photograph of a teenage girl of amorphous form and fanatical eyes who sat at a cheap little white dressing table. Her brown hair was in the ponytail that now lay grayed and lank in Marie's sack. The surface of the table was thick with objects, a pile of novelty hats, a mound of small trinkets, all said "Elvis Presley." The mirror was entirely papered over with his face. His face smiled from the girl's blouse and her toreador pants.

"Look here," said Marie. She showed Braxton a stained handkerchief that she took out of a small velvet box. "You see this spot? And this one? That's *his* perspiration. At one concert he fell right down on his knees in front of Momma and when she held this handkerchief out to him, he used it. He wiped his face on this." She put back the dirty cloth and held up a square of laminated plastic. "That's his hair in there. See those strands? Momma ran her fingers through his hair and that much got caught in her ring. At Fort Dix."

Braxton was earnest. "Marie. This is a lot of stuff. There're aspects of sales on these items that you probably aren't acquainted with. If you'll take a stranger's advice, you ought to get in touch with somebody who could offer you an expert's opinion, like an appraisal."

Marie nodded with a tolerant smile, as if to say she was way ahead of Braxton. "She had every single one of his 45s. There's a whole garage packed full of Elvis at home. I locked it all up in there. I guess somebody probably could open up a museum if they wanted to."

"That's what I mean."

"I just locked it up and left. Momma used to say she was going to mail it to Lisa Marie, that maybe Lisa Marie'd like to have all these memories of her daddy."

On the color television in the corner, two football teams had been getting up and knocking each other down for a long time. It was pitch-black night outside. Braxton had broken his mother's heart.

Marie began to slide her relics back into their bag. "Maybe I better drink some coffee," she said and giggled. "I think I'm just about smashed. When I was in junior high, sometimes I used to get drunk as a skunk, throwing up, passing out. Momma cried when she found out I was drinking. What's your name?"

"Braxton."

"Braxton? Braxton, that's a nice name. Long time ago in Las Vegas with my momma, I met three guys had actually legally changed their names to Elvis. One of them was black. One of them had gotten his fiancée to change her name to Priscilla and they'd come out there on the bus from Detroit to get married the same place Elvis and Priscilla did. But something went wrong, I forget what."

Braxton stood up. His leg was asleep. "All righty. Just sit tight." He told the waitress to bring coffee, then sprinted around the corner to the men's room—where he'd been desperate to go for half-an-hour—and stood skittery at the urinal, worried that Marie would wander out of the Casey Jones alone and drive away. A vending machine sold condoms. He couldn't believe how much they cost now. Back at their booth the girl hadn't moved. She sat spinning a key chain of a tiny Elvis thwacking his tiny guitar; she made the key chain dance on the edge of her coffee mug, and up and down on her mother's dead hair. Her bared shoulders and back were beautiful, curved like blonde bent wood, incredibly naked skin. His wife's skin, he now realized, had been too white. He'd loved his wife in spite of her very skin.

Marie was talking; she might have been talking the whole time he was gone. "I shut up the house. It's a duplex, you know the kind, and just told the neighbors, 'Look, will you rent this place out for me and I'll send for my stuff,' because I had to get out of there. I was going to start junior college this fall, but Momma was too sick. It was just her and me."

Pity settled in Braxton like cement. "No daddy?"

"D-I-V-O-R-C-E before I was born. She thinks he went to California. He didn't like Tennessee."

"You going out there to see him?"

"That's a joke. I don't even know who he is."

He shook his head. "My dad's gone, passed away."

She had wrapped the shank of hair around her wrist. Now she uncoiled it, fed it back into the bag.

Braxton took the bill. His wallet was filled with cash for his trip home; he left two fifties by mistake on top of the bill and Marie corrected him. He replaced the fifties with twenties as he borrowed a Virginia Slim from the girl. He'd somehow smoked his whole pack of Marlboro Lights. "California has a lot to offer," he told her. "Or Texas. I used to live in Corpus Christi, Texas. Now I live in D.C."

"I'm going to try Atlanta. I don't think I'd like Texas."

"D.C. either," said Braxton. He smiled right at her; the smile floated in her lagoon eyes and he watched it move. "How's this?" he said, his heart fast. He slid out of the booth, toppled to one knee. "How about we both get off for good in Memphis? I grew up in Memphis, it's okay. Tonight we'll drive over to Graceland for your momma and then we'll go stand on the bluffs and yell up in the sky at everybody dead. 'Hey up there, we miss you! Hi, Dad! Hi, Marie's mom! Hi, Elvis! We miss you.' And then first thing tomorrow—how's this?—We'll go get married! You and me. Why not? Want to? I'm free as a bird myself."

The girl swiveled her legs away from his. She frowned then shook her head. "No thanks. I'm not totally down on marriage like my friends. But I think marriage ought to be like..." she thought hard, "like meeting Elvis Presley. It's nothing to joke about."

Braxton hauled himself back into the booth, dusted his plaid trouser leg. "That's for damn sure," he said, drowned all of a sudden in grief. He would have left but he was too worn out to move, so tired he slumped down on his spine and closed his eyes.

"You know what? Braxton, you know what?" He heard Marie's voice, plaintive, and opened one eye. Slowly her butane lighter was raised toward her cigarette. She jerked back when its flame leaped at her. "This is true, I'll tell you something, Braxton. This is a true story, okay?" She was offering it like a gift to make up for saying no to marrying him. "One time my momma got asked inside Graceland. It was 1968. They were horsing around and they needed more girls. She couldn't believe she got asked. She and her friends hung out at the gates a lot and that night one of them got in and she got Momma in. She used to tell me this story at night, putting me to bed when I was little. About Graceland. She said in his house there were stars blinking up in the ceiling and mirrors and gold, just like it is now but new. They were all out back, sitting around the pool, Elvis and his friends, and the girls, even though it was the middle of the night. The guys had a bunch of lighters." She flicked hers back on. "They broke off the tips so the flames would shoot out and they shot them at each other's bottoms for a joke."

"Elvis did?"

"No. His friends. He watched. Then after they used the lighters up, Momma said they threw hundreds and hundreds of new flashbulbs into the pool and shot at them with BB guns so they'd explode. Elvis did that."

"Did the girls…What did the girls do?"

"They sat around and kept their eyes on Elvis. My momma tried to talk to the two girls beside her but she said they looked right through her like she was cheap glass. They sat around working at trying to fuck Elvis."

Braxton sat up in the booth and stared at her, shocked at the matter of fact profanity, then seeing the scene she'd described. In a minute he asked, "What was he like?"

Marie poured sugar from packets into her coffee. "Momma said he was better looking than you could ever imagine. And sad as rain."

Braxton and Marie sat, quiet, in their booth, and looked at each other. In the television's blue rays, waitresses ran back and forth. On the screen, football players ran back and forth. Braxton felt as sad as Elvis, poisoned by the blueness, weary from the liquor and the cigarettes. The short film of his life had reversed again, gone forward, thrown him—heavy with the years he'd tried to kick away—slung him back off the diving board, back down into the blue stinging water where he was aimlessly swimming divorced in D.C., sinking.

•   •   •

Outside in the parking lot of the Casey Jones Diner, the blue Cadillac turned the moon blue, turned the gravel silver blue.

Braxton read the car's front plate. THE KING LIVES ON. The back plate was Tennessee's. AMERICA AT ITS BEST.

Lights inside the Cadillac's trunk spilled over suitcases, boxes, and bedding. Buttoning a suede jacket over the thin halter, Marie turned slowly and dramatically to face Braxton. She whispered to him, "Elvis gave my momma this car."

Braxton's heart slid like a trombone from his chest. He whispered back, "Elvis? Elvis did? Is that really true?"

The girl handed Braxton the keys and then got in on the passenger's side. Dew from the steering wheel was cool in his palm. They sat there, white under the blue moon.

"Why?" he asked her.

She touched the piping on the dashboard with slow care. "Because Momma started crying right there by the pool. That night I told you about. And some of the guys tried to hustle her out quick before Elvis got bummed, but he said, "Wait a minute, how come she's cryin'?"

Braxton moved his fingers over the powder blue dash, over the shadowy chrome and white leather, up and down the steering wheel. "She was crying?"

"Because he looked so sad. And she was so scared when he asked her why, she couldn't talk loud and he had to get right in her face to hear her and she said, 'Because you're so sad.' She thought he was still sad because his momma had died and maybe he felt lonesome being home without her. Boy, that makes sense now."

Braxton slid the seat back, moved the mirrors, felt with his fingers for the ignition, held his hand there on the key, waiting, listening to Marie talk about Elvis and her mother.

"He made somebody take Momma home because she was upset. Then in a few days this Cadillac drives up to the door. The salesman drove it. My momma's daddy blew a fuse. He thought she must have—you know—with Elvis for it. But she hadn't even kissed him. And there was a card from Elvis that came with the car. It said, 'Don't be blue.' That's all it said. 'Don't be blue.' And it was a blue Cadillac to go with the card."

"Did he sign the card?"

"No. But it was him."

Braxton shook his head. "That's great, it's really great. I used to read where he was always doing stuff like that, giving away motorcycles and diamond rings. A Cadillac. Wow."

Marie put her hand on his. "Go ahead." She turned his wrist and the key turned.

The big convertible moved forward like lake water. One finger on the wheel led it out of the lot.

"Go ahead," she said again.

Slowly his foot pressed down, into the pedal, down, further down. The Cadillac floated in hasteless ease over the road's black waves.

Their hair stung at their faces. The wind stung too. Braxton was crying.

"Go as fast as you want," she yelled.

And then in a while she yelled, "Just don't kill us."

Too far away, too long ago, the bluffs of Memphis jutted out at the moon where the town's lovers had always parked to make love in their cars. There were stories that thwarted lovers had killed themselves by jumping from the bluffs into the Mississippi River below. Chickasaw Indian lovers had lain together on the bluffs long before La Salle had stood there discovering the river, before the townspeople had stood there watching Yankee gunboats sink their ships, before Braxton Cox had stood there with all his friends on the night before his wedding to the stewardess, the night he had flung a bottle of Wild Turkey up at the moon and called to the moon to join the party that he was sure would never stop.

He drew his foot back from the pedal. "We better turn around," he said. The three-point-turn was easy as sliding his finger through lake water.

"Stop a second," she said and he waited. "Go down there," she said and pointed at a road dark with trees.

The woods made almost no sound at all. He saw the car lighter's red eye, smelled the cigarette paper.

"We could do it if you want to," she said. "We could fuck."

He looked at her, shadowy in smoke. He said, "Know what we used to do when I was a kid? I mean, not when the sixties really got going in the seventies but before that. We'd neck. You hear of that? We'd neck for a long time. It wasn't actually too often that a girl would come out with what you just said, right off."

She shrugged. "A lot's happened since then I guess."

Braxton leaned back, his neck on the cool white seat. Stars were everywhere. "Too much for me," he said.

The girl crushed out her cigarette and moved over beside him. He cupped his hand beneath her ponytail and kissed her for a long time. Then he slid his hands inside the blue halter and pulled it down and kissed her breasts for a long time. Finally they got out of the car and went to the backseat. The leather seat was dew cold, snow white, so wide and long that he hardly had to bend his knees. Her short skirt bunched at his stomach. The little chains on her boot heels rubbed at his calves. When they finished, she said, "I saw a star fall. That was nice."

• • •

Back in the Casey Jones parking lot, Braxton asked her, "Atlanta, huh?"

"I guess so," she said.

"That was pretty great back there. I want you to know that. I'm serious."

She nodded. "That's all right." She opened a new pack of cigarettes. There were cartons of them stacked in the Cadillac trunk. "Listen, I'm going to ask you something, okay?"

He tensed. "Sure. What?"

"You think my momma was weird? Loving Elvis so much?"

"No, of course not." Braxton started to get out of the car but Marie seemed to be settling in to talk and so he sat back behind the wheel. "When I was real little, my momma took me to

Memphis to see Elvis's momma's grave and it's got this big statue of Jesus with his arms stretched out and two little angels with him. Momma was kind of hoping Elvis would show up at the cemetery while we were there, and see the blue Cadillac and remember how she was the girl who'd cried for him and he'd told her, 'Don't be blue.'" He didn't come and he was dead too just a year later. But I was pretty little and I got it in my head that the statue standing there with his arms out was Elvis. I thought it was really Elvis. Crazy Marie again, right?"

Braxton didn't want to hear any more about Elvis and Marie's mother. He was cold, tired, and depleted of will and hope. His hangover had started, he needed to get back to the bathroom. He needed to have been at his mother's house six hours ago to try again to make her understand how he could have lost his wife to a Brazilian. He felt hurt somewhere inside him deep and dull. "Yeah, I guess that's a little weird," he agreed. "But kids think funny things." He got out of the car and she got out too and came around to where he stood.

She said, "You ever see the Christ of the Ozarks? On Magnetic Mountain in the Ozarks?" He shook his head no. "Well, it's huge. The arms stretch out around seventy feet across. You know what? I thought that statue was Elvis too. The lady at the souvenir shop told my momma and me that the arms of that Christ were so big and strong you could hang six Cadillacs from each one with no trouble."

"Really?" Braxton gave her back the car keys.

"So that's what I thought. That Elvis had arms seventy feet wide with blue Cadillacs hanging from them on strings and when he saw my momma looking so sad for him, he snapped one of the cars off its string and gave it to her. I really believed that when I was little."

"Wow...." He didn't know what to say.

She hugged him good-bye and slid behind the wheel and closed the door.

Braxton pushed down the lock on her door. "You can't get into

Graceland in the middle of the night. We could get a motel and
go in the morning. Or, listen Marie, you could stay at my mother's
with me. She only lives about two miles from Graceland."

She turned on the ignition. "That's okay. Don't take it personally but I just feel like being on my own now, okay? Thanks
anyhow. See you around. Happy Thanksgiving."

The car backed away from him.

"Sure you don't want to get married?" he called after her.

"Sorry?" she yelled.

"Sure I don't look like Elvis?" he shouted.

She waved her arm as she floated past him, and he waved
back as long as he could see the blue Cadillac carrying her away,
enchanted maiden, to its master, the king of Graceland.

Braxton finally noticed that his wallet with four hundred
dollars in cash and his whole life on cards was missing. He didn't
know if he'd left it in Casey's diner or if it had fallen out of his
tugged-off trousers in the back seat of Elvis's car, or if Marie had
stolen it. But the wallet was definitely gone, like his wife, like the
future. He didn't notice until he was ringing the bell at his
mother's house where all the doors were locked and all the lights
were out, and he was looking for a key that he had lost long ago.

Precious

Winners and Losers

My wife Precious was always telling me how Buster was a late bloomer. She used to say, "Your dad was an early bloomer; you should have known him when he was a freshman at Carolina. That was the real Moochie." Buster would raise his eyebrow at her and she'd raise hers at him like they were talking in deaf language and nobody knew it, and then he'd shuffle back to his room. But I tell my boy Buster, in the game of life there are winners and losers and it's hard to switch teams after you run on the field. Buster never appears to be listening, but I feel like I want him to know.

Now when my only son's over here for weekends, he never comes out of his room. One time I bammed on his door and yelled, "What are you doing in there?" You know what he said? "Waiting to die." Can you believe that? At seventeen!

Actually I think I was a bloomer even earlier than college. It was high school that was the real me. I was revved to race back then, I was poured full of the juice of youth. I'll just come right out and say it. Everything on me quivered and bulged. Not a muscle, including the one we called Mr. Roto-rooter, that wasn't flexing of its own accord. It was all I could do to walk down the sidewalk without cramping into a pretzel or exploding like a tire. I was so pumped I had to jog in place. I had the feeling that if I didn't keep all those muscles moving, everything in me would get lockjaw.

Back then I spent my time under a barbell or under a car or trying to get a girl under me. I tell Buster, at least I *spent* my time. He doesn't appear to be doing anything with his but killing it. My mom had to stretch her arms across the door to hold me: "Moochie, listen to me, are you coming to your aunt's anniversary or not, are you coming home for supper or not, are you going to work Saturdays with your dad or not?" Oh, she had a life all planned for me but I sidestepped it. She thought I couldn't hold my horses and she was right as rain. "Mooch has ants in his pants," she told Precious. But it wasn't ants. I guess you could call it an anteater. That thing had a life all planned for me too, always pointing to where it just had to go in a hurry. I used to say, if I'd had it on a leash, it would have yanked my arm right out of the socket.

Along the way Somebody (and I guess it was God) poured the sands of time all over my motor. I know it was nothing personal. Some people think it was a rotten kind of joke for Him to play on his own pet creatures—human beings I mean—to rust them out with age so fast. But I feel I got a good shake and I'm not complaining. Not that I'm claiming I was any special pet of His either, but back when I was young He showered some confetti on my head, and I could hear the bands play, and a whole lots of nights I saw the sun come up. There's no doubt I was golden. Even Precious said so. Look, I was big, good-looking, white, and living in Hope Valley, U.S.A. I was passing high school with no sweat and everybody I knew in the world stood up and cheered when I ran onto the field wearing No. 48. Acne skipped right over me. My folks were nice as they could be. I had a big sister who was voted, "Girl: Best Looking" and "Girl: Best All-Around." In the locker room Billy Weatherspoon said to me, "Your sister's knockers are drivin' me ker-aazzee! I'd like to eat them like two big sundaes with cherries on top!" Of course I had to gut-punch Billy for saying that about Cottie, but the fact is he was right. She was a great looking girl if I do say so myself.

I'll even admit that one time I drilled a hole through the back of my closet and I watched Cottie taking a bath. Maybe that makes me sound like a pervert and I guess I'm sorry I told Precious about it. I suppose she's right, I'd punch Buster's lights out if I caught him sneaking a peek at his sister Ashley like that, but we're all only human. Hell, Dickey Moore *screwed* his sister Mandy at the drive-in and they both turned out okay in the end, more or less, I mean got married and had kids and all. The worst I ever did was that hand job while I was watching Cottie take her bath. She shaved her legs and under her arms. I was amazed at how she used tweezers on her nipples.

Our folks were as proud of us both as they could be. Cottie was cheerleader cocaptain and yearbook coeditor and I was a four-letter man every year at Hope High. I was All-State and national delegate for Young Republicans and it required six inches to list my achievements in the yearbook. I had for the motto under my senior picture some words of the poet Robert Frost that my mother found for me. The words were "Happiness makes up in height for what it lacks in length." Believe me, I took some flack for that. I won't repeat some of the gross things my friends wrote in my yearbook. I guess I should have gone with leave-a-beautiful-memory type stuff like everybody else. But we were always horsing around.

Back then it just never crossed my mind that I could die. I had a '56 Fairlane my dad got me, white convertible with red seats. I did things in that car you've got to love yourself to do. I'd pass between an Allied van coming south and an oil truck going north. I'd drag in the left-hand lane right up over the top of a hill on the bypass. I'd cut around a string of gutless geezers weaving behind a tractor. I'd go by six of them on two wheels, with empties rolling all over my floorboard and some girl slammed up against my shoulder screaming in holy terror. I guess if I found out Buster tried to pull a stunt like that, I'd ground him for good. (Not that he ever goes anywhere to get grounded from.)

I loved my car. I called it the White Knight and I washed it every other day. Lots of guys stuck racing stripes on theirs, or junk like those old black and pink fuzzy dice hung from the mirror. Billy Weatherspoon had decals of little blue feet that ran all over his Corvair. But I kept the White Knight pure. My mother said, "Moochie, if you could keep your room a tenth as nice as that automobile, I'd die a happy woman." She missed the point. My room was just a place to throw things and sleep in when I had to. Nobody but losers stayed in their rooms. I was so revved I needed a room on wheels. That car was *me*. Back before Precious, if I didn't have a girl down to her panties on those red seats, I had the White Knight jammed with my buddies and we were tearing up the town. Back then people had friends. I don't know what's the matter with Buster. I ask him, "Don't you have any friends? Where're your friends?" All I get's a slammed door.

Back then we'd order ten Big Boys at Shoney's and wheel out with the waitress chasing us, her tray spilling cokes. We'd flash a few moons at women in the parking lot at Crabtree Mall. We'd shoot the bulbs out of the marquee at Holy Savior Evangelist Tabernacle. We burned our share of rubber and I guess we raised some hell. But it was harmless. It wasn't the weird sort of stuff. Hating America never crossed my mind.

Buster says to me, "How can you like this disgusting world?" I say it's the only one I've got. He claims people like me "fucked it up and then passed it on." I don't like that kind of language and I don't like that kind of attitude. I tell him, "Damn it, Buster, you can't say, 'Well, the world's not perfect so I guess I'll give it a pass.'" Maybe it sounds gung ho or whatever you want to call it, but we did like the world, me and my friends. It was out there like something good you wanted to eat. We had no complaints. We'd landed in the best country on earth and we lived in Hope Valley and our motors were racing. We were glad to be alive, I mean if we'd thought about it.

And I don't see that we messed the world up either, even if we didn't do all this damn save the whales and gay rights and stuff. Maybe sometimes we got a little gross and loud and a little too revved with the cars and the guns and the girls, but we didn't set out to hurt anybody and it's a lie to say we did.

I think it was when my wife Precious heard about Dickey Moore's sister Mandy that she turned on me. After that I'd see her looking at me like I was from Mars. And that just wasn't fair. I mean, first of all, we're talking twenty years ago, and second of all, Mandy got in the car of her own free will.

What happened was, after Dickey told us about him and his sister doing it at the drive-in, a bunch of us took her out to the golf course one Saturday night after the football game and made her do oral sex on us. Maybe that sounds a little rough, but I don't suppose Mandy thought we were taking her out there to play a few holes of golf at midnight. I remember she said, "Y'all can just forget it, what do you think I am, a harlot from Charlotte?" And Billy said, "That's right, honeypie, and I'm a phallus from Dallas." Because everybody already knew Mandy'd been going all the way since ninth grade, including with her brother Dickey, and we'd heard she'd already done it with her mouth for Mr. Easton, the civics teacher, the night of the Junior Talent Show. So she let us strip her and she did Billy first.

Back then a sight like Mandy's big tits shot up through you like a rocket at Cape Canaveral. To me a girl's body was the best thing God ever made. Feeling the shapes under the tingly sweaters, touching that soft special skin, I was wild from it. Not that I was a sex fiend or something. It wasn't just girls that turned my motor over all day long. I could watch the jets and the wheat fields when the TV sign-off played the national anthem and get a thrill that nearly choked me. The same for football, like when you go for two up the middle. The same for the sun popping up out of the waves at the beach or the first time little Ashley came toddling toward me holding out her arms. Oh, and dancing. I always danced right under the band where I could feel like I'd dived down the throat of the sax or crawled inside the drums or I could surf on the air of the tune. The same for the way when Precious took me to her grandpa's farm, the carrots and radishes would pop out of the earth into my hand. All those feelings were as strong as seeing Mandy Moore's moony breasts with the nipples tight as thimbles. I was so alive it would kill me now.

But I'll admit that maybe we got out of hand with Mandy, and I'll admit it even though it's not like she brought us up on charges or anything. In fact she never said a single word 'til twenty years later and all of sudden she starts telling everybody she can waylay at the damn club, including my damn wife. I don't know, I'm not going to speak ill of the dead, and I guess I can't blame Mandy for wanting to get it all out, once they'd told her the bad news about her chemo not doing any good. I can sure sympathize. But I admit I wish she'd come to me before she dredged up all that old stuff to Precious and ruined my marriage. Mandy and I could have talked it all over if the past was preying on her.

When I think back, I do remember she cried her head off on the way home from the golf course that night and she said, "I hope y'all all have little girls some day and a bunch of animals do something like this to her and see how y'all feel then." Well, I guess Precious is right and I would go crazy if a horrible thing like that happened to Ashley. Except Ashley's not the sort of a girl that something like that *could* happen to, because she'd never jump into a car with five guys, all of them tighter than Dixie's hatband, and Wilson Hubbard actually tossing his cookies all over the back seat, and not think those guys were cruising for whatever they could find. Still it didn't seem like there were any hard feelings in the long run. Mandy married a guy from Southern Pines and we'd all see each other at the club and say hi. I sure didn't think she was holding a grudge the way she turned out to be, poor thing. Dickey was so all to pieces at her funeral that his wife had me take him out of the church. Right, here I was thinking Dickey was in a bad way and then I come home and Precious has packed her bag and left me.

Precious isn't her real name of course, but everybody in her family called her that and if she'd wanted me to call her Karen, she should have said something. It's not like I'm a mind reader. I met her at a KA mixer the end of my freshman year at Carolina. I pinned her in the fall and it was just the two of us from then on. I'd barrel down to Women's College every Friday in the

White Knight or she'd drive up with her girlfriends. Then the next year she transferred so we could be together. She was sweet as a dream of heaven. Just staring into her eyes gave me the same feeling I got from a first look at other girls' breasts, except with Precious it was peaceful at the same time because you knew you were doing something good because you weren't doing anything. Because she wouldn't. She'd pet 'til dawn but she wouldn't let me in. I mean there were girls at Carolina who'd haul you into the rhododendrons right in front of their housemother's eyes. But Precious wasn't like that. I was in constant pain. We'd French kiss for three straight hours and then I'd take her back to the Tri Delt house and I'd go back to KA. I could hardly stand up straight enough to walk her to the door. I never got her bra off 'til junior year. It was honest to god love. Still is.

College was great. Billy Weatherspoon and Dickey Moore and I all pledged KA and we raised some hell with a bunch of fantastic guys. I'll say this, we drank our share but we never burned the place down and killed anybody like those Greeks in the house on the corner did just a couple of years ago. We didn't flunk out either and we made a contribution. God gave me seven huge plays my last season including that eighty-four–yard touchdown against Duke. I'm not saying the classes didn't get a little tough at times. I had to drop a few and bust my butt to keep the old average in the plus column. The teachers at Carolina weren't as easy on a guy as maybe they were back in high school, and the truth is, some of them had never even heard of me despite my picture being in the paper just about all the time. But I handled it. Like Sinatra says in the song, "That's Life!" Surprise, surprise, the world doesn't owe us a living the way Buster seems to think. We're all taking God's course and it's no gut. Buster needs to learn that. I tell him, "The world's bigger than you are and you're not going to set it spinning." Especially not if he never opens the door to his room. Besides, Christ Almighty couldn't get people to act the way Buster thinks they ought to.

Precious was always saying Buster got her brains and she hoped to hell he did more with them. She used to get kind of mad if I went on about how college was so great because she never got to finish after she got expelled. A bunch of us had gone down to the beach fall of our senior year and climbed in through the window of somebody's summer house that was shut up. We had a cooler full of Buds. Precious and I lay on the porch all night and she let me rub it against her naked. I bet there were a million stars. When we got back to campus Saturday morning, she dropped me off because I was late to practice and she took the White Knight and got pulled for speeding. She'd drunk a little too much beer to be driving, I guess. Anyhow she threw up all over the cop's ticket book and he hauled her in. Precious hadn't ever signed out of Tri Delt for the night, and the whole thing got out of hand. She was just in tears when they expelled her. I told her, "What do you care about going to some old college? Let's you and me get married, how about that?"

Her folks hit the ceiling because they wanted her to finish her senior year but they gave in and announced our engagement in the papers. My folks went through the ceiling too and we had to postpone the wedding 'til after graduation. Precious cried her head off because now we weren't getting married right away and she was already missing a whole term even though she was dean's list and class secretary. We had a fight and broke up. I went wild for about a month and slept with a Tri Delt friend of hers, but I don't think she ever found out. Then Precious's dad was buddies with somebody in administration and they worked things out so she could come back the next year and we made up on Christmas Eve. She gave me some gold cufflinks I still wear and a giant stuffed Panda that's probably down in the rec room with Ashley's junk right this minute.

Christmas night Precious let me go all the way. The first time was in her grandfather's barn. We went out to their farm with her folks for Christmas dinner. We pulled the ladder up into the loft after us. I guess it sounds pretty romantic, Precious lying there under these scratchy old blankets, white as clouds in the sweet crunchy hay, and the voices of neighborhood kids singing "Silent Night" in the yard of the main house. But that's how it happened. I'm not telling anything special, just my life. In fact, I guess I'd say that was the highlight of it. But I didn't know it 'til now.

I graduated one Sunday and got married the next. Two hundred and fifty people sat in church and heard the preacher pronounce us man and wife. What a day. We drank a dozen cases of champagne and ten kegs of beer. Everybody said they had the time of their lives. Billy caught the blue garter and Dickey grabbed the trumpet from the band and played Taps on it. Then he played CHARGE!!! when the White Knight peeled off from the reception with a string of empties clattering on the asphalt, headed for the beach. Precious took the stationery Mom gave her that was engraved *Mrs. Randall Lionel Ryson III* and wrote her thank-you notes while we were down there.

In the fall Precious was planning to finish her last term but she totaled the White Knight so it was sort of the end of an era. By an honest-to-God miracle she only broke her leg, and kept the baby. But it was a bad break, compound fracture, and she was in traction a long time, and somehow she never re-enrolled. So like I say, over the years, every now and then she'd say something about how she wished she'd gotten her degree, but I sure never knew it was preying on her mind enough to make her do something crazy like leave me a whole lifetime after the fact. What'd she need that degree for anyhow, except to hang in the den? It's not like she had to go out and work. We were doing just fine. I got promoted to managing director (this was my dad's home insulation business) before we'd been married more than a year and we moved here to Hope Valley about three blocks from where I grew up. The company was called "The Comfort Zone," and it expanded like crazy, especially during the oil crisis, to where we had offices in three separate states. We made a lot of money keeping folks warm in the winter and cool in the summer.

And my part of that money came right home to Precious and the kids. Annex, pool, three cars, country kitchen, private lessons, private schools. It's not like I was out whoring and boozing all night like a few guys I won't name.

I thought we had a good life. Not that we didn't have our share of sorrow. Buster was born two weeks after I heard the news that Billy Weatherspoon had gotten killed in Vietnam. His mom couldn't even pronounce the name of the place where he died, it was so far away. That's why Buster's name is William Weatherspoon Ryson instead of Randall L. Ryson IV. Precious wanted to call him Surrell, after her grandpa, but that was just too weird. The night we heard about Billy, Dickey and I tied one on. We got Billy's old Corvair that was still sitting in his parents' garage waiting for him to come back. We drove it out to the Occa River and set it on fire with gasoline and pushed it over the bank. When those little blue feet decals sank under the water, Dickey played Taps on his horn from high school band. I don't know what got into us, and I guess we're lucky we didn't get thrown in jail because Billy's parents were pretty P.O.ed about the car, but they didn't press charges or anything.

There were some other bumps on the road. My sister Cottie got two divorces before she was thirty, and to be honest I don't think she's too happy with number three. They've got Dickey on these antidepressants since Mandy passed away. Wilson Hubbard developed a serious drinking problem and pretty much ruined his life; he dropped dead of a heart attack at forty-one, but by that time we'd more or less lost touch with him. Now, you could see why a wife might get fed up with Wilson Hubbard (and Wendy definitely did), but I'd like to know what the hell I did so wrong to deserve the last two years of my life with Precious doing me like that, and then the damn doctors hitting me while I was down.

A year after Buster, Ashley was born on Superbowl Sunday and she was a doll from the day she came home. I never had to worry about Ashley the way I did about Buster. Smart, pretty, sweet as heaven, good grades, class president, jazz gymnastics state-level finalist. Sometimes I go in her empty room and stand there and get tears in my eyes, if that doesn't sound too gushy. But I swear to god I think Ashley'd be living with me full-time if Precious hadn't gotten this feminist judge on her side. Buster doesn't even want to be here for the weekends but Ashley runs up and hugs me and sometimes she calls me up in the middle of the week just to check on me. I haven't told her about this damn cancer spreading all over the damn place. I don't want her worrying when there's nothing she can do. I haven't told anybody. I don't want Precious feeling sorry for me either, and I sure as hell don't want Buster telling me it's all because of the insulation my dad and I sold.

Ashley'll be heartbroken but she's strong and she'll be fine. But I'm in a constant worry about my son even though Precious doesn't think there's anything to worry about. Buster's a loner, lives behind a closed door. Who knows what he's doing in there? He'd get more exercise if they threw him in prison the way they did most of his heroes, because at least they'd make him do a few sit-ups. I bought him a new Jeep Cherokee but if I didn't drive it around myself when he comes over on weekends, the damn battery'd go dead. Buster's against the combustion engine. Brooding over fossil fuels never crossed my mind when I was seventeen, and I don't see why my boy has to throw his youth away on the sad state of the world. Honest to God, he's my own flesh and blood and I love him to death but the truth is, what Buster looks like and what he acts like, is a *nerd*. I don't know if that's what they still call it now, but I'm sure whatever it is, that's what they're calling Buster, and my heart just aches. I ask Ashley, "Sweetheart, why doesn't your big brother ever ask a girl out? Couldn't you fix him up with a friend of yours?" And she says, "Daddy, give it up. No way."

I'm not being hard on him because I want him to fit in like I did the way Precious thinks. I just don't believe he's happy. Hell, how could he be, locked up in his room with all the misery of the world on his chest, and no friends, not to mention no girl?!

Maybe this is going to sound sick for a father to say but I almost hope Buster's locked up in there with *Hustler* or something, giving himself a little solo action. I hope Ashley's not telling me Buster's not interested in sex!

Because if you ask me, sex is what we have to make up for having to die. That's my personal opinion. I guess you could call sex God's booby prize and I don't mean that in a sacrilegious way either. Okay maybe it doesn't last and maybe Precious and I weren't doing it much even before she turned on me, I guess over Mandy. Maybe we didn't have much going for the last five years or so. But I'll say this, we had our share. And well, hell, life can't stand still, the game's got to come to an end sometime. I said to Precious once—maybe it was like our fifteenth anniversary—that we were sagging like we were those wax candles of the bride and groom on a wedding cake. My pecs and her breasts were just sliding down our bodies. I tried to make a joke about how even if we'd been burnt away, at least we were lit. I thought that was pretty funny and she laughed too. Now I feel like I'm sitting on that wedding cake all by myself, pretty much melted down to a nub.

Today started out better. I was feeling okay. Ashley and I got back from church and had some nice sandwiches. I saw they were showing clips on TV before the Duke–Carolina game called "Highlights from the Past." Well, I figured I'd be one of the highlights so I asked Ashley to go see if she could get Buster to turn off that music of his. ("That's a great song," he says of this garbage where you can't understand a word of it except a few filthy things you wish you hadn't heard.) I told her, ask him to come out of his room and watch the highlights with us. Well, I was pretty amazed but she got him to do it. He scuffed into the den all in black (except his hair's pink and his skin's the color of a white tablecloth, and now I noticed he had a few more of those damn little rings stuck through his face). He slumped down against the paneling and said, "So? Bone cruncher time?"

I don't start anything 'cause I don't want him to leave. And sure enough they did show my eighty-four–yard run against

Duke. There I was, the *real* me, spinning and weaving and everybody in the stands on their feet. Buster got his sarcastic expression that made him look so much like Precious. He said, "Big Moochie Ryson, Jeezus, look at him go."

Ashley was her usual doll. She said, "Daddy, that's great!"

Buster made a joke of sticking his finger down his throat. Then he asked me, "You ever read a poem called 'To an Athlete Dying Young'?" I said I didn't think so unless I read it in college and couldn't remember. So he quoted at me, "'And silence sounds no worse than cheers / After earth has stopped the ears.'"

I asked him, "What does that mean?"

"That you have seriously worn your honors out, Dad. It's a garland briefer than a girl's. You should have died right then, right there in the end zone, with everybody cheering. Like the Greeks used to yell at the Olympic victors, you know, *Die now, die now!*"

"That's not very nice," Ashley said. She was combing my hair, which she's very sweet to do. "Why'd they do that?"

Buster slumped over so it was hard to make out what he was saying. "To, like, remind the winners how you'll never be this perfect again, how you only get these cheers once, okay? How it's a garland briefer than a girl's, but if you're dead you don't know the cheering's stopped, okay? You don't have to keep looking through the old photo albums, so die now, see?"

I said, "Well, thanks anyhow, Buster, but I'm kind of glad I didn't die then. For one thing, you wouldn't be around."

"Fine by me," said Buster.

"Oh Daddy, ignore him," Ashley told me.

But Buster cut loose. He talked more in the next half-hour than in the two whole years since the divorce. He told us he'd read this article in a magazine that proved it was the losers in high school that went on to personal happiness and great achievements in the world, while the implication was that if you were sort of a big shot, or whatever you want to call it, back when you were young, chances are you'd amount to nothing—

like you'd be a miserable misfit fixing used washing machines for nickels while the old high school losers you used to feel sorry for went off to be saints and movie stars and billionaires. I'm the first to admit that setting the world on fire never crossed my mind personally, but if that's what Buster wants, go for it, kid, nothing would please me more, as long as it makes you happy. But of course it was clear as day why this article meant so much to him, because, God help him, if there ever was a high school loser, Buster Ryson is it.

I told him his article was off-sides. I knew a lot of losers back in high school, and they weren't happy then and I'd be willing to bet my bottom dollar they aren't happy now. Not even if they won the Nobel Prize. Because they're still inside that same old loser head of theirs and it's telling them, "Who are you kidding? You're no winner." That's what I bet.

I told Buster, the fact is, back in high school I was president of our class and now I'm president of The Comfort Zone. I've got a bigger house than my folks, if you want to count things that way, and the only high-dive pool in Hope Valley. I had friends back then and I've got friends right now. I see Dickey Moore every other week. I wouldn't exactly call it flunking out of life. I said I wanted him to know I wasn't boo-hooing about where did all the roses go, I wasn't down on God for rusting my engine with the tarnish of time. Sure, you can't out-race time in the long run. But I wasn't trying to. I had just wanted to play the game. There's a shelf full of trophies on top of that TV, I said, and the guy that won them, won them, got out of his damn room and went and won them. I told him, I took the blows and did it my way, like Sinatra says, which is a great song, unlike some other songs I've heard talked about in this house.

I said, "The fact is, I was a winner and still am, whether you think so or not."

Buster raises his eyebrow just like Precious. He says, "Sure, Dad, and that's why Mom's engaged to marry somebody else."

Well, that news hit me pretty hard. It hit me like those guys in the Georgia game where they had to carry me off the field and I was out cold for almost an hour.

Right away, Ashley starts yelling at Buster about how he wasn't supposed to tell me about Precious getting engaged, and she even runs over and hits him.

Buster's red in the face and shouting back at her, "Right, like he's never going to find out!" And he stomps off back upstairs and the door-slam shakes the whole house.

I told Ashley not to worry. I pretended like I already knew anyhow, like I'd heard it at the club about Precious planning to marry somebody else. But I didn't know and I didn't expect it, I have to admit. Ashley told me the guy's name and it wasn't anybody I knew. She said he was from Knoxville and that they were all going to have to move there. Then Ashley started crying and saying her whole life was ruined because she didn't want to leave her school and her friends and me. I told her it wasn't ruined. I hugged her and told her that she was the most wonderful, beautiful, smartest girl in the world and that everything was going to be perfect her whole life long. Maybe it won't be, but I'd walk smiling into a fire to make it true.

I must have fallen asleep watching the game—I tire out pretty easily these days—and when I woke up another show was on and the house was dark. The kids had left but there was a note on the kitchen counter from Ashley saying, "I LOVE YOU DADDY." She'd made me some brownies wrapped in cellophane with a ribbon.

I took them back to the recliner and sat in front of the TV. But there was nothing I wanted to see. So I took down the old family photo albums. Maybe Buster's right. I'm living in the past—I look at the old pictures a lot lately. I look at my folks when they were young and my sister Cottie and my high school friends and college friends and our wedding. I look at lots of Buster and Ashley growing up. Mostly I look at Precious. And I remember my life with her, which was no great shakes, I guess, to her, or in Buster's grand scheme of things, but it had its moments. She can't pretend it didn't.

I remember running down that field in the Duke–Carolina game, right inside my body without having to think about where I was, the way you don't think about dancing because it's just a fact going on. I remember knowing I could make that eighty-four–yard run, like maybe a racehorse knows.

Even if that body's gone now, and taken the real me with it, and left some old geezer in this recliner with sixty different bottles of pills beside him that aren't going to do him any good, still I've got the highlights of the past.

I was a golden racer in those days and the world was full of gold. I remember the feel of the football tight inside my arm, sound coming at me across the field out of the band's twinkling brass, and Dickey Moore running out of the middle of the band toward me, the gold plume on his high white hat blazing in the sun, his horn raised, blowing CHAAAARRGGE!! I remember the stadium full of noise and friends, everybody in the world cheering, one cheer coming out of all the faces.

I remember things that break my heart and things that I'm ashamed of. I don't know if there's a heaven, but if there is, maybe I'll run into Billy Witherspoon and Mandy Moore up there and we'll tell her we're sorry and try to work it out after all these years.

I remember my sister Cottie's face on Christmas mornings when we were little. And my two children laughing together like sunshine in the blue of the pool.

Most of all, I remember the face of my wife as sweet as heaven in the sweet yellow hay that first time ever, the frost of her breath like clouds in heaven. I remember Karen my wife who was Precious to me.

Charmain

White Trash Noir

All of a sudden Dr. Rothmann, the foreman of my jury, says she wants to talk to the judge. She gives me a look when she walks by the defendant's table, straight in my eyes, and I nod back at her but I can't tell what she's thinking because there's so many different feelings in her face. But behind me my Mawmaw stands up and bows her head to her. The judge and the jury get up too and they crowd each other out of the courtroom and just leave us sitting here. My lawyer leans over and says, "Charmain, you have got to change your mind and take the stand." And I tell him, "No thank you."

Mr. Snow goes, "This is Murder One, Charmain. You just cannot kill your husband in this state if he played ACC basketball."

I go, "Well, this is Charmain Luby Markell and I'm not talking about my personal private life to a bunch of strangers in a court of law and have them turn it all into lies against me and mine."

I got this lawyer? He's young, just two years more than me, and halfway through our first talk in the jail I can tell he hasn't had a lot of Life Experience, which between you and I, I've already had way too much. Tilden Snow's his name, Tilden Snow III, and I think it's lazy for a family to use a name three times in a row when there're so many nice new names out there you can choose from. They even got little Names for Your Baby books at the checkout counters, which is where I got my Jarrad's name. That's what I call my little boy, Jarrad Todd Markell, even though his birth certificate says Kyle Lewis Markell Jr., totally because my husband's mother worships the ground her son Kyle walks on. Well, *did* walk on before I shot him.

So Mr. Snow wanted me to get up on the witness stand and tell why I shot my husband in the head and set him on fire in our backyard.

Mr. Snow chews at a cuticle; his nails are a mess. He sighs a long deep sigh and shakes his head at me. "Please won't you help me here, Charmain?"

Please won't I help him? Who're they trying to give a lethal injection to, me or Tilden Snow III? I go, "Mr. Snow—"

He holds up his hand like a safety patrol. "Tilden. I keep asking you, please call me Tilden. Mr. Snow's my daddy's name." I think he was trying to make a joke so I smiled and said I'd try to call him Tilden but I wouldn't take the stand and tell why I shot Kyle.

"Oh Jesus," he says. "Well, you better hope your friend Dr. Rothmann's telling the judge she's going to hang that jury."

I say, "What does that mean, she's going to hang the jury?" But he just pulls on his ears like he wishes they were longer and he runs off with the other lawyers after Dr. Rothmann and the judge, and leaves me to sit and wait, which is what I've mostly been doing since Kyle died. Which I admit he did do when I shot him.

I'm used to it now but the first time they hauled me into this courtroom, I was crying and grabbing on to my grandma Mawmaw so hard they had to prize my fingers from around her neck. I saw the way it was upsetting her how they had my hands and feet both hooked up to a chain. But Mawmaw whispered at me, "Don't you cry, baby doll, don't you let those folks see you cry," and I tried hard to stop and I did. The only other time I ever went to pieces was when Mawmaw brought Jarrad into the back of the courtroom and held him up for me to look at (he's two and a half now and he was nineteen months last time I seen him). He had a little toy basketball in his hands and I swear he looked like his daddy, maybe because he started to cry and his face turned purple the way Kyle's did when he got mad.

The first day I was in court the whole jury kept staring at me like somebody was going to test them in the morning. Right off I noticed this one lady on the front row, a soft pretty lady, small, with a sharp smart face. From day one, she looked right at me with her head cocked over to the side like a little hawk, sort of puzzling about me. They said her name was Mrs. Nina Gold Rothmann, except they called her "Doctor." She got to be the foreman of the jury even though she wasn't a man. And for two whole weeks of the State's making its case, she's about never took her eyes off me.

Now the State's done and it's time for our side to "shred them to pieces" according to Mr. Snow, except I'm not going to take the stand so there won't be much shredding likely to get done. Maybe that's why Doctor Rothmann's made them all go off to talk to the judge now. Maybe she's in there telling the judge just give Charmain Markell the death penalty so the jury can go on home. They must be about as sick of hearing about that gun and kerosene and Kyle's eleven points against Wake Forest as I am.

The first day of my trial I didn't like Doctor Rothmann. It's rude to stare the way she does. But after a while I kind of felt like we was almost talking to each other. I heard all about her life at what they call the vow deer, I believe. She had to tell about herself to get on the jury, or get off it, which a lot of them tried to because of their jobs or kids or whatever. They said she was a big doctor at the Research Center. She told how she was working on what we're all made up of, genomes, something like that. When you know their genomes, you can tell people what they're going to die of someday. Well, but I guess I don't need a Research Center to tell me that. Lethal injection. Least if the District Attorney Mr. Goodenough gets his way.

Anyhow this foreman lady's job of sorting out our genomes sounded hard but interesting and I could tell she cared a lot about it from the way she talked. At first I smiled at her just to be polite, but later on it was sort of personal because she was divorced and had a boy in college. And I thought that was kind of like me—I mean I've got one little boy and no husband anymore too. So a lot of days went by in court with me and Doctor Rothmann looking at each other. I started figuring out some beauty tips I could of given her if she'd come in Pretty Woman. She had three suits that didn't do much for her; the sleeves were too long so she just had them rolled up. Her hands were nice though; somebody did a good job on her nails, but not us—I never saw her in Pretty Woman and I do all their hands.

After a while I decided her eyes weren't mean, she was just thinking hard all the time, not like some folks on my jury that were taking naps with their eyes open. Not that I blame them. All that State's evidence was boring *me,* and it was my life. But Doctor Rothmann, she hung in there even with that old fat Mr. Goodenough mumbling about ballistics this and ballistics that for four solid hours. Isn't it something? I could not make myself listen.

After a week or so Doctor Rothmann got to be somebody I could kind of talk to in my mind in my cell at night, like maybe explain things to her that were all balled up inside me like string in a junk drawer, like she'd be smart enough to see how they'd look if they got untangled. When I looked at her over there in the jury box, I felt like she could see what was true. I tried to explain it to my lawyer Tilden Snow, but he said, "I don't trust Rothmann." He figured the D.A. must know something or he wouldn't have let her on my jury because he said usually the State avoids these Ph.D.s like the plague on account of they are soft on crime.

Yesterday I told Mr. Snow in the visiting room how deep down I thought the foreman lady was kind of sweet and he snorts at me. "She's about as sweet as a jar of pickled okra." I said I was surprised somebody rich as him even ate pickled okra but he tells me, "Charmain, I've got a grandmama same as you and she loved pickled okra."

I say, "I know you do because my grandma used to clean her house and your mama's house."

He says, "I know. Your grandmama was the White Tornado."

"Yes she was and still is. She quit your mama," I say.

He wants to know why but he's not surprised.

I tell him. "Your mama called her a servant and said how she had to iron your daddy's boxer shorts. And Mawmaw's like, 'No thank you, Mrs. Snow, I am not your servant and I am not about to put my hands in a strange man's underpants.'"

Mr. Snow—I'm sorry, I don't want to call him Tilden—laughed. He says, "I didn't know that. And here's something I bet you don't know. I remember you. Your grandmama brought you to the house with her one time while she was cleaning—"

I nod. "She brought me with her to a lot of houses because I helped her clean 'til I started at Pretty Woman."

"Well, one time when I was there visiting my grandma and I guess I was about six or seven, I asked you if you wanted to swing on my swing and then I asked you if you'd marry me. Do you remember that?"

"No."

"You don't remember that?"

"I'm sorry."

He shook his head like he couldn't believe I'd forget he wanted to marry me when I was four or five years old. Then he stacked up all his papers to go. He says, "Well, my grandmama was a bitch on wheels. And I bet the same can be said for your sweet Doctor Nina Rothmann."

People think you can't be nice and smart both but I don't see why. Mawmaw used to tell me and my brother Tanner, "I'd rather have sweetness and niceness in a child than a report card full of As," but why couldn't she get both? 'Course the last A she ever saw was the one I got in algebra in tenth grade. But I blame that on going out almost every night with Kyle who was a senior and the star of the basketball team. Rich as Tilden Snow was, even he wasn't popular like Kyle. So my grades slipped. Meanwhile my brother Tanner would probably still be stuck in first grade if all his teachers hadn't passed him along to get him out of their classrooms. I bet he's the only boy ever flunked conduct in elementary school.

Our grandma Mawmaw raised me and Tanner after Daddy and Mama got killed trying to beat a Food Lions truck through an intersection. She said they wasn't cut out to be parents anyhow, due to drugs, drink, and the NASCAR tracks. They dropped us off at Mawmaw's almost every night even before they got killed. Mawmaw said my mama was the only thing my daddy ever met that was as fast as him. He loved speed and speed killed him in the long run. And he took my mama along for the ride. Only twenty-four, both of them, which is how old I am now, so I guess twenty-four is just a real unlucky year for the Lubys in general, since that's how old my brother Tanner was three years ago when he held up the A.B.C. store while still on parole.

Poor Mawmaw, she used to tell me with my brother Tanner it was déjà vu right back to our daddy only worse. Daddy was Mawmaw's only child and she said he was one too many. Plus she said with Tanner she didn't have her strength like she used to. But she never quit. Thirty-five years at the job and she's still cleaning houses. Because of her I was never cold and I was never hungry and I was never made to feel no good. And I know my little boy Jarrad never will be either, if Mawmaw can just hold onto him against Kyle's mama Mrs. Markell's law suit. Kyle's mama getting her hands on Jarrad scares me more than a lethal injection. I mean, look how Kyle turned out. So bad his own wife shot him.

Way back when Daddy was fourteen and he robbed Mawmaw's purse, stole her car, and drove it down to Mardi Gras in New Orleans, she asked her minister at Church of the Open Door if the devil could of got her pregnant while she was asleep at night, 'cause she'd started wondering if Daddy was the son of Satan. But the minister said the Devil don't make personal acquaintanceships in the modern world. Well, that minister never met my husband Kyle Markell. And I wish I could say the same. When Mawmaw came down to the hospital after they pumped out my stomach, she told me the only way somebody *wouldn't* have killed Kyle sooner or later was they never met him. But I sure don't think Mawmaw figured it'd be me. I never was a violent person, never yelled, never cursed, and I never could stand blood. I couldn't even cut up a frog in biology. And when that Clemson guard whammed his elbow into Kyle's nose his freshman year and they couldn't stop the bleeding, I fainted dead away in the stands. I fainted other times too, like when Kyle had JuliaRoberts put to sleep just because of her seizures. That was my dog that had eyes like Julia Roberts. I'm convinced Kyle ran over her with the van and swore he didn't. I never wanted to hurt anything in this world 'til the day I picked up that gun and told Kyle to put down that basketball and shut the fuck up.

Anyhow, the reason I wouldn't go on the stand in my own defense was the samples Mr. Snow gave of what the District Attorney would likely ask me. I wouldn't tell that sort of thing to Mawmaw on my deathbed, much less testify on a Bible about it to everybody in my hometown. Like the weird disgusting stuff Kyle heard on the Internet that he kept trying to make me do in bed. And Mr. Snow said how they'd twist things all around so lies would look true and the true things sound like lies. So I kept telling the lawyer the same thing I used to tell Kyle. No thank you. He got real upset, the lawyer, I mean. To be honest it was nothing much compared to the way Kyle used to freak out on me when he was alive, which I guess it's my fault he's not anymore. All my lawyer does is grumble how I'm tying his hands behind his back. One day early on in the trial he said I had a sympathetic personality and was young and petite and pretty—the way his eyes shifted around behind his glasses when he said that I had the feeling he was coming on to me without even knowing it, which would be pretty strange considering, but he wouldn't be the first man that got strange on me at the wrong time. His idea was if I took the stand and started crying I could maybe win over the jury to go easy on me even if Kyle had played in the Sweet Sixteen.

Three weeks back, the night before my trial started my lawyer goes, "I don't want to scare you, Charmain—" (Sure!) — But he explains how unless I testify so he can bring up about the drug stuff and weird sex stuff and the 911 and the rest of it, I could get Death.

I'm like, "Well okay then, I'll take Death. But I won't take the stand."

He's like, "Great. You know who's gonna love this? The district attorney. You know why? Because you just lay down in the death chamber, Charmain, handed him the needle, and said stick it in!" He shakes this bunch of papers in my face. "Look at this, look at this, look at this!"

I say, "Excuse me but I heard you the first time."

"This is State's evidence. These are exhibits the State's gonna be showing to the jury and you don't think they're not going to have a seriously deleterious impact?"

Well, I didn't know what "deleterious" means but from the twitch in his mouth I could tell it wasn't good. I looked at the papers. Stuff like:

STATE EXHIBIT #7. ONE DESERT EAGLE MARK VII.44 MAGNUM CALIBER PISTOL, BLACK MATTE FINISH. SIX-INCH BARREL. FINGERPRINTS OF DEFENDANT ON GRIP.

STATE EXHIBIT #13. EIGHT-ROUND CLIP OF .44 MAGNUM SHELLS. TWO ROUNDS FIRED.

STATE EXHIBIT #28. EMPTIED KEROSENE CAN. FINGERPRINTS OF DEFENDANT ON HANDLE.

STATE EXHIBIT #51. TWO .44 MAGNUM SLUGS TAKEN FROM CRANIUM OF THE DECEASED.

STATE EXHIBIT #85. FIVE-PAGE LETTER OF CONFESSION TO SHOOTING ON MARRIOTT STATIONERY SIGNED BY DEFENDANT.

STATE EXHIBIT #97. ACC TOURNAMENT BASKETBALL WITH BULLET HOLE.

STATE EXHIBIT #103. PHOTOGRAPHS OF PARTIALLY BURNED CORPSE OF THE DECEASED.

I said it did look like they had plenty of exhibits. Tilden Snow just nodded like his head was on a spring. But he was right about them making the most of what they had. For two weeks, mornings and afternoons, that sour-faced district attorney, Mr. Goodenough, kept shaking plastic baggies with those exhibits in them in front of the jury's faces. He made it all sound like I was the original black widow spider. The worst was the pictures of Kyle's body. I didn't look at them. But the foreman-lady Dr. Rothmann turned gray as a old dishrag when Mr. Goodenough shoved them at her, and I'm not sure how much she even saw because she turned her head so fast.

I'd rather be dead anyhow probably. I mean, I already tried. And failed flat as I did Algebra II when I was going out with Kyle every night, which was a shame, I mean the algebra, 'cause it was kind of interesting. But at the time, I'm sorry to say, not as interesting as Kyle, who was already such a big basketball star at Creekside High he was on the news just about every week, leaping and dribbling and dodging and tossing. He could have had any girl he wanted in Creekside High and I was such an idiot I was glad he picked me.

Anyhow, I tried to die after I killed Kyle but I didn't. I woke up alive in the ICU and I could just hear Kyle laughing that snuffling way he had about how Charmain Luby never could do a single thing right. But I did try. I bought a shelf's-worth of every pill Wal-Mart's had on display, then I went to the Marriott and got most of them down with a bottle of vodka which tasted terrible because I'm not much of a drinker. I propped my letter to Mawmaw against the ice bucket and took out my silver-framed picture of my baby Jarrad (that Mrs. Markell got named Kyle Jr. on the certificate) and I lay down with the picture on the bed and cried myself to sleep. I felt like I was dying and they said I would of too if it hadn't been for the highway patrol knocking the door down and rushing me to the emergency clinic.

It was my brother's Mercury Cougar got the police there, which I didn't know was a stolen vehicle at the time I parked it out in front of the Marriott on Old 89, not that anything Tanner did would surprise me anymore. They had a whatever-you-call-it out for his car and it was a easy color to spot, Light Sapphire Blue, plus had a Pirates of the Caribbean flag from Disneyworld hanging on the antenna, plus Florida plates. They weren't even looking for me yet. So they saved my life and went for the death penalty.

I always wanted to stay in that Marriott. Or any Marriott. Even on our honeymoon Kyle took me to a Motel 6 at the beach. "I'm not paying good money for a bed in the dark." He wouldn't eat in nice restaurants either. "I'm not paying good money for something that's going to turn to shit in three hours." Kyle always called it "good money" and I guess what was good about it was he never spent it on me. He spent it on drugs and what he called "Antique Vehicles." He collected old junk motorbikes, cars and trucks, and anything else crappy that used to move and now couldn't anymore. He claimed their "value" was "going through the roof" someday and then he'd fix them and sell them for a fortune on the Internet. But he never did, surprise surprise. All he did was leave them there turning to red rust and weeds I couldn't get at to pull. Between his antique vehicles and his basketball court, he used up all the space in my yard so I couldn't grow a vegetable garden. He squashed my peonies under a 1952 Ford truck and he shot free throws standing on top of my tulip bulbs. Mostly up Kyle's nose is where the good money went. And I got Motel 6.

Where I really always wanted to stay at was the Polynesian Resort at Disneyworld. But considering what's happened, it don't take the Psychic Hotline to tell me Disneyworld's not in my future, because even if I don't get Death, I'll get Life.

My brother Tanner went to Disneyworld. Drove down to Orlando right after he got out on the A.B.C. Store thing. I wish he'd taken me with him. At least I would have seen the Magic Kingdom. Or I wish he'd never come back with that Mercury Cougar that stopped me from dying at the Marriott. Or I wish he hadn't come back at all, so I wouldn't have gone over to his trailer and seen his Desert Eagle Mark VII .44 magnum caliber pistol I shot Kyle with. (Mr. Goodenough has been talking for weeks about that gun, like it was the most important thing in my life so that's how I know so much about it now, because believe me at the time I borrowed it from Tanner, all I knew was it was black and heavy and if you pulled the trigger a bullet came out.) Most of all I wish I'd never eloped with Kyle.

I picked the Marriott because I figured as far as me and a nice motel goes it was sort of now or never, since I planned on meeting my Maker after those medications took hold—if there's even Anybody up there *to* meet, though I'd hate for Mawmaw to hear me wondering something like that. And you know what's funny—not really funny but freaky—is at first I was thinking, Ha Ha, wait'll Kyle gets this Visa bill, he'll turn totally purple, because on top of $129 at the Marriott, I had tore through Wal-Mart, looking like Kyle used to on the basketball court before they found out he was using cocaine. After I loaded up on medications, I bought Mawmaw a Hoover Deluxe because she brings her own equipment to the job, plus $326.59 worth of toys for her to put out under the tree next Christmas for Jarrad. It took me a long time to choose the toys and it was like I forgot I didn't have a long time. That's what was funny, I had completely forgot I'd killed Kyle, shot him in the head, and drug him out in the yard and set fire to him right under his basketball hoop with a big pile of brush and a gallon can of kerosene.

Then when I was lying on the king-sized bed in the Marriott swallowing those pills, it hit me how there was no way Kyle was ever going to pitch another fit over the Visa bill or the other million things he blamed me for, like his whole entire life, which I used to be dumb enough to think was my fault. And then it hit me how it was Mawmaw that was gonna get stuck with that huge Visa bill. And how it was Jarrad that was gonna get stuck with his friends saying his mama had murdered his daddy, which is worse than what I had to put up with in school because of my name and that was bad enough, calling me Toilet Paper and "Please don't touch the Charmain." Plus jokes about my parents being trash and road kill. Trying to write a letter for Jarrad to read when he was old enough was the last thing I remember.

My lawyer said a suicide attempt didn't look good for me in some ways, and did look good in others. The way it did look good was it showed I wasn't in my right mind and was full of remorse and confusion and maybe had acted "on impulse" and wasn't trying to get away with something. The way it didn't look good was I'd left a note for Mawmaw asking her to apologize to Mr. and Mrs. Markell for me and say I hoped they could forgive me for killing their son but not saying anything about how shooting Kyle was an accident, or self-defense, or spur of the moment, or too much to drink, or some other reason why it wouldn't be Murder One. Plus, setting fire to Kyle with kerosene—my lawyer said that had the look of a cover-up.

I guess it was a cover-up, just not enough of one. But it's true, I couldn't stand the idea of Mawmaw and Jarrad (when he was old enough) thinking I killed anybody, much less my husband, and I guess that's why I tried to get rid of his body. I figured if Kyle was just gone and everybody thought he'd run off to Hawaii or something, then Mawmaw wouldn't get her life ruined and Jarrad would have, I don't know, a chance, I guess. When I tried to explain my reason to Mawmaw in the hospital, she said my Mama and Daddy hadn't had half a brain between them but she had used to think I did have some brains. But I'd handed them over to Kyle to wipe his feet on. She said there *wasn't* no reason for acting the way I had, and I had to accept I'd acted crazy and move on from there.

But I will swear this on a Bible. I *never* thought Mr. and Mrs. Markell would drop by our house that afternoon (which is something they never did, and Kyle sure never told me he'd asked them to supper), and find Kyle only half burnt up. I figured that brush pile would burn on through the weekend—nobody lives near us and besides, Kyle liked to keep trash burning out back so you couldn't smell his marijuana. I'd figured by the time anybody showed up, I'd be gone to Heaven or probably Hell, considering, and Jarrad would be at Mawmaw's safe and sound, and when Kyle wasn't at Creekside Ford on Tuesday, because he had Monday off, somebody would call the house, and then one of his coworkers would come over and think he was gone. I *never* figured Mr. and Mrs. Markell would be wandering through my kitchen by four o'clock on Sunday, and they'd see the smoke and walk out to that brush pile. Because that is something parents should never have to see. Their son burning up in his backyard. And I do apologize for that.

Another thing that didn't look good for me was my brother Tanner and the fact that I'd borrowed Tanner's gun three whole days before I used it to shoot Kyle with. My lawyer called it "our elephant in the kitchen." Before Tilden Snow got to be my lawyer, I admitted in my statement that I took the gun out of Tanner's refrigerator and brought it home with me. "That gun implies premeditation, Charmain, which is why Goodenough's going for first-degree homicide." He (I mean Tilden Snow) couldn't stop trying to get me to say something that wasn't true about that gun. "Charmain, go back to that timeframe. I want you to let me know when I say something that correlates to your motivation." I swear that's the way he talks; sometimes even the judge looks at him like he's nuts.

But when Mr. Snow says, "Okay, go back," I say I'm not going anywhere. He doesn't listen any more than Kyle did. "Maybe you took the gun because you didn't want your brother Tanner to get in trouble with it."

I say, "No, I didn't."

"Maybe you took the gun because there'd been crime in the isolated rural area you lived in and you felt afraid to be in the house with Kyle gone."

I say, "All I *wanted* was to be in the house with Kyle gone."

He jumps on this. "So maybe you felt afraid to be in the house *with* Kyle and wanted that gun for self-defense."

I shake my head.

He sighs. "Maybe you weren't even aware you took the gun."

I say, "Now, Mr. Snow—"

"Tilden."

"How could I not know I took it? That thing weighs a ton."

He never did ask me to tell him *why* I took the gun out of Tanner's refrigerator. But he made that a rule from the very start. The day we met, he said, "Charmain, don't answer any questions I don't ask you. Don't tell me anything I don't tell you I want to know. Do you understand?"

I shrug. "Sure." And that was the end of honest communication. Honest communication is what the marriage counselor I got for me and Kyle two years ago said good relationships was based on. But that marriage counselor was a moron, plus started hitting on me every time Kyle went to the toilet (which was pretty much a lot and the reason why our money got sniffed straight up his nose). All I hope is, that moron's marriage-counseling office has already gone bust. It can't be real good for business when one of your patients shoots her husband in the head and sets fire to him. I told Mawmaw back when I quit the marriage counselor, "That man didn't respect me anymore than Kyle did."

That's when she said the thing that was haunting me from right then 'til a year later when I pulled the trigger on Kyle. She took my hands in hers that were like tree bark they were so rough, and none of the paraffin wax dips I give her could do a thing for them. She said, "Charmain, you listen to me. Since I was eleven years old I been cleaning out other people's toilets and the only way I can stand it is, I get the respect of the folks I work for and if I don't, I don't work for them no more. Listen to me, you got to *earn* respect. But when you do earn it, you make sure they give it to you. They can't make you turn any which way they want to. You got to learn that, honey. You're my only hope that thirty-five years on my knees with a scrub brush wasn't just a gob of spit in a week of rain. You got to learn that."

I said, "Mawmaw, I'm trying."

She said, "I know, baby. You're my hope. Because the Savior knows your brother Tanner is nothing but your daddy born again to torment me."

My lawyer felt about the same way about Tanner as Mawmaw. He said Tanner looked bad for us. First of all, he had a record of crime and violence that Mr. Goodenough could use to show a bad family background or bad genes or whatever. Second of all, Tanner had told the police he'd *advised* me to shoot Kyle and had said he'd be glad to shoot Kyle himself if I didn't want to. After he blabbed this total lie at the police station (and Tanner would always say any wild thing he could think of to get attention), for a little while the police got the idea in their heads that Tanner *had* shot Kyle. They kept trying to get me to admit I was just pretending I was the one had killed Kyle instead of my brother. They accused me of lying to protect him because he had a record and I didn't. The police chief came to the hospital after my suicide attempt, questioning me about that.

I go, "I'm sorry. But I am not a liar. And I wouldn't lie for my brother about something like this."

The police chief, with a little smile like life was one big joke, said, "Wouldn't you lie to protect him, Mrs. Markell? Isn't that a Luby family trait? I remember when your brother shot ya'll's cousin Crawder Luby in the chest at point blank range following an argument over a girl in the parking lot of Lucille's Steak House."

I say, "Tanner was never charged with shooting Crawder."

"That's exactly right. Tanner drove Crawder to Piedmont Hospital and tossed him out in front of the emergency entrance. Now when we came to interview your cousin Crawder, he claimed he had no idea who'd shot him. That's why we never could charge Tanner with that crime because his cousin that he *shot* stood by him. So, yes, Charmain, I think you Lubys will lie to protect each other."

"Well, I won't," I said.

Pretty soon they had to believe me because it turned out Tanner was off with Crawder the day I shot Kyle. They'd gone deep-sea fishing off of Wrightsville Beach and had run out of gas and had to be rescued by the Coast Guard. That's why Tanner'd given me his Mercury Cougar to keep 'til he came back. At least I thought it was his. Now I see he was hiding it out.

So then the police believed *I* shot Kyle and wanted to know why. Was it for money? Was there another man in my life? But by then Mawmaw had got Tilden Snow III to represent me and every time I'd open my mouth he'd say, "Don't answer that, Charmain." Mawmaw got him because she knew he and his daddy and grandpa were all lawyers, and they knew her from back when she was the White Tornado in their house. He took my case on what he called "pro bono."

According to my cousin Crawder, Tilden Snow III only did it because it was a good way for him to make his name as big as his daddy's, since newspaper and TV people were crawling all over us at my trial. That was a little bit because they said I don't look like your regular-type killer, plus had been a Teen for Christ, even if some big snoots in town called my family white trash, and Mrs. Markell didn't think I was good enough to marry her son Kyle since he'd been a big basketball star in high school and started out that way in college and scored eleven points at the NCAA tournament, Sweet Sixteen game. He could of kept on playing too if he hadn't got caught using cocaine.

But the other thing was two people in Creekside besides me had murdered somebody this same year and it's not that big a place. So we were getting a reputation. A Mexican man used rat poison on his wife, which folks thought was a accident at first because that part of town did have rats you couldn't kill with a pitchfork unless you hit them with a sledgehammer first. But then they found the rat poison in his wife's Maalox. Then Lucas Beebee (who was crazy and everybody in town knew it) used a chainsaw on a Jehovah's Witness and put her toes and ears in a flower arrangement on his mother's dining room table. A friend of the victim was there for the Beebee Easter buffet and recognized this woman's earbobs in the ears and called the police. So Kyle's murder was Number Three in a year, and instead of Creekside, North Carolina, which is our real name, they started calling us "Homicide, U.S.A." for a joke.

So Mr. Goodenough the D.A. said he was going to make an example out of me and he sure has tried. He's been elected district attorney in Creekside for twenty years running and they say it's mostly because of his name. I remember those campaign billboards from when I was little—HE'S GOODENOUGH FOR YOU.

At my trial, the D.A. said I had broke every vow I took in church when I promised to love and honor Kyle 'til death do us part. He said I was a black mark on the holy name of "Wife." Every chance he got he told the jury how Kyle had been a basketball star and played for the ACC because around here that's like saying you taught Jesus how to walk on water. He held up that souvenir basketball Kyle had from the Sweet Sixteen game that I'd shot a hole in and carried on about it almost like it was worse I'd shot the damn basketball than shot Kyle in the head. That's when I could see Dr. Rothmann on the jury start to fidget in her seat like she wanted to tell the judge to make the D.A. stop talking so much about how this was the very same basketball that Kyle had shot that three-pointer with, with two seconds left in overtime. Dr. Rothmann even rolled her eyes at the ceiling when the D.A. said how'd I'd cut short a promising young man's great career in pro basketball when even the newspapers knew it was drugs cut short Kyle's career when he had to drop out of college his sophomore year and no pro basketball team had given him the time of day since. He couldn't even have held on to his job at Creekside Ford if his uncle hadn't owned it.

Now my brother Tanner is so dumb he figured it would look better for me if he told the police he gave me the gun to take home because Kyle hit me all the time and I was scared of him. The truth is, I don't believe Tanner even knew I took his pistol out of his refrigerator that day.

And Kyle didn't hit me. Oh, he said he was going to hit me all the time, but he didn't have the guts. His style was more stuff like kicking my dog JuliaRoberts when I wasn't looking. Or pouring nail polish on my new winter coat and saying Jarrad did it when Jarrad was so little he couldn't even walk yet. Or making fun of me in front of his stupid buddies at Creekside Ford. Or smacking Jarrad in the face when he was a tiny baby, which is the one time I ever slapped anybody in life, which I slapped Kyle as hard as I could except it mostly just got his shoulder and he laughed at me.

So I couldn't help Tilden Snow with his plan to use the "battered wife syndrome." The only time 911 ever got called from our house was me getting the ambulance for Kyle when he sniffed too much cocaine and knocked over his trophy case and almost bled to death from broken glass. 'Course if I'd let him die that time maybe me and Jarrad would be in Disneyworld right this minute, staying at the Polynesian Resort.

I don't mean to make it sound like I wanted a fancy life. And maybe this is what I would of tried to explain to Dr. Rothmann if there'd been a way for her and me to talk. I could of took not having things, easy, no problem, if I'd had somebody that loved me, even liked me. Because you can hit somebody without laying a hand on them which is what Kyle kept doing to me. That's why I couldn't stop thinking about what Mawmaw said about how I was her only hope and had to earn respect. So I told Kyle he had to respect me more and not make me feel small. But he laughed at me and said, "Yeah well, maybe I would if you stuck a gun in my face."

So that's really why it all happened. That's why when I was over at Tanner's trailer and I saw that black pistol of his in the refrigerator, all of sudden I got the idea I'd do just what Kyle said. Next time he made fun of me, I'd stick a gun in his face.

So that Friday when Tanner carried Jarrad down to the pond to look at the ducks, I took his gun and hid it in my purse. Then on Saturday Mawmaw watched Jarrad for me and I worked all day at Pretty Woman. That night was bad because Kyle was trying to make me do stuff in bed I didn't want to. Sunday morning, he's mad at me. He's sitting on the couch in his underpants and wearing his old college basketball shirt, Number 56, click-clacking with that straight razor blade at his cocaine. I'm trying to get me and Jarrad dressed to go pick up Mawmaw for church and I'm late. Then Kyle tells me to nuke him a cup of coffee, and when I can't get the microwave to go off "Defrost," he starts laughing about "No-Brain Charmain." Then pretty soon he starts bouncing his souvenir Sweet Sixteen basketball off the living room wall like he was in a gym and not our living room.

Then he starts in on me about the Visa bill and what was I buying shoes for "that kid" for anyhow when he was so dumb he couldn't even walk yet so he must take after me? I'm looking at Kyle bouncing that basketball, while I'm standing there crying and Jarrad's crying too because I'm crying. I'm thinking, how dumb was I marrying this man when I was just sixteen when Mawmaw begged me to at least finish high school? How dumb was I not knowing maybe he was a freshman in college and a big basketball player, but he was still, excuse me, a total asshole?

So I'm standing in the living room, holding Jarrad. Kyle's yelling about the Visa bill, and my whole body fills up with the idea that year after year after year for the rest of our lives Kyle'll do the same kind of meanness to me and he'll do it to Jarrad too if I don't make him respect me starting now. And that's the first time I think about Tanner's gun since I took it. So I walk down the hall to our bedroom and I put Jarrad in his crib. Now he's crying at the top of his lungs, and I can hear Kyle yelling from the living room, "Shut him the fuck up!" I go get the pistol out of the bottom drawer of my bureau where I hid it and I walk back in the living room and I stick it in Kyle's face and I say, "*You* shut the fuck up."

He's surprised and his mouth falls open. But he's not scared. And then he laughs. "Hey, where'd you get that thing?" he says, pointing at the gun. "You planning to shoot somebody?" I don't say a word, I just keep looking at him. He says, "Well, No-Brain, if you're planning to shoot a pistol you got to take the safety off." He laughs some more and then he snatches the gun right out of my hand. He waves it in my face and says, sarcastic, "Here you go." He snaps this little lever on the side of the handle. "That's the safety." Then he hands the pistol back to me. "Knock yourself out."

Off in our room, Jarrad's bottle falls out of his crib and he cries harder.

All of a sudden Kyle starts throwing the basketball against the wall close to me. He breaks a lamp. Down the hall Jarrad screams like the world's gone crazy and Kyle turns purple. "I told you, shut that stupid kid up!"

I say, "You're scaring him."

Kyle screams, "I'll scare him okay!" And then he throws the basketball hard right at me and hits me in the head with it. Then he grabs the ball back and spins around to run down the hall. And that's when I pull the trigger. The pistol goes off. The noise was so loud it hurt. Most of the back of Kyle's head flies away. But he spins around and it goes off again and then it flings out of my hand. His knees bend, and it's weird, it's just like he's at the free throw line and is going for a basket. But then he drops the ball, which is all crumpled because I shot it, and his knees give way like the floor fell out from under him. He jerks over sideways and lands hard. The whole room shakes.

Down the hall Jarrad keeps screaming. All I can think about is, at least Jarrad didn't see it but the noise must have scared him. I run and go pick up my baby and I hide his eyes against me so he can't see Kyle lying there and we run out of the house. I drive Jarrad to Mawmaw's and tell her I can't go to church. I say I had a fight with Kyle and I can't talk about it now. Then I go back home and Kyle's still lying there with blood oozed out all around his head and his stomach. I have to run to bathroom 'cause I'm sick to my stomach. I don't know what to do. I just keep wishing I could make it go away. After a while I get an old blanket and wrap him in it. He's cold but I try not to touch him. I think I fainted. I don't remember the rest but I must of drug him out to the backyard and poured the kerosene on him and lit it.

That's the truth. If I could take the stand and tell Doctor Nina Rothmann the truth, the whole truth and nothing but, that's what I'd tell her.

But Mr. Goodenough made out how I'd plotted and planned to kill Kyle for his insurance policy and how I sneaked up and shot him in the back of the head from behind. Like I would *plan* for Jarrad to hear that gun go off so loud! The D.A. claimed how I tore up my own house to make it look like burglars so people would think I wasn't anywhere around and it was the burglars that set fire to my husband. But how I was so dumb I used my own brother's gun and left my fingerprints on it and on the kerosene can too and left them both right at the scene. The D.A. said I never meant to really commit suicide in the Marriott. It was a "ploy."

Mr. Goodenough spent a lot of time telling the jury, "Imagine the horror and anguish" of Mr. and Mrs. Markell when they saw their only son smoldering on a brush pile. Then he'd hold up the crime scene photos (that my lawyer tried to get excluded but he lost), and wave them right at the jury and shout, "Ladies and Gentlemen of the jury, just imagine!"

Both the Markells testified against me. They were the State's last witnesses. Mr. Markell slumped and looked beaten down. Mrs. Markell could scarcely sit still on the stand she hated me so much. 'Course that was true even before all this. I didn't like her either. She had spoiled Kyle so bad he told me himself how when he was little he would kick and slap her and she wouldn't do a thing about it if they were in public except give him what he wanted. On the stand Mrs. Markell said it didn't surprise her at all that I'd killed her son and she wouldn't rest easy 'til I had paid the price. They had to haul her off the chair she was shouting at me so loud even after she was excused. Her face looked just like Kyle's when he was yelling.

I'll tell you how I could rest easy even strapped down in the death chamber. That's if I knew Priscilla Markell had lost her case trying to get my baby Jarrad away from Mawmaw. I can't stand the thought of her screaming at Jarrad until he turns into a screamer too. And Tilden Snow has promised me he won't let that happen even if I do get the maximum. Which he's worried I'm going to get if all he's got on the defense side is character witnesses and the emergency doctor saying I really did try to kill myself judging from my stomach.

But some things you can't do. And letting Mr. Goodenough ask me sarcastic personal questions and twist my answers around into lies and make fun of me and say I don't deserve to be Jarrad's mama is one of them.

So that's all the far we'd got to in my trial by this morning. And that's when all of a sudden Dr. Rothmann calls over the bailiff and hands him a note and then the judge studies it for a minute at the bench and then the judge says we're taking a recess and he calls Counselor Goodenough and Counselor Snow to "come in his chambers," and they all leave us sitting here, waiting and waiting.

About an hour later, Tilden Snow comes back looking surprised but sort of smug. He motions for Mawmaw to lean forward and he whispers to us all this stuff about how Mr. Goodenough was backing down and dropping Murder One because otherwise he's going to get a hung jury and how if they could work it out would I agree to say I'd shot Kyle but I didn't plan to. Would I say I did it without premeditating and when I'd gone to pieces for a minute? I look at Mawmaw and she pats my hand. I tell him yes I will say that because it's the truth. Tilden Snow says I ought to thank my stars he got Dr. Rothmann put on my jury! I swear I think he even believed it was his plan all along, after he'd told me I was wrong for trusting her. He runs back off to the judge's chambers, all puffed up like a little rooster in a tan suit.

So we wait some more. After a while, Mawmaw leans over again from the row behind me and every now and then I can feel her hand patting me on the back. Right through my blouse I can feel the stiffness of her fingers and the calluses and rough spots on her hand like each one had a memory in it like a electric spark. I can see her mopping the kitchen floor of this house, and me helping her make the beds in that house, and us walking in the rain to the bus stop from this other house, dropping off the trash bags on the way. I can see her fingers working to tie the bow on my dress the day she took me to Tilden Snow's grandma's big house that they called Heaven's Hill. That was the day the little boy ran out the front door and hollered, "That's my swing. Get off of it." It was only after his grandmama came out with Maw-maw and told him to be nice to me because I belonged to the cleaning lady that he said, "I'm Tilden Snow. You want to marry me?"

I said to him, "No I don't." And I looked over at Mawmaw 'cause I was worried she'd be mad but she was smiling like I had said the right thing.

So I'm feeling all these memories in Mawmaw's hand while she rubs my back. Then the jury comes back with the judge and all, and Dr. Rothmann stops in front of me for a second and looks right in my eyes. And I nod at her and behind me Mawmaw stands up and gives her a little bow.

After a lot of talking, the judge tells me to stand up and I do and say I'm guilty and I get fifteen years. The first thing I think is, I'll get out in time for Jarrad's high school graduation. My lawyer says with parole it could even be less than ten. Kyle's mama is so mad she smacks her husband on the arm. Then they come over to take me out. I turn around and I grab of both Mawmaw's hands and I kiss them. I say, "I'm sorry, Mawmaw, I'm sorry I'm sorry."

She says, "You hang on, baby."

So I do.

Lucy

Maniac Loose

H olding a yellow smiley-face coffee mug, Lucy Rhoads sat in her dead husband's bathrobe and looked at two photographs. She had just made a discovery about her recently deceased spouse that surprised her. Prewitt Rhoads—a Booster of domestic sanguinity, whose mind was a map of cheerful clichés out of which his thoughts never wandered, whose monogamy she had no more doubted than his optimism—her spouse Prewitt Rhoads (dead three weeks ago of a sudden heart attack) had for years lived a secret life of sexual deceit with a widow two blocks away in the pretty subdivision of Painton, Alabama, where he had insisted on their moving for reasons Lucy only now understood. This was the same man who had brought her home Mylar balloons proclaiming "I Love You," white cuddly Valentine bears making the same lying vows, and an endless series of these smiley-face coffee mugs—all from the gifts, cards, and party supplies shop he owned in Annie Sullivan Mall and called "The Fun House." This was the same man who had disparaged her slightest criticism of the human condition, who had continually urged her, "Lucy, you need to stop turning over rocks just to look at all the bugs crawling underneath them."

Well, now Lucy had tripped over a boulder of a rock, to see in the exposed mud below, her own Prewitt Rhoads scurrying around in lustful circles with their widowed neighbor Amorette Strumlander, Lucy's mediocre Gardenia Club bridge partner for more than fifteen years; Amorette Strumlander, who had dated

Prewitt so long ago at Painton High School, who had never lived anywhere in her life but Painton, Alabama, where perhaps for years she had sat patiently waiting, like the black widow she'd proved herself to be, until Prewitt came back to her. Of course, on his timid travels into the world beyond Painton, Alabama, Amorette's old boyfriend had picked up a wife in Charlotte (Lucy) and two children in Atlanta before returning to his hometown to open The Fun House. But what did Amorette Strumlander care about those encumbrances? Apparently nothing at all.

Lucy poured black coffee into the grimacing cup. Soon Amorette herself would tap her horn in her distinctive pattern, *Honk honk honk* pause *honk honk,* to take Lucy to the Playhouse in nearby Tuscumbia so they could see *The Miracle Worker* together. Lucy was free to go because she had been forced to accept a leave of absence from her job as a town clerk at Painton Municipal Hall in order to recover from her grief. Amorette had insisted on the phone that *The Miracle Worker* would be just the thing to cheer up the stricken Mrs. Rhoads after the sudden loss of her husband to his unexpected heart attack. "I always thought it would be me," said Amorette, who'd boasted of a heart murmur since it had forced her to drop out of Agnes Scott College for Women when she was twenty and kept her from getting a job or doing any housework ever since. Apparently, Lucy noted, the long affair with Prewitt hadn't strained the woman's heart at all.

In fact, Lucy wasn't interested in seeing *The Miracle Worker;* she had already seen it a number of times, for the Playhouse put it on every summer in Tuscumbia, where the famous blind deaf mute Helen Keller had grown up. The bordering town of Painton had no famous people to boast of in its own long, hot, languid history, and no exciting events either; not even the Yankees ever came through the hamlet to burn it down, although a contingent of Confederate women (including an ancestor of Amorette's) was waiting to shoot them if they did. A typical little deep south community, Painton had run off its Indians, brought in its slaves, made its money on cotton, and then after the War Between the States, gone to sleep for a hundred years except for a few little irritable spasms of wakefulness over the decades to burn a cross or sometimes to send a student to march with Martin Luther King, or more often to campaign against anything that might destroy the American Way of Life.

In its long history, Painton could claim only three modest celebrities: there was Amorette Strumlander's twice-great grandmother who'd threatened to the shoot the Yankees if they ever showed up; she'd been a maid of honor at Jefferson Davis's wedding and had attended his inauguration as President of the Confederacy in Montgomery. Fifty years later, there was a Baptist missionary killed in the Congo either by a hippopotamus or by hepatitis; it was impossible for his relatives to make out his wife's handwriting on the note she'd sent from Africa. And thirty years ago, there was a linebacker in an Alabama Orange Bowl victory who'd played an entire quarter with a broken collarbone.

But of course none of these celebrities could hold a candle to Helen Keller, as even Amorette admitted—proud as she was of her ancestor who'd known Jefferson Davis. Indeed no one loved the Helen Keller story as told in *The Miracle Worker* more than she did. "You can never ever get too much of a good thing, Lucy, especially in your time of need," Mrs. Strumlander had wheedled when she'd called to pester Lucy into going to the play today. "*The Miracle Worker* shows how we can triumph over the dark days even if we're blind, deaf, and dumb, poor little thing."

Although at the very moment that her honey-voiced neighbor had phoned, Lucy Rhoads was squeezing in her fist the key to her husband's secret box of adulterous love letters from that same deceptive Amorette, she had replied only, "All right, come on over, Amorette, because I'm having a real dark day here today."

Still Lucy wasn't getting ready. She was drinking black coffee in her dead husband's robe, and looking at the photos she'd found in the box. She was listening to the radio tell her to stay off the streets of Painton today because there was a chance that the streets weren't safe. In general the town of Painton didn't like to admit to problems; the motto on the billboard at the town limits proclaimed in red, white, and blue letters, "There's No Pain in Painton. The Cheerfulest Town in Alabama." There was always a patrol car hidden behind this billboard with a radar gun to catch innocent strangers going thirty-six miles an hour and slap huge fines on them. If Deputy Sheriff Hews Puddleston had heard one hapless driver joke, "I thought you said there was no pain in Painton," he'd heard a thousand of them.

The local billboard annoyed Lucy, as did the phrasing of this radio warning; she thought that a town so near the home of Helen Keller had no business suggesting life was "cheerful" or that the streets were ever safe. The reporter on the radio went on to explain rather melodramatically that there was a maniac loose. A young man had gone crazy at Annie Sullivan Mall on the outskirts of Painton and tried to kill his wife. Right now, live on the radio, this man was shooting out the windows of a florist shop in the mall and the reporter was outside in the atrium behind a cart selling crystals and pewter dwarves. No one was stopping the maniac because he had a nine-millimeter automatic assault weapon with him, and he had yelled out the window that he had no problem using it. The reporter had shouted at him, "No problem" back at him and then urged the police to hurry up. The reporter happened to be there broadcasting live at the mall because it was the Painton Merchants Super Savers Summertime Sale for the Benefit of the Painton Panthers High School Foot-ball Team, State Semi-Finalists, and he'd been sent to cover it. But a maniac trying to kill his wife was naturally a bigger story and the reporter was naturally very excited.

Lucy turned on her police scanner as she searched around for an old pack of the cigarettes Prewitt had always been hiding so she wouldn't realize he'd gone back to smoking again despite his high cholesterol. He'd never hidden them very well, not nearly as well as his sexual escapades, and she'd constantly come across crumpled packs that he'd lost track of. Lucy had never smoked herself, and had little patience with the members of the Gardenia Club's endless conversation about when they'd quit, how they'd quit, or why they'd quit. But today Lucy decided to start. Why not? Why play by the rules when what did it get you? Lighting the match, she sucked in the smoke deeply; it set her whole body into an unpleasant spasm of coughing and tingling nerves. She liked the sensation; it matched her mood.

On the police scanner she heard the dispatcher rushing patrol cars to the mall. This maniac fascinated her and she went back to the radio where the reporter was explaining the situation. Apparently the young man had gone to the mall to shoot his wife because she'd left him for another man. According to the maniac's grievance to the reporter, his wife was still using his credit cards and had been in the midst of a shopping spree at the mall before he caught up with her in the Hank Williams Concourse where they'd fought over her plan to run off with this other man and stick the maniac with the bills. She'd fled down the concourse to the other man, who owned a florist shop at the east end of the mall. It was here that the maniac caught up with her again, this time with the gun he'd run back to his sports van to collect. He'd shot them both, but in trying to avoid other customers had managed only to hit the florist in the leg and to pulverize one of his wife's shopping bags. Plaster flying from a black swan with a dracaena plant in its back gouged a hole out of his wife's chin. He'd allowed the other customers to run out of the shop but held the lovers hostage.

Lucy could hear the sirens of the approaching patrol cars even on the radio. But by the time the police ran into the atrium with all their new equipment, the florist was hopping out of his shop on one foot, holding to his bleeding leg and shouting that the husband had run out the back door. The police ran after him while the reporter gave a running commentary as if it were a radio play. As the florist was wheeled into the ambulance, he told the reporter that the maniac had "totally trashed" his shop

"Terminator style." He sounded amazingly high-spirited about it. The reporter also interviewed the wife as she was brought out in angry hysterics with a bandage on her chin. She said that her husband had lost his mind and had nobody but himself to blame if the police killed him. She was then driven off to the hospital with the florist.

Lucy made herself eat a tuna sandwich although she never seemed to be hungry anymore. When she finished, the maniac was still on the loose and still in possession of the nine millimeter gun that he'd bought only a few months earlier at the same mall. News of the failure of the police to capture him was oddly satisfying. Lucy imagined herself running beside this betrayed husband through the streets of Painton, hearing the same hum in their hearts. The radio said that neighbors were taking care of the couple's four-year-old triplets, Greer, Gerry, and Griffin, who hadn't been told that their father had turned into a maniac in Annie Sullivan Mall. The couple's neighbors on Fairy Dell Drive were shocked; such a nice man, they said, a good provider and a family man. "I never thought Jimmy'd do something like this in a million years, and you ask anybody else in Painton, they'll tell you the same," protested his sister who'd driven to the mall to plead with her brother to come out of the florist shop, but who had arrived too late.

The reporter was obliged temporarily to return the station to its mellow music program, *Songs of Your Life*, playing Les Brown's Band of Renown doing "Life Is Just a Bowl of Cherries." Lucy twisted the dial to OFF. She did not believe that life was a bowl of cherries, and she never had. In her view, life was something more along the lines of a barefoot sprint over broken glass. She felt this strongly, although she herself had lived a life so devoid of horror that she might easily have been tricked into thinking human existence was the bowl of sweet fruit that her husband Prewitt had always insisted it was. The surprised reaction of the Mall Maniac's neighbors and family annoyed her. Why *hadn't* they suspected? But then, why hadn't she suspected Prewitt and

Amorette of betraying her? At least the maniac had noticed what was going on around him—that his wife was stockpiling possessions on his credit cards while planning to run off with the florist. Lucy herself had been such an idiot that when years ago she'd wanted to leave Prewitt and start her life over, he'd talked her out of it with all his pieties about commitment and family values and the children's happiness, when at the exact same time, he'd been secretly sleeping with Amorette Strumlander!

Lucy smashed the smiley mug against the lip of the kitchen counter until it broke and her finger was left squeezed around its yellow handle as if she'd hooked a carousel's brass ring. There, that was the last one. She'd broken all the rest of the mugs this morning and she still felt like screaming. It occurred to her there was no reason why she shouldn't. She didn't have to worry about disturbing her "family" anymore.

It had been twenty-one days now since the death of the perfidious Prewitt. Last Sunday the Rhoads' son and daughter had finally returned to their separate lives in Atlanta, after rushing home to bury their father and console their mother. These two young people, whom Prewitt had named Ronny after Reagan and Julie after Andrews, took after their father, and they thought life was a bowl of cherries too, or at least a bowl of margaritas. They were affable at the funeral, chatting to family friends like Amorette Strumlander about their new jobs and new condo clusters. They liked Amorette (and had Lucy not distinctly recalled giving birth to them, she could have sworn Amorette was their mother, for like her they both were slyly jejune). Ronny and Julie were happy with their lifestyles, which they had mimicked from trendy magazines. These magazines did not explain things like how to behave at a father's funeral, and perhaps as a result Ronny and Julie had acted during the service and at the reception afterwards with that convivial sardonic tolerance for the older generation that they had displayed at all other types of family functions. Amorette later told Lucy she thought "the kids held up wonderfully."

Lucy was not surprised by her children's lack of instinct for grief. Their father would have behaved the same way at his funeral had he not been the one in the casket. "The kids and I are day people," Prewitt had told his wife whenever she mentioned any of life's little imperfections like wars and earthquakes and pogroms and such. "You're stuck in the night, Lucy. That's your problem." It was true. Maybe she should have grown up in the North, where skies darkened sooner and the earth froze and the landscape turned black and gray, where there wasn't so much Southern sun and heat and light and daytime. For life, in Lucy's judgment, was no daytime affair. Life was stuck in the night; daytime was just the intermission, the waiting between the acts of the real show. When she listened to police calls on the radio scanner, the reports of domestic violence, highway carnage, fire, poison, electrocution, suffocation, maniacs loose in the vicinity of Annie Sullivan Mall, always struck her as what life was really about. It suddenly occurred to her that there must have been a police dispatch for Prewitt after she'd phoned 911. She'd found him by the opened refrigerator on the kitchen floor lying beside a broken bowl of barbecued chicken wings. The scanner must have said: apparent heart attack victim, male, Caucasian, forty-eight.

Prewitt had died without having much noticed that that's what he was doing, just as her day children had driven off with whatever possessions of Prewitt's they wanted (Ronny took his golf clubs and his yellow and pink cashmere V-necks; Julie took his Toyota) without having really noticed that their father was gone for good. If Prewitt had known he'd be dead within hours, presumably he would have destroyed the evidence of his adultery with Amorette Strumlander, since marriage vows and commitment were so important to him. But apparently Prewitt Rhoads had persisted in thinking life a bowl of imperishable plastic cherries to the very last. Apparently he had never seen death coming, the specter leaping up and grinning right in his face, and so he had died as surprised as he could be, eyes wide open, baffled, asking Lucy, "What's the matter with me?"

Amorette Strumlander had been equally unprepared when she'd heard about Prewitt's sudden demise from their Gardenia Club president Gloria Peters the next morning. She had run up the lawn shrieking at Lucy, "I heard it from Gloria Peters at the nail salon!" as if getting the bad news that way had made the news worse. Of course, Lucy hadn't known then that Prewitt and Amorette had been having their long affair; admittedly that fact must have made the news harder on Amorette. It must have been tough hearing about her lover's death from Gloria Peters, who had never once invited Amorette to her dinner parties where apparently Martha Stewart recipes were served by a real maid in a uniform. In fact, that morning after Prewitt's death when Amorette had come running at her, Lucy had actually apologized for not calling her neighbor sooner. And Amorette had grabbed her and sobbed, "Now we're both widows!" Lucy naturally thought Amorette was referring to her own dead husband Charlie Strumlander, but maybe she had meant her lover Prewitt.

Honk honk honk pause *honk honk. Honk honk honk* pause *honk honk.*

Amazingly it was two in the afternoon and Lucy was still standing in the middle of the kitchen with the yellow coffee mug handle still dangling from her finger. She quickly shoved the photographs she'd found in the bathrobe pocket as Amorette came tapping and whoohooing through the house without waiting to be invited in. She had never waited for Lucy to open the door.

"Lucy? Lucy, oh, why, oh, good lord, you're not even ready. What are you doing in a robe at this time? Didn't you hear me honking?" Mrs. Strumlander was a petite woman, fluttery as a hungry bird. She swirled around the table in a summer coat that matched her shoes and her purse, and patted her heart as she was always doing to remind people that she suffered from a murmur. "I have been scared to death with this maniac on the loose! Did you hear about that on the radio?"

Lucy said that yes she had, and that she felt sorry for the young man.

"Sorry for him?! Well, you are the weirdest thing that ever lived! You come on and go get dressed before we're late to the play. I know when you see that poor little blind, deaf, and dumb girl running around the stage spelling out 'water,' it's going to put your own troubles in perspective for you, like it always does mine."

"You think?" asked Lucy flatly, and walked back through the house into the bedroom she had shared with Prewitt. She was followed by Amorette who even went so far as to pull dresses from Lucy's closet and make suggestions about which one she ought to wear.

"Lucy," Amorette advised her as she tossed a dress on the bed, "just because this maniac goes out of his mind at Annie Sullivan, don't you take it as proof the world's gone all wrong, because believe me most people are leading a normal life. If you keep slipping into this negative notion of yours without poor Prewitt to hold you up, you could just slide I don't know where, way deep. Now how 'bout this nice mustard silk with the beige jacket?"

Lucy put her hand into her dead husband's bathrobe pocket. She touched the photos and squeezed the key to the secret letters into the fleshy pads of her palm. The key opened a green tin box she'd found in a little square room in the basement, a room with pine paneling and a plaid couch that Prewitt considered his special private place and called his "study." He'd gone there happily in the evenings to fix lamps and listen to vinyl big band albums he'd bought at tag sales, to do his homework for his correspondence course in Internet Investing in the Stock Market. And, apparently, he went there to write love letters to Amorette Strumlander. Lucy had never violated the privacy of Prewitt's space. Over the years as she had sat with her black coffee in the unlit kitchen, watching the night outside, she had occasionally fantasized that Prewitt was secretly down in his study bent over a microscope in a search of the origins of life, or down there composing an opera, or plotting ingenious crimes. But she was not surprised when, the day after her children left for Atlanta, she'd unlocked the "study" door and discovered no mysterious test tubes, no ink-splotched sheets of music, no dynamite to blow up Fort Knox.

What she had found there were toy trains and love letters. Apparently Prewitt had devoted all those nights to building a perfect plastic world for a dozen electric trains to pass through. This world rested on a large board eight feet square. All the tiny houses and stores and trees were laid out on the board on plastic earth and Astroturf. In front of a little house, a tiny dad and mom and boy and girl stood beside the track to watch the train go by. The tiny woman had blonde hair and wore a pink coat, just like Amorette Strumlander.

Lucy found the love letters in a green tin box in a secret drawer built under the board beneath the train depot. There were dozens of letters written on legal pad, on pink flowered note paper, on the backs of envelopes, hand-delivered letters from Amorette to Prewitt, and even a few drafts of his own letters to her. They were all about love as Prewitt and Amorette had experienced it. There was nothing to suggest to Lucy that passion had flung these adulterers beyond the limits of their ordinary personalities, nothing to suggest *Anna Karenina* or *The English Patient*. No torment, no suicidal gestures. The letters resembled the Valentines Prewitt sold in his gifts, parties, and cards shop in downtown Painton. Lacy hearts, fat toddlers hugging, fat doves cooing. Amorette had written: "Dearest dear one. Tell Lucy you have to be at the Fun House doing inventory all Sat morn. Charlie leaves for golf at ten. Kisses on the neck." Prewitt had written: "Sweetheart, You looked so [great, scratched out] beautiful yesterday and you're so sweet to me, I couldn't get through life without my sunshine."

Beneath the letters at the bottom of the box, Lucy had found the two Polaroid pictures she now touched in the bathrobe pocket. One showed Amorette in shortie pajamas on Lucy's bed, rubbing a kitten against her cheek. (Lucy recognized the kitten as Sugar, whom Prewitt had brought home for Julie and who, grown into an obese flatulent tabby, had been run over five years ago by a passing car.) The other photograph showed Amorette seated on the hope chest in her own bedroom, naked from the waist up, one hand provocatively held beneath each untanned breast. After looking at the pictures and reading the letters, Lucy had put them back in the box, then turned on Prewitt's electric trains and sped them up faster and faster until finally they'd slung themselves off their tracks and crashed through the plastic villages and farms and plummeted to the floor in a satisfying smash-up.

Now, in the bathroom listening to Amorette outside in the bedroom she clearly knew all too well, still rummaging through the closet, Lucy transferred the key and the photos from the bathrobe pocket to her purse. Returning to the bedroom, she asked Amorette, "Do you miss Prewitt much?"

Mrs. Strumlander was on her knees at the closet looking for shoes to go with the dress she'd picked out for Lucy. "Don't we all?" she replied. "But let time handle it, Lucy. Because of my murmur I have always had to live my life one day at a time as the Good Book says, and that's all any of us can do. Let's just hope this crazy man keeps on shooting people he knows and doesn't start in on strangers!" She laughed at her little joke and crawled backwards out of the closet with beige pumps in her hand. "Because there are sick individuals just opening fire whenever and wherever they feel like it, and I'd hate for something like that to happen to us in the middle of *The Miracle Worker* tonight. Here, put that dress on."

Lucy put on the dress. "Have you ever been down in Prewitt's study, Amorette?"

"Ummum." The dainty woman shook her head ambiguously, patting her carefully styled blonde hair.

"Would you like to see it now?" Lucy asked her.

Amorette gave her a curious look. "We don't have time to look at Prewitt's study now, honey. We are waaay late already.

Not that jacket, it doesn't go at all. Sometimes Lucy....This one. There. Oh, you look so pretty when you want to."

Lucy followed her dead husband's mistress out to her car. Amorette called to her to come along: "Hop in now, and if you see that mall shooter, duck!" She merrily laughed.

As they drove toward the interstate to Tuscumbia through Painton's flower-edged, unsafe streets, Lucy leaned back in the green velour seat of her neighbor's Toyota (had Amorette and Prewitt gotten a special deal for buying two at once?) and closed her eyes. Amorette babbled on about how someone with no handicaps at all had used the handicapped parking space at the Winn-Dixie and how this fact as well as the mall maniac proved that the South might as well be the North these days. Amorette had taken to locking her doors with deadbolts and might drop dead herself one night from the shock of the strange noises she was hearing after dark and suspected might be the sounds of burglars or rapists. It was then that Lucy said, "Amorette, when did you and Prewitt start sleeping together?"

The little sedan lurched forward with a jolt. Then it slowed and slowed, almost to a stop. Pink splotched Amorette's cheeks, until they matched the color of her coat, but her nose turned as white as a sheet. "Who told you that?" she finally whispered, her hand on her heart. "Was it Gloria Peters?"

Lucy shrugged. "What difference does it make?"

"It was, wasn't it! It was Gloria Peters. She hates me."

Lucy took one of Prewitt's left-behind hidden cigarettes out of her purse and lit up. "Oh, calm down, nobody told me. I found things."

"What things? Lucy, what are you talking about? You've gotten all mixed up about something—"

Blowing out smoke, Lucy reached in her purse. She thrust in front of the driver the Polaroid picture of Amorette's younger self, flash-eyed, cupping her breasts.

Now the car bumped up on the curb, hit a mail box, and stopped.

The two widows sat in the car on a residential avenue where oleander blossoms banked the sidewalks and honeysuckle made the air as sweet as syrup. There was no one around, except a bored teenage girl in a bathing suit who roller-bladed back and forth and looked blatantly in the car window each time she passed it.

Lucy kept smoking. "I found all your love letters down in Prewitt's study," she added. "Didn't you two worry that I might?"

With little heaves Amorette shook herself into tears. She pushed her face against the steering wheel, crying and talking at the same time. "Oh Lucy, this is just the worst possible thing. Prewitt was a wonderful man, now don't start thinking he wasn't. We never meant to hurt you. He knew how much I needed a little bit of attention because Charlie was too wrapped up in the law office to know if I had two eyes or three, much less be sympathetic to my murmur when I couldn't do the things he wanted me to."

"Amorette, I don't care to hear this," said Lucy.

But Amorette went on anyhow. "Prewitt and I were both so unhappy and we just needed a little chance to laugh. And then it all just happened without us ever meaning it to. Won't you believe me that we really didn't want you to get yourself hurt."

Lucy, dragging smoke through the cigarette, thought this over. "I just want to know how long?"

"Wuh, what, what?" sobbed her neighbor.

"How long were you screwing my husband? Five years, ten years, 'til the day Prewitt died?"

"Oh Lucy, no!" Amorette had sobbed herself into gasping hiccups that made the sound "*eeuck*." "No! *Eeuck. Eeuck.* We never...after Charlie died. I just didn't think that would be fair. *Eeuck. Eeuck.*"

"Charlie died a year ago. We've been in Painton fifteen." Lucy squashed her cigarette butt in the unused ashtray. She flashed to an image of the maniac smashing the glass storefronts that looked out on the concourse of the shopping mall. "So,

Amorette, I guess I don't know what the goddamn shit 'fair' means to you." She lit another cigarette.

Amorette shrank away, shocked and breathing hard. "Don't you talk that way to me, Lucy Rhoads! I won't listen to that kind of language in my car." Back on moral ground, she flapped her hand frantically at the thick smoke. "And put out that cigarette. You don't smoke."

Lucy stared at her. "I do smoke. I am smoking. Just like you were screwing my husband. You and Prewitt were a couple of lying shits."

Amorette rolled down her window and tried to gulp in air. "All right, if you're going to judge us—"

Lucy snorted with laughter that hurt her throat. "Of course I'm going to judge you."

"Well, then, the truth is," Amorette was now nodding at her like a toy dog with its head on a spring, "the truth is, Lucy, your negativity and being so down on the world the way you are just got to Prewitt sometimes. Sometimes Prewitt just needed somebody to look on the bright side with."

Lucy snorted again. "A shoulder to laugh on."

"I think you're being mean on purpose," whimpered Amorette. "My doctor says I can't afford to get upset like this."

Lucy looked hard into the round brown candy eyes of her old bridge partner. Could the woman indeed be this obtuse? Was she as banal of brain as the tiny plastic mom down on the board waving at Prewitt's electric train? So imbecilic that any action she took would have to be excused? That any action Lucy took would be unforgivable? But as Lucy kept staring at Amorette Strumlander, she saw deep down in the pupils of her neighbor's eyes the tiniest flash of self-satisfaction, a flicker that was quickly hidden behind a tearful blink. It was a smugness as bland and benighted as Painton, Alabama's history.

Lucy suddenly felt a strong desire to do something, and as the feeling surged through her she imagined the maniac from the mall bounding down this residential street and tossing his gun to her through the car window. It felt as if the butt of the gun hit her stomach with a terrible pain. She wanted to pick up the gun and shoot into the eye of Amorette's smugness. But she didn't have a gun. Besides what good did the gun do the maniac, who had probably by now been caught by the police? Words popped out of Lucy's mouth before she could stop them. She said, "Amorette, did you know that Prewitt was sleeping with Gloria Peters at the same time he was with sleeping with you, and he kept on with her after you two ended things?"

"What?"

"Did you know there were pictures, naked pictures of Gloria Peters locked up in Prewitt's letter box too?"

Mrs. Strumlander turned green, actually apple green, just as Prewitt had turned blue on the ambulance stretcher after his coronary. Amorette had also stopped breathing; when she started up again, she started with a horrible-sounding gasp. "Oh my god, don't do this, tell me the truth," she wheezed.

Lucy shook her head sadly. "I am telling the truth. You didn't know about Gloria? Well, he tricked us both. And there were some very ugly pictures I found down in the study too, things he'd bought, about pretty sick things being done to naked women. Prewitt had all sorts of magazines and videos down in that study of his. I don't think you even want to hear about what was in those videos." (There were no other pictures, of course, anymore than there had been an affair with Gloria Peters. The Polaroid shot of Amorette's cupped breasts was doubtless as decadent an image as Prewitt could conceive. Every sentiment the man ever had could have been taken from one of his Mylar balloons or greeting cards.)

"Please tell me you're lying about Gloria!" begged Amorette. She was green as grass.

Instead Lucy opened the car door and stepped out. "Prewitt said my problem was I couldn't *stop* telling the truth. And this is the truth. I saw naked pictures of Gloria posing just like you'd done and laughing because she was copying your pose. That's what she joked about in a letter; how he'd shown her the picture of you and she was mimicking it."

"Lucy, stop. I feel sick. Something's wrong. Hand me my purse off the back seat."

Lucy ignored the request. "Actually I read lots of letters Gloria wrote Prewitt making fun of you, Amorette. You know how witty she can be. The two of them really got a laugh out of you."

Unable to breathe, Amorette shrank back deep into the seat of her car, and whispered for Lucy please to call her doctor for her because she felt like something very scary was happening.

"Well, just take it one day at a time," Lucy advised her neighbor. "And look on the bright side."

"Lucy, Lucy, don't leave me!"

But Lucy slammed the door, and began to walk rapidly along beside the oleander hedge. She was pulling off fistfuls of oleander petals as she went, throwing them down on the sidewalk ahead of her. The teenage girl on roller-blades came zipping close, eyes and mouth big as her skates carried her within inches of Lucy's red face. She shot by the car quickly and didn't notice that Amorette Strumlander had slumped over onto the front seat.

Lucy walked on, block after block, until the oleander stopped and lawns spread flat to the doorsteps of brick ranch houses with little white columns. A heel on her beige pump came loose and she kicked both shoes off. Then she threw off her jacket. She could feel the maniac on the loose right beside her as she jerked at her dress until she broke the buttons off. She flung the dress to the curb. Seeing her do it, a man ran his power mower over his marigold beds, whirring out pieces of red and orange. Lucy unsnapped her bra and tossed it on the man's close-cropped emerald green grass. She didn't look at him, but she saw him. A boy driving a pizza van swerved toward her, yelling a war whoop out his window. Lucy didn't so much as turn her head but she took off her panty hose and threw it in his direction.

Naked to her panties, carrying her purse, she walked on until the sun had finished with its daytime tricks and night was back.

She walked all the way to the outskirts of Helen Keller's hometown.

When the police car pulled up beside her, she could hear the familiar voice of the scanner dispatcher on the radio inside, then a flashlight was shining in her eyes and then Deputy Sheriff Hews Puddleston was covering her with his jacket. He knew Lucy Rhoads from the Painton Town Hall where she clerked. "Hey now," he said. "You can't walk around like this in public, Mrs. Rhoads." He looked at her carefully. "You all right?"

"Not really," Lucy admitted.

"You had something to drink? Some kind of pill maybe?"

"No, Mr. Puddleston, I'm sorry, I've just been so upset about Prewitt, I just, I just…"

"Shhh. It's okay," he promised her.

At the police station back in Painton they were handcuffing a youngish bald man to the orange plastic seats. Lucy shook loose of her escort and went up to him. "Are you the one from the shopping mall?"

The handcuffed man said, "What?"

"Are you the one who shot his wife? Because I know how you feel."

The man tugged with his handcuffed arms at the two cops beside him. "She crazy?" he wanted to know.

"She's just upset. She lost her husband," the desk sergeant explained.

Prewitt's lawyer had Lucy released within an hour. An hour later Amorette Strumlander died in the hospital of the heart defect that Gloria Peters had always sarcastically claimed was only Amorette's trick to get out of cleaning her house.

Three months afterwards, Lucy had her hearing for creating a public disturbance by walking naked through the streets of Painton, the Cheerfulest Town in America. It was in the court-room across the hall from the trial of the Mall Maniac, so she did finally get to see the young man. He was younger than she'd thought he'd be, ordinary looking, with sad puzzled eyes. She smiled at him and he smiled back at her, just for a second, then his head turned to his wife who by now had filed for divorce. She still had the scar on her chin from where the plaster piece of the swan had hit her in the florist shop. The florist sat beside her, holding her hand.

Testifying over his lawyer's protest that he'd tried to kill his wife and her lover but had "just messed it up," the maniac pleaded guilty. So did Lucy. She admitted she was creating as much of a public disturbance as she could. But unlike the maniac's, her sentence was suspended, and afterwards the whole charge was erased from the record. Prewitt's lawyer made a convincing case to a judge (who also knew Lucy) that grief at her husband's death, aggravated by the shock of the car accident from which her best friend was to suffer a coronary, had sent poor Mrs. Rhoads wandering down the sidewalk in "a temporarily irrational state of mind." The lawyer suggested that she might even have struck her head on the dashboard, that she might not even have been aware of what she was doing when she "disrobed in public." After all Lucy Rhoads was an upright citizen, a city employee, and a decent woman, and if she'd gone momentarily berserk and exposed herself in a nice neighborhood, she'd done it in a state of emotional and physical shock. Prewitt's lawyer promised she'd never do it again. She never did.

A few months later, Lucy went to visit the maniac at the state penitentiary. She brought him a huge box of presents from the going-out-of-business sale at The Fun House. They talked for a while, but conversation wasn't easy, despite the fact that Lucy not only felt they had a great deal in common, but that she could have taught him a lot about getting away with murder.

Flonnie

The Rising of the South and
Flonnie Rogers

Flonnie Rogers lived with my grandmother since the beginning of time. Flonnie said she had herself raised, without much help and with a lot of backtalk, my mother and her nine brothers and sisters. She hoped to do as much for us grandchildren even though we were worse than the first batch had been. She was five feet tall and may have weighed as much as ninety pounds.

Flonnie said that before the War she had been a slave on a big sugar plantation where everybody was starved to death and beaten to death by a cruel master. Sometimes she said that if we didn't quit aggravating her peace of mind, she was going to send *us* off to be starved and whipped by this horrible man. Other times she said that when she was just a little skinny girl of twelve, she had stove in that master's head with the wood axe and sliced him into two separate pieces that tried for two minutes to walk off in two separate directions and then dropped dead as a door nail at her feet. She said she had done this because she couldn't abide the man's aggravation any longer. She advised us to watch our step.

It was often while Flonnie was out in my grandmother's big backyard wringing chickens' necks for supper that she reminisced about hatcheting her old master. Whipping the hens in a feather-flying arc over her head, she suddenly slapped them down on a wood block and whacked their heads off, with the very axe she had used on that awful plantation owner.

Not until later did I learn that there had never been any big sugar plantation in Piedmont, North Carolina (and Flonnie boasted that she had never been out of the county, and never intended to go). Besides, no matter how old she was (and it was none of our business), she couldn't possibly have been old enough to have been a twelve-year-old slave when the Civil War started, not unless she was the oldest human being alive. Maybe she was.

My grandmother said that Flonnie had showed up at the house one day to start a job that no one had realized they were offering her, had moved in with a tin trunk and two brown shopping bags, and had continued to intimidate the family every since. After my grandfather had died, and the ten children had grown up and left the house, Flonnie and my grandmother lived there alone for another quarter of a century.

Grandchildren came to the house to visit and stayed as long as we could. The neighborhood had once been rich and now was poor and people still did things there they didn't do in the new parts of Thermopylae anymore. People kept chickens in their backyards and chamber pots under their beds, raised vegetables, rocked in big swings that hung from chains on the front porch, walked in the long evenings up and down the sidewalk, saying, "How you? Nice evening. Take care now."

The house was enormous, with a cellar and an attic piled with rusted treasure, which Flonnie could never see the magic in. The dining room was the largest room in the house. Sometimes I would sit by myself at the end of a table meant for twenty. I'd stick my feet behind a rung of the dark, high-backed, cane-bottomed chair and take a cloth napkin from its tarnished silver ring with my grandfather's initials on it. In a semi-circle around my lunch plate there would be small dishes of sliced cantaloupe, sausage patties, hard strips of country ham, cold biscuits, butter beans, corn, snapbeans with fatback, okra and cold fried chicken—leftovers from last night's supper and this morning's breakfast. Flonnie and my grandmother kept cooking for the family that had moved away.

Grandma slept in the room where my grandfather had died. At the end of the upstairs hall, Flonnie slept in a cubicle she'd curtained off by two quilts hung on a rope. Along that hall there were five empty bedrooms by then, but she wouldn't take one of them. Those of us children who were frightened of the dark or bothered by the cold in one of those rooms, Flonnie begrudgingly would allow to sleep in the bed with her, if we promised not to fret and wiggle. Those who tossed and turned would be left outside the door for the bogeyman to pick up.

Beneath her loose-spring bed she kept her tin trunk; it was locked and full of secrets. She would never tell us what they were, except it might be rattlesnakes and it might be ghosts. Both her sheets and her long nightgown were starched cotton, sharply creased and cold and white as ice. Her hair was white too; it astonished us when she took off the tightly knotted hand-kerchief with my grandfather's initials sewn in it, and unwove dozens of braids until the hair stood stiffly out around her head like a halo of icicles.

Astonishing too was the way she reached inside her mouth with a funny grin, pulled out her teeth, then dropped them in the glass of water she always brought up to bed with her.

At ten o'clock when the Lord was expecting to hear from her, Flonnie said prayers on her knees, one hand clinched tightly around the back of a grandchild's neck to insure that we did the same. "Show the Lord some respect. He won't truck with a wig-gler. A whiner neither." Then she sang us lullabies that scared us to death.

Way down yonder, in the meadow,
Lies a poor little baby.
Gnats and flies picking out his eyes.
Poor little thing is crying Mammy.

"Did his Mammy come to save him?"

"No, she never did. You want to know why she left her own little baby boy there with his eyes eaten up and bobcats gnawing off his toes?"

We both did and did not want to know.

"Because that child had that self-same day tromped all over her fresh-mopped floor." Or that child had sassed her back, or messed with her flour sifter, or whatever offense whoever Flonnie was talking to had most recently committed.

In bed if we made the slightest movement, she would jerk the sheets away and say, "Hush!" If we moved again, she would send us to the bathroom, convinced that we were fidgeting because of incontinent bladders. To our mortification, she accused five- and even six-year-olds of planning to mess up her sheets in the middle of the night. The bathroom was dark miles and miles away, down the stairs, across the house, along a black corridor past the kitchen. The worn linoleum on that corridor was like frozen snow under our bare feet. Feet that bobcats crouched in wait for.

• • •

Flonnie called my grandmother "Miz Hayes" and my grandmother called Flonnie "Flonnie." For fifty-five years they lived in the same house, raised the same children, and cooked (on two stoves—one black wood-burner, one white gas-burner) the same three meals daily. In the end, they were closer to each other than to anyone else. They tormented one another as only the intimate can.

Flonnie could read while my grandmother could not. We knew that Grandma wasn't taught to read because she had worked at the tobacco factory from the time she was eight up until the time Grandpa had seen her walking home along the railroad tracks and had told his brother, "I plan to marry that girl." We all knew that story and knew we weren't supposed to embarrass Grandma by reminding her that she had never had a chance to get educated the way the rest of us had. But we had no idea how Flonnie had learned to read; she told us it was none of our business.

Every night the two women would sit in Grandma's chair and Flonnie's chair, close to the stove in the corner of the sitting room, with the stove's pipe stuck out behind it into a hole in the blue flowers of the wallpaper. Every night Flonnie would slowly take up the tiny gold-framed glasses that were looped by a piece of twine to the thin plastic belt on her dress. Slowly she'd unfold *The Thermopylae Evening Star* and begin to read to herself, the paper held in front of her (and my grandmother's) face. "My my my!" she'd mutter in a loud whisper. Then she'd shake her head. "What's happ'ning to this world?"

Minutes would go by, we playing Chinese checkers on the floor, the clock with its owl face metallically ticking, Grandma shelling butterbeans, a paper bag on her lap, a pan beside the leg of her rocker. Suddenly shaking the pages into a flurry, Flonnie would gasp, "Good lord a mercy!" as if she'd just read that Mars was going to smash into downtown Thermopylae the next morning.

"What?" I'd ask. But Flonnie would shake her head and return to her paper. Then in a few more minutes she'd start to laugh, a low snuffling sound that seemed to escape against her will.

"What's so funny?" my cousin would ask.

"Nuthin'," she'd reply, the whites of her eyes elaborate with innocence.

My grandmother had two revenges. One was never to give Flonnie the chance to refuse to answer her. She did this by pretending to be oblivious of the fact that there was a newspaper full of pathos, humor, and catastrophe being deliberately rattled in the face of her ignorance. Grandma's counterattack was to get up and turn off the radio in the middle of one of Flonnie's baseball games. Flonnie had never been to a live game, nor ever given the slightest indication that she wanted to go to one, but for some reason—perhaps simply to irritate my grandmother—she liked to listen to that lethargic litany of balls, strikes swung on and missed, the drone infrequently broken by a rising staccato of activity. "It's a long drive out to left field. Up up up…Carrboro's going back back. He's…*got it!* An unbelievable catch by the young rookie." Flonnie couldn't afford to turn the radio back on because to notice that my grandmother had walked to the big mahogany set and snapped it off would be to admit she knew Grandma was trying to get her goat. So occasionally she had to go to bed without knowing whether Carrboro had gotten it or not.

When my cousins and I came to visit, Flonnie was always sending us on errands. She said they were to keep us out from under her feet while, with a baseball cap over her knotted handkerchief, she hoed in her vegetable garden or she washed down the porch that wandered around three sides of the old frame house, or she slapped dough until the kitchen was a storm of flour to make the biscuits that were on the table whether there were three for dinner or thirteen. When she was not in a bad mood, she gave us the lace patterns of dough left after she'd finished cutting out the biscuits. We'd wad the dough into tight balls that got dirtier and dirtier until finally we ate them or threw them away.

Whenever Flonnie called us "honey" or "honeylamb," we knew we were going to be sent on an errand, for the rest of the time she called us "child" or "young 'un" or assigned us an arbitrary name, usually a cousin's. "I'm not Jimmy, I'm Philip."

"It's no never mind to me what you callin' yourself. Carry that dog out this kitchen 'fore I toss it in my stove and fry it quicker'n you can say Jack Robinson."

The most frequent errand was, "Honeylamb, go on up to the corner and get your poor old Flonnie a can of Tuberose. Her legs are giving her the misery today. Sciatica's got them both." (Who, or what, Sciatica was, she never explained.)

Sometimes, in addition to snuff, we were sent for groceries listed in her small crabbed handwriting. Or she piled a wagon with empty bottles on which we were to collect for her the return deposits and trade them for more Coca-Colas. She loved Cokes and the worst mistake you could make was to drink her last cold bottle in the refrigerator.

As we set out on these excursions to the corner store, she yelled warnings and threats at us from the front steps. She told us that the police chief was hunkered down behind the toy counter at the Five and Dime, just waiting to catch children who wasted time looking at toys. She said the Children Robber was hiding behind the ice cream freezer at the grocery, looking for boys and girls to steal and sell to factories in China.

And sometimes she asked us to run across the street and hand Mr. Overhill fifteen cents toward her burial insurance. "Don't you dare drop it, you hear, and make sure he put my name down in his book. Flonnie Rogers. Watch him mark it down."

And sometimes she yelled at us to run quick and knock on Miz Cawthorne's door and tell her to run out back, Elwood's robbing her clothesline again. Flonnie told us that Elwood was special. "Those touched in the head, they belongs to the Lord." Flat-haired, gap-toothed, with a wide pasty lunatic face, Elwood was probably in his late thirties in those days. He sported an Eisenhower jacket and bright orange tennis shoes. For reasons mysterious but delightful to us, he coveted the voluminous undergarments that Mrs. Cawthorne, a widow of my grandmother's age, hung out on a line in her backyard. Whenever he'd snatch one of her three-sectioned pink girdles off the line and hook it on over his baggy blue jeans, Mrs. Cawthorne would tear out of her porch door and chase him down the street, waving at him one of the fly swatters that the funeral home gave away as advertisements. If Flonnie spotted us off behind the hedges watching Elwood try on a big lace slip, she'd yell, "Y'all, go tell Miz Cawthorne! It's Elwood." Or, if her Sciatica wasn't troubling her legs, she might run over there herself and beat at him with her broom.

"You! You stop acting like a fool and put Miz Cawthorne's drawers back on the line like they belong. I'd be shamed of acting like a fool the way you do!" Awed by Flonnie (as were we all), the big man would burst into awful sobs, hand over the underwear, and scuttle clumsily away around the side of the house.

The degree to which Flonnie awed as well those outside the family circle became clear to me on our first bus trip together. We were going to see her sister. I'd never known she'd had relatives and was surprised to learn there were people in her life besides us.

"You never said you had a sister," I accused her.

"Whole lots more things I never told you 'sides that. And not fixing to neither."

"I bet a million dollars you're going to say it's none of my business."

"Lord hates a betting boy, much as a boy that talks sass to grown people."

But the revelation of a sister had opened up whole patterns of previously unconsidered possibilities, and I went recklessly on. "How come you never got married and had your own children, Flonnie?"

"Hush!"

"But how come?"

"Because I'm not studying to marry no fool. And all the men I ever come across or 'spect to, this side of the grave, were nuthin' but aggravating fools. And I never come 'cross a boy neither that wasn't a fool and a aggravation to start out with and grown into worse if the law didn't catch him and throw a noose around his neck first."

"Why would they throw a noose around his neck?"

"To choke him 'til his tongue stuck out all swollen and his eyes bulged loose from his head."

"But why?"

"For pestering folks."

Flonnie never sat with me on the bus nor would she let me come to the back to sit with her. Nor could she tolerate to see a young black man sit down in the front of the bus (as a few were beginning to risk doing in the late fifties). "Get up out of that seat and come on back here 'fore I take hold of your hair and slap you cross-eyed," she would say to total strangers, three times her size and a third her age. I was terrified that one of them might

someday pick Flonnie up and snap her like a twig, or that the bus
driver might arrest her and take her off to the state crazy house
where she'd said they'd taken Elwood and would take everybody
who acted up in public. She said they chained people to walls
and never turned them loose 'til they were nothing but bones
and you could see the marks where they'd dug their fingernails
into the stone, trying so hard to get free.

But none of that ever happened on the bus. The young men
would usually try smiling at her and smoothing her over—"Now
granny, now granny." Then they'd either get up and go to the
back with her, shaking their heads, or they'd ignore her and stay
where they were. And Flonnie, disgusted, would shove me
sharply down into an empty seat at the front, and leave me there.
My ears hot red, I kept my neck craned back to be sure she didn't
get off at the back door when the bus stopped, leaving me all
alone in a foreign neighborhood.

Flonnie was a royalist in her politics and a moral aristocrat.
She would, she said, have no truck with trash, black or white,
and was of the opinion that there were very few people in the
world, black or white, who weren't trash. Her sister had married
trash, as I learned on my first visit, for Flonnie made her sister cry
by saying so. Trash pure and simple was her judgment of an uncle
of mine who had run off up North and forgotten to take his wife.
She said the same of the town's mayor, of people who made
movies, two of my cousins, the woman that owned the corner
grocery, Richard Nixon and Lyndon Johnson, her dead daddy,
Khruschev, Jayne Mansfield, Chuck Berry, and Franco of Spain.
Her distinctions were based on a sense of class, not ideology. Had
Flonnie lived in France in 1789, she might have marched
proudly with the Bourbons to the guillotine.

There were a great many things it was trash to do—mock-
ing the poor and mentally disturbed, popping gum out loud, not
keeping your word, sassing-back, eating like a hog, forgetting
your place, bragging, breaking wind, and most of all failing to
show the appropriate respect. "I'd better not catch you showing

no respect to the Lord," she would warn us when on Sundays, setting aside her weekday kerchief and her snuff, dressed up in a red straw hat and black patent shoes, she herded us into some relative's car to go to the white church, moving us along behind my grandmother with painful prods of her large black patent leather pocketbook, and leaving us there to walk to the bus stop. She refused to let us go with her to her church.

In time I learned that Flonnie's refusals—which as children we believed to be personal, just arbitrary rules imposed for the same incomprehensible reasons that all grown-ups had for saying "No"—were not personal to Flonnie at all. They were the rules of the town and of the South and, in other guises, of the whole country. Flonnie's pride was to refuse to give them the chance to make her acknowledge that she had no choice but to obey their rules, just as she had refused to notice the sudden silence of the radio.

The knowledge came to me in time; I heard it in school, how we had lost "the War," I read it on separate water coolers "White" and "Colored." And for a time I hated the South for not letting Flonnie Rogers and me ride together to visit her sister, for making her ignore the bathroom that said "Ladies" and use the one that said "Women," when if ever there was a Lady in Thermopylae, her name was Flonnie Rogers.

I left the South as soon as I could and Flonnie called me trash for bad-mouthing my home.

I came back for my grandmother's funeral. Flonnie had cleaned the two dark draped front rooms that nobody ever went in and told us if we trekked dirt across the good rug, she'd skin us alive and sell what was left to the butcher. She had picked out of the closet and starched and ironed the dress that went to the funeral parlor for Grandma to wear. "Miz Hayes," she said, "was not trash. And that's what that particular dress says. And the Lord will know it when He sees her coming in the gate."

My aunts and uncles told Flonnie they would be selling the house soon so she would have to leave it. She had lived there longer than any of them, lived there more than half a century, and had no ownership in it. Some of them invited her to move into their homes. She said no. She said she had family of her own.

When the time came to leave for the funeral, Flonnie walked into the parlor where Grandma's children and grandchildren and friends were waiting for the undertaker to tell them which of the cars they should ride in. She was wearing her red straw hat with a black rhinestone pin stuck through it and a shiny black coat with big double buttons and a fox-like collar.

"I'm going, Clayton," she said to my oldest uncle.

"'Course you are, Flonnie," he said. "You ride on with Mrs. Hackney and the children in their car."

"No," she told him. "I hired my own."

The car Flonnie hired was a brand-new black limousine, so grand it rode first, just behind the hearse, in the procession to the church that she had never before attended. I was in the car behind hers, and I could see her sitting by herself exactly in the middle of the wide seat, the top of her red hat in the rear window, a bright flame of red like a revolutionary flag.

Patty

Love and Other Crimes

Maybe saints don't care about their reputations—of course, any saints you ever heard of managed to get themselves written up in books—but when it comes to the rest of us, we've all got some notion of who we are that we'd like the rest of the world to agree with. Some folks think they're especially nice or generous or sexy, and they can't stand it if people don't treat them that way. With me, it's my brains. I admit I think of myself as smarter than most. Whenever the *Hillston Star* mentions that I'm the youngest police chief our small Piedmont city ever appointed and that we have the lowest per capita crime rate in the Southeast United States, I take a personal pride in the notice, and I give my brains the credit. It goes the other way as well: if there's a homicide, I take that personally too, because I think potential murderers ought to worry so much about my coming after them that their ugly impulses just shrivel away and they decide against killing people in Hillston.

Now other types of reputation are low on my list, including the one that around here they call social prominence. I don't live in the best part of town and I don't belong to the Hillston Club like all the people who do live in the best part of town, and nobody's ever asked me to join it. So I was only in the Hillston Club on this particular night because I was curious about why Patty Raiford had invited me to her fifth wedding. She and I weren't what you'd call close. But then her wedding turned out not to be exactly on an intimate scale anyhow—more like Haver

Stadium for Homecoming, so I didn't take it as a bid to get personal. Besides, she'd sent the invitation to "Chief Cuthbert Mangum, c/o Hillston Police Department, Cadmean Building, Please Forward," and my name isn't Cuthbert; it's Cudberth, which my mother possibly mistook for Cuthbert, but still anybody who knows me knows I live at River Rise, and everybody in town just calls me Cuddy.

Patty'd had good luck with the weather. It was a late-summer night, hot and clear with a full North Carolina moon the color of a ripe peach. A moon that looked like it was going to come in through the french doors of the Hillston Club like a balloon that God was sending Patty to tell her congratulations. The moon would have fit right in with the rest of the decorations. It was clear from the size of the flower arrangements that the bride was a party-thrower of robber-baron proportions and willing to treat even folks she didn't know to at least a hundred thousand dollars worth of bands and booze on the flimsy excuse of her getting married again.

Money was nothing to Patty; she'd been born with plenty, and when that ran out, she'd collected more from various husbands, and spent a considerable portion of it throwing these type of fêtes. People said Hillston'd be a lot duller without Patty Raiford's parties, and probably it would be for them. She was such a favorite with the *Hillston Star* that they referred to her in headlines by her first name only, like she was Elvis. For her wedding announcement they had a big picture of her in a floppy lace hat under the caption, PATTY TO TIE KNOT # 5 WITH SEAFOOD KING.

The knot was tied by the elderly minister at First Presbyterian Church. He was brought out of retirement to officiate at Patty's fifth, and seemed to have some doubts about its permanence, judging from the warnings in his homily. (But since he'd officiated at weddings one through four it was hard to blame him.) Maybe it wasn't an accident when he flipped his Bible up into the choir stall, startled by the blast of trumpets Patty had hired to strike up some loud Handel as she raced out of the church. She'd had a fleet of buses waiting to take her guests from there to the Hillston Club, which is where about two hundred of us were still celebrating at midnight when—as the *Star* put it the next day—"the joyful festivities turned to tragedy in one horrible moment."

While we were still in the joyful festivities part of the evening, I'd strolled through the ballroom looking for a fellow police officer, Justin Savile the Fifth, the most likely of my friends to get invited to this event. But I didn't see him. Not having a date to dance with myself and tired of analyzing the crime rate (all the country club set appeared to think they could politely talk about to a chief of police), I took a bottle of champagne onto the verandah, and out there under Patty's big moon listened to the Jimmy Douglas Orchestra play slow songs to keep people on the dance floor. They weren't succeeding; there was a problem with the air conditioning and it was too hot for guests who hadn't fallen in love that very night to want to sway up against each other to the tune of "Unforgettable." Most of them crowded instead around large tables that ringed the walls and kept on drinking, smoking, and laughing loudly together.

I heard somebody in the shrubs between the verandah and the pool, and turned to see a man about my age headed up the steps. He was a tall, blond fellow with a tan, who looked like he'd taken off weight too fast, and seemed lost inside his green polo shirt. Just as he stumbled past me with a polite apology, there was a sudden drumroll inside the ballroom. We both moved over to the french doors where a spotlight turned our attention up to Patty. She was leaning over a little balcony that jutted out from the end of the room off the second-floor. Across its rail there was a banner that promised in gold letters JOE AND PATTY FOREVER. Together the blond man and I watched the bride shake a blue lace garter over her head then spin it down at the squad of men in tuxedos waiting below. As they grabbed for the garter, it fell to the floor near a huge ice sculpture. They scrimmaged for it in a violent huddle.

The man in the polo shirt muttered in that soft slur of the wealthy South, "You'd think it was a basketball in the last five seconds."

I nodded companionably. "Final Four too."

We watched as one of the younger males got hold of the garter; he held it aloft like a scalp, then ran off with it. Patty clapped for him, then announced from the balcony that she and Joe were leaving for a few minutes to change for their honeymoon drive to the Carolina coast. The man in the green polo shirt ground his teeth. As he hurried away toward the side of the verandah, a business envelope stuffed in the rear pocket of his khakis fell out.

"Hey, you dropped something," I called after him.

He picked it up, said, "Thank you so much," and was gone. If I'd known who he was, I would have stopped him.

• • •

The first time I met Patty Raiford was a few years back, when Justin Savile dragged me along to her "divorce party" at her big family home on Catawba Drive. For some reason, no matter who she was married to, everybody always referred to Patty by her maiden name—Raiford. I guess it was less confusing, considering how often she changed husbands. Between those husbands, Patty always went back to the family house she and her brother Pascal had inherited from their folks. Her brother lived there by himself, except when Patty got divorced.

She had dubbed this particular divorce party "Nostalgia Night"—husband number three was on his way to becoming a sentimental memory—and everybody was supposed to dress up as their favorite childhood television show. Patty was Cher. Justin came in a Nehru jacket as "The Man from U.N.C.L.E." I didn't want to come as anybody, so I just wore my summer police chief's uniform and said I was Andy Griffith on Mayberry, RFD. Could be that's why folks ran up and asked me to do something when

Patty's husband number three arrived with a U-Haul and tried to load into it various pieces of furniture that he claimed were his. He was dragging a chair through the door with Patty's brother still sitting in it yelling for help. I made the ex-husband put everything back, and Patty got the last laugh by dropping a drawer full of women's panties down on his head from a second-floor window, shouting rather coarse suggestions (I guess facetiously) about what he could do with them. Turning a black-purple that didn't look good for his blood pressure, he'd stomped off, idly threatening the lives of everyone at the party.

Patty's laugh was appealing, I admit, though she didn't look a thing like Cher. So I invited her to dinner a couple of times, but I got nowhere. She was always devastated but busy, and next thing I knew she'd married number four. According to Justin, she and Four apparently had gotten together at that very Nostalgia Party. A couple of years later, she'd divorced Four and gotten herself engaged to Joe Raulett, the Seafood King. And I was invited to her wedding c/o the Police Department.

Number five was a change of pace for Patty. All her previous husbands had pedigree. Famous old Southern families had produced both No. 1, an all-star quarterback with a drinking problem, and No. 2, father of her twin sons, a New Orleans portrait painter of considerable private means (just as well because all his portraits looked like his mother and nobody wanted to buy them). No. 3, the one with the U-Haul, was a millionaire heart surgeon addicted to tennis. No. 4 was Wilson Tedworth Junior, vice president of the bank his daddy owned and apparently everybody's favorite of all her spouses.

But No. 5, Joe Raulett, the Seafood King, was a self-made man. By his own admission, he "came from nothing," but by his own boast, he came fast, far, and hard. He now owned a chain of big blue restaurants dotted through the Carolinas, all called "Neptune's" and all with the same menu of fish and crustaceans fried "in 100 percent pure Georgia peanut oil"—as we were told in his bright blue television ads.

No doubt that's why at their wedding reception there were so many mounds of lobster tails and crab claws, and why at the end of the high-ceilinged ballroom, right below the little balcony from which Patty had thrown her garter, there was this statue of Neptune. It stood seven feet tall and was carved out of blue ice and stood in a vat the size of a communal hot tub packed with dry ice so it steamed. You could tell it was the Greek god of the sea because he had a spiky ice crown on his head, and in his right hand he raised a big ice trident skyward. A circle of irregular icicles around the base appeared to represent the foaming waves out of which the ocean god was rising butt-naked. His private parts had been tastefully minimized by the artist. All night long I overheard drunken guests making cracks about whether or not the groom had personally posed for the thing. Not many of them even knew Joe Raulett. The few relatives from his side of the family were huddled together in one corner, drinking iced tea and worrying about the long drive home.

My wedding invitation had invited me to Patty's "fifth and final marriage," but maybe she'd made the same rash pledge last time too and maybe then the big banner had read PATTY AND WILSON TEDWORTH JUNIOR FOREVER. According to Justin, Patty had always had lots of men in her life and many of them had come to some kind of grief. Even her dad had gotten killed in a car crash while speeding to pick her up from an eighth grade dance. When she was in college, two boys—a cadet down from West Point and a Deke at Haver University—fought a duel over her. An actual old-fashioned duel with real pistols. They shot each other in the cemetery behind the football stadium on Sunday morning, after discovering at an ΣAE party on Saturday night that Patty was engaged to both of them. The cadet died in the hospital, and the frat boy almost did. The incident made her famous all over the state, and after that it was like men just got in the habit of violence where she was concerned.

Now, long after Patty had gone off to change out of her wedding outfit, the guest who'd got hold of her blue lace garter was tearing around the room wearing it on his head like a laurel wreath, while two rivals snatched at it as he dodged by them. So I guess I ought to be glad she'd said no when I'd asked her out to dinner since it was clear dating Patty was like sneaking a stack of sirloins past a pack of starving Doberman pinschers; you didn't want to do it unless you were heavily insured. 'Course, in what Patty and Justin called "their circle," suitors could afford premium policies. Their circle circled the best part of town, where I didn't live, and it cul-de-saced here on Catawba Drive at the Hillston Club. It was the circle where you golfed all day and partied 'til you puked all night, and the names of its members were the names you saw on Hillston street signs. Justin's pals still call themselves "The Young Circle" but I think it's time they dropped the label. Not even Patty Raiford could ring up five husbands fast enough to belong in something that makes them sound like they're still in prep school.

But younger, prettier women just faded away in comparison with Patty, and they seemed to know it. When she walked back into the ballroom in her travel outfit, I saw a half dozen men shoot over to her like a floor full of tacks sucked into a magnetic field. She wouldn't dance with them, and they sulked back to watch the Atlanta Braves on a portable TV in the foyer. A few of the baseball fans' abandoned wives came over to where I was standing by the french doors onto the verandah. They called back to Patty, "Oh, come look at this moon!" as if they'd never seen a moon before in their lives, or at least never expected to see another one. Or maybe it was just a tactic to get Patty away from where their husbands were. These women got so overcome by the moon that they gave high-pitched shrieks, ran past me across the verandah, and jumped into the club pool in their cocktail dresses.

The shrieks of the swimmers did bring out my friend Bubba Percy, star reporter (according to him) of the *Hillston Star*. Bubba was a big, pretty man with Bambi eyelashes, a pudgy face, and the kind of glossy hair they make TV commercials about. His byline was one of the most popular in the state, but he was even more conceited about his looks than his talent. Before he saw me, he pulled out a little comb and worked on his hair.

I stepped clear of the shadows. "Bubba, vain as you are, I'm amazed you'd come out here, because those girls have so splashed up the water in that pool you won't be able to see your reflection in it."

Undisturbed, he gave his cuff links an admiring glance. "Cuddy, if you were as good-looking as I am, you'd make it a law so every stop sign in Hillston had your picture on it. 'Bout to arrest somebody?"

"No, the bride invited me."

He was surprised. "Yeah?" Bubba unbuttoned his gold brocaded vest and fanned himself with the lapels. "Hot in there," he informed me. "That ice dick of Joe's is melting off his statue. Their air conditioning doesn't kick in soon, the old Seafood King's gonna turn into the Seafood Queen." He looked over at the women paddling around in the pool. "Women'll do anything," he said after a while.

"Just about."

We watched as a third young woman, Blue Sunderland, who looked like her baby might already be a few weeks overdue, cannon-balled into the deep-end with an explosion of water that crashed over her two friends' heads. They came bobbing up to her. All three laughed. Bubba clamped a cigarette in his white teeth and grinned. "Yep, women'll do anything. Men won't. You ever notice that?"

"Men are boring," I agreed. "You covering society news for the *Star* now?"

"Captain Pig, I wouldn't miss one of Patty's weddings for another week in the sack with Hillary Clinton. We go way back."

"You and Mrs. Clinton?"

"Me and Patty." He rolled the cigarette with his tongue from one side of his mouth to the other, but didn't light it. "Yeah, Patty gave me a blow job in a hot-air balloon once. Over the

State Fairgrounds. Everybody thought I was just up there by
myself having an epileptic seizure."

I didn't bother to answer. Bubba was famous for his tales of
outlandish and physically risky sexual adventures, which might
or might not be true—the one about him and my mother certainly had no basis in fact; my mother never went anywhere but
the Baptist Church and the A&P, much less got it on with Bubba
Percy, as he had claimed, out on the observation deck of the
Empire State Building one New Year's Eve.

I offered him some champagne and he took the whole bottle.
"You notice I don't bother saying I don't believe you."

"Believe me. It was real. Me and Patty, hot-air balloon." He
pointed his champagne bottle at the sky in a toast. "Now look at
me, not even married once, and look at her, number five, and
she's only thirty-eight."

I agreed. "There's no denying Patty's predisposed to a faith in
connubial bliss that defies her statistical experience."

He laughed. "How you talk, you silver-tongued Pig-Chief.
You at the wedding?"

"Yeah. Her poor brother Pascal. He's given her away five
times and he keeps getting her back."

Bubba pointed at somebody inside. "Doesn't look happy
about it either."

It was Patty's brother coming into the ballroom like he was
looking for something he couldn't find; maybe somebody to
dance with. He was a stocky man in a black velvet dinner jacket.
I said, "Aren't they supposed to be twins? He sure doesn't have
her looks."

"Yeah. Pascal got the brains and Patty got everything else."
Bubba and I stood watching the party while we drank our
champagne.

I asked his opinion. "You think five's the lucky number? You
think it's Joe and Patty forever like their banner says?"

Bubba gave me the local gossip: Patty's circle was hoping for
the best. That meant they figured she'd be divorced again by

Christmas. They couldn't get over her break-up with Wilson Tedworth Junior, who'd always been called Dink, for reasons Bubba
felt free to speculate on. That meant they'd had no hopes for that
marriage either. The young circle said Patty'd been truly crazy
about Dink, but the problem had turned out to be that Dink was
just truly crazy, and there'd been "a few episodes." That meant he'd
tried to kill any man who'd talked to her since the honeymoon.

Bubba said "the final episode" that had broken up marriage
No. 4 had happened right here where we were standing. One
Sunday Dink Tedworth had suddenly swerved off the golf course,
raced his electric cart around the pool and onto the verandah,
careened through the lunch crowd, and crashed into a golf pro
who was drinking bloody marys with Patty. It ended both the golf
pro's career (his hip was broken), and Dink and Patty's marriage.
In court, Dink apologized and got off with a warning from the
judge, who happened to be a friend of his father, Tedworth
Senior, President of Central Carolina Trust.

According to Bubba, Dink got "the royal screw" in the
divorce settlement. The divorce judge didn't like the Tedworth-
family-friend judge who'd given Dink a break on the assault
charge, so he gave Patty her freedom, Dink's house, and most of
his assets at Central Carolina Trust. The consensus of the young
circle was that Dink had been a good sport about being told to
hand it all over to Patty. Gallantry to women and insouciance
about money—both were big parts of their code.

A year had gone by since the Tedworth divorce, but the
young circle said Dink was still not reconciled to the loss of his
wife. So for months they had been enthusiastically predicting
trouble at her wedding to Joe Raulett, the Seafood King. Bubba
had come in hopes of seeing "fireworks." He got his wish.

•   •   •

I walked back to the verandah with a plate of shrimp to find
Bubba still transfixed by the breasts of the wet, pregnant Blue

Sunderland. Her friends hauled her out of the pool, then the three of them ran off onto the adjoining golf green, where they stripped down to their bras and panties and stretched out beside the ninth-hole flag. "Look at that." Bubba flicked his unlit cigarette into the night and angled for a better view. "I'd love to make it with Blue Sunderland, wouldn't you?"

"Bubba. Give it a rest."

"Aw, lighten up, Porcus Rex. It's just the old Eurocentric sexist rhetoric fighting extinction." He greedily popped another cigarette in his mouth.

I pointed out, "You don't even light those things."

He shook his head, careful not to mess up the wave in his auburn hair. "Nah, I quit. I travel too much and North Carolina's about the only place you *can* smoke anymore." He pointed back at the crowd inside. Between the cigarettes and the dry ice steaming up from the Neptune statue, it looked like Patty was close-dancing with her new husband in a rain forest. The Seafood King was a good-looking man—sort of like Ted Turner with the prematurely gray hair and the Clark Gable mustache. But he was an awful dancer.

Suddenly Bubba gave a sharp whistle, grabbing my arm in melodramatic style and spilling my champagne. "Step back from the fan," he warned. "Tedworth's here."

"Your pal Dink? At Patty's wedding? That's tacky."

"Damn right. Justin would have a fit. This is black tie and Dink's in a damn polo shirt!"

Bubba shoved me through the french doors and pointed out Patty's fourth husband over near the Neptune statue. He turned out to be the tall blond man who'd come out of the bushes onto the verandah earlier and stood next to me watching Patty throw the garter. Not only was he underdressed, he was drunk and crying and hauling at Patty. Patty's brother Pascal was ineffectually trying to pull Tedworth away, and Patty was yelling about why didn't Dink just drive his golf cart through the wall and smash into them like last time! It was obviously this sort of thing the circle was talking about when they mentioned that Patty and Dink Tedworth had "episodes."

The fact that Tedworth was crying (which presumably he hadn't been doing when he ran down the golf pro) made the scene more embarrassing than it would have normally been. Southern men are often drunk and often hauling at people, but they don't cry in public unless their mothers have died or their alma mater's lost a bowl game. At my side, Bubba gave a disgusted snort. "Look at that, he's bawling his eyes out!"

Tedworth managed to drag the five people pulling at him halfway across the ballroom before they pinned him to the floor. Rather than leave well enough alone, Patty ran over and told the Jimmy Douglas Orchestra to play "Can You Feel the Love Tonight?" from *The Lion King*, which must have had some special meaning because Tedworth went nuts and threw a vase of flowers at her, instead hitting the Neptune statue so icicles flew off the waves at its base. A half dozen men piled on top of him like they were sacking the quarterback, and Patty leaned over them and shouted into their midst with what smacked of sarcasm, "I can feel the love tonight, Dink. How 'bout you?"

At this point, the groom, Joe Raulett, rushed into the middle of the scene, but Patty's brother stopped him before he could reach the huddle. Tedworth got loose and took a swing at them. The others piled back on top of him. Bubba and I looked at each other, shrugged, ran inside, and pulled the top layers off the drunk man. Hauling him to his feet by his green polo shirt, I warned him, "That's enough, Dink." He seemed to give some thought to the possibility. "You okay?" I waved my hand in his face. Weaving, he nodded; he had the glazed look of a dying bull and jerked his head dully from one cluster of gawking guests to another. His nose was bleeding, and his wiping at it wasn't an improvement.

Patty suddenly appeared beside me and took my hand. "He's fine," she assured me. She raised my arm as if I'd just won a boxing match. "Y'all know Cuddy Mangum, our chief of police? And I didn't even call 911." Faces nodded hello. Her husband and brother fought to hold onto Tedworth's arms; all three turned red and grim from the struggle.

Bubba grinned. "Man, Patty, you still bring it out in them, don't you? Well, that was fun. Now if Dink had just had dueling pistols..."

Just then Tedworth broke loose and lunged toward Patty and me. He told Patty he was so sorry, he loved her but he was going to have to hurt her. Then he toppled into me, apologizing with a bizarre pattern of polite pats.

Patty pulled me away from him. "Come on, Cuddy, let's dance." She called to her brother. "Pascal, do something about Dink."

Dink told Pascal Raiford not to touch him, but Joe Raulett grabbed hold of one of his arms and Raiford took the other. On his way out, the Seafood King urged me to indulge his bride. "Dance with her, Chief Mangum. We've got it under control here." He called out to the crowd. "It's under control. Everybody get on back to having fun." The groom kept his hand in a hard squeeze on Tedworth's arm as he and his wife's brother fast-walked the drunk away like they all three might be going to fox-trot together as soon as they found an open spot. I had to admire the Seafood King, he was a take-charge kind of guy and wasn't going to let his new wife's ex-husband ruin his expensive party. I lost them in the crowd.

Bubba picked up two champagne bottles and a plate of jumbo shrimp, and with a kiss blown at Patty, headed back out-side, no doubt to the women lying on the golf course.

Patty wrapped her arm around me as she steered me nearer the band. "Where'd Bubba go?" she asked.

"Ran off after three young bridesmaids doing water ballet in the swimming pool."

"Oh them." She puffed them away with a dismissive breath. "You gonna dance with me or not?"

As she and her husband both seemed to think it was such a good idea, I figured why not. She was a good dancer; a palm's pressure on her back was enough to lead her into a complicated pattern without a falter. And she had a warm generous hand that felt at ease in mine. Maybe that easiness was the source of Patty's appeal; she was at home with men. After all, she'd been with a man since the womb—her brother Pascal was a twin—and she had given birth to twin boys herself.

As other couples joined us on the floor, and the band segued into another syrupy show tune, I said I was sorry Dink Tedworth had to cause such a scene at her wedding.

"Ummm." She shrugged as if to add, "What else can you expect?"

"You know I saw your ex outside a while ago; he didn't act all that drunk. How'd he get so wasted so fast?"

She lifted her shoulders again, slipping off responsibility. "He doesn't drink," she said. "I heard you were a great dancer."

I guess we weren't going to talk about how her fifth husband was now tossing her fourth husband out of her wedding party. "Who told you?" I asked her.

She smiled as we deftly side-stepped a couple loudly counting out the box step as if they'd be marched in front of a firing line if they messed up. "Justin Savile."

"Justin?"

"A dancin' champ, he said." I gave her a spin and a reverse dip. She laughed. "He was right."

I looked around. "Where is Lieutenant Savile tonight? Weren't y'all friends?"

She frowned with a little smile. "Well, I asked him, but he and Dink go way back, so he sent his regrets."

"Ah," I nodded. "Opposed to your divorcing Dink Tedworth?"

"Opposed to my marrying Joe."

"Too bad," I said. "I know Justin loves any chance to wear those patent leather ballet slippers with bows on them."

She laughed the laugh that had made me want to take her to dinner a few years ago. She said, "He even has buttons on his trousers instead of zippers." I wondered how she knew that, but maybe it was common knowledge in the circle. She walked her fingers along the back of my neck. "Justin said it was some big dance competition you won."

"It was a Shag contest at a law enforcement convention."

"Good enough for me. Okay, Cuddy, let's show 'em how to do it." We'd already had two dances together and I offered to let somebody else cut in, but she pulled me over to the band leader and squeezed his hand. "Jimmy, honey, play me and the police chief a fast old shag, okay? Like 'Kansas City,' something like that."

Jimmy Douglas shook his head in mock despair. "Patty, how many these honky tunes you gonna make me run tonight?"

Patty gave the musician a little back rub. "You just play something fast. You know you love me, Jimmy. I'm your best customer."

He laughed. "Well, that's true."

"But I'm settling down. This is my last wedding." She crossed her heart with two fingers.

"Then I hope it's a good one." Douglas smiled and turned back to his band. They took off in a hurry with Little Richard's "Tutti Frutti," and Patty and I stayed with them. We must have been doing okay, because the other dancers fell back, and made a circle around us and clapped when it was over.

"How 'bout another one?" Patty panted. I just nodded, not wanting to admit I was out of breath. The band kicked into "Sea Cruise." She and I were good together, no doubt about it, and were headed for a big finish when we got preempted. Somebody screamed. Loud.

I had Patty on an outswing and let go of her too fast as I spun around in the direction of the scream. She skidded into the couple behind us. Then she looked up, and she screamed too. The band stopped playing with the sharp squeal of a distressed clarinet. Everybody was staring up toward the ceiling. At the end of the room, under the balcony, Wilson Tedworth Junior hung head first on top of the giant ice Neptune statue, with the points of the crown stuck in his neck and his head dangling in air. Two forks of the huge trident were poked through his midriff. Blood spurting over his green polo shirt spread in bright lines down the sides of the sea god, turning the blue ice to purple.

For two or three seconds, it looked like Neptune had lifted Tedworth up over his head, ready to pitch him somewhere. He stayed there poised in air, while the whole room went dead quiet, for what was only seconds but felt longer. Then the statue's head and arm snapped off, and Tedworth crashed down, splattering vivid red on the ice as he fell. The statue toppled over sideways and shattered. Tedworth landed with a loud thud on top of the hors d'oeuvres table and bounced off. The table held dozens of glass platters and punch bowls and candlesticks and vases. Most of them broke.

By now we had a stampede headed for a look. It wasn't easy to push them back. Once I got close, I knew Dink Tedworth was dead. He looked right at me, but his eyes were blank. When I yelled for a doctor, two guests stepped forward and said that's what they were. I looked up at the little balcony right above us on the second floor. It was empty. The banner JOE AND PATTY FOREVER was hanging sideways from a rope. Tedworth must have ripped it loose as he plummeted headfirst onto the ice statue ten feet below. The two doctors agreed with me that he was dead. He'd gone over that rail in one of three ways. He fell, he jumped, or somebody pushed him. I was going to have to find out which one.

• • •

It was a relief to the guests to have the police chief already on the scene, and after I got them corralled, they called 911 for me and shut the french doors to the ballroom so no one could get in or out. I appointed a few guards, who lunged for their stations, full of importance. Everyone else stood staring at Patty as she stepped out of the crowd and asked me, "Is Dink dead?"

I nodded yes. With a long look at my face, she nodded back at me, then sat down carefully in the nearest chair.

As I ran out into the lobby, and up the curving stairs to the second floor, I was chased by the hysterical club manager, who kept telling me he was Mr. Bowe, as if that would explain everything. We ran through an empty dimly lit dining room and reached a door that led into the small balcony area from which Tedworth had fallen. Nobody was there. Mr. Bowe (a prissy little man torn between horror and an institutional effort to pretend nothing was wrong) prattled on compulsively about how the balcony was a musicians' gallery modeled on an eighteenth-century royal governor's mansion in Virginia. It was used only once a year when a brass quintet played fanfares to introduce the new crop of Hillston debutantes, daughters of local doctors and merchants, who would never minuet again in their lives.

In the thick dust on the balcony floor I could see dozens of smeared footprints. According to the tremulous manager, the entire club was thoroughly cleaned once a week, but a glance at the cobwebs suggested that "thorough" didn't include this little area. On the other hand, there was no dust at all on the rail over which Tedworth had taken his tumble, but Mr. Bowe felt confident that his staff must have wiped off the rail before attaching Patty's banner.

Mr. Bowe was frantically opposed to the notion that Tedworth had accidentally leaned over the rail and lost his balance; it conjured such nightmares of lawsuits slapped on the club by the Tedworth family that he had to press his satin handkerchief against his eyes to squeeze out the image. Balling each of his small hands in the grip of the other, he urged me to consider suicide. "I'm afraid we have to face it, poor Mr. Tedworth jumped to his death, heaven help him. You saw how he was acting. We all saw it. And there have been other…well, there have been incidents, even here at the club. Incidents."

"Yeah, I heard about the golf pro."

"If you want my opinion, I think poor Mr. Tedworth, and I always liked him, I think he jumped to spoil his former wife's wedding reception."

"That'll do it," I agreed.

He peered at me anxiously from behind his handkerchief. "Don't you think he jumped?"

I was shining my pen light into the corners. "Maybe somebody pushed him."

The little club manager turned the color of key lime pie. Pushed him? That would be even more sordid. He had to go take an aspirin; at least he said he needed an aspirin but he looked like he needed a fistful of Valium to me.

Among other dusty things on the floor, I noticed a dead infant mouse, a little strip of leather half the size of a match, a folded sheet of nice white blank paper, and a piece of moldy sandwich. I made the embarrassed Mr. Bowe leave them all where they were. As he walked me back through the dining room, I saw a little red chair knocked over near one of the rear windows, and under it there was a bottle of champagne spilled out on the carpet. The manager was nearly in tears when I stopped him from picking up the chair. "You can't touch things, all right, Mr. Bowe?"

Alarm fluttered through him. "Why? You're not bringing in the police, are you?" I reminded him again that I was the police. He waved his shiny white handkerchief in a frenzy as he led me back downstairs, like a nervous escort leading a surrender party.

While of course none of Tedworth Junior's family had been asked to come celebrate Patty's wedding to Joe Raulett, many of his friends were there, being friends of Patty's as well. Women collected at tables, crying; men at the bar, talking too fast as they narrated to one another what all of them had just seen. Patty still sat staring straight ahead in the chair where I'd put her. Her husband Joe was holding his ribs like he was going to be sick as he paced around making calls on a mobile phone. Pascal Raiford, sweaty and shaky at the same time, was trying to help out by putting the wedding presents in shopping bags then removing them when they didn't fit. Dr. Honeycutt was amazed that he had played golf with Dink only two days before. He kept insisting,

"You sure couldn't have predicted any suicide and I don't believe it was one." He was contradicted by his wife Caryn, who assured me that Dink was so despondent over losing Patty that his close friends were "seriously worried" about him.

I sat down beside Patty. Two women had joined her and kept rubbing her hands as if they were trying to keep her circulation going.

I leaned toward her. "I'm real sorry, Patty. But I've got to ask you a few questions." She took a drink of the water her friend held out, and nodded at me. "Did you have any other conversation with Tedworth tonight—other than what we all heard?" She said no. "Do you know what he meant by he was going to have to hurt you?" She shook her head no. "Did you understand him to mean he might—"

"Kill himself? He did, didn't he?"

The women around Patty nodded eagerly, murmuring, "Yes. Of course he did. Don't blame yourself. He just couldn't move on without you. He came to say good-bye.'"

She burst out crying. "I'm just so damn mad at him."

Pascal Raiford hurried over and pulled his sister into a hug. I asked to talk to him, and when we'd stepped aside, I questioned him about where Dink Tedworth had gone after he and Joe Raulett had dragged him out of the ballroom. Pascal told me that Joe had taken Dink into the men's room to do something about his nose bleed, and that he, Pascal, hadn't seen either of them again until Dink fell off the balcony. Like Dr. Honeycutt, Pascal was sure Dink's death was an accident and not suicide, although he admitted that at times lately Dink seemed to be on the verge of a nervous breakdown, and that he had been behaving erratically at the bank where they were both vice presidents.

I could finally hear sirens as Joe Raulett strode toward me, pointing at his watch, urging me to let their guests go home. I said I was sorry, but we needed names and addresses for their statements. Patty's new husband was making an effort to keep his voice pleasant, but the strain gave his face a waxy look. "You count the band, there're still two hundred people here. They're exhausted."

"And Tedworth's dead." I sat Raulett down. "I need to ask you some things. Pascal Raiford says you took Tedworth into the men's room—"

Raulett interrupted to ask if it wasn't obvious that Wilson Tedworth had killed himself and had come to Patty's wedding reception expressly to do so.

"I don't know that it's obvious," I told him. There was an unbroken bowl of crab claws on the floor. I leaned down and took a couple. "That true, you took him to the men's room?"

Reluctantly Raulett told me that yes he had led Tedworth into the men's lounge, where the man had drunkenly tried to clean himself up, after which he'd agreed to depart from the club without further trouble.

"He did?" I ate a crab claw. "Sort of a change of mood for Dink."

Raulett tightened his arms around his midriff. "Maybe he knew he'd made an ass of himself. I told him if he didn't get out, I'd have him arrested."

"Did he? Leave?"

Raulett loosened his tie. "I thought he did. He left the men's room."

"But you didn't watch him leave?"

"I'm not a crossing guard. I kept trying to wash off the damn nosebleed he'd gotten on me, and he wasn't in the lobby when I came out of the john."

"And you went straight back to the ballroom."

"Yes." He shook his head distractedly. "I think so."

I looked at him awhile. "He make you mad, Joe?"

"Damn right." Raulett jumped to his feet, and pointed at the verandah. "The guy's a nut. You heard what he did a couple of years back right out there?!"

I nodded. "Ran over the golf pro with his cart. Yeah, I heard."

"Right. A nut. The things Patty and I had to put up with—" He started toward where Patty's brother was leading her out of the room.

I sat him down again. "Just a second. Tedworth say anything that suggested he was getting ready to kill himself?"

After a struggle, Raulett admitted, "Just how he loved her and she was too good for me. But I wouldn't put it past him," he added angrily.

"Seems like shoving *you* over the rail would have done the trick better. Left him around to enjoy Patty." I ate another of the Seafood King's crabs and wiped my hands on the little napkin that said "Joe and Patty" above today's date. "You see him fall?"

"No. First thing I heard was everybody screaming."

"See anybody up there on the balcony tonight?"

"Well, just Patty when she threw the garter. But that was before Tedworth busted in on us. Oh, and Mr. Bowe's people put up the banner."

"You ever up on the balcony yourself?"

"No. Why should I be?" He strode away from me to console his guests for the ruined party.

• • •

So Justin Savile, head of our homicide division, had to show up after all at the wedding he had refused to attend because he'd known Wilson Tedworth Junior since kindergarten. Although I'd roused Justin out of bed after midnight, he'd arrived at the Hillston Club in half an hour dressed in a three-piece seersucker suit with a blue bow-tie and socks to match. He hugged Patty and told her how sorry he was about Dink. Then he came over to look at the blood-soaked body with me.

"I knew this wedding to Joe Raulett was a bad idea," Justin told me by way of greeting. Justin's convinced he has psychic insights. Maybe he does. Or maybe he's just a really good detective. "See what I mean?" He lifted the corpse's hand, and let it fall. "Accident?"

"Probably not." I pointed at the railing of the balcony. "Hard to accidentally fall over that." Looking at the body, I suddenly remembered something. "He had an envelope sticking out of this back pocket earlier tonight—it fell out, I told him he'd dropped it, and now—" I checked all his pockets. It wasn't there.

Justin looked at the dead man sadly. "Suicide note?"

I said, "Maybe not."

Justin sharply turned his head up to me. He knew what I was saying. Then he pulled the cloth back over his old schoolmate.

While Justin worked his way through the guests huddled in the lobby, forensics gathered what evidence they could. In a fret, I hounded them to hurry their photos. The cause of death was disappearing on us fast. Even if Tedworth's blood was cooling, it was warm enough to melt the broken-off pieces of the ice statue stuck in the side of his neck and poking out of his ribs. Our medical examiner Dr. Dick Cohen kept yawning as he made notes. He couldn't get over why so many Hillston corpses had to pick an ungodly hour like this one to croak in; he took it personally.

"That's right, Dick, they're dying just so you'll have to haul yourself out of bed in the middle of the night when you haven't had eight straight since you left Brooklyn."

"It's the God's truth. I can't sleep down here in the South."

"Well, since you're awake, what'd Mr. Tedworth officially die of? And don't tell me he choked on a piece of ice."

Dick Cohen speculated that Tedworth had expired after the sharp point of a triangle of ice four inches long punctured a carotid artery in his neck while simultaneously two eight-inch prongs of an ice trident perforated his lung and heart. Carefully pulling the pieces of ice out of the body, he packed them in iced containers.

"Any chance of suicide?" I asked him.

He scratched at his black stubble. "Nutty way to kill yourself. 'Course, you can't tell with a drunk. I had one cut off his own head with a circular saw." He hauled himself wearily to his feet. "Come see me at the morgue."

Tedworth's distraught parents arrived, having been called by the idiotic club manager. Justin took them into the office and tried to console them.

The ambulance attendants had hoisted the body bag onto the gurney when Bubba Percy ran in from the verandah. I'd forgotten he was still out there. Bubba was now looking like he'd done a few cycles in a washing machine. He was barefoot and bare-chested, his hair and pants were soaking wet; the rest of his clothes were missing. I said, "Those three ladies roll you for your wallet?"

Bubba quickly took in the scene. And its significance. "I fuckin' missed it, didn't I? I just heard somebody killed himself. Who?" As he'd asked the room at large, nobody bothered to answer him. Undeterred, he loped with squishy steps after the gurney, leaving behind big puddles of water, and before the attendants could stop him, he zipped open the body bag. I yanked him back from it.

"Dink Tedworth. Goddamn it!" Bubba was squirming with annoyance. "I can't believe I missed the whole fuckin' thing. What'd he do, shoot himself in front of Patty? Is that it?"

I told Bubba he'd have to wait to read about it in the *Raleigh Sun* because a reporter from that paper had already left to file his story. He growled at me and went racing after Dick Cohen.

We couldn't find the missing envelope that should have been in Tedworth's pocket and no one had seen it. Justin's team asked the same questions of one hundred and eighty-seven people and got the same answers. He sent everyone home to start nursing their hangovers. None of them had seen Wilson Tedworth Junior from the moment he was escorted out of the ballroom until half an hour later when Caryn Honeycutt (the doctor's wife) screamed as she caught sight of him dropping through the air. The drummer of the Jimmy Douglas Orchestra did think he'd caught a glimpse of a couple on the balcony shortly before Tedworth fell; they looked like they were necking. But the drummer wasn't sure; the little balcony was all the way across the ballroom, and it was dark, and it was none of his business. Nobody admitted to being one of that hypothetical necking couple.

The feeling around the Hillston Police Department was that Justin Savile could get anybody to blab anything; he could coax the sexual fantasies out of a mother superior under a vow of silence. So I believed him when he said the guests and staff weren't going to be much help. There had been a few people in the lobby during the half-hour before Tedworth's fall, but they hadn't noticed him coming out of the men's room and climbing the staircase to the second floor. They were Braves' fans who had hauled a TV out there; it was the fourteenth inning with the bases loaded, and they wouldn't have noticed if their wives had danced by naked shaking tambourines.

While of no use as witnesses, the guests were all too eager to offer theories. They explained that where Patty was concerned, "jealousy was a real issue for Dink"—something I'd already guessed. We heard a dozen more times about the golf pro. We also heard how on their honeymoon, Dink had cracked a man's head open on a granite bar top in St. Kitts for presuming to buy Patty a piña colada. This man had needed fourteen stitches and a check for $25,000 in order to recover from his injuries. A week after their first Christmas, Dink had smashed open the door of a hotel suite in Charlotte, expecting to find Patty there with a stranger. It turned out she was in fact visiting her sister in Savannah just as she'd told him. Instead, he'd terrorized an Israeli diamond salesman taking a shower. Tedworth claimed he'd gotten an anonymous phone tip telling him to go to that room of that hotel, and he'd apologized and paid for the door.

According to their friends, things had just gotten worse after Patty left him and took up with Joe Raulett, though ironically enough it had been Dink and her brother Pascal who had sponsored Joe's membership in the Hillston Club, where Patty had met him. Dink had clearly regretted the introduction. Once, finding them kissing at the Pine Hills Inn, he'd challenged Joe to a fight and when his offer was declined had smashed his rival's face into a plate of tortellini. He'd paid for the damages. I asked Justin why Patty hadn't gotten a restraining order against her former husband. Justin shrugged. "I guess she expects it. Back in college, these two guys actually fought a duel and one of them got—"

"Killed. I heard."

But while on the one hand the guests conceded that Dink Tedworth was "insanely jealous" of Patty (emphasis on insane), and "maybe had a problem with his temper," on the other, they were quick to defend him against the assumption that he'd also had a problem with his drinking. They wanted it understood that Dink didn't drink, by which they presumably meant he didn't drink all the time, the way most of them did. His atypical intoxication tonight explained why he had lost his balance and fallen off the balcony, as a few of them insisted. Or had lost his mind and jumped off the balcony, as most of them feared.

The majority of these guests had—like Justin—preferred Dink Tedworth (one of them) to Joe Raulett (not one of them), although they had nothing specific against the Seafood King except that his Cadillac was the bright blue color of his restaurants, and so was his cummerbund. Some dismissed him as new money—most of theirs was at least fifty years old—but they didn't doubt that he loved Patty. They just worried that this tragic thing with Dink was going to get the new marriage off to a bad start. Bless her heart, sighed Caryn Honeycutt, Patty seemed to be living under a curse like the Kennedys or something. Why if you counted her father, this was the third man who'd gotten himself killed over her. Mrs. Honeycutt sounded a little envious to me.

By three A.M., we'd sent almost everybody home. Justin was leaving to take the Tedworth family back to their Tudor mansion a block away. He came to say good-bye and found me poking around under the collapsed food table, looking for that letter of

Dink's. He couldn't resist pointing out that my tuxedo pants looked like they'd been made in the sixties and worn every night since. I allowed it was possible. Justin sighed, "Cuddy, is this another one of those Rubin's Rentals on Tuscadora?" He flipped open my jacket and read the label, which indeed did say just that. "Why don't you at least *buy* a tux?" (Justin's were custommade.)

I swatted away his hand. "The day I see you in a polyester Hawaiian shirt is the day I buy a tux."

I walked him out to the lobby where Joe Raulett was bluntly informing Mr. Bowe that the Hillston Club had better not bill him for all the breakage when the table collapsed. Dink Tedworth had caused that breakage and he hadn't been on the Rauletts' guest list and wasn't their responsibility, so the club could forget it, he wasn't paying a cent. Flushed and trembling, Mr. Bowe fluttered over to the Honeycutts and, raising a pale little eyebrow, whispered, "If Mr. Tedworth had been alive, he wouldn't have dreamed of not offering to pay for those damages."

The Seafood King was surprised when I told him he could not take off on his honeymoon in the morning, in fact couldn't leave town until after the coroner's inquest. He accused me of bullying him because he didn't have the social clout of the Tedworths. Patty turned and stared at him as if she'd mistaken a stranger for somebody she knew. Then she told him, "Let's go home, Joe. Everybody's tired." I certainly was.

Bubba Percy caught up with me as I headed for the car lot by the tennis courts. By now the moon was gone, and a hot black wind was whipping leaves off the enormous oak trees that shielded the club from outsiders. Bubba had on a waiter's jacket over his bare chest. He was shivering in his soaked pants. "Dink didn't shoot himself," he told me.

"Nope. You lose your clothes?"

"Maybe didn't even jump. Fuckin' tripped. You see him?"

"Bubba, if it's any consolation, I missed it too."

He pulled a pack of cigarettes from the waiter's pocket, and this time lit one and took a deep drag. "Dink Tedworth's caused scenes before."

"Yeah," I nodded impatiently. "The golf pro. The guy in St. Kitts. Yeah yeah yeah."

Bubba leaned on somebody's BMW and got conversational. "One night Raulett was making out with Patty in his car right out there on Catawba Drive, and Dink drives up behind them and rams them. They jump out, and Dink's BMW shoves Raulett's Cadillac straight down the hill into a power line pole. It took out the lights in North Hillston for six hours."

"I hadn't heard that one."

He smoked with great pleasure. "Yeah, well, you want news, come to a newsman."

"Why didn't the lovebugs stay home 'stead of going at it in public all over town? Considering Dink's well-known 'problem with jealousy'?"

"Pig Chief, you can't let people intimidate you. Well, I got my headline. NEW HUBBY'S ICE MAN KILLS PATTY'S EX. Like it?" He squeezed water from his pants. "Ask me what I was doing all that time."

I looked him up and down. "Go home. Sky's gonna let loose."

"Come on. Ask me. I swear, Blue Sunderland and me. We got it on."

I found my car keys. "I'm happy for you."

He grinned, shaking his wet hair like an Irish setter, and jabbered on despite the fact that I was loading evidence bags into my trunk and not paying attention. "Sixteenth fairway. Blue Sunderland. *And* her girlfriends watched. I'm not kidding. Then they pushed me in the pool and we messed around. We were sitting on the side, and who knows what could have happened, maybe a four-way, but somebody chucks some ice out the window at my damn head, hurt like hell, blood everywhere, and that kind of broke the mood, and then before I can get it going again Blue's husband runs out looking for her, yelling about somebody's dead."

I slammed shut the trunk.

He added, " I heard the sirens but I figured some geezer'd just had a stroke."

"Bubba, good-bye."

"Yeah. I better get a photographer over here." His teeth were rattling.

"Where's your car?"

He pointed at his new convertible, felt in his pants for his keys, then cursed. "Damn it. I left my jacket by the pool. I hope nobody took my damn gold vest. I got it at Harrods in London."

I opened my car door. "I thought maybe you stole it the last time you went to the Liberace Museum."

Bubba grinned, having fun again. "Yeah. I went with your mother. And she was a wild woman once we crawled under his white baby grand." I watched him trot off just as a bombardment of thunder let loose. Rain splatted out of the black clouds like God had turned them upside down, like He'd changed his mind about celebrating Patty's fifth wedding with that big pink moon. Bubba broke into a gallop; his brand new convertible was fast filling with rain, which couldn't be all that good for his white leather seats.

●　　●　　●

The clouds came to a standstill right on top of Hillston and it rained all night. Fat drops were still rolling morosely down my office windows on Monday morning when Justin came in with the report from forensics.

He pulled off his raincoat, revealing yet another new outfit, an ivory linen suit that he didn't buy on his salary. I licked chocolate glaze from my doughnut as I asked him, "Justin, don't you think you're looking jest a little too massa-of-my-old-Kentucky-home for a cop in Hillston, North Carolina, in the new millennium?"

"You're just jealous. And given your misguided loyalty to your regular haberdasher—K-Mart—I can understand why." He threw his Panama hat on a chair and tossed a pad of notes at me. He'd found Dink Tedworth's BMW where he'd parked it last night; it looked like he'd been living in it. There were a lot of pictures of Patty in his glove compartment but no suicide letter.

I looked through Justin's notes. There were thirty-two different people's fingerprints on the balcony. The only clear shoe print was one of Mr. Bowe's. Tedworth's blood—perhaps from his earlier nosebleed—was on the rail. At some point last night somebody'd been up on that balcony sniffing cocaine: there were traces on the piece of folded white paper left behind, and it hadn't been lying there long enough to get dusty. Also interesting: there were not only no prints on the balcony rail, there were none on the champagne bottle spilled on the carpet by the dining room window. Justin said forensics thought they looked wiped. I asked if Dink Tedworth was the cokehead.

"Nope." Sipping his espresso out of his porcelain cup, Justin gave me a computer handout of a print match. "A partial off that paper. Guess what, Patty's brother Pascal has a very bad habit. He didn't want to say anything last night, but when I told him I had a match with his Navy file, he admits he was on the balcony at the party—"

"Indulging in an illegal substance?"

"I'm afraid so, but he doesn't want Patty to find out. Now Pascal says when he headed back from the balcony after his snort up the nose, he saw somebody standing there in the dark in that dining room."

"Who?"

"He says it was Dink. He says this was early on, before Dink caused the scene on the dance floor. He says Dink was drinking champagne right out of a bottle. Now Pascal wonders if Dink was trying to get up the nerve to jump because he tried to talk to him and Dink told him to go away and tell Patty to have a good life, or words to that effect. Pascal's changed his vote to suicide."

"Join the crowd." I looked out my window at the rain beating on umbrellas moving down below. "Dink kills himself in front of Patty?"

"It happens."

"I know it does." I ate another chocolate doughnut out of sadness at the way people work so hard at breaking their own hearts.

Justin handed me a folder. "But Patty was just one of Dink's problems, I'm sorry to say." Justin said he had pushed Pascal Raiford hard on what he'd meant last night about Dink's behaving erratically at work and Pascal had finally broken down and confided that Dink had recently gotten himself into "real trouble" at Central Carolina Trust.

"Why didn't Pascal mention any of this last night?"

"Wanted to protect Dink's name, he said. Plus, he admits he didn't want to say he was up on the second floor, scared we'd get on to his coke habit." He tapped the folder. "But this bank business was going to come out anyhow. Dink messed up seriously bad."

He sure had.

Justin explained that this morning Pascal Raiford had taken him to the bank where he and Tedworth Junior had both been vice presidents, and he'd talked with Tedworth Senior. It turns out that while Dink never spent much time at Carolina Trust, preferring the golf links or tailing Patty around town, he'd spent enough time in it to skim off a million dollars, and had fudged the books successfully for two years to hide the fact. His father had confirmed it. Dink had robbed them blind.

Justin flipped through the file. "My problem is, Dink didn't have the brains for big-time embezzling."

I pointed out, "He got caught."

"But after two years. It was just last week he got caught."

In fact, only six days ago there'd been a blowout at the bank when the "misappropriation of funds" was traced back to the owner's son. Lawyers were called into a long meeting with

Tedworth Senior, as a result of which Tedworth Junior was yanked off the golf course and confronted with the evidence against him. Dink had immediately confessed. He acknowledged that he'd gotten in way over his head and had been too embarrassed to admit it, having always been a disappointment to his father anyhow. When asked to return the funds, he claimed to have lost the entire million dollars in bad investments. His father instructed him to take a "leave of absence" 'til they sorted things out. If Tedworth Senior hadn't been the majority shareholder of Carolina Trust, Junior might have been in jail now, and alive.

Justin said Pascal was the person whom they'd sent to the golf course to bring Dink back to the bank so they could confront him. "Pascal said it was the hardest thing he ever had to do. And Patty doesn't know about it and he hopes she doesn't have to."

"Why should Patty care?" I asked. "She divorced the guy."

"Well, maybe so, but Dink never stopped loving her. Dink's dad said Dink made a will *after* the divorce and still left her everything." Justin swung his raincoat over his shoulders like a cape. "'Course, she'd already taken most of it anyhow."

"Right." I lobbed the doughnut bag in the trash. "Go find out about those bad investments. You don't just lose a million dollars."

"Sure you do," said Justin, whose family was real old money and had misplaced most of it somewhere between now and the Revolutionary War.

•   •   •

On my way to the morgue I ran into our assistant D.A. She'd just read Justin's report and leaned toward suicide. She said Dink Tedworth had a long history of violent and irrational behavior. We had a temperamental man who'd lost his wife, his money, his job, and his reputation, and who had mixed (we'd discovered) champagne with enough barbiturates to make a hippopotamus sail over high hurdles. I couldn't argue with any of it. But I was still fretting over those wiped fingerprints and that missing letter. The assistant D.A. said I was always fretting and should give it up and take her to dinner.

Our medical examiner Dick Cohen sat in the morgue hunched over Dink Tedworth on the autopsy table. He was shivering, even in his bulky sweater. The man leaves Brooklyn for the South because he hates the cold and then spends all his time in a freezing morgue. He turned Tedworth's jaw to the side, and with a plastic pointer showed me the hole in his neck. "A point of that ice crown went right in here." There was a huge bruise on the jaw and teethmarks through the lip.

Dick wanted me to take a closer look at the wounds in the rib cage. He was always wanting me to miss things so he could explain them. But this time I got it right away. There were three wounds in the chest; not two, three.

Dick's narrow balding head gave its unvaried nods. He touched two gashes on the corpse. "The two forks from the trident did these." Then he moved the pointer to a third hole off at an angle. Something thicker and deeper than the trident prongs had gone 8.38 centimeters into the chest cavity, penetrating the pericardium and puncturing the tricuspid valve. It was that wound that was critical. "So what was it?" He pulled his glasses down on his nose to add weight to his question.

We checked through the death scene photos. It wasn't the third prong of the trident because I found a shot that showed the third prong, broken off, lying on the floor beside the collapsed hors d'oevres table, nowhere near the body. We examined Tedworth's bloody polo shirt again. There were definitely three separate rips in it, and all had faint traces of the blue dye that had coated the ice statue.

"How 'bout these?" I pointed at a photo showing the base of the Neptune statue with its circle of high jagged spears of ice that were supposed to look like ocean waves. Dozens of the spikes lay broken on the floor.

Dick looked begrudgingly at the photograph. "Doesn't work. They came off the statue's base. Tedworth got stabbed by the head and arm, seven feet up from the base. And he landed a good yard from the base." He used his pointer on the photo. "So there's no way one of those spikes…"

I threw the pictures down. "You stupid idiot!"

Alarmed, Dick stepped back. "Hey, no need to—"

"Not you. Me!" I started dialing Bubba Percy at the *Hillston Star* on my mobile phone. Waiting, I told Dick, "It's murder. Somebody used one of those big pieces of ice from the base, then chucked it out the window at the pool and hit Bubba Percy on the head with it."

"Hope they didn't mess up his hair." Dick sneezed.

• • •

At the Hillston Club, there was nothing even the rich could do to stop the rain, which had soaked the golf course, flooded the tennis courts, and frustrated the young circle, who, swinging their rackets and clubs, paced impatiently in the lounge, glaring out at the torrent. Mr. Bowe, the nerve-wracked manager, scurried among them, apologizing for the weather and for the intrusive yellow police tape that kept them out of the bar as well.

Nobody at the *Star* knew where Bubba Percy was. I left my fourth message for him to call me immediately. Headed upstairs to the balcony, I ran into a pleasant looking man who said he was Dink's lawyer. He gave me the interesting news that yesterday Dink had made an appointment to see him this morning, claiming it was "urgent." The lawyer asked about our investigation, and I told him most people seemed to be leaning toward suicide. He was adamant. "No way Dink killed himself at Patty's wedding reception, no way."

I asked him what made him so sure and he answered, "Bad taste."

I patted his shoulder. "I couldn't agree with you more."

Mr. Bowe the manager took me furtively into his office and whispered that possibly this wasn't relevant and it was true that Mr. Raulett was a club member—though a very recent one and perhaps the admissions committee regretted their decision anyhow—but late last night he had seen Mr. Raulett down in the kitchen pressing an ice pack on some terrible-looking bruises on his ribs. And so Mr. Bowe thought I might wonder—as he did—how did Mr. Raulett get those bruises when he hadn't been part of the subduing of Mr. Tedworth on the dance floor? I nodded. Mr. Bowe nodded. He fluttered away.

Up on the second floor, I found Justin waiting for me with a pallid Pascal Raiford. In the daylight I could see more of his resemblance to his sister Patty, but she'd definitely come out ahead in the looks department. Justin had bad news from Tedworth's bank; it seemed unlikely that anyone would ever find out how and where Dink had lost the million dollars; he'd destroyed any records. But Tedworth Senior was going to replace the money personally and there would be no public exposure of Dink's crime after his death.

I whistled. "That's a dad for you."

Pascal now confided to us that Dink had pretty much told him he was going to commit suicide. He'd said so last night up on the second floor

I got a little nasty sounding. "Mr. Raiford, is there some reason why you're handing out vital information like this on the slow installment plan?"

Rattled, the pudgy banker turned toward Justin. "Please try to imagine how tortured I've felt. Wanting to tell the truth. But wanting to spare Dink's reputation, for Patty's sake."

I turned to Justin. "For Christ sake, did she divorce Tedworth or not?"

Justin ignored this and asked Pascal exactly what Dink had said.

"He said, 'I can't go on without her, I don't want to live without her.'"

I asked, "And what did you say?"

Pascal mumbled, "Go home and sleep it off."

I asked him why he hadn't taken Dink home himself if he believed this was a genuine suicide fret. "I should have," he admitted. "Oh god, I should have." I sent him off to give his statement.

By the overturned chair, where the champagne had been spilled, I picked up an ashtray, leaned out the window, and tossed it into the pool below. It was an easy throw. Meanwhile Justin cut a square out of the still damp carpet to take to the lab. Mr. Bowe saw us and had a fit.

Another piece fell into place. On our way downstairs, Justin stopped at a club photograph on the wall. It showed a golfing foursome a few years back, holding a small trophy. There stood Joe Raulett and Wilson Tedworth Junior, side by side and smiling, with Pascal Raiford and Dr. Honeycutt on either side. Justin pointed at Raulett's tasseled golf shoes in the picture. "That's it!" he told me, chagrined. "That tiny strip of leather you saw up on the balcony? It's part of a shoe tassel. And you know what—" He opened his briefcase and flipped through last night's crime scene photos to one with Joe in it. "Damn it, I noticed his shoes last night but I didn't put it together." He was stabbing his finger at Raulett's shoes. "Tassel loafers with a tuxedo?" With the magnifier you could see the tip of the groom's shoe; it had black tassels. Raulett had been on that balcony last night and had lied about it.

"So it's another duel over Patty." Justin said. "*Cherchez la femme, mon capitaine.*"

"Talk American," I ordered him.

After Justin left, Bubba Percy came bouncing into the lobby. "Bubba, don't you answer your pager? I've been calling since—"

"Listen to this!" Bubba had just heard from Patty's "best friend," Amanda Dixon, one of the young matrons in the pool with Blue Sunderland last night, that Patty had only married Joe Raulett for "spite" and was still in love with Dink Tedworth. This morning Patty was all to pieces on the phone to Amanda, blaming herself for driving Dink to suicide by torturing him. (Clearly, her best friend saw no reason to preserve Patty's privacy.)

"Torturing him how?" I asked.

Bubba took me aside enthusiastically. "Whenever Patty saw Dink following her, she'd put the make on some jerk like that golf pro, just so he'd go nuts. Patty was the one—listen to this, Cuddy—"

I gave up trying to stop him.

"It was Patty who got Amanda to call Dink and drop that anonymous phone tip about her banging somebody in the Charlotte hotel. You know, Christmas before last when she was in Savannah. Patty did it just to see if he'd drive to Charlotte and make a fool of himself."

Bubba had my attention. "Patty married Joe Raulett just to upset Dink Tedworth?" He nodded. "Well, I'd say she succeeded."

"You heard it here." He tapped my shoulder with his rolled-up newspaper.

"Hang on. I need to talk to you." I grabbed his arm. "Last night in the pool with those women—"

"It was wild."

"Bubba, shut up! Didn't you say something to me about somebody chucking ice in the pool? Did you say ice? I need to know, was it from that Neptune statue? Was it dyed blue?"

Bubba stared at me; he knew from my eyes he was now holding the end of a major piece of string. He played it out, watching me carefully as he talked. Yes, last night while he was sitting at the edge of the club pool with "the Three Graces of Hillston," somebody had actually thrown a "stick" of ice from somewhere and hit him on the head with it. Maybe it was blue; it was too dark to see much. It was like an icicle as thick as his fist and a foot long, and it had broken on his skull. A long piece had actually stuck in his hair, and when he pulled it out, it had blood on it. It could have killed him. With a deep sense of injury Bubba bent over and showed me a very tiny scab beneath his thick wavy hair.

I made Bubba come out to the pool in the rain to show me where he'd been sitting, and from where he thought the ice had been tossed. He pointed up at the side of the second-floor of the club. "'Round there somewhere," he said with a shrug. "How should I know?"

"What'd you do with the ice?"

Baffled, he was trying hard to hide it. "Are you kidding? I took it home and stuck it in the freezer for a souvenir. What do you think? I dropped it in the pool."

I looked at the rain spattering into the big rectangle of warm empty pool water. "Bubba, please tell me you haven't washed your hair since last night."

He was indignant. "I wash my hair twice a day. Look at it."

"Did you touch anything after you grabbed that icicle? I don't mean women, I mean your clothes. Did you wipe—"

"Okay, what's up, Mangum? It's a homicide, right? Somebody killed him with that stick of ice?"

"Did you wipe the blood on your clothes?"

He decided he'd find out more if he helped. Dramatically, he struggled to remember. "I think I leaned over, let's see, and wiped my hand on something....Yeah, it was my gold vest. I had a fit and said to myself, 'Why the hell did you do that, you paid three hundred—'"

Without listening to more, I rushed him back inside the club. "You're going with Pendergraph here—" I called over an officer. "Wes! —And get him that vest."

Bubba balked. "I took it to the dry cleaners this morning."

"Goddamn it! Go call them quick! Stop them from cleaning it."

Pendergraph made a move to hurry Bubba, but Bubba dug in. "Mangum, come on, fair's fair. You owe me. Off the record." He stared at me solemnly, but I knew he'd be on the phone in a nanosecond with whatever I told him so I just walked away.

He yelled after me. "She killed him, Patty killed him?" The club manager walked into the lobby, heard this, pressed his yellow handkerchief against his mouth and scurried back to his office.

• • •

I told our assistant D.A. we had a homicide and couldn't have dinner. There was blue vegetable dye from the statue and type A blood and type O blood on Bubba's brocade vest. The type O was Bubba's; the type A was Dink Tedworth's. There was also blue dye and Dink's blood on the section of carpet fabric we'd removed from the second floor.

Someone had taken an ice spike broken off from the base of the Neptune statue in the fight and, concealing it, followed or led Dink Tedworth upstairs, stabbed him in the heart, then tossed the ice out the window, figuring it would soon melt, destroying the evidence. Instead, it had landed on Bubba Percy; for the only time in his life the reporter was in the right place at the right time. The murderer had dragged Tedworth onto the balcony and shoved him over the rail so that he'd crash down onto the statue. (The struggle to lift him over the rail in the dark had looked like a "necking couple" to the Jimmy Douglas drummer watching from the bandstand.) Afterwards, the killer had spilled champagne over the carpet stain and wiped the bottle clean of prints. Hurrying back into the ballroom, he'd joined the horrified crowd clustered around Dink's body.

The assistant D.A. said, "Who's the someone?"

I admitted I didn't know for sure, but I had someone in mind. She said, "Meet me at Pogo's and tell me about it."

I said I had to go pick up some shoes first.

• • •

Patty Raiford Raulett was alone at the Raifords' eighteen-room Colonial on Catawba Drive. Her twin sons were in New Orleans with their father. Her brother Pascal was at the bank.

And when I asked for her husband Joe, she said he was off clos-
ing a deal. I expressed surprise that Joe would be doing business
the day after he'd gotten married, since he'd planned to be at the
beach on his honeymoon. Not to mention that his wife's
ex-husband had died the night before.

Patty shrugged. "Can I help?"

"Matter of fact, I want the tassel loafers Joe was wearing last
night."

She gave me a look, then flung my raincoat over a brocade
chair. "I'll be right back." She took her bloody mary and left.

I wandered around a mammoth living room crammed with
handsome furniture that looked old and expensive. There were
pictures of Patty everywhere. There must have been five photos
of her for every one of Pascal, even though it was his house. But
then there'd been five marriages of Patty's for every one of Pascal's (and I'd heard that the one marriage he'd had had only
lasted six months).

She returned with the loafers and her bloody mary. I held up
the piece of leather we'd found on the balcony floor. It fit the
torn tassel on the shoe. I said, "I need to talk to your husband."

Patty motioned for me to follow her. "Well, you're welcome
to wait. What have Joe's shoes got to do with this?"

We went out through a sun room onto a patio. I said, "Nice
garden."

"Thanks. Pascal tries to keep up the old family style without
the old family income." (And she didn't even know what her
brother was shelling out for cocaine.) The rain had stopped, and
we sat down under an umbrella on the patio. There was a green
plastic alligator floating in the pool with a *Vogue* magazine lying
on its stomach. A maid suddenly appeared beside us. She poured
me an iced tea and gave Patty another bloody mary. Patty
squeezed her hand thankfully and she left. Did they have a sig-
nal, or had the maid been looking out the window, waiting for
when to bring the next drink?

I said, "The shoe means your husband was up on the balcony

last night. So when he tells me he wasn't, I wonder why he lied. Also I wonder where he got those bruises I've heard are on his ribs, since it wasn't in the scuffle on the dance floor."

She didn't beat around the bush. "You think Joe killed Dink?"

"That what you think?"

"No. I think Dink jumped."

I let that go for now. "A friend of yours told Bubba Percy you deliberately set out to make Dink jealous even after your divorce."

"Amanda Dixon?" She didn't seem angry at her gossipy friend.

"Apparently. If it's true, didn't you worry something like this might happen? Or was it more important to keep on being the North Carolina belle of the ball? Isn't that your reputation?"

She blushed. "That's not very nice." We looked at each for a while. I waited. She stared sadly into her bloody mary, and whispered. "I never thought he'd kill himself. That's the God's truth."

"How 'bout old Joe?" I held up his tasseled loafer. "Were you using Joe to make Dink jealous?"

"Miz Raiford?" We were interrupted by the maid returning with a cordless phone. She didn't say who was on it. Patty answered, said, "Hi, Joe," and told him to come home right away, that I wanted to see him. She hung up and said he'd be here in about twenty minutes.

She stirred her drink with the celery stalk. "It's my fault Dink jumped."

I said, "He didn't jump. He was murdered. Bubba Percy wonders if maybe you killed him."

"Bubba thinks he has a sense of humor."

"He says women'll do anything."

"He's right." She made an effort at a smile. "They will. But I didn't kill Dink."

"Your brother Pascal says Dink told him flat out last night that he was going to kill himself, but Dink's lawyer thinks he wouldn't have done it in front of people at your party because it'd be in bad taste. Is that right?"

She nodded. "Everybody always said Dink had the best manners."

"Except for that little problem with his jealousy." I put on my sun glasses; it made it easier to watch her face. "Somebody had already stabbed Dink in the heart before he went over that rail."

She took this in, shaded her eyes to look at me.

"So does your husband know you married him just to spite Dink? A thing like that could annoy a groom."

Patty wasn't liking me as much as she had on the dance floor. "You're pretty sarcastic."

"Murder rubs me the wrong way."

She spent the next half-hour asking me questions, a few of which I answered. Meanwhile I kept looking at my watch. After forty minutes, I called the desk sergeant and told him to send a car out to find Joe Raulett. Patty followed me back through the huge cool house, promising me that Joe was just stuck in traffic. The maid was mopping the floor of the marble foyer and pointed silently for me to walk around her. I asked her if that had really been Mr. Raulett on the phone. She turned to look at Patty. Patty gave a tiny nod and the maid said, yes, it was Mr. Raulett on the phone, and she went back to her mopping.

At the door, Patty said, "So Bubba Percy thinks I murdered Dink?"

My raincoat felt sticky and heavy in the hundred-degree August sun. I nodded. "But he also says the two of you had oral sex in a hot-air balloon over the state fairgrounds."

She smiled and closed the door.

●　　●　　●

Justin yawned as I took another bite of jelly doughnut. "Admit it, Patty pulled a fast one on you."

It was true. I don't know who she was talking to on that cordless phone, but it wasn't Joe Raulett because he'd already left town on a plane to San Juan. Where he'd gone from there, we still hadn't found out. Justin studied me for a while. Then he said, "You're not happy. It's that stupid envelope in his pocket, and for all you know it was Dink's damn phone bill."

It's a strange thing. We had nothing in common, and yet Justin knew me better than anybody else in my life. (Admittedly my relatives are dead and I live alone.) I said, "Yes, I'm not happy. So where did that letter go?"

"More to the point," he looked at me, "where did Joe Raulett go?" He threw a dart at the photo of my predecessor, Chief Fulcher, that I kept on the door for just that purpose.

I said, "If it was the honeymoon, kind of tacky to leave the bride behind." I headed back to the big house on Catawba Drive.

The maid didn't look happy to see me. Patty, her bloody mary in hand, didn't look any happier. She said Joe really had said he was coming home and she was as surprised as I was that he'd fled the country. She had no idea where he'd gone.

I got sarcastic on her again. "Well, where'd he tell you he was going when you helped him pack and waved him off to the airport and then sat there with me pretending he'd be back any minute?"

She refused to admit she'd known Joe was headed for the airport. And there was going to be no way to prove it. Then she'd tried to get me to look at things differently. "You can't call this murder. Joe and Dink got in a fight about me and Dink fell over the rail. It could just as easily have been Joe who got killed."

I asked, "Would you care? Or is it just to the victor go the spoiled?"

"You're not very nice," she told me again and closed the door on me.

I called Bubba. The *Star* broke the story with a big photo of Patty.

SEAFOOD KING MURDERS PATTY'S EX
AT SOCIETY WEDDING
ANOTHER MAN KILLED FOR LOVE OF FORMER CAMPUS QUEEN

Patty was back in the news. Dink Tedworth had died for love of her. And Joe Raulett had killed him. The assistant D.A. felt she had a case. A waiter at the club remembered seeing Raulett and Tedworth headed up the lobby stairs together. A fingerprint of Raulett's was found on the overturned chair. A guest recalled Raulett's threatening Tedworth's life in a restaurant once. Pascal Raiford admitted he'd had his suspicions of the Seafood King all along. None of the young circle were surprised—after all, that blue cummerbund. But I still wasn't happy. I wanted the satisfied feeling I get when I bid five no-trump and I make five no-trump. And I didn't have it. Why hadn't a tough man like Raulett toughed it out, admitted the fight, and claimed that Dink's fall over the rail was an accident? The whole town knew how often Dink had attacked him in public. Why run away?

•   •   •

The petite and pompous Hercule Poirot, another great believer in brains, says that it's always the little gray cells that solve murders. But in this case, it was what the little gray cells forgot. I had a call from Rubin's Rentals on Tuscadora. They wanted their tuxedo back, which I'd stuffed in my closet after coming home the night of Tedworth's death. I'd forgotten all about it.

Justin and I were headed out to dinner and I told him I wanted to run the rental into Rubin's while he waited. Justin was checking the garment's pockets. I told him I'd already gotten all the change out, but I could lend him a dollar if he was desperate. "Jocular," he said. Then he stuck his hand in a little diagonal side pocket of the jacket that I hadn't even known was there and he pulled out an envelope. "I guess you don't use a cigarette case," he said. "That's what the pocket's for." He handed the envelope to me. "Here you go. Look familiar?"

"Patty" was written on the front in a big sloping script. Yep, here it was, the envelope missing from Dink Tedworth's khaki pants, the envelope I'd torn the Hillston Club apart for. Justin shook his head. "You'd be lost without me...." I pulled over to the curb. "Shut up and let me think." I flashed back to how Tedworth had lunged against me after I'd broken up the fight on the dance floor, and how he'd patted me so many times while apologizing. He must have put the envelope in my jacket then. But why? Justin wondered if maybe he'd been so out of it with pills and alcohol that he'd believed he was returning something *I'd* dropped. But I decided that Dink had put the letter there deliberately, because he knew I was the police chief, and that I'd make sure Patty got it.

I read the letter to Justin. Then I sent him over to Central Carolina Trust to arrest Patty's twin brother Pascal for murdering Dink Tedworth.

• • •

The next day Patty burst into my office without waiting to be announced. I have to admit she looked good angry. Justin was with me but she didn't say hello to either of us. She said, "Pascal's in jail! Is he some kind of witness? Why won't they let me see him?"

"Hi, Patty." I smiled at her. "Guess what, you were right. Joe didn't kill Dink." This took her aback and she stopped talking. I said, "But Joe *was* up on that balcony and he did have a fight with Dink. However, he left Dink up there alive as can be. Somebody else came along and killed your ex. Oh, and you won't like this, but it wasn't *Cherchez la femme*; it was that other phrase, Follow the money."

Now she looked at Justin. "What is he talking about?"

I answered for myself. "I'm talking about Dink and your brother Pascal, about the million dollars they embezzled from

Carolina Trust. Honey, it didn't have a thing to do with you. You're back down to only one guy dead for love of you."

Justin hurried over to her and helped her into a chair. He looked at me frowning. I told him to go ahead and tell her what we'd learned since I'd seen her last. He tried to do it gently.

The truth is the murder did have a lot to do with Patty. Dink had gotten himself into such a state by the night of her wedding that he'd crashed the reception to see her "for the last time"— not because he was going to kill himself, but because (as he put it in his letter) he planned to "face the music in the morning" by pleading guilty to embezzlement. He also wrote her that he was sorry to have to hurt her but he planned to tell her brother Pascal that if Pascal didn't turn himself in at the same time, Dink would have him arrested. Because Pascal had been his partner in the embezzlement.

In fact, Pascal was the head man, the know-how behind the computer wizardry that had made all that money disappear without the bank's ever noticing. We'd gotten the confession out of Pascal that morning. At the end of Justin's interrogation (I listened behind the glass), Patty's brother had been almost bragging about his clever scheme. He'd admitted that because he'd needed the junior Tedworth's access to bank codes, he'd lured him into his plot. In fact, Dink hadn't completely grasped how criminal what they were doing was: Pascal had persuaded him it was really just a game on paper and that they could put everything back whenever they wanted to. Dink had always loved Pascal because he was Patty's twin and because Patty loved him. And so he'd given Pascal the information he needed. Once involved, Dink was trapped not by the money, but by the specter of his father's ever finding out.

Pascal, on the other hand, did want the money; he not only had expensive tastes, he was investing in the fast-growing Neptune restaurant chain owned by a new golf buddy of his, Joe Raulett. Unfortunately, it was around the same time that Dink's marriage broke up and Joe Raulett went after Patty. Pascal couldn't let Dink find out that the embezzled money was going to buy shares in the hated Seafood King's business, that Pascal and Joe were building Neptune Restaurants as fast as they could with money that belonged to Central Carolina Trust.

So Pascal told Dink that he'd lost all the money investing in bad stocks, that he hoped Dink could forgive him, that they had to forget the whole thing had ever happened and pray the bank never found out.

But the bank found out. And, because of Pascal's cleverness, the trail of embezzlement led back to Dink alone. When the outraged board called in Pascal and told him to go to the golf course to get Dink, he almost panicked and fled himself. Luckily he didn't. For as it turned out, he didn't even have to beg Dink to keep quiet about his involvement. Dink volunteered! Since the bank didn't suspect Pascal, Dink would take the full blame on himself and leave Pascal out of it "for Patty's sake." And Dink might have stuck to this noble sacrifice had he not discovered that—far from losing the money—Pascal had used it to get filthy rich in partnership with the Seafood King who'd stolen Dink's wife.

He found out because he spent a lot of time spying on Joe Raulett. He even broke into Raulett's Cadillac the night before the wedding to see what he could find there. He was hoping for something to turn Patty against her future husband. What he found were contracts in a briefcase that made it clear even to someone of his simplicity that Pascal Raiford owned 19 percent of Neptune Inc., for which he had made payments of $738,000.

At the wedding reception Dink found Pascal, blew up at him, and told him that he wouldn't protect him anymore—that Pascal had lied to him and betrayed him and that if he didn't return the money and turn himself in, Dink would call the police on him in the morning. Poor Pascal, he hadn't been kidding when he'd told us he was "tortured" that night at the club. Buying time, he'd told Dink that he'd do as he asked in the morning but that they mustn't ruin Patty's party. Then he followed Dink around, watched him getting drunker and more upset. He tried to stop him when he rushed onto the dance floor and grabbed at Patty. What if Dink drunkenly shouted out the truth right then and there? Pascal couldn't risk it.

So, fortified by cocaine, Pascal seized the opportunity, the way you have to if you want to get ahead in business these days. After Joe Raulett strong-armed Dink into the men's room, Pascal snatched up one of the thick icicles that had been knocked off the statue's base when Dink had thrown the vase at Patty. He saw Dink run back into the lobby from the men's room, spot Raulett, and chase him upstairs. Pascal followed them. While he watched from the shadows, the two men started fighting. Dink bruised two of Raulett's ribs with a kick. Raulett slammed Dink in the face with the little red chair, knocking him out. He left him lying there on the floor by the windows.

Pascal ran over and stabbed Dink in the chest. He threw the ice stick out the window. He dragged the body to the balcony, toppled it over the rail, and ran downstairs to join the crowd. He was even luckier than he'd hoped, the body not only hit the statue, it was speared on it. Pascal then did what he could to make everybody think, first, that Dink's death was an accident, then when that didn't work, that he'd committed suicide, and then, as a last resort, that he'd been killed in a fight with Joe over Patty. The Hillston Club set was predisposed to believe that men would fight to the death for love of Patty. It was something they were used to, even admired. She had that reputation. And Pascal almost got away with it.

When Justin finished the story, Patty sat there looking older. Maybe she didn't like it that this was a murder about money—as tacky as a sky-blue cummerbund or a rented tuxedo. Maybe she didn't like it that Raulett had left town not so much from fear of being accused of murdering a man in a fight over her, but because he figured he'd be going to jail once the truth about the embezzlement came out. He'd taken Pascal's money knowing full well where Pascal had gotten it, and we could prove that now.

I had to tell her she couldn't even have Dink's letter because we needed it for the trial, though I did have a copy made for her. As Justin walked her out, I said, "So long, Patty," but didn't expect an answer and didn't get one. She didn't like me, even if I was a good dancer.

•   •   •

We finally tracked Raulett to Belize. Over the phone, Justin persuaded him that he could avoid implication in first degree murder if he came home and testified against Pascal—not that he had a home to come to, at least not a home with Patty because she'd filed for divorce.

Just before Pascal's trial started, I ran into Bubba Percy at Pogo's. I was alone in a booth, waiting for the assistant D.A., and Bubba was (so he claimed) waiting for Blue Sunderland, who by now had had her baby and was cheating on her husband with Bubba (so he claimed). The star of the *Star* sat down with me uninvited, bringing his dinner plate with him.

"Life is good, Hog Cop," he said, wiping his pretty mouth after slurping the sauce from a gelatinous chicken wing. "So, listen, I've got an auto-correct for you on Patty's love life. She's dating Caryn Honeycutt's husband and they aren't even legally separated."

I said, "Bubba, I don't care."

"You know what Blue told me? Patty used to sleep with her own twin brother. She and Pascal got it on." He checked his hair in the mirror across the aisle. "Here's my theory. Pascal's in love with Patty and just puts up with all these other men because she always comes home to her brother in between. But she's really in love with Dink Tedworth, and Pascal finally can't stand it. So that's really why he whacks him. Not this dumb embezzlement stuff. Love."

"You're a real romantic, you know that, Bubba? The truth is, 'Men have died and worms have eaten them. But not for love.'"

"Who said that?" Bubba dipped his comb in my water glass.

"Rosalind."

"Rosalyn Carter?"

"No, Rosalind *As You Like It.* But Rosalyn and Jimmy Carter now, there's a couple that really did believe in love."

"And you don't?" He ran the comb through his curls. "You take away love and you take all the horror and misery and violence out of life. Then what am I going to put in the paper?"

"You got me there."

Meredith

Fast Love

It was love at first sight out of the corner of my eye as she flew past the showroom window where I stood eating a double-cheeseburger and trying not to hear Dalton Longfielder bore our only customer with exaggerations about his racing a 560-horse-power Mustang down in South Carolina last Sunday. It was love in a blur too. At first I thought maybe something rabid or mentally defective was after her. I didn't think of muggers; we didn't have crime in Toomis in the Seventies. As our billboard for some reason still brags, Toomis is "the Safest, Smallest Industrial Town in Piedmont, North Carolina." Our industries are the state mental hospital and a snuff factory. If you live here, you don't notice the smell.

So she ran by at six in the evening on an October day, and when nothing else followed her, I did. Destiny can't be ignored, no matter how highly unlikely it might look at first sight—as my grandmother told me when she bought her bus ticket to go march against the death penalty and my father caught her and put her in the (mental) hospital.

This blurred object of my sudden affection looked highly unlikely because the women of Toomis all walked on the few occasions when they weren't driving their cars; they didn't run. And in mid October—whether it was forty degrees or eighty degrees—they wore wool plaid skirts with cardigan sweaters looped over their shoulders. She, on the other hand, had on white shorts with red stripes and red shoes with white stripes and a T-shirt with a portrait of Margaret Mead the anthropologist on it. Her red hair in its ponytail leapt all over the place like a fire chasing her down the street.

She was beautiful from a rear view; I don't mind mentioning that I noticed because I'd already decided to marry her. We Wintrip males have a long family tradition of choosing a bride in the twinkling of an eye, although I believe I was the first to spot one on the run. My great-grandfather saw his future wife stabbing at a bully with a pitchfork as she stood atop a hayrack with her skirts tucked up. Grandpa saw Grandma trying to leave town in the back of a snuff truck. My father first glimpsed my mother as she and her fiancé were winning a Tri-Delta shag contest. And I fell in love in a flash with the first female jogger anyone ever saw in Toomis, North Carolina. I had loved only once before—unhappily—and now as I panted toward the town limits, a stitch in my side, a throb in my back, fear tingled through me. Would this girl break my heart as Betsy Creedmoor had done long ago?

I lost the jogger just on the ridge of the first long upgrade of Route 55. The double-cheeseburger and calf-high Frye boots did me in. After the spasms ended, I crawled along the shoulder until I felt well enough to walk back to Wintrip Motors where Dalton Longfielder, my dad's other vice president, amused himself by hurling me to the ground on the pretense that he'd already called an ambulance to rush me off for rabies shots. He laughed like a hog choking on table scraps. He'd seen the girl too. "Nice bod," was all he could think of to say.

Dalton is my sex, race, and age. So much for what we have in common besides being vice presidents of Wintrip Motors. His brain is thick and spongy. He sports a forty-eight–long maroon polyester blazer, a crew-cut, and ought to clip the hairs in his nostrils. My dad likes Dalton; in the summer they'll lie side by side in shorts under a car with their legs sticking out like the legs of two Greek soldiers in love. They like cars. They like football; they say that in their time they crunched a lot of cartilage playing defense for the Toomis Tigers (the high school team). Dad wishes Dalton were his son. So do I. The truth is, in high school, team sports were never that compelling for me. Instead I had a talent for chess, debating, and bicycling—enthusiasms that struck my father like a collapsed lung.

Senior year, when my life was in shambles over Betsy Creedmoor, the track coach lured me into the sprint. As it happened, I was good. I'd always been a runner. From childhood on, wherever I was supposed to be, I ran there fast. I ran after what was required of me. I ran after the school bus. I ran after the footballs my father was always kicking at me in the backyard. I ran like the wind out of necessity. I was always late because I was always off at the movies or reading or daydreaming about going someplace far from Toomis and saving the world, like my grandmother had wanted to do when she'd hidden in the back of the snuff truck. Toughs in the neighborhood, murderous with the baffled envious rage that the stupid feel for the intelligent, would bolt out at me from behind bushes and try to mutilate me. When we were twelve, Dalton Longfielder chased me through the Baptist nursery school playground with a branch of poison sumac that he planned to rub in my eyes. I was jumping three-year-olds like they were hurdles.

So you might say life trained me as a sprinter. I even lettered in track. Now I planned to use that training to win a wife. Sunday night I pawed my tennis shoes out from under the bed. Wearing them Monday, I was on the watch for my future bride as soon as I had hurried from my "other job" over to Wintrip Motors where from five to eight P.M. on weekdays and all day Saturday, I worked for my dad. I did it for the money and for my mother who begged me. Maybe she thought that if my dad's only child refused his command to come to Wintrip Motors as a VP, he'd put me in the mental hospital too, like he did to his own mother.

When Dad first heard about what he called my "other" job— which is state social work—he told me I was nuts. He let me know *social* meant *socialist* and *worker* meant Red Square and he knew what he was talking about because he was always right about everything. Then he jack-knifed to a stop (we were driving home from my college graduation), swelled into a frenzy, and announced he was going to beat the commie crap out of my head with a pistol butt. By the time he got his glove compartment open, I'd done the quarter-mile in four seconds less than my old coach's best hopes. Plus done it wearing an academic gown. My mother was standing beside the highway screaming, "He doesn't mean it!" But I didn't know if she meant me or my dad and didn't want to take the chance.

Although it was the seventies, my father was a man of the fifties. In the fifties, and not just in Toomis, people were still scared to death that the Communists might take over and brainwash Americans into thinking they had a right to other people's property—especially the property belonging to these people who were scared to death of the Communists. Nearly all the parents that my parents knew shared their fear that children were going to *catch* communism. They thought it was like polio, only there wasn't a vaccine. So when I was nine, Dad made me sell glitter-dusted Christmas cards door-to-door because the money went to help fight the Red Menace. From my father's point of view, I obviously hadn't sold enough, for Russia had gotten me in the end and mesmerized me into preferring social services to the showroom of Wintrip Motors. It was for my mother's sake ("Let your father," she begged, "hold up his head in Toomis!") and also so I could pay rent and wouldn't have to live at home, that I moonlighted at Wintrip Motors.

Thank god I did and that Wintrip Motors hogged the side of Main Street where Meredith Krantzsky jogged. Meredith Krantzsky. That was her name, although horribly enough it was Dalton Longfielder who introduced her to me. My own attempt to meet her had been thwarted by my grandmother's best friend.

Wearing my sneakers, I'd been in a nonchalant crouch by the showroom door at six o'clock Monday. Suddenly *she* flashed around the corner of Parritt's Diner and flew toward me. As she neared the end of the block I could see gold specks in the green of her eyes. She was altogether as beautiful as I'd suspected from my original blurred impression.

I trotted forward, casual. "Mind if I run along with you a little bit?"

She turned, arching a copper brown eyebrow at my seersucker jacket and best paisley tie.

I ran beside her. "My name's Blake Wintrip. Felt like…little exer—" But then I tripped over the wheel of a baby stroller coming the other way, and while I spiraled around to catch my balance, old Miss Carthage spied me from the bus stop bench. She clawed me to a standstill to tell me she'd spent the morning visiting my grandmother at the mental hospital. I couldn't get past her without knocking her down. By the time I could unclench Miss C.'s relentless fingers, my bride-to-be was disappearing like a sunset through the intersection of Maple and Main, where all at once she turned, smiled at me, and then ran on. My heart burst.

Miss C. pushed up my eyelids and stared at my pupils. "Blake, are you all right? Heaven's sake what's the matter with you? Your face is a deep plum purple, almost a heliotrope." Miss Carthage is an amateur painter and has even sold dozens of her pictures for outrageous prices since Southern primitivism got to be fashionable. Her first name's Lavinia and that's how she signs her paintings, Lavinia, in the same kind of printing as Vincent Van Gogh. My grandmother calls her "Vin" and she calls Grandma "Frankie." They founded the Ladies Art League, to which my mother now belongs, and Miss C. drives their canvases up into the Appalachians where the gift galleries sell them to tourists. Miss C. poked at my ribs. "Are you sick, honey?"

"I'm in love," I told her. "I'm about to propose."

"Wonderful! Frankie will be so relieved. She always said that Betsy of yours belonged in Mercy much more than she did." (The mental hospital was called Mercy for some reason and everyone used that name for it to avoid mentioning the word "mental.") "Who's the lucky lady?"

"There she goes." I pointed with a sigh as the red ponytail bounced away toward the horizon.

Miss C.'s tactless remark about my former girlfriend was a reference to a sorrow from which only time and an inadvertent discovery of the truth had cured me. My high school girlfriend, Betsy Creedmoor, temporarily lost her mind during senior year under the pressure of being forced by her mother to pretend to be stupid for popularity's sake. Betsy was brainy, and in our town in the seventies the intellectual life was frowned upon for females. (For males too, as far as that goes.) Betsy's breakdown—she would sit for hours with her bare feet in the gutter outside Toomis High, drawing designs on her legs with lipstick—was the angel's sword that drove me out of Paradise. The sight of her beautiful vacated eyes sent me from the garden of ignorance into a life of social work among children of Cain.

That was the way my grandmother put it when I went to Mercy to ask her what I ought to do about Betsy. She sat at her easel, hummed her old marching song, "We Shall Overcome" and thought a long while. Finally she told me I had to let Betsy find her destiny by herself and I had to go find my own. "Trust to time, Blake; it'll either kill you in the end or you'll get what you want or you won't give a shit." I told Grandma I was going to the state university and study injustice. Okay, she said, but get over the notion that the world should make sense, much less be fair. Grandma was in a position to know. Here she was, perfectly sane, locked away to weave placemats and play solitaire with worn-out cards in a mental hospital. Here was Betsy Creedmoor deteriorating beyond repair and declining to speak any language but pig Latin, while her mother accused me of cruelty when I pleaded with her to get her daughter medical help.

"Blake, Blake," cried Mrs. Creedmoor, "why do you persecute me and my Betsy so? Why are you trying to lock our little girl away in a snake pit with a bunch of old crazy people? When you're the one who's followed her around like a little puppy dog ever since fifth grade. She was so happy and popular 'til she took up with you."

Mrs. Creedmoor had never liked me. Her feelings were requited. She had two-toned hair and arms as brown as her golf bag. She smoked four packs of cigarettes a day; even when she was doing the dishes, she would pinch her cigarette with a sudsy hand and stick it in a seashell ashtray over the sink. When I told her Betsy was probably manic-depressive, she'd sigh, "Oh, what makes you talk that ugly way? Why, she's just worked too hard turning herself into a silly bookworm like *you.*" And as this woman was speaking, her sixteen-year-old daughter stood for hours weeping at her reflection in the hall mirror with her fingers stretching her mouth into a howling grin.

Betsy missed so much school because of her nervous breakdown that her grades slipped into the norm. This did, in fact, enhance her popularity. She gave up debate club and stopped playing chess with me at lunch. Instead she'd wander the high school grounds with other girls, collecting as they wafted by, a huddle of large retarded boyfriends—among them Dalton Longfielder.

With her mother's blessing, Dalton escorted Betsy to the senior prom where she was a Silver Bell at the Snow Queen's Court. (Winter Wonderland was the theme.) There, all misty in a trance, she walked by me as if we'd never met, and by midnight she lay thrashing like a silver fish in the backseat of Dalton's stripped Ford. (A "friend" told me he saw them.) In the yearbook, Betsy won "Most Popular." Eventually, I began to realize that although Betsy really had lost her mind, it wasn't going to make any difference to the people she'd be around. The Sigma Chi boozehound that she eventually married never even noticed something was wrong until she'd gone completely catatonic after their baby was born.

I went to State on my grandmother's recommendation and against my dad's wishes. He showed me a Toomis newspaper editorial calling the university a "radical infested swamp where leftists and homosexuals meet to hide their shame from God's all-seeing eye." The truth is, Toomis has been about a decade behind all century long. While other places had hippies in the sixties, we had beatniks. While the New Left was ripping the ragged social fabric into headbands, we lay on the campus green playing Pete Seeger songs on bongos. By the time State got around to burning the Marine recruiting stand, it was almost the eighties and everywhere else was back to toga parties and panty raids.

At State I gave up running, except to the john, and divided my time between studying injustice and drinking beer. I slept with three girls, but I never fell in love. I thought I was still in love with Betsy Creedmoor. My only consolation was that Betsy had broken up with Dalton Longfielder and replaced him with the future Sigma Chi dentist who wore pastel knit shirts with alligators over the left nipple and who lugged his golf bag to classes. Betsy had enrolled in State, according to her mother, to work on her M.R.S. degree.

She spoke to me only twice during those four years. Freshman year, I was standing in the quad listening to a famous old socialist who kept running for president and trying to get people to arrest him. The twelve of us listening were cheering him as Betsy ambled by with a varsity weightlifter. She said to me, "I kid you not, never take life to heart." That was all. And then in our last term as seniors, I happened to squeeze past her coming out of Slaughterhouse Five, a foul college bar. This time she said, "Check and mate, buddy." But her eyes weren't focused and she may not even have been talking to me.

As Grandma says, "Trust to time." Here I was, only three years after I graduated, wishing Dalton Longfielder were off with Betsy celebrating their anniversary with a bottle of Asti Spumante. If so, I would have been spared the agonizing sight awaiting me at Parritt's Diner when, a few days after I had first tried to introduce myself to the girl of my dreams, I saw her in a booth with that hulking maroon blazer of Dalton's leaning across at her and only his two chili dogs between them. I recognized her at once, despite the fact that now she was sitting still and wearing a dress. When I reached them, Dalton was regaling her with the news that Richard Petty's pit crew could change two tires and fill a gas tank in 12.5 seconds flat. He punched me chummily in the stomach, and after I caught my breath, rubbed his knuckles in my hair. I grabbed the table edge to keep myself from stabbing forks into his cabbage-size hands.

"Meredith Krantzsky meet Blake Wintrip, then forget him, he's married, six kids, impotent, queer, and got VD. *Huhgawr, huhgawr, huhuhuh.* Bye, bye, Blake." Dalton prided himself on his witty urbanity.

"We've sort of met," she said and looked up from her tuna salad. "I've got a bone to pick with you. I know your grandmother, Frankie Wintrip, I spend a lot of time with her, and—"

My heart cramped with dread. She didn't look insane, but of course they'd let poor Betsy Creedmoor run loose through life too. She said, "I work at Mercy. I'm a psychiatric social worker and your grandmother shouldn't be in there."

I said, "I'm not sure anybody should be in there. Nice to meet you. I'm a social work field coordinator."

She smiled. Right then I could tell there was a chance she eventually might like me.

Dalton shoved a chilidog in his basketball of a face. "Shuh-muhhhowwtoommmamph."

"What?"

Meredith handed Dalton a fistful of napkins. "He said I moved to Toomis from Memphis. Actually it was Atlanta."

Dalton was holding both chilidogs in one hand and eating them as he talked. He said something about driving to Atlanta and having a steak at a nice place the name of which he couldn't remember.

I found out (because Dalton idiotically bragged about it) that he had simply muscled his way into Meredith's booth uninvited. Thank God she hadn't asked him.

That evening in my old high school track shorts I was doing knee-bends in front of Parritt's Diner. I'd called in sick to Wintrip Motors; Dalton answered the phone and I told him my VD had flared up.

At last, through the red and yellow rustle of leaves on the sidewalk, I saw Meredith Krantzsky jogging toward me. I saw her, and in a weaving line behind her, all whooping and sniffling, the eleven members of the Ladies Art League of Toomis. Among them old Miss Lavinia Carthage with a stopwatch was high-stepping along like an ibis in a hurry. My mother scurried beside her in Bermuda shorts with the obligatory cardigan sweater looped over her shoulders. Crouching in the diner doorway, I pretended to relace my sneaker until this extraordinary procession thundered by. Later I learned from my mother that the Art League ladies "just loved Meredith to death" and were now all crazy about the jogging to which she had introduced them when they'd invited her to Newcomer's Brunch.

Reports (and there were plenty) that my mother was out every evening trotting through the streets of Toomis with a throng of elderly female amateur painters hit my father like a karate chop. When Mom started serving broiled fish and raw broccoli for supper, Dad told her succinctly, "You've gone crazy, Elizabeth."

"Then lucky my jogging instructor is a mental health expert," giggled my mother from the floor where she was doing sit-ups, her feet in their new Adidas stuck under the settee.

My father pawed through the refrigerator like a grizzly bear. "And I don't like the sound of that girl's name. Krantzsky. You know what kind of name that is? A you-know-what, I bet you a ten dollar bill." He took his gray flat-top of a head out of the fridge with a chicken leg in his mouth. "Works in a nut house, doesn't she? Some kind of left-wing nut."

I cleared the table. "If you don't like the nut house, why'd you put Grandma in there?"

"You're out of line, Mister," he told me. He always talked as if he thought we were in a western movie together.

I said, "I'm going to ask Meredith Krantzsky to marry me."

"Oh Blake, I love her to death!" My mother looked me over critically. "She's going to tell you to eat better and get more exercise."

"It's a small price to pay," I said.

"Marry her and you're fired," my dad promised me.

I gave my curtain line while skipping backwards out the door. "Hey, Dad, better not tell Dalton that she's a you-know-what. Because he's trying to date her too."

I put on a confident air but the truth was that three weeks had passed since my first sight of my fiancée and not only were we not engaged, we had never sat down together. But we ran together every evening. And I trained, for love, like a fiend. I went on my mother's diet. I gave up beer. October flared the trees into the bright color of Meredith's hair. Indian summer did its best for me, holding back the chill, keeping the evenings crisp and slow. Good jogging weather. We exchanged life stories as we ran through the long southern twilight. She'd had her own version of Betsy Creedmoor. He was a flautist named Matthew she'd lost track of after he was arrested in Katmandu for smuggling mescaline. She'd gone to a college that was full of those subversives that my father longed to pistol whip. She liked movies, she played chess.

One evening the two of us ran out to Mercy Hospital where we saw my grandmother and Miss Carthage jogging around the lawn plotting price hikes to spring on the Appalachian gift galleries who bought their folk art. I took Meredith's hand and said to my grandmother, "How do you like her?"

"Marry her," she said.

Meredith laughed. "Frankie, you cut to the chase."

"Damn right she does," agreed Lavinia Carthage. "And they call her wacko? What a world."

Meredith said to them, "Should I marry Blake?" The two elderly painters shook their heads yes. I kissed them both. And then I kissed her.

The following Saturday, Dalton sat down in my booth at Parritt's Diner. He twisted my biceps with his horrible hand. "Hey hey hey," he said as Meredith came into view. "There's that girl from Memphis. What was her name? Merry, right. Been saving her for a rainy day, watch and learn, wimp."

I shoved him back into the booth. "I catch you around her, I'll shove your jaw up into that cavity where your brain's supposed to be, you stupid asshole."

Dalton stared at me as if I had just stepped out of a UFO. He had bullied me for more than twenty years and I was threatening him! First he started that awful pig snort laugh of his, then it changed to a puffing sound, then he took a swing at me. I ducked under his fat fist and socked him in the stomach with a lifetime of injustice behind my punch. By the time he crawled to his feet, I was shooting out the door, kissing Meredith as I raced by her.

Just out of Dalton's reach, I taunted him all the way up that long incline on Route 55. He never made it to the top.

Meredith Krantzsky and I were married that June. We waited 'til we got Grandma Frankie released from Mercy so she could be at the wedding. We bought a house with an extra bedroom for her. Sometimes Mom stays with us too. When the baby comes, we'll have to get a bigger place.

My dad was always quoting Joe Namath at me. "When you win, nothing hurts." And he was right.

Angie

The Power

It all started with one of Badger's screwy theories, which he told me the first night we met. I'd noticed the little weirdo in the crowd at the Mick Bar because he had on a hat and not many men wear hats indoors in the South anymore. Or outdoors either. Not many men wore hats up north even back thirty years ago, which is when my dad went bust with his hat store on East 34th. My dad loved hats more than money, as he proved time and again. What happened to him taught me a lesson: between love and Chapter Eleven there's a short straight line. It was a lesson reinforced by my ex-wife and her lawyer. Ever since my divorce, I don't give love the time of day. As far as I'm concerned, you can take love and hand it back to the French along with the snails and the Jerry Lewis movies.

But because of my dad, I spot this guy Badger in his classic folder Panama with the dropped brim and I notice he's reading. Skinny and squirmy, he's at the bar, bits of newspapers all over the counter and sticking out of the pockets of a nubbled mohair jacket that he'd probably pulled from a bin at a thrift store. He was flicking his cigarette ashes into an empty longneck and reading *The Dialogues of Plato* in a paperback so old the price on the cover was fifty cents.

Badger isn't bad-looking and only maybe ten, twelve years older than I am, but his outfit made him look twice my age, a good fit with the Mick, which is a fifties retro sports bar named after Mickey Mantle. I happen to be a sports agent or believe me

I wouldn't hang at the Mick, but it's where sports people pass the time down here in this Carolina town I'm stuck in. It's loud and smoky and not cheap, in a worn-out building with a brick front the color of tobacco, always crowded because it's across the street from the old stadium. Tap Upchurch, the guy that owns the place, got sent up to the Yankees for a single season back in the late fifties. He never made it off the bench so he moves down South and opens a bar named "The Mick" after his hero Mickey Mantle, who I guess spoke to him a couple of times. He's got a bat that Mantle hit one of his nine grand slam home runs with and a towel Mantle wiped his face on. He keeps this towel in a plastic case above the bar because he loves Mantle so much.

Since 1959, farm team players have hung out at the Mick waiting for the big time to come save them. These days a few women show up alone and turn out to be stringers for ESPN, but mostly it's the same old Mick full of men, the same old-timers bragging about the same old memories to the same old bartender. It's got boiled eggs floating in pickle brine and a Wurlitzer juke-box with Rosemary Clooney hits and a cigarette machine telling you to buy unfiltered Camels for 25¢ a pack even though the machine now charges over three bucks for cigarettes and doesn't sell Camels anymore anyhow. Of course plenty of people in North Carolina still smoke, claiming they're helping out the economy, and I admit I started back myself when I got down here. But most local smokers don't sit around in noisy sports bars wearing Panama hats and reading Plato. So I pick Badger out of the crowd right away, and before long he's telling me this theory of his about Marilyn Monroe and the Great DiMaggio.

Later I find out that Badger is kind of the mascot of the Mick and uses it like a temp service, picking up odd jobs from the regulars. Ten years ago he moved down here alone from New York where Tap thinks he was some kind of a teacher until he'd "run into personal problems" and lost his job. Tap didn't know the details, didn't know Badger's real name. Nobody did. When Badger's not running errands, he sits around reading ancient philosophers and asking other customers questions about the meaning of life—he calls it "the fundamentals." That's why he's called "Badger"—because of how he latches onto things and won't get off them. He'll keep after you like you were a slot machine and he couldn't stop pulling the handle. These are not questions like "Think the Braves can take the Series?" These are more like "Is the entire universe just a dream of love in the mind of God?" Well, a lot of people don't want to be bothered trying to answer this type question over a beer in a loud bar, so there was an empty stool on either side of Badger when I saw him that first time.

I figure it was because of my dad's loving hats so much that I sat down next to him and said, "Nice Panama." Or maybe it was because I hadn't been back South all that long and didn't really know anybody in town except these two clients of mine who play triple-A ball and one of them doesn't drink and the other one's on lithium but not enough of it. Or maybe it was because Badger was reading a paperback, which my mom was always doing before she died. Anyhow, the little weirdo lets go with this huge smile when I sit down beside him and then out of the blue he asks me if I believe in irresistible impulse.

I said, "For example?"

He said, "Jimmy Stewart, remember, defending Ben Gazzara for killing the bartender in *Anatomy of a Murder*."

I said, "Didn't it turn out that guy pulled a fast one on Jimmy Stewart and there was nothing irresistible about it at all?"

He said, "Jump back, Jack," which maybe meant, "Point well taken." Then he turned and tapped the magnet pin-up of Marilyn Monroe that was stuck to the old cigarette machine behind him. Marilyn looked right at home in the Mick with her big red fifties mouth and her white fifties dress blowing up around her thighs from the whoosh of the Manhattan subway she was standing on.

I said, "Marilyn Monroe."

He said, "Yeah. Irresistible impulse. Happened to Joe." Then Badger tells me his theory that Joe DiMaggio murdered Marilyn

Monroe because even after she'd broken his heart he couldn't stop loving her and went crazy whenever he saw her with another man. And this was because Marilyn Monroe had been, quote, "at the height of her power" when Joltin' Joe had fallen for her and so there was nothing he could do to resist his feelings. Badger told me he could produce "a labyrinth of circumstance" to back up this theory and he started smoothing out clippings from his pockets that I guess were going to prove his point. He had a couple of baseballs in his pockets too and they rolled down the sticky bar counter at Tap Upchurch who rolled them back without looking up. Later I found out Badger gets the players to sign these balls so he can sell them in front of the stadium across the street—except if he can't find the players he just signs them himself.

Instead of doing the smart thing—excuse myself and leave— I buy him a beer and say how I'd recently read a book claiming it was the Kennedys who'd done away with Marilyn Monroe. Badger was ready for that one. "Yeah, I read that too, and you know how those rumors got started?"

I took a stab at it. "J. Edgar Hoover?"

"Nah. DiMaggio started them. He had pals in the L.A. police that helped him plant the evidence against John and Bobby, the whole rat pack. Because deep down in a synergistic sense they did kill her, and Joe knew it." Badger snatches my lapel so tight he wrinkled the wool. "Joe was a gentleman, a great human being, and why shouldn't he hate those smug bastards? They treated the woman he loved like a goddamn hooker. Am I right, Ricky?" His eyes were hot as a gas pilot.

Curiosity dragged me in. "Why are you calling me Ricky? My name's Jordan."

He patted my face in an admiring way. "I look at you, I see Ricky Ricardo. I mean when he was nice and young, nice-looking guy before Lucy plowed him under. Hey, Ethel, hey, Ed, where'd Lucy go?"

But I still don't hop off that stool. I guess it's like my mom used to tell my dad about all his businesses going bust, "Cariño, you never know the time to say good-night." Instead of heading for the exit, I ask Badger why DiMaggio's plan hadn't worked. I mean if the baseball hero was so tight with the L.A. cops, why hadn't they ever accused the Kennedys of killing Marilyn Monroe? Because nobody had even suspected the Kennedys until they'd been dead for thirty or forty years. Badger patted my hand like we were a couple of close friends, when he didn't even know my name, which by the way is Jordan Cole Jr. "You oughta know better than that." He shot his eyebrows up and down, like why couldn't I see the obvious? "The Kennedys had the wherewithal to make problems disappear. Like Mary Jo in the back of that car, you know what I mean?"

Well, my dad didn't like the Kennedys either because he always blamed JFK's hair for destroying the hat business, so maybe that's why I ordered Badger another longneck. I told him it was a little funny to me that somebody who worshipped the Great DiMaggio the way he did should accuse the man of murder. Badger came back to his opening remark. "Irresistible impulse. We can't blame Joe."

"Are you blaming Marilyn for getting herself murdered?"

He thought about this a while, then shook his head. "We can't blame Marilyn. My friend, never underestimate the cosmic power of love. Plato had the skinny on that." He tapped his paperback. "*Symposium*. There's nothing you can figure out that Plato wasn't there first. All the Greeks knew what love could do."

"Cosmic power of love?"

"When a woman like Marilyn's at the height of her power, it's like an earthquake. Buildings are going over."

I said, "Niagara Falls."

He smiled from ear to ear. "Babaloo!" Then he slid a few newspaper clippings toward me. "On a lesser plane, now, on a *much lesser* plane from Marilyn and the Yankee Clipper, it was the same thing with O.J. and Nicole." He tapped at an article with a headline about the O.J. Simpson murder trial. "Same thing, right?"

"I'm not sure I follow you."

He gave me an impatient punch on the arm. "Nicole. Extremely hot. She was at the height of her powers too."

"So O.J. couldn't help it?"

"Nobody can help it. Like Medea tells Jason. Euripides—" Badger waits, so finally I nod like I know what the hell he's talking about. His eyes flare up. "She tells him, she's out of control, 'With more love than sense, I left my home for you, I killed for you, and you dare to leave me, basest of men?'"

"Medea had a rough time, sounds like."

He folds his clippings carefully. "Jane Russell said it all, Ricky. When love goes wrong, nothing goes right."

I agreed with that much. "You're right, love's a troublemaker," I told Badger. "Love and I have nothing to do with each other personally."

"You never know," he warns me and tips his hat.

•   •   •

So that was back in April. Now it's August, and career-wise everything's going great. I'm sitting in the Mick talking over a big new contract with my hyperactive client, the triple-A pitcher named Ronny Lamar Rome, and with us is naturally Badger. By now he's like my shadow. Okay, maybe he's a little weird but at least you can mention the Eighth Avenue Line or the West Village or the Belmont track without getting a blank stare. Over the last few months, I've bought him a few beers and a few meals and sent a few errands his way, and the result is he hangs around me like he had emphysema and I was a tank of oxygen. After he got bounced from his apartment and moved to a one-room, I let him store some stuff in my garage, and since that time Badger's got it in his head we're really close friends. I hear him telling regulars in the Mick how I'm his "best bud." Well, I figure, what's the harm. He doesn't have any family; at least if you ask he won't answer your question but points up at the sky like they'd all gone to heaven at some point. He thinks the two of us have a lot in common: we've traveled (a lot of folks in this town haven't even been out of the state), we watch movies on TV (what else is there to do around here?), and we're both, according to him, "unshackled by natural bonds to tellurian gravity"— whatever that means. Badger's brainy. I mean he can read Plato in Greek. I've seen him with the books.

In May I took a trip to Madrid. My mom was born in Mexico and my dad met her in Madrid when she was on vacation there and he was stationed in Spain and falling in love with hats. They were always talking about how they met in Madrid. So I figured what the hell, might as well see what the place looks like. While I'm there, Badger calls me long distance from a pay phone with a bag full of quarters and tells me these museums to go to. So while I'm changing planes in London I buy him this T-shirt that says MIND THE GAP and he says he can't get over how I remembered him. He wears the T-shirt all the time. He's got it on tonight along with the brown Borsolino fedora I gave him out of a box of my dad's unsold hats I've got stored in my garage. One of these days I'll take them to the thrift store.

This night in August it's about ten P.M. when the pitcher Ronny Lamar Rome moves off to get his Polaroid taken with some drunk frat boys. Badger's gassing on about how baseball's the only thing in America that's like Greek plays. "Baseball and the ancient Greeks understand the nemesis of inevitable chance. The fate of who you love. Oedipus marries his mother, what does he know?" I'm nodding like I couldn't agree more but about to wrap things up when out of the blue he plucks hard at my sleeve and points to the door. I look over and see Angie Schuelenmeyer standing there. Badger shakes his head, pretty agitated. "Hey, Jordan, 'member my telling you how there's love goddesses wreaking havoc on the earth?"

I said, "Not really."

"Sure you do, you figured the Kennedys killed Marilyn—"

"No, I didn't say—"

"And I explained it was Joltin' Joe. 'Cause when women are at the height of their powers, hang on, boys, you're taking a ride on the Atom Smasher. You remember the Atom Smasher at Rockaway's Playland?"

"Not really. Rockaway Beach? Queens?"

"Yeah, Woodyallenville, I grew up there. Love's a roller coaster and you can't get off."

So then he starts in on Marilyn Monroe and the Yankee Clipper again; by this time I'd heard a hundred different versions of his screwy theory on "the cosmic force of love power," but DiMaggio murdering Marilyn was his favorite. "Irresistible impulse," I said.

He smiled. "Babaloo! Well, Angie over there," he jerked his head at the door, "she's got the power."

I looked again at the woman coming into the Mick. "You know that's Zane Schuelenmeyer's wife."

"I sure do. Like you said, Niagara Falls. Five-point-five billion gallons of water could land on your head every hour, you dally too long with the Maid of the Mist."

"What are you talking about?"

Badger gets his gas-pilot intense look. "Jordan, you need to point out the post-lapsarian implications of big falls to Ronny Lamar Rome, otherwise..." Suddenly the little weirdo picks up an imaginary club and starts bashing in an imaginary somebody on the tabletop. He doesn't stop 'til I shake his arm. It was a pretty good imitation of a homicidal maniac completely losing it. You can see why a lot of people in the Mick just steer clear of him.

I ask him, "Is something going on with Ronny and Angie?" He just points.

I watch my star pitcher Ronny Lamar Rome wheel around from the frat boys and follow Angie doing her "keep your eyes on my hip bones slipping out of their sockets" type walk she has, which she does all the way over to our booth where she stops and looks right through me. (What else is new?) Then Ronny slides back into the booth and she scoots across the vinyl after him and runs her hand up his leg. Right away I can tell I've got a situation on my hands. The fact that all of a sudden I can't see Ronny's hands and that Mrs. Schuelenmeyer is moving around on him like she's riding a mechanical bull indicates to me that the situation is by no means a new one. I don't need Badger whispering "Jump back, Jack" in my ear to let me know I have somehow dropped the ball and need to pick it up fast and throw it out of the park because the ball is in the nature of a crate of TNT with a quick fuse.

Here's the deal. Devil Rays brass is flying into Raleigh-Durham to finalize on the two Triple-A clients I represent. This deal is totally green-lighted except the brass wants to watch my two guys in one last game before we sign. Naturally, one of my two guys is Ronny Lamar Rome, the pitcher with the 1.85 ERA who's now got his hands under the skirt of Zane Schuelenmeyer's wife. Naturally, Zane Schuelenmeyer is the other guy. The only way it could be worse is the way it is: Zane Schuelenmeyer was the catcher when this pitcher threw three shut-outs and two no-hitters this season. The only other way it could be worse is that I suddenly see Zane walking into the bar. Which I do. This is a bar where everybody knows everybody, right? It's not like there's more than one baseball hangout in this boonie town, so where else did Angie think her husband was going to come looking for her?

If Zane makes it to the booth, even he's bound to notice that his wife is by now pretty much doing a slow dance on his friend Ronny Lamar Rome's lap. But I luck out. Like he was stealing second, Badger shoots across the room and gets himself in the doorway between Zane and the booth. He pulls the big catcher off to a corner where he can't see what the rest of us are seeing, and keeps him there autographing baseballs while I try to reason with the lap-dancing wife.

Angie's one of those red-haired Southern girls. She's got, well, Badger later called it an "indiscreet" face. Plus, a long full body it's hard to look away from. She's got attitude too. So when I say, "Angie, you wanna climb off Ronny? I see Zane headed this way," she tells me, "Jordan, all you see is your 15 percent of Zane headed this way." Okay, I *am* counting on those commissions and God knows I've earned them. But at least maybe she thinks about her 85 percent and she gets off Ronny's lap.

Tonight Angie's wearing a kind of retro-fifties outfit like she'd coordinated herself with the Mick Bar—a red halter top with white pedal pushers and white sandals with stiletto heels. She leans that halter over into Ronny's face as she swings out of the red vinyl booth. "I need to go to the toy-toy," she tells him like it was an invitation to heaven, then she walks away doing some kind of salsa dance to Rosemary Clooney singing "Mambo Italiano." Ronny had leaned out of the booth so far to watch her go, he was defying gravity. He would have been in the ladies room with her in a flash if I hadn't grabbed his wrist (non-pitching arm) with both my hands and twisted.

"Oww," he says surprised.

"Ronny, you do know that's Zane's wife?"

"Angie, yeah, so?" He shrugs, ruffling his hair, which is dyed a greenish yellow and styled like he'd slept on it wrong and just woke up. On the looks scale, Ronny Rome is definitely at the "extremely hot" end of things. He claims to have slept with a thousand women and I'd believe him if I thought he could count that high. He has an easy strut to his walk and big brown sleepy eyes that he uses on females so fast that sometimes the one coming to his front door and the one leaving it run into each other and I have to "handle" the crossover for him.

"Yeah, so, Angie," I say. "Look at me, Ronny, you're pitching tomorrow. Zane's catching and the two of you are gonna play so fantastically that these gentlemen flying up from Tampa are actually going to give you millions of dollars. Millions, Ronny. Of which I am going to take fifteen percent plus the seventeen thousand you already owe me."

"Whatever."

"Angela Schuelenmeyer is off-limits, banned, no-no, taboo. You get it?"

He smirks at me. "Hey, talk to her, she's free, white, and twenty-one."

I smirk back. "No. She's not free, she's married. And she's twenty-seven. And Zane's your friend. More important, listen to me, he's your catcher."

"Whatever." Ronny's not listening. He's running his tongue around the lip of his glass like it was Angie Schuelenmeyer.

"Where's Kristi, Ronny?"

"Who?"

Kristi was his last girlfriend. Last and obviously past. She's a local model. In the outfield at the stadium, there's a big billboard of Kristi lying on wall-to-wall carpeting she wants you to buy. Just a few months ago, Ronny asked me to set up a date with her and I had. Like Badger says, there's a lot to being an agent.

I knew I needed to move fast. Now, unlike most of this boonie town (where Time doesn't stand still, it lies down and takes a nap), I *can* move fast. Maybe I was born in the South, but my dad took us to New York when I was nine to see if men would buy more hats up north. They wouldn't. But I grew up in Manhattan, midtown, off Lex, right above my dad's third Cole Hats store that went bust. I picked up a lot of speed there. My mom always said New York wasn't as fast as Madrid, or Mexico City either. I don't know about that, but compared to down here, Manhattan is one big blur going by. I never would have come back to the South if I'd had any choice because, like my mom said, this place is slow as syrup, and likes it that way. She says she would have lost her mind down here if it hadn't been for all the books. Rednecks treated her like crap because she was from Mexico and had an accent. The hell with them.

My whole goal in life is to get back to New York. Like I said earlier, I'm a sports agent—you know, like Jerry Maguire, except do I have Cuba Gooding Jr. dancing in the end zone? No. I've got Ronny Lamar Rome disappearing underneath a bar booth with his catcher's wife. I deserve better. I'm good at my job. In fact, according to my ex-wife the tennis star, I'm better at my job than I am at my life. I give everything I've got to my clients. Last year, I kept my bulimic ice skater on the circuit even after her shoplifting hit the tabloids. (It was Godiva chocolates; they caught her in the store with a twelve-pound Millennium "Ultimate Party Favor" in her duffel bag. $375.00 retail.)

Last year was a bad time. My whole life went south and I had to follow it. My mom died. Two months later my dad took off after her like he was running for a bus. She was the only thing he loved more than hats. My wife left me, and the agency's new boss Emili—with an "I"—Miller-Dunn tells me we're downsizing and I'm getting transferred to our branch office covering the South. This woman actually said to me she figured I wouldn't mind leaving New York because of my "recent broken ties"—by which she meant not just my mom and dad dropping dead but my wife divorcing me because she's having an affair with Emili Miller-Dunn. On a scale of one to ten, the whole year was in negative-one-thousand for Jordan Cole Jr.

But I need the job, so I go South in my dad's old apple-green Pontiac that I've still got the New York plates on. One night I come out of the Mick and some A-hole's slapped a bumper sticker on it saying WE DON'T CARE HOW YOU DO IT UP NORTH. Well, Bubba, you ought to care! Wake up and smell the double espresso—not that you could ever get one around here, or the *Times* either.

I work hard, handle the NASCAR racers and the bass fishermen and the stunt artist that jumps his dirt bike over eighteen-wheelers when he isn't in jail. Then a few months after I get to Carolina I meet these two new triple-A players, Schuelenmeyer and Rome, at their agent's funeral. From then on I'm counting the days 'til I fly to Manhattan and tell Miller-Dunn I no longer work for her lousy agency because I'm the competition. I quick sign the pitcher and catcher on the side, figuring the minute I sell them to the majors, I'm on the plane to JFK. Zane

Schuelenmeyer, the catcher with the wife, is batting .413. Ronny Lamar Rome, the pitcher with the wife on his lap, can throw a fastball 105 miles an hour. With Zane catching, Ronny sometimes gets seventeen, eighteen strikeouts a game. The problem is, without Zane catching, Ronny is just as likely to rip a base bag out of the dirt and chuck it at the umpire. He takes more handling than the bulimic ice skater, which is saying something.

Ronny's always calling me. "Jor, I need you to handle this thing for me, okay?" Usually he wants me to get rid of a girl. It's too bad he didn't call me the first time he laid eyes on Angie Schuelenmeyer. I could have told him that back in Georgia his buddy Zane, the best catcher in the minors, put a shortstop in a wheelchair for life because this guy got his hand inside the top of Angie's bikini at somebody's pool party. A wheelchair for life. I mean, they were both slinging their fists and everybody said it was an accident, but hey, that doesn't make the guy a shortstop again.

Zane's a Georgia boy from a town with a smaller population than the last apartment building I lived in when I lived in New York. What Einstein had in brains, Zane's got in body, and sort of vice versa. He's six-foot-five, two-thirty, pumped—and he didn't buy his muscles at a drugstore either, he worked on them. He doesn't drink, smoke, or take any kind of pills except vitamins. He's got no bad habits I know of except his wife. Zane and Angie got married in high school. They have exactly zero in common except they both think she's the hottest ticket in town. In which opinion obviously they're not alone.

Thank God Angie's made it into the toy-toy when Zane finally spots me, Ronny, and Badger in the booth, and ambles over. I say, "Hey there, Zane, big game tomorrow, right?"

But he clearly could care less about his future in the majors and had nothing but Angie on his mind. "Y'all seen Kitten?" He calls his wife Kitten, and I guess you can call a Bengal tiger "kitten" if you want to.

Badger suddenly pipes up. "Matter of fact your wife was in here looking for you, Zane."

"She was?" The catcher frowns and I stop breathing.

"Yeah, Angie got worried waiting at home for you so she came here. She said if we saw you to tell you she went back to the house. Right, Jordan and Ronny?" After this amazing lie, the nut smiles at Ronny Lamar Rome, so there's nothing I can do but jump in and say, "Yeah, that's right, isn't it, Ronny?" and stomp my loafer into Ronny Lamar's instep to shut him up. The pitcher had his mouth open and could have said anything.

"Kitten went on back home, Ronny?" asks Zane slowly.

"Wherever," Ronny shrugs without looking at him.

"Well, I guess she better be there. I'm going on back then," Zane tells us, thank God, before the door to the ladies room opens and Angie mambos out of it. But instead of leaving, he just stands there frowning. Zane's got a big handsome freckled face that's almost always squeezed into that frown, like the world's going by him too fast. Weird, because a 100-miles-per-hour fast ball doesn't bother him at all. He can catch one. He can hit one. Two weeks ago he hit a grand slam off a fastball. But Angie has a different kind of speed.

I hop up and yank at the catcher. "Come on, Zane. Badger, let's walk Zane out."

After we hustle Zane Schuelenmeyer outside the Mick and I shove him into his white Caddy and wave him off, I slam Badger against the brick wall. "Are you psychotic? Suppose Zane'd started to wonder why Angie was looking for him in a bar when he doesn't drink?"

Badger laughs richly as he hugs me. "I love you, my friend, but you gotta understand character. Zane doesn't hypothesize."

I shake him again. "Suppose Angie'd waltzed out of the john?"

He wiggles loose and picks up the Borsolino, smoothes the brim. "She did. She went out the back. Zane was talking to you. She's meeting Ronny at the Marriott."

I stare at him horrified. "Who the hell told you that?"

"*Cogito ergo sum*, Ricky," he grins.

I grab a fistful of his London Underground T-shirt. "Don't mess with me, Badger."

He puts his hand around my fist and pats it. "She slipped a Marriott card key down Ronny's shirt on her way to the can."

I stare at him some more. He nods.

"Shit!" I say.

He points at his T-shirt. "Time to Mind the Gap, right?"

Once when Badger was grilling me about the philosophy of a sports agent (like I have time to ruminate on a philosophy while I'm lugging a fifty-two-inch TV over to Ronny's mother's or taking some bass fisherman's large-mouth to the taxidermist), I told him an agent does what's written on that London T-shirt: "Mind the Gap." A good agent minds the gap between his client and his client's best interests. And he does it not out of love but because he takes 15 percent. A gap is when clients do things that hurt them—like eat chocolates, like make a play for their catcher's wife in a sports bar where everybody knows them. Things like that. When the gap widens so much nothing can bridge it, your client falls through. Deal falls through. You don't go to New York.

"Game's over," I say and light up a Marlboro. I admit I felt defeated.

Badger mooches from my pack and lights up too. "You oughta quit smoking, Jordan," he says to me, "a guy with his life ahead of him."

"What life?"

"You're still in love with that girl, the tennis player, your ex. Maybe you could get her back."

"Badger, don't go there. And you don't want to force me to choose between you and cigarettes either. Zane gets home, Angie's not there, game's over."

"That's no tautology," Badger says, God knows what he means half the time. Then he shows me this damn Swiss army gizmo he carries around with everything on it from a little ruler to a big knife. "I don't want you to worry. I ripped up his back tire while you were getting him in the car. He'll be a while getting home. Babaloo."

I swear, I was almost glad I'd put up with the little weirdo all this time. I told him to quick take my car to the Marriott and get Angie to go home before Zane got back there. I'd waylay Ronny.

So we do that. I tell Ronny that Angie can't meet him tonight and Ronny throws a ketchup bottle at the wall 95 mph and knocks off the Mickey Mantle bat and gets ketchup all over it so Tap Upchurch has a fit and throws him out. I ride with Ronny home to his contemporary off in the woods with its deck out over a deep lake. He calls the place the sex shack and he's built it in the middle of nowhere because he likes his privacy so he can "do it naked under the stars." He tells me I'll have to fix it so he can sleep with Zane's wife without Zane's noticing. "I gotta have her," he tells me. "I'm totally in love here." I take his car and the keys to his truck so he can't leave the house. (It's not like you can whistle down midnight taxis in boonieville.)

Badger's waiting for me at my place to tell me how he intercepted Angie at the Marriott and followed her back home with some baseballs for Zane to sign so he was there when Zane drove in after he'd finally gotten his tire changed. Badger said Angie did a good job following his lead, claiming how she'd been out earlier looking for Zane at the Mick. So all's well except Badger also tells me that to get Angie to leave the Marriott, he had to give her a note he wrote in Ronny's handwriting (which he was good at from faking all the baseball autographs) going on about how much he loved her but their love would have to wait 'til tomorrow. This upset me. "Tomorrow? The Tampa scouts are coming to the game tomorrow! Couldn't you have said, 'Our love will have to wait 'til Friday, our love will have to wait 'til NEVER?'"

"Love," says Badger, "is the Euclidean lever that moves the planet Earth." I threw him out of my house.

Naturally, I'm up all night worrying about whether Zane Schuelenmeyer has found that love letter from "Ronny" and slaughtered Angie while she slept, which would mean he wouldn't be available for tomorrow's game, and probably neither would Ronny Lamar Rome, who'd probably be slaughtered in his bed too, and there goes my little midtown office with the sign I've already done the layout on: "The Cole Agency. Tomorrow's Stars Today." At four A.M., I even drive over to the Schuelen-meyers' brick colonial in the Colony Club Estates, but there're no police cars or ambulances in the driveway.

• • •

Well, like they love to say down here, tomorrow *is* another day. Pregame practice starts, Zane shows, and so does Ronny because Badger takes him back his car and his keys, and so do the two big shots from the Devil Rays who treat me like dirt but what the hell, they sign with me or they don't sign. Zane, frowning, asks me if I think anything funny's going on with his wife Kitten and I say absolutely not, he can trust me on that. Zane hits a home run in the first that he dedicates to his Kitten (he dedicates all his home runs to her or his mother or to Jesus Christ), and a triple in the third that bounces off Ronny's ex, Kristi, where she's lying on the wall-to-wall in the big centerfield billboard. Ronny throws eleven strikeouts by the fifth. These Tampa guys have got the caps off their signing pens.

And that's when Badger starts grabbing at me and pointing. I turn and see Angie striding through the stadium with her red hair bouncing in the sun. Her eyes are so green you can see them twenty rows away. She's got on a man's white shirt tied under her breasts and her tan stomach bare above this short white skirt. She walks like girls in an old print my dad kept on the wall of his hat store on 34th—one of those Depression pictures of Manhattan working girls strolling down the sidewalk, out on the town, all of them wearing hats. You could see their strong thighs under their thin dresses. Angie had that kind of feel to her, an over-flowing kind of feel, like you could pour her out like honey warmed on the stove.

She's headed for the dugout where Zane's picking up a bat and Ronny Lamar Rome is sitting on the bench blowing big pink bubbles of gum and then slowly sucking them back through his lips like they were Angie Schuelenmeyer. Before she gets down to the dugout, half the stadium is looking at her, including the Devil Rays brass. They want to know who is she? "Zane Schuelenmeyer's wife," I explain while kicking at Badger who naturally is stuck to my side like a bare sweaty leg to a leather car seat. Today he's wearing a black homburg of my dad's and a T-shirt with Aristotle on it. He holds the homburg on with both hands and shoots off in that fast ferret way of his. He stops Angie when she's still a good fifty feet away. I see her hand Badger a note as she points to Ronny. Ronny spots her and starts crawling over the back of the dugout to get at her. And do what? He's in the middle of a goddamn ballgame!

Zane notices Angie and strikes out on three pitches, with two outs and two men on. She leaves the stadium while he's swinging away, and when he's done he hurls his bat into the dugout, maybe at Ronny's head. Inning's over and Ronny and Zane have to take the field. Ronny slings a warm-up pitch right at Zane and smacks him in the face mask with a curve ball. "What's the problem?" asks the top Tampa guy.

"No problem," I guarantee and excuse myself. As I climb the bleachers, ahead of me I see my future disappearing like the Manhattan skyline on a foggy night. "What's the problem?" I ask Badger, snatching the note from Angie out of his hand and reading it. It's addressed to "Baby Big Boy" and it's pure porno passed off as ever-lasting love. It instructs Ronny to come straight home to his lake place after the game where she'll be lying waiting on his bed. "Don't shower," it says. "I love your pitching smell."

I kill myself hopping over bleachers to chase Angie down before she can take off in the new powder blue BMW convertible that Zane will actually be able to afford if I can get these goddamn contracts signed. Badger's right behind me when I throw myself in front of her car (which is a lot nicer than the old apple-green Pontiac of my dad's that I'm still driving). At least she stopped. I try not to shout. "Angie, you wanna use your *head?* You want Ronny ending up in a wheelchair like that shortstop in Georgia?"

Angie looks at me. There's a first. She says, "Come here, Jordan."

I step 'round to the driver's door. It's hard to explain but there's so much brightness to her, she's hard to look at. She says, "I need you to do me a great big favor."

I scowl at her. "What?"

All of a sudden she reaches up, pulls me down by my tie, and kisses me on the mouth. I jerk away like I've been electrocuted, which is what it felt like. She says, "I need you to be nice and take care of Zane, okay? I'm leaving him for Ronny."

I'm having trouble breathing. "You can't. You blow this deal and you'll be getting 85 percent of *zero* on either one of these guys."

"Hey," she says like she made it up, "money can't buy happiness."

"Angie, neither can Ronny Lamar Rome. Trust me on that."

She stares at me some more. "Anybody ever tell you you look like the guy on *I Love Lucy?*"

It wasn't what I expected. "Yeah," I say. "Badger."

She smiles over at Badger and gives him a wave. "Badger's got brains, okay. I am crazy about Badger. He appreciates a woman's need to be somebody. And you know what, Jordan, for a good-looking man, you don't have a clue." She pulls sunglasses out of her cleavage and puts them on.

"What are you talking about?"

She laughs and starts her engine. "See what I mean?"

I guess she would have run me over if I hadn't vaulted out of the way. She drives across the parking lot at 50 miles per hour and slams to a stop in front of the Mick. One for the road, I guess.

I just stand there wondering what she and Ronny think her husband's going to be doing while she's sniffing the pitcher's armpits out at his sex shack beside the lake. I jump when Badger gives me a pat on the shoulder from behind. He can sneak up on you like he did it for a living. "I told you Angie had the power," he says. "It's Joltin' Joe time. Two guys on the track and here comes the Silver Comet. Head-on collision, my friend, jump back. They're all in the grip."

I light a cigarette to make myself breathe. Okay, Badger was right. Something had to be done. I think fast and come up with a plan. Badger will handle the Angie end, I'll take care of Zane and Ronny here at the stadium. I explain what we need to do.

Fortunately, while Angie's porno ramblings to Ronny "Baby Big Boy" Rome go on for four pages of personalized lavender stationery, all that the last page says is, "Win win win!!! Your prize is waiting on your bed—Love kisses love 4ever! A—"

On the other side of this page I get Badger to write the beginning of a note in Angie's handwriting and address it to Zane. He does a great job, you can't tell the difference.

Zane honey—
'Member Tabby, my old best girlfriend from high school? Her Mama called me—Tabby just got hurt pretty bad totaling her car so I'm driving to Tenn. to see her—She's in the I.C.U. Don't worry about me. I'll get back soon as I can. I'll call—(Over)
Win win win!!! Your prize is waiting on your bed—
Love kisses love 4ever! A—

I reason this way. Zane won't remember Angie's old friend who moved to Tennessee (it was actually Badger who dreamed up the name Tabby), but he'll figure that over the years his memories of poor old Tabby have slipped through his porous brain. And there'll be no way for him to trace her since Tennessee is large and she has no last name or even real first name. As for the prize waiting on the bed—which is no doubt the naked Angie sprawled out at Ronny's sex shack panting for the sweaty pitcher's return—I'll substitute a different kind of trophy and leave it on Zane's own bed. There's a lot of stuff from my marriage packed away in boxes in my garage and somewhere in it is a loving cup inscribed WORLD'S BEST HUSBAND. My tennis star wife gave it to me four years ago (obviously this was before she divorced me to move in with Emili Miller-Dunn). That cup'll make a great prize for Zane.

I'll say this for Badger, he just says, "Yes." I tell him if we pull this plan off, I'll give him 10 percent of my fifteen. He tips the black homburg but shakes his head. "I don't care about money. I care about love. You're my best friend, Ricky. Babaloo!" And he hugs me. Well Jesus but still.

So Badger shoots off in my car. The idea is for him to race over to my place in the Pontiac, pick up the trophy, zip to the Schuelenmeyers' colonial in Colony Club Estates, break in, and plop the WORLD'S BEST HUSBAND cup down in the middle of their king-sized bed. (I warn him to watch out for Angie's Lhasa Apso, Lover.) Then he barrels across town to the bypass and shows up at Ronny Lamar Rome's lake house. His job there is to convince Angie to leave town for a week, how he does it I leave up to him—he can tell her how Ronny's waiting for her in Atlanta, tell her her mother's dying, tell her whatever he wants, just get rid of her.

By the end of the week I'll have the two contracts signed with the Devil Rays, and by that time Ronny (who's got a serious case of what they currently call attention deficit disorder) will probably have forgotten all about Angie because I will have fixed him up with one of the hot bimbos he was pestering me to fix him up with before Angie swung into view.

As soon as Badger drives off, I run back into the stadium where Ronny has gotten himself out of the sixth, but not without letting two runs score, so now the game's all tied up. I tell the Devil Rays big shots that my boys are saving the best for last. They look skeptical. I get Ronny off by himself in the dugout and slip him the first three pages of Angie's sex-memo. He's looking at that lavender paper like it's lined with cocaine and he's Darryl Strawberry.

I tell Ronny how I handled things for him with Angie. She loves him too but she can't come to his house. She'll be waiting for him at the Marriott instead, in a hot tub suite in his name.

"I want her to come to the lake," he says.

"Too risky. And she wants you to stay away from Zane. Oh and the other message." I tell him Angie says if Ronny can get twenty strikeouts in this game, she'll be the angel flying him up for his first look at Paradise tonight at the Marriott. (You have to talk to Ronny like a country western song.)

"Hey damn thanks, Jor." He grins and smacks me on the back. I point out that to get twenty Ks, he has to strike out nine more batters in the remaining three innings. "Okay," he shrugs.

Then Zane comes back from the locker room john and I get him off by himself. He wants to know where Kitten went and what was she handing to Badger? I give him the last page of Angie's lavender stationery with the news about Tabby's terrible car crash.

"Angie didn't want to bother you during the game. She asked Badger to give you this." I have to be patient while Zane studies the note, which he does frowning and moving his lips. Then he reads aloud, "'Tabby, my old best girlfriend from high school,'" and shakes his head puzzled. "Tabby? What friend Tabby?"

I try to be helpful. "Tabby?... Oh wait, that's right, I remember Angie telling me one time about an old friend of hers named Tabby. Seems like she said she moved to Tennessee or something."

Zane thinks as hard as he can, a painful sight. "Yeah, Tabby, yeah, I kinda remember." His big freckled face goes all sad and sweet. "Poor Kitten. Her friend Tabby got in a car accident and she's gone driving off to Tennessee to see if she can help out."

I squeeze his forearm which feels like a piece of the Alaska pipeline. "That's Angie for you," I say. "Always thinking of others."

He frowns. "Yeah. She's got a heart big as...as...big as—"

I help him out. "She's got a big heart."

Slowly he smiles. "She sure does."

"You're a lucky man having such a big-hearted wife."

"You know what, Jordan, I'm gonna hit another home run and dedicate it to Tabby's pulling through."

"Zane, that's a great idea."

I climb back into the grandstand and sit down beside the Tampa brass; the bald one looks at his watch. "Where you been the last twenty minutes?" he wants to know.

I tell him, "Minding the gap."

Zane Schuelenmeyer hits a double in the eighth and a grand slam homer in the ninth, his second of the season. He's four for four. He catches a pop-up unbelievably far back in the stands (the crowd's on its feet) and he throws out on a steal the only guy that gets on base in the last three innings.

As for the other nine guys that come up to bat against us, Ronny Lamar Rome strikes them all out for a grand total of twenty Ks. He throws five fast balls in a row that clock over a hundred. This game widens his strikeouts-to-walks ratio to eight to one, which is up there with Pedro Martinez. He gets a standing ovation when he leaves the mound in the ninth.

The Devil Rays sign.

We celebrate at the Mick. I don't see Badger, but my Dad's old green Pontiac is parked out in front of the bar with the key in the ignition. Still no Badger when I take Zane home. Zane's upset when he sees Angie's packed a bag (in a hurry too) and taken her Lhasa Apso, Lover, off with her. But he bursts into tears when he sees the WORLD'S BEST HUSBAND loving cup on his bed. "She's the sweetest girl in the world," he tells me. I agree.

Of course Ronny Lamar Rome gets upset when the world's sweetest girl is not waiting naked in his hot tub suite at the Marriott that I reserved for him. He throws his shoe through the television. But I'm at the Marriott just a few minutes later with room service and an exotic dancer named Sierralyn, who's as close to a life-sized Barbie doll as it's possible to get and still walk upright. I had to pay a limo service three hundred bucks to drive her in fast from Charlotte, which is where Ronny first saw her last spring in a cage at the Inferno Club. I tell Ronny I know he's serious about Angie, but she just couldn't take the chance of Zane's getting wind of their love. Give it time, and in the meanwhile be nice to Sierralyn, who drove all the way from Charlotte to congratulate him. I leave them with Ronny showing her how he can pop open a champagne bottle with one thumb.

If Sierralyn doesn't work out, I've got Kaylee, a Tampa TV personality, on a back burner.

Everything's going great. The next morning I'm getting calls from talent that a month ago wouldn't use my back to wipe their cleats on. I quit Emili Miller-Dunn by fax. She calls me personally (there's a first). She says my wife's left her too. It was a good day for Jordan Cole Jr.

Then a week goes by and Zane's flipping out because Kitten hasn't gotten in touch with him at all and he's supposed to leave for Tampa today. I lie and claim that Angie called me from Nashville and told me she couldn't reach Zane because there must be a problem with his answering machine. I promise him she's fine.

Then I go seriously looking for Badger. I haven't seen him since I sent him to Ronny's lake house to do something about Angie and I'm beginning to think I need to know what he did. I ask around in the Mick, but nobody's seen Badger since the afternoon of the "big game" (as it's now referred to, the game that sent Rome and Schuelenmeyer to the majors), when somebody remembers seeing him in a booth with Angie Schuelenmeyer. Meanwhile, Tap Upchurch doesn't care what happened to Badger because his autographed Mickey Mantle grand slam bat is missing from over his bar and it was worth, he says, eighteen thousand dollars. While I'm trying to get Badger's home address out of Tap, Zane all of a sudden runs into the Mick. He's looking for me. With a frown, he shows me this note postmarked Nashville that he just got from "Kitten."

The note says that Angie and her dog and "Tabby's mom" are taking Tabby "up North" because there's a plastic surgeon "up there" who's the only one who can "do something" about Tabby's face, which according to the note was "ruined" when she went through the windshield of her car. (The note is actually on Angie's lavender stationery so I figure Badger must have stolen some out of her bedroom when he planted the loving cup on the bed.) I have a little trouble breathing as I read this forgery, which Zane takes to be sympathetic on my part. I think fast. I advise him to fly to Tampa tomorrow as planned and let me locate Angie for him. I say there's no knowing exactly where up North she's taken Tabby for plastic surgery, but I predict she'll call home as soon as she possibly can. I hope he's had his answering machine fixed. He says he's got voice mail now. He frowns. "She oughta keep on calling."

"Angie probably just doesn't want to leave Tabby's side," I suggest. "You know how warm-hearted she is."

Zane frowns deeper. Sooner or later even he's gonna notice something's weird.

Something's weird, all right. When I get home that night, there's a letter for me from Badger—also postmarked Nashville. In it he sends congratulations; he read in the paper that I got a great deal for Schuelenmeyer and Rome with the Devil Rays and he knows how much those contracts meant to me. In a P.S., he says that Angie won't be a problem. Then he adds, "I'm headed out West. If you need to, tell the authorities I stole the car. But if you can avoid it, I'd appreciate it. Remember: Some people go over the Falls and survive. Your friend, Curtis Dawson."

Three days later, I'm packing up my house for the move to New York. I'm still worrying where the hell is Angie, and what the weirdo meant: if you need to, tell them I stole the car. And what about that stuff about surviving the Falls? Plus, it's the first I've heard of Badger's real name, which rings a tiny bell but I can't think why. Then that night I get a heartsick phone call from Zane Schuelenmeyer, who's crying into the receiver; he needs me down in Florida right away. Angie's left him. I say, "How do you know?" He tells me—from a letter in her car. I'm an agent; he's my second biggest commission (Ronny's the biggest); I hop on a plane the next day.

In Tampa here's what I find out. Yesterday morning Zane wakes up at his rental and finds his wife's powder blue BMW convertible parked in his driveway. In it there's a letter from Angie taped to the steering wheel. (Except I know it's not from Angie, it's from Badger. Of this, I suddenly have no doubts at all because in it Angie is claiming she has an "irresistible impulse" to be on her own. The letter explains how she's brought back the convertible BMW to Zane's house because she didn't feel like she had a right to keep it. She claims she got the address from me. She goes on about how she'd meant to explain everything in person to Zane but she lost her nerve before she could knock on the door. So she walked to the station and took a bus "out West." She hopes someday Zane will forgive her and understand why she has to have her freedom. That's why she's leaving him. There's nobody else, nobody. And never was. It's a personal thing. When Zane is ready for a divorce, go ahead and get one with her blessing. And please go on with his life and become a superstar. She'll be pulling for him. It's signed, "Love kisses love 4ever, Kitten and Lover." The car is otherwise clean and empty.

Zane has gone completely to pieces at his wife's leaving him (and taking their dog), but fortunately there's a three-day break before he has to play against the Red Sox and we're able to put him back together. Ronny Lamar Rome is actually a big help. Ronny manages to keep his mouth shut about being so in love with Angie himself that he was trying to steal her away from his best friend. He keeps telling Zane it's the best thing for him and Angie both until Zane starts to believe it. Meanwhile Ronny confides in me that it's now clear to him why Angie never showed at the Marriott to take him to Paradise. She got on "some type of woman kick" about personal identity and is probably now "drivin' around the country like goddamn Thelma and

Louise." He actually believes that Angie's left Zane because she has to have her freedom, but I'm getting a different idea.

Flying back to Carolina from Tampa, I keep thinking over the screwy theories I've heard from Badger in the past year, about the cosmic power of love, how DiMaggio killed Marilyn and the rest. I'm up all night thinking. The next morning I go to my garage and pull down the boxes I let him store there. Two of them are full of old out-of-date clothes. Inside the third box are mostly philosophy books, including five copies of a book by Curtis Dawson, Ph.D., that's called *Agape and Filia in the Dialogues of Plato* and was published by some college in the midwest about fifteen years ago. (Later on I look up the Greek words on the Internet and find out they mean "Love and Friendship," which I guess Badger had a thing about figuring out.) Underneath the books I find some letters from a woman named Nina, plus lots of black and white photographs—the kind actors use for auditions—of a really good-looking woman with a sexy smile. At the bottom of the box is a yellowed New York tabloid folded over. I see a young Badger staring out at me from the first page, which I read. I remember where I heard his name before.

After a while, I go to my computer, get on the Web, key in "criminalrecords.com." I ask it about Curtis Dawson in the state of New York. They fill in some details and lead me to others. Badger's wife's name was Nina. She was an actress. Or wanted to be. She was sleeping with a bartender in the restaurant where she worked, on 92nd Street near where Badger had just gotten a job teaching philosophy. When the guy brought her home at three A.M. one night, Badger was waiting on the apartment steps. He beat them both to death with a piece of lead pipe he picked up out of the garbage on the sidewalk. The guy that came along and pulled him off them cracked Badger's skull open with the pipe to calm him down.

The next twenty years Badger spent in a hospital for the criminally insane upstate. That's where he finished the book on Plato. At his trial, the prosecutor had fought the temporary insanity plea; he thought it was a bunch of bull to claim Aphrodite made you do things against your will. But apparently the jury decided (like a lot of regulars at the Mick decades later) that the way Badger talked about the power of love meant that he was crazy. They decided he hadn't premeditated anything, that he had murdered under an irresistible impulse.

So I think awhile and I bag the photos and letters and the old newspaper and take them to the dump with my trash. Mind the gap, right? If what I'm thinking turns out to be true, nobody's ever going to think of Badger. And there's no way they can say I did it; you can't get from the stadium to Ronny's and back in twenty minutes, much less kill somebody while you're gone. (And I've got the Devil Rays brass checking his watch, saying, "Where you been for twenty minutes?")

The rest of Badger's things I box back up to go to New York along with my dad's hats and my mom's books in Spanish and the leftovers of the marriage that my wife didn't want. Okay, these boxes are kind of my family, I guess, if that doesn't sound too weird, and I might as well hang onto them, what the hell.

Back in my living room, I unpack a nice crystal glass and pour myself a drink from one of the bottles of good scotch that the Tampa brass sent me. I sit and think through what must have happened when I sent Badger to take care of Angie Schuelen-meyer. I shouldn't have said, "take care of," maybe. I figure Angie's down there at the bottom of the lake off the deck of Ronny's sex shack and she's been down there around three weeks. And Mickey Mantle's autographed bat that Tap Upchurch says is worth eighteen thousand dollars, I figure that's at the bottom of the lake too. Maybe Angie gave Badger a hard time about her plan to leave Zane for Ronny that afternoon and brought back bad memories, or maybe it was just the way she looked at the height of her powers. Or maybe it was just because Badger didn't want to let me down, his best friend.

He must have driven the powder blue BMW convertible to Nashville and sent the cards from there to Zane and me, and then driven the car to Tampa and he left it in Zane's driveway with the good-bye letter. I don't know where he meant by heading "out West," but if he went to California, there're so many crazies out there he'll fit right in.

Then, a few days after I looked through his belongings, I got a good-bye letter of my own from Badger, postmarked Tampa, Florida. I think he sent it from the bus station because inside was a strip of four photos, the kind you get made in the machines they have in stations, where you sit on a seat and look at a mirror. In each shot Badger's got on a different one of the hats of my dad's that I gave him. The brown Borsolino fedora. The Dobbs felt wide brim. The Harris Tweed trilby. The plaid golf cap. In each shot Badger has that huge smile he had when I first sat down beside him at the bar of the Mick. And he's holding Angie's little dog Lover in his arms.

The letter's not very long.

Jordan,

I want you to know I love you, my friend. You treated me with kindness. You were generous. If I went too far to repay you, I apologize. But maybe someday she'll come back to him. Love is the lever. Go to New York. Tennis is a good game to watch there.

Curtis Dawson

I keep the strip of photos but I burn the letter. Right, sure, Badger. You don't come back from the bottom of a lake.

•   •   •

The night before I fly to Manhattan, I drop by the Mick to say so long to some of the regulars. I get a shock. They're having a sort of good-bye party for me, balloons, cake, a photo of the Mick with their signatures all over it. They give me a great big cheese in the shape of North Carolina and throw in a lot of ribbing about me being a big cheese now and looking down on the good old boys. They joke about how I'll never come back to town. It's probably true. I never will. Then somebody asks me about Badger and I hear myself saying he sent me a postcard a few days ago explaining that he's moved to Chicago because he's got family there and they got in touch with him after all these years. The regulars say they're surprised to hear it. They didn't think Badger had anybody but me.

They talk about him for a while. All his weird theories about love power and how he read books in Greek and always had a hat on because he had some kind of scar on his head that must have embarrassed him. They want to know if I ever got Badger's real name and his story out of him. I say I never did.

I'm leaving when I notice Tap Upchurch has now got a baseball signed by Ronny Lamar Rome on a stand above the cash register. I figure the autograph's in Badger's handwriting. I'm looking at it when Tap comes over and points out that the Mickey Mantle autographed bat is back on the wall next to the towel in the plastic case. Tap says a few days ago he was cleaning and he found the bat rolled under the bar into a far corner. He must just not have seen it before. It's fine, he says, except for that stain from the ketchup bottle that Ronny Rome threw at it the night before the big game. He asks me, "Remember that night, Jordan?" I say I do, but I'm not really listening. I'm wondering am I all wrong and Badger never touched that bat? Could Ronny be right? Was it a woman identity thing with Angie? Did maybe Badger get her into a deep discussion that afternoon here at the Mick or maybe out on the deck at Ronny's sex shack and did she maybe decide to go be free on her own? Is it possible they drove out of town together in her blue convertible, talking about fundamentals? Maybe she meant it when she said she was crazy about him because he knew how to appreciate a woman. Maybe they got to discussing Plato in the Mick that night and decided to spend the rest of their lives philosophizing together.

I'm waving good-bye when Tap stops me and reaches under the bar. He thinks he oughta give me something, since didn't I

give it to Badger in the first place? He pulls out the black homburg, the hat that Badger was wearing the last time I saw him,
when I asked him to go take care of Angie.

I ask Tap where he got it.

He shrugs, "I found it on the floor beside the bat, go figure
how it got there."

"Go figure." I take the hat from him, straighten the brim,
brush the crown. Tap says, "Boy, Jordan, that little nut Badger
used to say some weird shit, didn't he?"

I say, "Hey, what do we know, maybe the entire universe *is*
just a dream of love in the mind of God." I fit the homburg on
my head and head for New York.

Mona

Miss Mona's Bank

Everybody knew about the two robbers half an hour after they got here. Everybody knows about everything in Thermopylae, and everything isn't very much, let me tell you. First of all, it was their license plate. What little you could make out through the dirt wasn't North Carolina or anything close to it. Turned out to be New Jersey, called at the bottom "The Garden State," which I judge was a northern style of joke since I once took a Trailways bus through New Jersey when the Junior Civitans went to New York City and gardens was the last thing we saw.

Second of all, it was one of those old Volkswagen buses painted like a dream where you went crazy. So if Newton had only been on the job at noon (which of course he wasn't), those two robbers would have gotten arrested like everybody else from out of state that failed to notice the 20 mph sign under the big sugar maple at the z-curve in Route 33. Newton would have given them tickets for speeding, faulty muffler, obscured plates, and the rest of the usual. If that had just been the case, the engagement of Miss Mona Leggett and Judge Skye would still be on, their friends would be going to their wedding after all these years, and maybe Miss Mona would really be retiring like she promised, and maybe I'd be getting my promotion. Maybe I'd be Horton Caldwell, Bank Manager, instead of what I still am—just a clerk. Still.

But Newton was at the Gulf station putting his patrol car through "The Works" wash and wax drive-through for free. So the robbers breezed into town.

According to Lovie Clay, they rolled down their windows at her when she pulled up next to them at the Main Street light and they yelled out, "Hey!" at her like they wanted to drag. "Where's a good spot to grab a bite around here?" Except I can't do accents the way Lovie can; she made them sound like *Law and Order.*

Lovie sent them to the Three Chefs lunch counter where her sister was one of the chefs. They'd already tried the Old Hickory Lounge at the Holiday Inn but it doesn't open up 'til five, and besides, only the older one was wearing a tie. It was a black tie, wide, with tiny pink women all over it, plus a pink shirt, a shiny old black-and-white checked sports jacket, stained black pants with one of the cuffs come loose so it kept catching in the shiny pointy-toed shoes he was wearing without any socks. Plus he had two glass rings on his fingers and a pork-pie hat with a white feather stuck in it. He was fifty or sixty, I guess, and short, and he looked like the walk across Main from his van over to Three Chefs and from Three Chefs over to the bank to rob it was as much outdoors as he'd seen in a long time. He was so white he was blue.

The young one was tall with sort of greasy blond hair hanging down to his shoulders. He had a good body, with blue jeans stuck into yellow work boots and to match that off an orange T-shirt with a photograph of five strung-out dope addict types on it: he explained in court it was this famous British band. "Alternative rock," he called them. Well it was an alternative to anything most people were used to in Thermopylae, that's for sure. I grew up on a farm but at least I know there's a world out there.

"I mistrusted those two robbers right off the bat," Lovie boasted, but she wasn't alone. I heard talk came to a complete stop when they took their stools at the Three Chefs. Lovie followed them there. She'd follow a squirrel to bury a nut if she thought she could get anybody to listen to her talk about it.

"Pastrami on rye," is what the young one asked for.

"We don't carry it," Lovie's sister Reba told him.

"Which?" he asks, sarcastic.

Reba took offense. "Neither one." She drags out an old menu. He had to settle for a B.L.T. while the old one had coffee and half a box of Valentine's candy he took off the shelf behind him.

Then, "Nice town," the young one said.

Lovie butted in as always. "You folks just passing through?" She was only fishing since nobody figured those two were planning on settling down in Thermopylae and opening a pastrami stand. They said, that's right, they were just passing through. Then they paid their bill, walked down to the corner, and tried to rob Miss Mona's bank of everything in it.

It's not really Miss Mona Leggett's bank. Or even any Leggett's bank anymore. It used to be her daddy's and her granddaddy's bank but now it's a chain and Mr. Waverly of Hillston is president of this particular branch. But Miss Mona has been the manager for twenty-five years and Mr. Waverly just lets her have her way because he's so impressed with how the Leggetts go back to before the Revolutionary War. Miss Mona is the last one left. They ran out of men in Korea when Captain Percy Leggett got shot down and that just left his baby sister Mona and she never married. Of course, nobody could figure out what she was waiting for when she'd been engaged to Judge Skye for fifteen years.

Miss Mona lives for our bank. But she's living in the past. She admits she doesn't want a thing changed except the light bulbs. So if anybody happened to have a suggestion for modern improvements, they might as well keep them to themselves. She'd still be on the gold standard if the law allowed. When First Savings almost went under in 1975, Miss Mona just refused to let customers withdraw their accounts. "I wasn't about to allow a run on this bank, not about to." I must have heard her tell that story ten thousand times since I started with First Savings three years ago. I guess she did save the bank, but only because nobody in this town's got the backbone to defy Miss Mona, even to get their own money away from her. So you can imagine how far I got proposing marketing ideas with some snap to them—like promotional inducements. She wouldn't even have balloons for children, much less a CorningWare set for opening a new account. I had a lot of ideas that weren't even new, but I got nowhere because she's turned her back on the times. "This is not an appliance store, Horton, and it's not a fairground. This is a bank, nine to four. Anyone who cannot hold onto his money outside those hours deserves to lose it."

The only thing I ever managed to get past her was a burglar alarm connecting us to the police station, which Mr. Waverly agreed to after First Savings in Raleigh was robbed. Of course he waited 'til Miss Mona went on vacation to Savannah before he sent the security company over. He's so scared of her he wouldn't mention the word retirement if she lived to be a hundred and came to work naked with weeds sticking out of her hair. Not that it's likely. There's never a hair loose on Miss Mona's head. She gets it done in Hillston every Saturday and once a month they color it blue for her. Lovie Clay was the first one to say Miss Mona looked like the picture of Andrew Jackson in the Old Hickory Lounge, even her permanent wave. Then some folks started calling her Old Hick, not to her face though.

So when the two robbers from New Jersey walked into the bank at 2:35 at least I had the alarm. When it happened, Miss Mona—wearing the red corsage of roses Judge Skye sends her every Valentine's—was waiting on Wilma Hawick. Over at the back, Reverend Ballister's widow was dumping stuff out of her big pocketbook onto a desk. I was counting cash receipts for Horace Crieff and Jimmy Coldstream was after him. We all stopped short when those two waltzed in whistling, each one carrying a Wal-Mart's bag.

The fishy old one with the naked-ladies tie gets in line right behind Wilma. The younger one with long hair hangs back by the doors. Wilma waits tables at the Pancake House and she had her tips in a bag of loose change that took Miss Mona some while to add up, which she does twice.

After Miss Mona finished counting out Wilma's silver, she says, "Next please!" I could tell she was already biased against the robbers because the old one was in her bank with his porkpie hat on and the young one had an unlit cigarette in his mouth. The old one hands her a folded note. She shakes it back at him with her blouse cuffs starched stiff and white as a block of ice. "You want me to read this?" she asks him in her sharp voice. She always talks like she's got an Army behind her. The young one lights his cigarette. She's been waiting for this and she wheels on him. "Put that out! No smoking in this bank!" He throws down his butt on the speckled marble floor and grinds it out in a sarcastic way.

Miss Mona calls over to him, "Please place that cigarette in a proper container, young man." She points at an old brass spittoon that was probably her grandfather's. The young one tries to stare her down but gives it up and picks up the butt and flicks it into the spittoon. As soon as he does, Miss Mona reads his friend's note. Out loud. "Hand over all the bills in the drawers. I got a gun. So does he." She slides her bifocals down on her nose. "What do you mean, hand over all your bills?"

"Look, don't play cute, lady," the old one snaps at her and quick reaches in his Wal-Mart's bag and pulls out an automatic pistol. "EVERYBODY! THIS IS A ROBBERY!"

Wilma screams. "Lord God, Lord God, help me!" She runs straight over to hug old Mrs. Ballister, but Mrs. Ballister beats her off with her big pocketbook. Then Wilma tries to climb up Horace Crieff like she was a cat and he was a tree. Horace and Jimmy both had thrown their arms high in the air. So had I. Mrs. Ballister watched it all like it was NYPD Blue.

The young robber pulls a gun out of *his* Wal-Mart bag. "No freak, no hassle," is what he said. Wilma sat down on the marble floor and started crying.

"Let's have it, lady," says the old one, shoving the bag under the teller's grille at Miss Mona. The whole time, of course, I was killing myself trying to stretch my leg out far enough to reach that alarm buzzer built into the floor. It was about an inch from Miss Mona's foot but she'd forgotten all about it. I got a charlie-horse trying and the old one waves his gun at me. "Watch it, buster, stand still." So I had to straighten up. But I tried clearing my throat at her, raising my eyebrows, twitching my fingers and tapping my foot, anything to call her attention to that buzzer. Everybody else in the whole bank was staring at me except Miss Mona.

She slid the bag back under the grille at the old one with a look like he'd just tried to deposit a sack of cow manure. She crossed her arms. "Put those guns away and get out of my bank."

The young one snorts a laugh. His partner yells, "Shut it, Jack!" His pasty face was getting red as a tomato and he pokes it right up against the grille. "Look here, lady. Get this through your fugging head, this is a fugging bank robbery, okay? No joke, okay? For real. Real gun, okay?" He points it at her.

Wilma was on her feet and racing again. "He's gone kill us all! Don't shoot us, please don't shoot us! Lord God, y'all, some-body do something!" This time she tried to climb Jimmy Cold-stream. She pulled his arms down out of the air where he was holding them and tore a rip in his shirtsleeve. While Wilma had everybody's attention, I quick slid my foot over and pressed the alarm buzzer with my toe. It made me break out into a sweat to do it but I could almost hear the bell bellowing at the police sta-tion and help on the way. I just prayed it arrived before Miss Mona got us all killed.

Holding Wilma away from him as best he could, Jimmy Coldstream yelled at Miss Mona, "Ain't you better do like he say?"

"Certainly not," was her answer.

"Bernie, let's go," shouts the young one in a high-pitched way. His gun was jerking in his hand like it was trying to get away from him.

Bernie turns to him. "Jesus Fugging Christ, can you believe this old bag?"

Miss Mona claps her hands over her head loud. "Wilma. Be quiet!" Wilma stopped on a dime, sank back to the floor, and lay there petting herself. Old Mrs. Ballister looked at us all like we were prizes on *Let's Make a Deal*.

Miss Mona snapped her fingers at the old guy Bernie like he was a bad waiter and she was tired of waiting. She said. "Watch your language. Now, let me tell you something. I have managed this bank for twenty-five years and never have I lost so much as a single penny and I don't plan to start now by 'handing over bills' to you. You may fire that gun if you are such a fool the death penalty doesn't bother you. Or you may leave the way you came in. Right this minute. And that goes for you too, young man." She points at Jack over by the doors. "So if you're going, go. If you're shooting, shoot."

The robber named Bernie stared at Miss Mona for so long without breathing that his eyes swelled. She stared back like she had all day. Then finally he let his breath go off in her face and he turned around and walked away. The young one named Jack ran over to my window and poked his gun through the bars. "Okay, let's have yours!"

Miss Mona stepped in front of me and shoved me back. "Mine is the only drawer with bills in this bank," she tells Jack. "This boy has no cash to give you."

It was an outrage. I'm not a boy, I'm twenty-four years old and of course I have my own cash drawer. But Miss Mona looked right at Jack and convinced him otherwise. His face fell like a child that dropped a Popsicle in the dirt. He and Bernie stared at each other for a while. "Now what?" asks Jack.

The old one shrugs, shoulders close to his neck. "Fug 'em," he says.

"Yeah," says Jack. "Hell with it."

Then they skipped backwards out the doors. The whole thing took about five minutes, but it felt a whole lot longer. Soon as they were gone, Wilma screamed like a factory whistle 'til her breath gave out. Mrs. Ballister trotted over to open up the doors and watch the robbers running down the street. "Right on Main," she calls out over her shoulder.

"Catch them!" I yelled at Horace and Jimmy. But they stayed where they were.

"Horton!" Miss Mona stopped me. "Get Newton." She was as straight and still as a hero on a horse but her cheeks were pink.

"I already set off the alarm!" I yelled at her. "I set it off! It was right there under your foot."

"Never mind that. Call Newton at Hot Hat Barbecue. If he's not there, go down to the Gulf station and get him. Horace, you go out there and find somebody who saw their car." Miss Mona was like somebody who'd finally gotten the big battle she was waiting for so she could boss everybody around. "Jimmy, take Wilma home. Wilma, go home and lie down."

Of course, they all jumped like she *was* Andrew Jackson. Mrs. Ballister even kissed her hand, cooing, "You were just wonderful, Mona. I was so proud. And just think I almost waited 'til tomorrow to come over here."

"Did you find your checkbook in that purse yet?" Miss Mona asks her, business as usual.

Newton was at the Gulf station, leafing through the dirty magazines while his cruiser radio outside was going a mile a minute calling for him to come in. It's a scandal that a man like that can get elected to a public trust even in a boonieville place like Thermopylae. Once I pried the centerfold out of his hands and told him we'd been robbed, he jumped into action like he was being filmed. He left most of his tires at Culloden and Main and scared everybody in town with his sirens and lights going like the whole place was on fire. After he jumped the curb and just about drove through the bank window, he kicks open the doors and runs in with his gun out before I could stop him.

"Where'd they go?" he shouts.

"Right on Main," says Mrs. Ballister.

Horace Crieff runs back inside. "They left on South 33 in a yellow van with curly lines painted all over it."

"How much'd they get?" Newton asks Miss Mona.

"Not a red cent," she tells him. "But they intended to commit robbery. Put that gun away and go catch them. Horton will go with you to identify them."

We saw the van on the shoulder about six miles south of town where they'd boiled over. Jack was under the hood hopping, trying to screw off the radiator cap with his bare hand. Bernie tried to hide under some grungy blankets in the back of the van when we pulled up behind them. That van was the dirtiest, most littered-up motor vehicle I ever saw. They told us they lived out of it. It looked like they'd been joined by hogs. Newton arrested them and cuffed them together and told them he was licensed to shoot to kill if they made a break for it. Bernie said, "Jesus Fugging Christ."

That night I walked past the police station on my way home from talking about the robbery at the Old Hickory Lounge bar, except Lovie Clay did most of the talking, when she hadn't even been in the bank. So I hear Jack standing by the window of his cell, singing a love song with his guitar. He sounded pretty good and turns out he was a professional entertainer or at least trying to be if he could find any work. Turns out Bernie played keyboards with him, plus was his manager or agent, the one that was supposed to find him the work except he couldn't. They explained it all the next day in front of Judge Skye. How show business up North was fixed so a newcomer couldn't get a break. How they were heading to Florida to try their luck at a resort where people sing while you're trying to eat. Bernie had finally got Jack signed for three weeks in Miami, but they ran out of money in North Carolina and lost their heads and decided to rob our bank to buy gas. They laid it on pretty thick about how sorry they were. Bernie claimed they'd been planning to mail back our money as soon as they "clicked" in Miami.

Lovie Clay got so excited when she found out the robbers were in show business, she got their autographs in case Jack ever got his break and turned into somebody. Lovie always wanted to be a star on Broadway and she even subscribed to *Variety*. But it's clear the piano at the Old Hickory Lounge is as close as she's ever going to get. If I have to listen to her sing "You Light Up My Life" one more time...

The robbers pleaded guilty before Judge Skye. Their public defender made a big deal about how neither one had any kind of previous record and how it ought to be obvious this was the first time they'd ever tried to rob a bank, considering how they'd let Miss Mona talk them out of it. It turned out the guns weren't even real; they'd stolen them out of Wal-Mart's and all they did was squirt water. You sure couldn't tell it from looking at them though.

There was a lot of talk in Thermopylae about why Judge Skye did what he did that morning, with Mona Leggett sitting there right in front of him, taking time off from the bank for the first day in twenty-five years. It was one of three things. Either his love for her was entirely worn out and he was looking to end things in a hurry. Or two, he was trying to put her in her place before the wedding so she wouldn't run all over him the way she does everybody else in town. Or three, he figured she'd think what he did was funny. If it's three, Judge Skye ought to be impeached off the bench, because anybody who thinks Mona Leggett's going to laugh about somebody trying to rob her bank with a squirt gun has no right to be handing down judgments in a court of law.

"It appears to me," says Judge Skye, "that there has not been a robbery at First Savings." He actually winks at Miss Mona. "The bank manager wouldn't allow it."

"Bless her!" sings out Mrs. Ballister.

The judge hit his gavel a soft one. "Even if the bank manager says she thought those guns were real, she says she did *not* feel intimidated or in fear of bodily harm." He actually grins at her. "She did *not* feel assaulted or even threatened by the defendants."

Miss Mona had been looking at Jack and Bernie like she could already see them strapped to side-by-side electric chairs. Now she's starting to look at the judge the same way.

He has to drink water to stop from chuckling. "Therefore as there has been no robbery and no successful attempt at robbery—"

Wilma stood up. "They scared me. They scared Horton too." She points at me. "He was shaking in his pants. But not Miss Mona!"

"Bless her!" shouts out Mrs. Ballister, just like she was back in her husband's church.

"Wilma, be quiet." Miss Mona takes over the courtroom. "You too, Mrs. Ballister."

Judge Skye thanks her for restoring order in his court, then he hands down his so-called sentence. He sentences Jack and Bernie to entertain every afternoon for two months at the elder care hospital down the road and warns them that if they don't show up every day they'll get two years in prison.

The robbers just about fell on their knees from joy, thanking the judge like he was Billy Graham, because Newton had told them they were going on a chain gang. There haven't been any chain gangs in this county for fifty years, but those two didn't know that because they had a scary view of the South that they'd gotten out of old movies on cable.

"Court is adjourned." The judge stood up and so did I and Newton started hollering, "But Judge!"

Miss Mona just sat there like she was carved out of the same marble as the bank floor.

According to Lovie Clay, it was only an hour later that Judge Skye received back his engagement ring, enclosed without a note in a bank deposit envelope. Lovie said Miss Mona had Jimmy Coldstream drive it over to the judge's house and leave it in his mailbox. I know she didn't take it herself because she was back in the bank telling me I couldn't offer a gas grill to the first five customers to buy a $25,000 five-year CD. Her red roses corsage was in the trashcan next to her desk.

She never mentioned that robbery or Judge Skye again that I ever heard.

When Lovie started telling the bank robbery story—how Bernie got Jack a job singing nights at the Old Hickory Lounge after they finished up at the hospital and how they made it down to Florida finally and next Christmas sent the Lounge a crate of grapefruits, she always starts off, "I remember the day they robbed Miss Mona's bank..." And every time she does, somebody in Thermopylae corrects her, "Lovie, you mean the day they *tried* to."

Miss Mona is still Miss Mona and Judge Skye is out of the picture and I am still just a clerk. My only hope is Mr. Waverly, the branch president, whose wife's been dead for three years. I saw him and Miss Mona doing the fox trot at the bank Christmas party. Of course, she was leading.

Betty

A Deer on the Lawn

Mrs. Ed Glazer didn't think it would be right for her to leave her husband because, after all, he had supported her financially through twenty-two years of her wishing she could leave him. Of course, he'd never known how she felt. For a long time, she wasn't even sure why she wanted to leave him. He was a good provider. She had everything she could reasonably expect in a material way from a supermarket manager in a small town in North Carolina. She had a walk-in deep freeze, HBO, airplane tickets to Florida twice a year to visit Lana, their only child, which was more than Lana wanted to see her anyhow. She had a pedigreed poodle and a part-time maid, who, though she was what Ed called "slow in the head," was still a help around the house, and company.

Betty Glazer liked her house and her maid—and her car and her life weren't too bad. The problem was she just didn't like Ed. On their wedding day, she'd thought she liked him, but she'd been mistaken. As she later realized, at eighteen you can make a lot of mistakes. The youngest of Betty's three brothers, for example, had drunk a pint of bourbon while out fishing when he was eighteen, and he'd steered his motorboat straight into a bridge piling and blown himself up. Sometimes Betty felt as if it were her life that she'd blown up when she was eighteen; her bridge piling had been marrying Ed Glazer because they'd been high school sweethearts and voted Best-Looking Couple in the yearbook. They hadn't even graduated when everybody started asking them, "When's the wedding?" And so they'd started to say, "Pretty soon now," and the next thing Betty knew she was walking down the church aisle in a dress she couldn't remember picking out and making all these promises she hadn't thought through.

Then as it turned out, she didn't like Ed. She didn't like his big ears, or his loud shirts pushing up against her dresses in their crowded closet, or the way she could hear him even down in the family room when he cleared his throat, always three times in a row. She didn't like the way he stabbed his food or snatched up the phone so fast or scared her pets. The sight of his long pink toes wiggling in the carpet tufts while he watched TV gave her a headache from trying not to run out of the room. Then after what the family called "the accident," Betty stopped trying to convince herself that she liked her husband at all. As far as she was concerned, it was his fault their little boy was dead. Still, she'd made the best of things for almost twenty years, 'til last fall when Ed stuck a huge stuffed deer he'd shot out there in the front yard. It was like her feelings about "the accident" had been a quiet private ember, and that deer had been like pouring kerosene on that ember, turning her heart into a bonfire. She hated him and the big deer both.

In their subdivision, a few neighbors had animals planted out in front of their houses—rows of ducks or swans or a burro saddled with petunias. One even had a deer on the lawn, but it was a little deer made out of bright painted plaster. Ed Glazer was the only one who had a real antlered stag that he'd shot and stuffed and polyurethaned standing right in the middle of his front lawn. It was the biggest thing Ed had shot so far, and he was so proud of it that he and Betty's brothers had gotten a taxidermist to weatherproof it so he could show it off on his lawn. It looked so realistic that people slowed down when they went by to see if it was alive.

Betty liked the house a lot better when Ed wasn't in it inching his hairy toes at her through the carpet while she was watching Romance Classics. So she was always agreeable when he wanted to go off hunting with her brothers. Ed thought she was a good sport about being left alone. He loved to hunt and bought everything he could possibly need for shooting things, including a red-and-white Winnebago in which every fall he drove to the nearby mountains where Betty's brothers had a cabin. He owned six rifles, a crossbow, and three orange insulated jackets. He loved packing up his equipment, making plans with her brothers on their portable phone.

She hated listening to the warm-up hunting stories he and her brothers told, the same ones over and over. Ed's favorite was about the rich Texan who shot eighteen elk in Yellowstone National Park and then told the game warden hauling him off to jail how it was worth it. Her brothers liked the one about the dumb city fellow who got stopped on the Interstate with a cow strapped to his fender and told the highway patrolman it was a moose. They also liked the story of the hunter who was so dumb he fired at a stag that was tied upside down to a pole and killed the guy carrying the front end. And another hunter who was so dumb he shot a horse that was painted purple. They laughed their heads off.

Betty hated the stories. Ed thought that was sentimental and womanly of her; in fact, he liked the way she would cry all night over a dead little bird. Betty preferred little animals to big ones. Kittens and hamsters and puppies. She especially liked little newborn things. She'd loved her twin babies more than anything in the world. They'd been so delicate, their tiny hands no bigger than little pink fish. Their little boy Larry had never grown up because a car had killed him when he was two years old. That was the accident they never talked about.

It happened in the street right in front of their house and the old man driving the car hadn't seen Larry, who'd run right out in front of him. Betty didn't blame the old man. From her window, she'd seen Larry crying and running to get away from Ed because Ed was in the yard, teasing him by shooting him with the water pistol. The little boy had raced screaming away from Ed, right out into the street in front of the old man's car. The police said it was nobody's fault. But Betty thought they were wrong.

Now their daughter Lana was twenty-two, big and healthy, taller than her mother, with wide strong hands. Lana was much more like Ed than Betty. She said she didn't really even remember her brother Larry so how could she miss him? She moved down to Florida where she and her husband Pete were long-distance truckers together. They didn't have time to come back to North Carolina to visit their folks. To scrape by, they had to stay on the road as long as they could keep awake. Taxes and gas were killing them. They said they didn't have time to have any babies either. Betty was crushed when they told her she wasn't going to get the little baby grandchildren she'd been waiting for. When she heard the news, she crazily thought of divorcing Ed right away and marrying the first man she met while she still had time to have another daughter who would want children. It broke her heart to think there'd never be a pair of short fat little pink arms around her neck. But it didn't seem right to walk out on a mistake like Ed after living with it so many years, plus accepting room and board.

Betty had lots of pets, a gerbil, a parakeet, and a dozen tropical fish. But her great love was her miniature poodle, Robert Goulet. She called him "Robbie," and her husband called him "Ghoul." Robbie and Ed hated each other. Betty liked it when Robbie growled at the doorway to keep Ed out of their bedroom. Robbie didn't like Jackie Louise either, the mentally handicapped maid Ed had gotten through the Methodist Church. And Jackie Louise was scared of him, but she was scared of most things except Betty.

Jackie Louise did the ironing while she watched the soaps, laughing and crying whenever the actors did, though according to Ed she didn't have the foggiest idea what was going on. Betty thought Jackie Louise worked hard and tried her best; she'd try so hard she'd soak herself with sweat and grind her teeth and even get tears in her eyes. She did a good job on Ed's short-sleeved shirts, squeezing around the tiny buttons on the collar and front pocket. When Betty did Ed's shirts herself, she'd break out in a hot rush of anger and just iron right over the little buttons. But Jackie Louise had infinite patience and would iron all day until Ed's shirts hung from every doorknob and off the backs of every chair as if dozens and dozens of Ed Glazers had invaded Betty's split-level home and were holding her hostage.

One late spring morning, Jackie Louise was ironing and Betty was looking out her picture window at the deer on her lawn. Rain smacked at the window; the rain had been going on for four days. She made a wish that the rain would soak through the polyurethane coating on Ed's stuffed deer and dissolve it into a big soggy lump. Robbie ran into the room, jumping to be picked up; while Betty held him, he growled out the window at the deer. He hated it too. Once he'd bitten it on the leg, and then Ed had sprayed roach-killer around the deer's ankles; the poison made Robbie so sick he vomited on their bedspread and Ed threw him against the wall.

The deer had fourteen-point antlers. Ed had gotten it last fall using a spray can of artificial female deer rutting odor that drew the bucks "like nobody's business." He loved the story about the hunter whose buddies sprayed two whole cans of the deer rut all over him while he slept in a tent, and how that stag tried to rape the man in the middle of the night.

Betty was sure her neighbors thought Ed was nuts to put his deer outside on the lawn instead of cutting off its head and attaching it to the wall over the TV set in the family room like the man two doors down had done. All last winter that stag's insides had lain stacked on the shelves of Betty's walk-in deep freeze beside the huge slabs of cow that Ed hauled home from the supermarket he was manager of. She wouldn't cook the stag steaks. It was the first time she'd refused to do her duty as a wife, but the sight of that frozen deer heart in her freezer made her sick, it was so big. Finally, Ed gave all the meat away to her brothers, and their wives fixed it. They said it was delicious. It's just a matter of taste, they added, to make Betty feel better.

Betty put Robbie down and he ran off, chasing Ed, who was leaving for the day. Betty kept looking out her window instead of checking on the big rolled roast defrosting right now in her microwave. All she wanted to do was stare. Everything else was too complicated. Outside, her daffodils had been beaten to the ground by the rain, as if Ed's stag had trampled them. The stag standing there on her lawn reminded her of those television ads for life insurance in which as soon as the husband dies, this big deer shows up like his ghost and wanders all over the yard and the house, poking his antlers in and out of rooms, watching over the dead man's wife and children. Suddenly it felt to Betty as if Ed were out there in the rain staring at her with those marble deer eyes, and she'd never get to be home by herself. TV seemed to think women wanted men around them all the time: they wanted huge strange men with shaved heads shooting their sinewy arms up at them out of the washing machine, or men flying in through their kitchen windows with emergency supplies of plastic bags, men crashing holes in their walls to show them a new cleanser, men tearing laundry apart to make a point, tiny men rowing back and forth in their toilets to install deodorizers. Whereas maybe women just wanted to get away from it all for a while. Betty certainly did.

She heard a scratchy panic noise like her gerbil made when he was trying to outrun his exercise wheel. It was Robert Goulet at the front door screen, furiously wet, slick as a white guinea hen and shivering a spray of rain all over the floor. How had he gotten out? She swooped him into her arms and yelled at Jackie Louise for the first time in their relationship. "Look at him! Did you let him go out by himself?!" Betty was beside herself. She grabbed her husband's freshly ironed shirts out of the stunned maid's hands and wrapped them around the crying poodle.

Dismay opened Jackie Louise's mouth but nothing came out except a whimper that sounded almost exactly like Robbie's.

When the phone screamed at her, Betty thrust the dog at her maid. "Keep him warm!" she said.

The phone was Ed in his truck on his cellphone. He wanted to tell her he'd just remembered it was their anniversary so he didn't want Betty to have to cook. He'd take her to the Pompey Lounge. She said she couldn't talk, she had to take care of Jackie Louise and Robbie. Ed remembered that he'd let Ghoul out when he left for work. He said he'd forgotten to bring him back in. "Honey, it's just a dog," he crooned.

Betty turned around, hanging up the phone in time to see Jackie Louise staring at the microwave oven. The fatty roast, left too long, started boiling from the inside out, exploding like gummy buckshot all over the oven glass. Jackie Louise screamed over and over. Robert Goulet jerked out from the tangle of Ed's shirts and ran away. Betty ran to the maid, slipped on Ed's wet shirt, and fell to the clean floor, hitting her head so hard she actually cracked her skull.

Late that afternoon, Ed found Betty unconscious on the floor, blood in her hair and Robbie curled up beside her. Jackie Louise hadn't called an ambulance, or anyone else; she'd run out into the rain and walked five miles to the clinic on Eisenhower Boulevard, the place from which Ed had gotten her through the Methodist Church. She was hiding in the basement behind some old metal beds.

In the ICU, Ed was all choked up; he had to keep clearing his throat as he told Betty's brothers that she couldn't leave him, that she was his high school sweetheart and he'd never loved anybody but her. He couldn't get over the fact that he'd already bought a dozen roses and a huge box of chocolates for their anniversary and now Betty was unconscious and couldn't enjoy them. The doctor told him not to worry; it was a hairline fracture that would heal and a concussion that wasn't dangerous and she'd be all right. They'd just keep her here a few days to be on the safe side.

When it came time for Betty to leave the hospital, the doc-tor warned Ed that she was still a little emotionally under the weather and would need time. Ed didn't think so. He thought she'd be her old self as soon as she got home. But when Betty came home, she couldn't make herself even try to be her old self.

Jackie Louise would never stay again in the Glazer house, although Betty brought her there in the car twice. But as soon as she saw that deer on the lawn, she'd start yelling. She seemed to think she had blown up Robert Goulet in the microwave or in the television. Every time someone would turn on the TV at the charity clinic, Jackie Louise would scream her head off. They had to keep her out of the lounge altogether, even though she enjoyed the art supplies.

Betty's brothers' wives found her another housekeeper who was much better anyhow. But Betty didn't seem to care what happened to the house, or anything else. The doctor wanted Ed sleeping on the couch to "give his wife some time," but Ed only lasted a week, and then he insisted Betty let him "get some honey." She let him, but she couldn't stop herself from crying, and Ed finally lost his temper and yelled at her and the doctor both. Then the doctor said Betty needed a change of scene. So Ed sent her to the beach with her brothers' wives. It rained most of the time and her sisters-in-law played bridge while Betty and Robbie sat on the porch staring at the sea.

She wasn't any better when she came home. In August, Ed sent her to Florida to see their daughter Lana. But Lana didn't really want her there. She and Pete were on the road all the time, and pretty soon they made Ed come take Betty home. They said all she did was sit in the hot trailer and stare out the window.

When Betty got home this time, Ed had let all her tropical fish die. He'd forgotten to feed them. It was when she was burying her fish that Betty made a sudden decision. It cheered her up enormously and she went to her little son Larry's grave and took him some carnations and thought about her idea some more. The next morning Betty was a new woman who Ed mistook for her old self. She cleaned her house top to bottom, she cooked a wonderful dinner for Ed, she ironed his shirts, she shopped, she smiled. Ed was thrilled. He told her brothers that his sweetheart was back at last.

Betty's great mood lasted all week, into the start of hunting season when Ed was headed for the mountains to try for another deer. He was meeting Betty's brothers up in the mountains at their cabin and Betty helped him get the Winnebago ready. She encouraged him to go even when it started to snow and he was worried about leaving her alone. She said she'd be fine; she even laughed. Go have fun, she told him, get another deer for the lawn. She held up Robbie and waved his paw good-bye as Ed drove off.

Thirty miles out of town, the Winnebago skidded sideways on a horseshoe curve, rolled over into a ravine, and blew up. It was the next morning before they even found Ed in his charred neon orange jacket. One of Betty's brothers was a state trooper. He said it was very hard to tell after the fire but it looked as if maybe something had gone wrong with Ed's brakes, like somehow the fluid had drained out. The investigators said it was an accident and nobody was to blame. Betty's brother felt terrible breaking the news to her. He knew she and Ed had been married since they were high school sweethearts and voted Best-Looking Couple in the senior class. Betty told her brother that she couldn't feel anything. They said she was in shock.

Lana and Pete drove their truck up to North Carolina for Ed's funeral. The truck was full of dishwashers they had to deliver to Richmond so they couldn't even stay overnight.

Holding up both Robbie and the new Persian kitten she'd just bought, Betty waved Lana and Pete off as they pulled out of her driveway. She stood at the empty spot where Ed's deer had been and where it had killed all the grass. She was thinking maybe she would plant a flowering fruit tree there as soon as spring came round again. The lawn looked too empty. Lana's truck disappeared around the corner, taking with her, as a memento of her father, the big stag that had once stood in the middle of the lawn, keeping watch over Betty with lidless eyes.

Mattie

Invitation to the Ball

"A dinner invitation once accepted is a sacred obligation. If you die before the dinner takes place, your executor must attend."
—*Ward McAllister, the man who made up*
"the Four Hundred"

Mark told Tugger Whitelaw, Chanler's best friend, that something had to be done, and that he'd found a girl, the perfect girl, to do it. Mark had been warning Tugger for months that Chanler was in a bad way, that he was getting weird about this woman in the painting at the Parnassus Club. And when Tugger saw how Chanler was acting, he'd agreed to help Mark.

Afterwards, Tugger told his fiancée that he blamed himself for what had happened. He should have seen it coming. After all, the girl Mark had found for Chanler was a Southerner and so was Tugger and maybe he should have read her signals better. "But we're from Charleston," explained his future wife. "And Mattie was from New Orleans. Those places don't play by the same rules."

Tugger told his fiancée, a sweet woman, "Mattie didn't play by any rules at all. Mattie was a pirate."

• • •

That day when it all began, Mark and Tugger found their friend Chanler seated in front of the painting of Mrs. Rawlings at the Parnassus Club, in the high-ceilinged, oak-paneled bar. The three young men had joined the private arts club although none of them were in the arts. But then few of its members were anymore. The Parnassus was off Fifth Avenue, an easy walk for their group from midtown brokerage and law firms and it served large classical cocktails that appealed to them.

Mark led Tugger over to where Chanler was seated in front of the life-sized portrait. "Channie," he said, "we need to talk."

Chanler, ruffling his sandy hair, straightening his expensive thin glasses, asked what had happened to Mark that they needed to talk about?

It was true, Tugger affably noted, they'd been talking about Mark's problems all through prep school and Yale together, for Mark was temperamental, profligate, too good-looking, and much poorer than his friends, and was often in trouble for one of these reasons or another.

But Mark said this time it was Chanler's problem they needed to talk about.

"What problem?" Chanler asked.

"Channie," Mark began, tasting his martini. "We're all worried about you. Aren't we, Tug?"

"Sure are." Tugger smiled to show that his concern for his best friend was benign.

Turning his face back to the painting he'd been looking at, Chanler asked, "Worried about what?"

"This." Mark pointed at the picture of the woman over the mantelpiece. "You're like Dana Andrews in *Laura*. Isn't he, Tug?"

Tugger slowly nodded, trying to back Mark up.

Chanler was surprised. "You mean, the old movie?"

"Yeah. Dana Andrews fell in love with Laura's portrait, remember? Laura." Mark sang a line of the song.

Popping cashews in his mouth, Tugger tried to help. "Kim Novak played her."

Impatiently, Mark the movie-lover grabbed the silver bowl of nuts. "Not *Vertigo*, jerk." He glowered at Tugger's ignorance. "Gene Tierney, Laura. This cop had a fixation on her portrait. Like you, Channie, okay? You're spending way too much time with old Mrs. DeWitt Rawlings here."

Chanler considered the above-the-mantel portrait of Mrs. Rawlings in front of him. "I thought *not* having a fixation on a woman was my problem."

It was true that friends of Chanler Swaine, and he was famous for having the most friends of anyone in his young group, were always telling him he didn't want things enough. Of course, this same equanimity was what made him so pleasant to be around. Born into an enviable trust fund, blessed with reasonable looks and brains, Chanler Swaine appeared to be entirely satisfied with his life—a state of mind that was, if not unnatural, certainly unusual. Didn't even the rich always want more money, the successful more success, didn't the beautiful labor to make themselves more beautiful? His friends wanted more. Tugger wanted to lose weight and marry his Charleston sweetheart. Mark, with his wavy black hair and startling blue eyes, so handsome that women stared at him in public places, wanted a great deal of money. Chanler, on the other hand, appeared to want nothing. With the same ambling vagueness that he played his little old-fashioned tunes on the piano, his long fingers wandering softly over the keys, he seemed to stroll with his gentle irony through life, without knowing or caring that it was a race to be won or lost. But if Chanler tended to drift, he did so in the direction of virtues that his friends had come to rely on. He had been a gentle and generous boy; now he was a gentle and generous man. But he had never been in love.

Until now. Chanler had suddenly developed a bizarre infatuation with Mrs. DeWitt Rawlings, or rather with her portrait, which hung in the Parnassus Club, above a green marble mantelpiece ripped a century earlier from some hapless Veronese palazzo. In this painting, the "ravishing" Mrs. Rawlings (as the nineteenth-century social arbiter Ward McAllister had christened her) stood in a gold gown on a curved stairway, half turned toward the viewer as she were about to whisper something intimate. It was a famous painting and was one of the prizes of the club's collection. Absurdly enough the artist himself, Jacob Zanski, had in 1887 applied to the same club for membership and been blackballed. Chanler, who was now on the membership committee, had discovered the reason for the blackball against

Zanski in the archives's old minutes, where "Jew" was written beside the immigrant's name. A hundred years ago, as Chanler noted with his quiet irony, prejudices were so sure of themselves that they kept records.

The night that it all began, Chanler sat facing the portrait of Mrs. Rawlings so that her strange low-lidded seductive green eyes stared straight down into his. He couldn't seem to keep his eyes off a woman a hundred years older than he was. He was drinking a Champagne Diana, (brut champagne with a shaving of lime and dash of Cointreau, named for Mrs. Rawlings), and asked his friends to agree she had beautiful ears. Even Tugger, who'd resisted Mark's alarm, grew concerned.

"This wasn't," said Tugger, "what we meant when we said go find a girl."

Chanler hoped they weren't about to match-make again. Apart from Mark and Tugger (who was having trouble getting his childhood sweetheart from Charleston to move to New York), Chanler was the only bachelor left in their group. He'd once been on the verge of proposing to a bond trader named Belinda, but the moment had passed. Asked why, he admitted that when he wasn't with Belinda, he couldn't remember what she looked like. But as Mark now pointed out, he spent so much time gathering information on Mrs. Rawlings' life in the Gilded Age and so much time staring at her portrait here at the club, that obviously he could pick her ear lobe out of a large crowd in a fog. "We're getting a little worried about you, aren't we, Tug?" prodded Mark.

"A little," Tug agreed and gave Chanler's arm a friendly rub. "I mean, Mark likes old movies and I like old musicals, but there's such a thing as too much of the past, Channie. I don't even know why we joined this place. The old farts here just snooze and complain about their prostates."

Now in general Chanler's young group had nothing against the past; in fact they thought of themselves as stylistic reconstructionists. Like their grandparents, they knew how to dress and how to fox trot. They even put on fancy dress balls for charity, just as their great-grandparents had done. Tugger enjoyed his Broadway revivals and his Porterhouse steaks; Mark loved his film noir, his braces and Panama hats, his martinis and cigars. But Channie's falling in love with a woman in a fin-de-siècle painting was taking social neo-classicism too far.

"What's wrong with my admiring Mrs. Rawlings?" Chanler asked.

"Well," Tugger shrugged apologetically, "she's dead."

Mark eagerly agreed. "You finally pick somebody and she's been dead a hundred years. You see the problem, Channie?"

"She's only been dead since 1951," Chanler smiled.

"Half a century later, that's still a problem." Mark stroked his new mustache with tan, well-manicured fingers. "Not that you should have married Belinda. I mean she turned out to be a real class-A bitch, right? I'm just going to have to find you the right girl. Now can you leave Mrs. Rawlings alone long enough to get some sushi with us?"

But Chanler told them to go ahead; he'd eat at the club. They left him staring at the portrait.

•　•　•

That night Mark telephoned Tugger. "So, okay, Tug? Am I right?"

Tugger admitted that Chanler did appear to be falling in love with a painting, and if Mark did know the "perfect girl" maybe he should invite her to come meet their friend. The very next week, Mark asked Tugger to bring Chanler to the club at a certain time because the girl would be there.

At the appointed time, Tugger and Chanler were sitting together in front of the portrait of Mrs. Rawlings. Mark spotted them as if coincidentally, and told Chanler, "I want you to meet somebody tonight. You're gonna thank me."

Chanler gestured no. "Don't try to fix me up, Mark. Do Tugger instead."

"Not me," said Tugger. "I'm going to propose to Nancy again as soon as I lose some weight." But Mark was already hurrying down the wide stairs, presumably to bring back the girl for whom Chanler was going to thank him.

Chanler asked Tugger, "Has he got some woman hidden down in the coat room?"

"Maybe you'll like her."

Chanler confessed that he'd never seen a contemporary woman in the same class as Mrs. Rawlings.

Tugger gave the woman in the painting a closer look. "Well, she is beautiful. Are those real, those jewels sewn on her dress?"

Chanler explained that Mrs. DeWitt Rawlings's husband had inherited a large copper mine at a time when there was no income tax. "They're real. But," he added, "you should have seen Alice Vanderbilt at the same party. She was 'The Electric Light.' Her whole head was covered with diamonds."

"What party?" Tugger asked. Chanler pointed at the portrait's title. "Mrs. Rawlings as Dido. Mrs. Vanderbilt's Ball, 1883." It had been a fancy dress affair, which was why Mrs. Rawlings was costumed in this jeweled outfit: she'd come as the Queen of Carthage—or at least as the fashionable tailor Lanouette's bizarre notion of what that ancient queen might have looked like. Chanler explained to Tugger how this picture—painted a year after the ball—commemorated Diana Rawlings's great triumph at the most famous party ever given in New York City, the dance and dinner on which Alva Vanderbilt had spent $250,000 in order to break into Society. Chanler told Tugger that $250,000 in 1883 would be about four and half million dollars today.

Tugger was amazed. "For a party? Four and a half million?"

Chanler agreed that it was no small change, even for a Vanderbilt. But it had been worth every cent to the social-climbing Mrs. Vanderbilt because it had forced Mrs. Astor to pay a visit to her home, and where Mrs. Astor went (and she went wherever a man named Ward McAllister advised her to go), the Four Hundred followed.

"But what exactly is it about Mrs. Rawlings that you like so much?" Tugger persisted.

Chanler's answer surprised him. "She's a pirate," he said.

"You mean like a thief?"

Chanler shook his head. "No. I mean like a pirate captain, flying her own flag, breaking rules. The opposite of me."

"Or me," agreed Tugger. "Or anybody else in here." He gestured around the private club where the members chatted at one another in a room that had been designed by Stanford White and left alone ever since. The men were mostly old and looked and dressed and talked alike. "No rule-breakers here."

Chanler nodded. Yes, he said, the most powerful rule of Society is that Society rules and that it is impossible to break its rules without dreadful penalties. "But, of course," he added, placing his long thin legs on the leather chair across from him, "rules only have power over those who agree to believe in them." A portly man across the way frowned fiercely at Chanler's feet, and he quickly removed them from the chair. He smiled. "See what I mean? But pirates do as they please and get away with it."

"And what did Diana Rawlings do that was so piratical?" Tugger asked.

"She murdered her husband," smiled Chanler.

Tugger thought he was joking. "She what?"

"She murdered her husband. I can't prove it yet, but I've been researching and I'm sure she did it. And got away with it." Chanler squeezed his arms to his chest, his mild gray eyes brightening. "That's what makes her so beautiful."

"You're nuts." Tugger frowned; Mark was right: their friend was in the grip of a strange fixation. "It makes her beautiful—that she's a murderer?"

Chanler thought a bit. "She's letting you know she's going to act on her desires. It's in her eyes in the painting. See how she looks right at you."

"Not really," said Tugger, hoping Mark would come back soon with the girl.

Chanler took something from his pocket and showed it to Tug. It was a small framed photogravure that he'd found at the antiques fair at the Armory. It was a photo of Diana Rawlings taken for the society pages ten years after the death of her husband; in it she sat in a fashionable group at the races at Saratoga. Behind her, Chanler pointed out, stood the artist Jacob Zanski. "And Jacob Zanski knew she was a pirate. He saw it from the beginning, and he put it in this portrait."

Tugger, alarmed, listened as Chanler pointed out details of the painting of the woman in her long golden ball gown. The dress was beaded with hundreds of small rubies, emeralds, and pearls, low-cut and strapless, except for two thin strands of rubies curling over her shoulders. Her head was a flame of auburn hair, piled high and sprinkled with rubies. She wore no necklace, and the white nakedness of her neck and bare arms was, even today, a shock to viewers. On her right hand, the one resting on the newel of the marble banister, she wore a bracelet of intricate design, of rubies twined in gold. The dress had cost more money than a thousand mill workers could have earned in 1883 in a year of long, back-breaking days at a thousand looms.

Chanler said the dress had caused a sensation at Mrs. Vanderbilt's ball. So had the fact that Diana Rawlings (who was not one of the Four Hundred) had arrived at the party unescorted by her husband (who was). Indeed, no one in the Four Hundred had ever heard of Diana before she had married DeWitt Rawlings only six months earlier. His own family had been surprised, and not at all pleased by the marriage, and had tried to keep it as quiet as possible. They'd thought DeWitt, an amateur archeologist, would never marry anybody, much less a shop girl half his age, however beautiful.

But while Diana had arrived at the Vanderbilts essentially uninvited, she'd been escorted there by the Reverend DeLancey, rector of a large Fifth Avenue church, who had come dressed as El Cid, and by his wife, a lumber heiress, who'd come as Bo Peep. Between these pillars of society, Mrs. Rawlings had walked past

the guards into the white limestone chateau, up the marble stairway lined by rows of footmen in maroon knee britches and pow-
dered wigs. She had swept into the ball to join the thousand
guests dancing under a canopy of roses—every rose for sale that
day in all of New York City. Beneath the circular frescoed ceiling, she'd offered her hand to Alva Vanderbilt as if she'd done so
daily for the past dozen years; she had explained that her husband DeWitt sent his regrets, he'd been unexpectedly delayed
returning from an archeological trip to Greece. Alva Vanderbilt
accepted her hand. What else could she do? Despite the shock of
Diana's décolletage and the fact that no one really knew who she
was, if this Dido was all right with the Reverend and Mrs.
DeLancey, well then how could she be wrong?

Because of that ball—Chanler explained to Tugger—Diana
had climbed into a world where she was to live unchallenged until
her death sixty years later. She managed to remain there from that
night on, even when, the very next day, her husband was found
lying dead on the terrace of the family's country house, having presumably fallen, or jumped, from the balcony. "But," said Chanler,
"he didn't. She'd killed him just before she went to the ball."

Tugger tried to stop himself from eating the mixed nuts.
"Channie, you sound weird, you know that?"

"There were rumors of murder even back then, but nobody
ever—"

But at that moment, Mark interrupted. "Channie? I'd like
you to meet somebody."

Chanler and Tugger turned and saw the young woman. She
stood at the top of the stairs beside Mark. Even Tugger could see
the shocking resemblance, even in her tailored black suit and
pageboy haircut. She had the same slender figure and cream-
white glow to her skin as Mrs. Rawlings. The same auburn hair
and the same green, oddly tilted eyes that Chanler couldn't look
away from. Mark was grinning as Chanler hurried to his feet,
pulling Tugger with him. Mark said. "Mattie, this is Tugger
Whitelaw."

"Tim," insisted Tugger.

"And Chanler Swaine, the guy I've been telling you about. This is Mattie."

She smiled. "Mark says you know just about everything there is to know about my great-grandmother." As she held out her hand, Chanler noticed the bracelet she wore. He couldn't believe it. She laughed, "Well, I don't know a thing." Her laugh was low and conspiratorial and her voice had a soft Southern sound.

"Your great-grandmother?" Chanler kept staring at her.

"I'm Mattie Rawlings." She pointed at the portrait. "Look at that. Just like you said, Mark. It *is* my bracelet." She spun the bracelet with its gold-tangled rubies, showing it to them. Tugger asked her where she'd gotten it.

Mattie smiled at Tugger. "From my dad. He told me it had belonged to his family, but he didn't say it was in a famous painting. That poor darling hated old memories." She invited them all to sit down. "So, Chanler, will you tell me everything there is to know about Diana Rawlings?"

Chanler said he'd just been explaining to Tugger that Mrs. Rawlings' husband had been found dead the morning after the Vanderbilt ball and that there had been rumors that Diana had been having an affair and had murdered him.

Mattie laughed. "Why do men think just because a woman's capable of adultery, she's capable of murder too?"

"You gotta admit, Tug," Mark grinned as they followed Mattie and Chanler into the club dining room. "Mattie's right for him. Like Bogie says, the stuff that dreams are made of. Look at Channie!" Chanler was talking to the young woman with an animation unusual for him. She nodded, smiling as they went.

"I guess," said Tugger dubiously. "I don't know. I thought the idea was to get him away from this stupid painting, not bring it to life."

•　　•　　•

Chanler Swaine was the chairman of the BGC—Ball for a Good Cause—Committee. This formal dance was held every Christmas. The good causes varied but the guest list stayed pretty much the same and invitations were avidly sought by socialite New Yorkers of twenty- and thirty-something age. A few weeks after their first dinner together, Chanler invited Mattie Rawlings to be his date at this year's ball. She accepted, and made quite an impression on the group, and other invitations followed. Tugger congratulated Mark on finding such a perfect girl for Chanler. The young couple got along beautifully; everything that Chanler liked, Mattie liked as well. She shared his taste in restaurants, furniture, and friends. She liked to hear cabaret singers and to walk in the park, she liked the History Channel and she collected things like old autographs and Art Deco lacquers. In fact, had Mattie been trained like Gigi since childhood to take her place as Chanler's mate, she couldn't have been more perfectly suited, although very different in personality. She didn't even mind having dinner once a week with his mother, whose sarcasm had reduced earlier dates of Chanler's to tears; Mattie appeared to enjoy the undeclared war of thrusts and parries at the upper–East Side townhouse.

But she had her own life too; in fact, she would occasionally be unavailable for an evening out or she would go away for a weekend, or spend the afternoon at Belmont racetrack with Mark Toral and others in their group who liked the sport. Mrs. Swaine told Tugger that Mattie's independence was reassuring. Chanler's family had money, and fortune hunters were not unheard-of.

Tugger asked his friend one evening over drinks, "Is Mattie a pirate too?"

But Chanler was puzzled. "A pirate?" He seemed to have forgotten his theory about Mrs. DeWitt Rawlings; in fact to have forgotten the woman in the painting entirely. Mattie had effaced her.

Later that same evening, Mark came into the club and for some reason tried to pick a fight with Chanler. After Chanler left to meet Mattie, Mark sat in the bar drinking and bad-mouthing Chanler to Tugger. He said, "What does Channie know about life? He's richer than God."

"Not really," Tugger modestly protested.

"Not really," Mark mocked. "All his bills go straight to his mommy."

Tugger was surprised at the sarcasm that had started slipping into Mark's voice when talking about Chanler. He objected on his friend's behalf. The resulting fight caused a rift with Mark that Chanler himself had to repair, asking Tugger a week later please to overlook Mark's caustic tone; their friend, he said, was under pressure at work and in financial trouble.

"He always is. Why do you always defend him?" Tugger asked.

Chanler smiled. "Well for one thing, he introduced me to Mattie."

They were in the club bar and Tugger sat looking at the portrait of Mrs. Rawlings. Finally he asked, "Where did Mark say he met Mattie?"

"The Yale Club."

"She went to Yale? When?"

"No, she was just there." Chanler played a slow imaginary tune with his fingers on the leather arm of the chair. "Thank God."

Tugger shook his head. "She's from New Orleans. Mark worked at that bank in New Orleans, remember?"

"Tugger, what are you getting at?"

"Maybe they met there."

"So what?"

Tugger gestured at the painting. "You know more about the Rawlings family than Mattie does."

"God, the way you and my mother harp on 'family.'"

"Are you going to marry Mattie?"

Chanler stopped his silent tune, turned to his friend. "Is that a problem?"

Tugger looked at him. "I hope not."

Three months later, Chanler proposed to Mattie.

Chanler's mother sweetly let the girl know of her fears that someone would try to marry Chanler for his money. Mattie sweetly replied that she hoped Mrs. Swaine would do everything in her considerable power to thwart such a tragedy. But even Mrs. Swaine, something of an East Side fixture and by her own proud admission a snob, could have no objection to her son's choice on the basis of family. She knew the name Rawlings. It was true that society had lost track of them since they'd gone downhill. It was true that the Rawlings house on 53rd Street had fallen to the wreckers' ball, their country estate had been turned into a girls' school, and who knew where the gold gown of Dido, so heavy with real jewels, had gotten to. Nevertheless, the name Rawlings had been in the Four Hundred, and still meant something, at least to New Yorkers like Mrs. Swaine. She still believed it took four generations to make a gentleman, which made Mattie's father, DeWitt Rawlings IV, a gentleman twice over, even if he had drunk himself to death in a succession of cheap rooms in New Orleans, having long since squandered what little of the copper fortune his family hadn't managed to mislay in a century of stock market crashes.

Mrs. Swaine examined Mattie on her past and Mattie passed the test. She was, she said, the last of the Rawlings, the only child born to her father in his late middle age. She confessed to her father's seediness, she admitted to her poverty with refreshing candor. She said that after his death, she'd come to New York and now worked at Sotheby's and roomed with two other young women in a Chelsea walk-up. She told Mrs. Swaine that she was well aware of the financial distance between them. She said that Chanler had proposed to her three times already and that she had declined. She said she still was hesitant to say yes.

It was this reluctance that finally won over Chanler's mother, who confessed to Tugger that she'd originally thought Mattie a gold-digger but that the gold had been lying around for the picking a long time, untouched, and what fortune hunter of Mattie's generation would have the patience not to pounce at once? Tugger tried to persuade himself that she was right. Chanler was his oldest friend.

•   •   •

At Christmas, a year after they met, the public announcement of the Swaine-Rawlings engagement was made at the Ball for a Good Cause, to which Chanler and Mattie came dressed as DeWitt and Diana Rawlings. Mrs. Swaine's friends were struck by Mattie's beauty and congratulated Chanler on his choice.

Tugger's girlfriend from Charleston flew up for the event and they came as Nick and Nora Charles, although everyone thought they were Fred Astaire and Ginger Rogers.

Mark came alone, drank too much, and announced that he'd lost his job. Everyone was embarrassed.

In the end it was Mrs. Swaine herself who insisted on (and financed, for Mattie didn't have a cent) the formal wedding at the big Fifth Avenue church. She also paid for the big reception at the Parnassus Club. Her wedding present to Chanler was a townhouse a block away from hers. She said it would be ready when they came back from their month-long honeymoon cruise in the Mediterranean. She commissioned a portrait of Mattie, painted by a famous society artist, dressed for the BGC as Mrs. Rawlings.

Tugger's girl came North to attend Chanler's wedding with him; he told her that if she'd marry him, he'd move back home to Charleston with her. She said yes. As for Chanler and Mattie's wedding, the ceremony itself was perfect, but things went wrong at the reception. Tugger's toast as best man was filled with such curious fears for his friend's happiness that people commented on it. They also couldn't help but notice Mark's quarrel with the bride off in a corner (where no one could hear what they were arguing about), which was broken up by Tugger, with whom

Mark then also quarreled. Afterwards, Tugger and his girl left the party without waiting for the ceremonial tossing of the garter and bouquet.

There was another tense scene when Chanler overheard the older Mrs. Swaine's remarks to the younger Mrs. Swaine about finances; Chanler's mother said merely that all of Chanler's money was under her control. In the event of a divorce, or even an indiscretion, Mattie should expect to leave the marriage as unencumbered by wealth as she had entered it. Chanler told his mother that she was insulting his bride. Mattie had to defend her new mother-in-law to her new husband by saying she wasn't offended at all.

A third episode occurred when a drunken Mark boorishly kept cutting in to dance with the bride until Chanler finally had to ask two other friends to take him home. Mark broke a chair as they dragged him out. Chanler's mother told Chanler that his friend Mark Toral was no gentleman, even if he looked like one. Looks might serve, she said, as a successful substitute for class these days, but only as long as one stayed sober.

It was soon after Mark's eviction that Mattie realized that she'd lost her heirloom ruby bracelet. She was as close to frantic as anyone had ever seen her. The ballroom was searched but to no avail. Sadly, despite its value, the bracelet wasn't insured.

But by morning when the newlyweds left to fly to Athens, Mattie had recovered her typical composure. She was conciliatory toward Tugger when he showed up at the airport to apologize for his behavior at the reception. She even kissed him on the cheek, then went off to buy magazines so that he and Chanler, the two old school friends, could be alone. It was then that Tugger gave Chanler a special wedding present; it was a daguerreotype of Mrs. DeWitt Rawlings that he'd found through an autograph dealer. Dated the night of the Vanderbilt ball, and in fact taken during that event, the picture showed Diana in her Dido gown, looking exactly like the Zanski portrait now in the Parnassus Club, down to the rubies in the hair and the ruby bracelet on her wrist.

Chanler was touched. He and Tugger reconciled and embraced, reminding one another that they'd always be friends.

On the flight to Athens, Chanler didn't mention Tugger's thoughtful daguerreotype because he sensed that the bond between him and Tugger made Mattie uncomfortable. For the same reason, he didn't ask what Mattie and Mark and Tugger had fought about at the wedding reception. Chanler was never one to invade another's privacy.

• • •

A week after their honeymoon ship sailed out of Athens, Mattie gave Chanler his wedding gift from her. They had had a good morning climbing among the ruins of Delos and then Chanler had returned to the ship to read while Mattie went alone into Mykonos for an afternoon's shopping. She was gone so long that she almost missed the last tender back aboard. Now as their cruise liner was pulling away from the hills of white houses; the newlyweds watched from their private balcony. They lay side by side on deck chairs whose cushions were as blue as the sky and the sea.

"Are you happy, Mr. Swaine?" Mattie asked him, raising her champagne flute to his. He nodded; he'd never been this happy before in his life.

She toasted him. "I just wish Daddy could have lived long enough to meet you and know how happy you were going to make me."

He took her hand and kissed the wrist near where she had once worn the ruby bracelet. She must be, he thought, still upset about its loss; she had held on to so little of her past. He'd seen only a few things in her apartment that had to do with family: two photos, her father's watch and cufflinks, a few old books, a few letters her father had written, a few that his father had written him. But Mattie didn't talk about her father often; she'd once described "memory lane" as "nightmare alley."

She leaned over, kissed Chanler, then handed him a beautifully wrapped package. "Here, honey, happy wedding." Her present for Chanler was the part of her past that had brought them together. She said that sorting through the jumble of odds and ends stored by her father, she'd found an old suitcase. There'd been something in it she'd thought Chanler would like.

Chanler carefully opened the package, taking out a battered travel journal, its leather covers cracked and dry. In faded ink, in thin, regular script, it was dated 1883, and inscribed "DeWitt Rawlings, Vol. 3." Chanler looked up at Mattie, thrilled. The diary belonged to Diana Rawlings's husband, DeWitt. He read the first entry aloud.

> After the remarkable ruins at Mycenae, Eleusis is a disappointment. Still, it is fresh territory for us, and Trimmer is confident we shall have a successful dig. I miss Diana dreadfully. It is difficult that we should be separated after so brief a time together.

"Yes, it's my dad's grandfather," Mattie said. "His journal from the Greek dig. The amateur archeologist had kept a diary on the Mediterranean voyage to ancient sites that had taken him away from his new bride. He'd left after only six months of a marriage that had shocked New York society and horrified the Rawlings family.

> Diana understands I couldn't say no to this trip, having waited so long for a respite in my responsibilities to the family business. Trimmer's team is the absolute best in the archeological field, and I am learning at such a great rate that he pleasantly jokes that all the new copper my father dug up robbed the academy of a good digger of old bronze.

"It's the perfect present for me," said Chanler.
Mattie smiled. "Well, my goodness, what else from the

perfect wife?...Don't stay out here long, Channie. With that sun-burn you'll get a chill. And a storm's coming."

"Thank you," he smiled.

Mattie turned, her white caftan caught by the Mediter-ranean breeze, and blew a kiss, her turn reminding him of the painting of Diana. Behind her, the Mediterranean sun was like a great blood orange sitting on the blue plate of the ocean. Then she was gone, headed to the ship's spa, she told him, to make her-self beautiful for the captain's table tonight. Chanler teased that it was a waste to spend so much time at that spa day after day; what could they do to improve her?

Alone he settled in his deck chair and, fascinated, reopened the journal of Diana Rawlings's husband. On the surface DeWitt was a contained, ironical man, whose meticulous notes on bro-ken shards of the Peloponnesian past filled the bulk of his diary. But now and then from the yellowed pages flared his passion for his young wife.

> Diana says she has received not a single visit from anyone in my family. Their snobbery and cruelty disgust me. How can they not see her value? I know they still think me mad for marrying her, and no doubt had Father not passed away before I met her, it might well have cost me his estate. But I would happily trade all the copper in this earth, and a thousand times more, for Diana. Before her there was nothing and, without her, nothing again.

As he read, Chanler could see that DeWitt was not blind to his wife's shortcomings, her vanity, ambitions, propulsive desires. But he loved her so much that everything in her nature gave him pleasure:

> Diana has met a painter who has flattered her into a commis-sion. Zanski his name is. How she likes to have her beauty appreciated. And why shouldn't she?

Letter from Diana waiting here at the hotel, sent on from Athens. She talks of nothing but an idiotic ball that Alva Vanderbilt is planning, at God knows what cost to poor Willie. My darling obviously would give her soul to be invited and wants me, even from this distance, to manage to get her there; adorned, no doubt, like Cinderella in some astonishing gown for which Lanouette will triple-charge her. I've decided to write Ted DeLancey to ask the favor. He and his wife go everywhere; indeed one wonders when the good rector has time to compose his sermons. And they could take her along.

This morning, we unearthed a bronze mirror, nearly intact, with a figure of Eros at its base. A great excitement.

Chanler was mesmerized by the journal. Here were the people only hinted at in the public records, only summarized in the microfiche of old newspapers where he had first searched for the facts behind the painting of Diana. He read on, page after page of the dead man's diary, finding among the lists of Attic amphora fragments, DeWitt's poignant expressions of love for his wife.

Then near the end of the entries, Chanler came to a page that stopped him cold. He read it several times. The sun had gone down, and his burn was chilling him in the cooler air. What he read suddenly changed everything.

After hurriedly dressing, Chanler got out the little daguerreotype of Mrs. Rawlings that Tugger had given him at the airport and took it to the ship's library where he'd noticed a magnifying glass beside a globe. With the magnifier, he carefully examined the sepia figure of Diana Rawlings in her ballgown. Chanler had guessed right. She was wearing the bracelet at the ball.

He had caught Diana Rawlings in a lie that would have convicted her of murder. At the inquest that followed her husband's death, Mrs. Rawlings had testified that she'd had no idea that DeWitt's ship had already docked before she left for the Vanderbilt ball. Nor, she had sworn, had he come to their Fifth Avenue townhouse at any time while she was away attending the ball.

She said she assumed that DeWitt had gone straight from the pier to their country home, where he must have somehow fallen to his death during the night. She said it was not until the police officers arrived the next morning with news of his accident that she had had any idea that her husband was not still abroad.

But DeWitt had been inside the Fifth Avenue house with Diana before she left for the ball. And Chanler could prove it.

He hurried to the bridge and asked the captain a question: would it be possible to verify a specific piece of historical maritime information? Was there a way to find out if the time listed for a ship's docking in New York harbor on a certain day in 1883 was the scheduled time, or the actual time? Yes, the captain thought it would be possible to assist Chanler, who was staying in the most expensive suite on the cruise. In fact, it took only fifteen minutes on the computer to learn that the 1883 ship in question had actually arrived three hours *ahead* of schedule.

With the computer printout, Chanler hurried back along the hallway to their suite. The predicted rain was blowing in, the seas swelling, and he had to catch his balance against the bulkhead as he went. As he came around a corner, he saw a dark-haired man heading into the elevator. Two women getting off it turned back to look at the man; for an instant Chanler had the oddest sensation that he recognized the back of the man's head.

Back in his stateroom, he placed a ship-to-shore call to New York, to Tugger Whitelaw. He'd forgotten the time change and he waked Tugger out of a deep sleep. There was a great deal of static on the line. Chanler said he needed Tugger to check something out for him about Diana Rawlings. About the investigation into whether or not she'd killed her husband. Tugger was happy to do it. They set a lunch date at the Parnassus Club—just the two of them—as soon as the Swaines returned from their cruise next week.

Chanler asked how Mark was doing. Tugger said he hadn't seen their friend lately; someone at the club had mentioned that Mark was on vacation somewhere. Tugger admitted that he and

Mark hadn't even really spoken since Chanler's wedding. "We had sort of a falling out."

"Oh?" Chanler said. "About what?"

"About Mattie, to tell you the truth," Tugger blurted out.

Chanler said he didn't want to hear any more insinuations about his wife.

"Channie, I'm sorry, but I'm going to tell you this one thing about that bracelet of hers and I don't care if you want to hear it or not." Tugger had to talk over Chanler's objections but he managed to say what he'd learned only a few days ago about Mattie's bracelet. "I can show you the letter Tiffany's sent me," he ended.

There was a long pause. Then finally Chanler said softly, "Well, they're wrong."

Tugger said, "No they're not. If Tiffany's doesn't know, who does? You ought to stop focusing so much on what Diana Rawlings did a hundred years ago and concentrate on what your own wife's doing right now."

Chanler asked Tugger to fax him the letter from Tiffany's to the ship. He gave him a number. Then the storm suddenly cut the connection and the operator wasn't able to get through again.

Chanler sat on the bed, trying to decide what to say to Mattie. In the end, he decided to say nothing.

•　•　•

An hour later, when Mattie finally returned from the spa, Chanler was still seated on the bed in his khakis and T-shirt, still looking at the Rawlings journal.

"I guess you like your present," she said.

"Yes. Thank you," he said, staring up at her through his round glasses. "Did you read it?"

"Glanced at it," she said, coming close. "Pretty boring. Why aren't you in your tux?"

Chanler held up the diary. "It's not boring. Diana lied at DeWitt's inquest. I can prove it."

She leaned over, took off his glasses, kissed him. "You know, Mark was right. You're kind of nuts on the subject of my family."

He put the glasses back. "And I know why she lied."

Mattie was looking at herself in the mirror. "Why?"

"Because she murdered her husband. I'm sure now."

Mattie's head pulled quickly back. "Oh Channie, come on, not that again you don't know that..."

"Yes, I do. Now I do. Diana Rawlings killed your great-grandfather." He took a long breath. "If that's who he was."

Mattie turned and stared at him with that strange, straight-on look that was so like the look of Mrs. Rawlings in the painting. "What's that supposed to mean?" He didn't answer her and finally she shook her head. "First you're madly in love with Diana Rawlings. Now she's a murderer. And the truth is she's just a painting." Slowly Mattie smiled and shrugged. "Okay. So what convinced you she killed him? Tell me while we get dressed."

Chanler followed Mattie to their bedroom. "Dewitt found out she was having an affair."

Mattie picked a red dress from the closet. "Oh?...Who with?"

"Jacob Zanski."

"Who?" Mattie sat at the vanity, began applying make-up.

"The portrait painter. Remember?"

"...Oh, right. The painter."

"Yes. Jacob Zanski. They were lovers. Listen to this." And sitting on the bed, Chanler read to her from DeWitt's journal.

I cannot shake off Corinne's—["That's DeWitt's older sister," Chanler explained]—disturbing letter. Her distasteful innuendoes about Diana and this Zanski fellow....Why shouldn't she walk with Zanski in the park, or picnic with him by the lake for that matter? But Corinne cannot bear the thought that the bulk of father's estate should go to Diana, or to our children should we have any. I've written my sister to keep her base suspicions to herself.

Mattie looked into her vanity mirror, at Chanler standing behind her. "That's it?" she frowned. Both spoke to their reflections in the glass. "That's your proof? All that means is DeWitt's sister tried to make him *think* Diana was having an affair. It doesn't mean she was. Heaven's sake, why shouldn't they picnic in the damn park? And even if she was sleeping with the painter, so what?"

Chanler looked in the mirror. "Well, she'd been married less than a year."

"You know what I mean, honey." Mattie handed Chanler the pearls his mother had given her the night before the wedding. He fastened the clasp. "How do you get from that to she murdered him?"

Chanler held up the journal. "Because of this. Listen. 'This evening in a shop in the Plaka, I found the most extraordinary bracelet, rubies set in twists of gold. Very Byzantine.'" Chanler paused, looked up at her. "Your bracelet, Mattie, the one you lost at our reception, right?" He read again. "'The shopkeeper, a fat, keen-eyed woman absurdly claiming direct descent from Agamemnon, soon had me at her mercy, and I bought the bracelet for Diana. So I've said my good-byes at the site—Trimmer was so kind as to be disappointed—and we sail in the morning. My return should put a stop to Corinne's gossip. I'll take Diana to Alva and Willie Vanderbilt's party myself." Chanler straightened his glasses, looked at Mattie.

Mattie shrugged at the mirror. "I guess I don't get your point."

His mild gray eyes moved down the line of her perfect neck to the white cream of her shoulder. "You don't? Remember, Diana told everyone she didn't even know that DeWitt had returned to the States before she went to the Vanderbilt ball. But she had to know because he'd brought her the ruby bracelet from Greece. You see? And she wore it the night of the ball. That means she had to have seen him before she left for the ball."

Mattie reminded Chanler that he'd told her himself that the portrait of Mrs. Rawlings as Dido at the Vanderbilt ball had been painted a whole year after the event. No doubt someone had found the bracelet in DeWitt's effects, had given it to his widow and she'd added it to her costume whenever she'd sat for the painting. Perhaps she'd done it as a sentimental tribute to her dead husband.

Chanler shook his head. "No. She wore it to Alva Vanderbilt's ball."

"How do you know?"

"Tugger."

Mattie turned impatiently away. "Oh, honey, great. Tugger."

Chanler then showed Mattie the daguerreotype of Mrs. Rawlings taken at the Vanderbilt ball, the gift from Tugger that she had not yet seen. He pointed out the bracelet clearly visible on Diana's wrist.

She frowned angrily. "Tugger gave this picture to you at the airport? Why didn't you show it to me?"

Chanler made a gesture of apology; he said he hadn't wished to remind her of the unpleasantness between her and his friend by mentioning Tugger at all. Slowly Chanler took out his dress suit. "I have a theory about *how* she killed him." He watched as Mattie slipped on the red dress.

She turned for Chanler to do her zipper. "You'll have to tell me later," she said. "We're going to be late to dinner."

While Chanler was in the bathroom, the phone rang; from the other room, Mattie told him to go ahead and shower, she'd answer it. When he returned, she was perfectly made-up and waiting serenely. She said the phone had just been their steward, reminding them that they were to go to the captain's table.

At dinner, Mattie was at her most charming and Chanler was congratulated on his marriage to so engaging a young woman. "Thank you," he said to the ambassador's wife on his right. "I was in love with her before I even met her. Wasn't I, darling? In love with your ghost?" he said across the table to Mattie.

Mattie smiled at him. "Don't be spooky, darling."

She left the table soon after that, saying she thought she'd go to the casino for a while alone; she knew Chanler didn't like gambling. Why didn't he join the bridge players and she'd meet him there?

When she found him in the card room an hour or so later, she suggested they have a nightcap in the Perseus Lounge at the stern of the ship. There were rarely many people there this late, and she loved listening to Chanler play his romantic old songs on the white baby grand.

They stayed until after the bar closed. Even before that, the storm had driven the other passengers back to their cabins. Waves sprayed the decks outside and wind rattled the glass windows and doors. Although Mattie was cold, she didn't want to leave; she draped Chanler's tuxedo jacket over her shoulders. She kept filling his champagne glass as she asked him questions about why he was so sure Diana Rawlings had murdered her husband. It was a subject he couldn't resist.

He told her that he'd studied Diana's history for a year and he was sure that she was having an affair with the man who'd painted her portrait; in fact Chanler suspected she'd been lovers with Zanski *before* she married DeWitt Rawlings. The painter's studio was across the street from the milliner's shop in which Diana had worked until she'd met and married DeWitt so that, with his money and his name, she could make not only her own way in society but her artist lover's way as well. Zanski had talent but no money or social position. Diana wanted both.

But things went wrong. First, DeWitt's sister Corinne saw the lovers together and wrote to her brother about it. Worse, Diana found out she was pregnant. She knew that if anyone calculated carefully enough (as apparently no one ever did, not until Chanler worked out the arithmetic a hundred years later), it would be clear that she'd conceived while her husband was inconveniently on the other side of the Atlantic at his archeological dig. It would be clear that the child was Zanski's, not Rawlings's.

Still, Chanler said, DeWitt was so deeply enamored with Diana that she might have somehow managed to squirm out of her dilemma. But something catastrophic happened the night of the Vanderbilt ball. The betrayed husband arrived back in New York too soon and was confronted with evidence even he could no longer ignore.

Chanler showed Mattie the computer printout showing that DeWitt's ship had docked in the New York harbor on March 26, 1883, a good six hours before Diana would have left with the DeLanceys to walk around the corner to the Vanderbilts on 52nd Street.

"And that means?" asked Mattie, pouring him more champagne.

"That means DeWitt came home completely unexpected and caught Zanski and Diana in bed together, or doing *something* together that a husband couldn't pretend was something else. Something that meant his sister Corinne was right. Something that meant divorce."

Mattie jumped as the wind slapped open one of the glass doors to the bar observation deck, sucking the flapping curtains out into the rain. Chanler had to throw himself against the door to get it closed. He was, he told her, a little drunk, and he suddenly felt very sleepy. He suggested they go back to their cabin.

"First finish your story," Mattie smiled. "It's fascinating. So DeWitt came home that night, and saw the lovers together?"

Removing his glasses to rub his eyes, Chanler nodded. "Okay. Here's my theory. DeWitt confronted them and Zanski left the room. DeWitt made it clear the marriage was over. Maybe he lost his temper and flung that ruby bracelet at her. Diana saw herself losing everything. Social position. Wealth. A future for herself, for her unborn child, Zanski's child. I think she made her decision quickly. Her best hope was if no one ever knew Dewitt had been there. Either the servants weren't at home or she avoided them or she bribed them. She pushed her husband down the stairs, or hit him with something."

Mattie nodded. "Why? To stop the divorce?"

"To stop everything the divorce would cost her."

Mattie stared out at the black night. The wind smashed a deck chair against the glass, startling them. "And then what?" she asked. "Diana picks up his body, hails a hansom cab, hauls him out to their country house, and tosses him off the balcony? Then hurries back and dresses for the ball? Oh, honey, come on!"

Chanler smiled at his wife sadly. "No, I think Jacob Zanski did all the dirty work for her. I think Zanski took care of it while she put on her gold gown, sprinkled rubies in her hair, and set out with Reverend and Mrs. DeLancey to the Vanderbilts' ball. Funny, if she hadn't been so vain that she couldn't resist wearing the Greek bracelet, her secret might have been safe forever."

Mattie laughed. "Sweetheart, sometimes I think Diana Rawlings' life is more interesting to you than your own." She yawned, turned the empty champagne bottle upside down in its bucket. "So she steps over her husband's body and heads off to the Vanderbilts. Pretty gutsy lady."

"Very gutsy lady," Chanler agreed.

Mattie ruffled his hair. "That invitation to the ball must have meant a lot to her. You never wanted anything that much, did you?"

He looked at her solemnly. "Except you."

"Darling, you've got me." She showed him the channel-set, multiple-carat diamond wedding ring that they'd bought at Tiffany's. "Poor Diana, you think she *enjoyed* the Vanderbilt ball after all that?"

Chanler said he thought that Diana Rawlings had enjoyed it greatly and that after her triumph, she had returned to her town-house at dawn and calmly waited there to be brought the shocking news of her husband's death in the country. Of course, questions were raised, rumors of adultery were bruited about. But in the end, DeWitt's death was ruled an unfortunate accident. And in the end, despite Corinne Rawlings's long legal battle to contest her brother's will, Diana and her newborn baby, DeWitt Rawlings II, inherited everything. Diana never married Jacob Zanski. Their son never knew his father was not a Rawlings but an immigrant portrait painter. Maybe the lovers didn't dare risk marriage. Or maybe their passion was killed by the murder they concealed. Maybe it just wore itself out.

"And that," concluded Chanler, unsteadily rising to his feet, "is the end of the story. Mrs. Rawlings died in her bed, a grande dame of ninety. Her grandson DeWitt III lost most of the family fortune in the '29 crash. His son DeWitt IV drank away the rest."

"My dad."

"So you tell me." Chanler loosened his tie.

She turned to him. "You keep making these pointed remarks. I have the feeling we're talking about something we're not talking about, Chanler. But then, that is your style."

Chanler made his way to the curved glass of the stern, looked out at the storm waves spuming over the rail. He thought he saw the shape of a man on the observation deck behind some cable housing, but it made no sense that anyone would be out in that kind of weather, and when he looked again whatever he'd seen was gone.

Mattie asked him, "Does it change how you feel about your beloved Mrs. Rawlings, now that you've proved she's a killer."

Chanler turned, his eyes on hers. "No, it doesn't change a thing. Funny."

Mattie said. "Everybody's dead. The money's gone. I didn't inherit a cent."

"You certainly didn't. Just the bracelet. And you lost that." He waited for her to say something, but she just looked at him with a strange focused stillness, like a cat's. Finally, he added, "Here's something else that's funny, Mattie. Zanski died in his early forties. In his will, he left a dozen paintings 'to his son.' But since he didn't have a son, as far as anybody knew, and since Diana certainly wasn't about to admit that her little boy was Zanski's heir, all the paintings went to some distant Polish cousin. You know how much the last Zanski portrait sold for at Sotheby's?"

She shook her head impatiently.

"Three and a half million dollars," Chanler replied. "Actually, I thought you would know, since you work there and I got that figure from a Sotheby's catalogue in your apartment."

She shrugged. "I guess it didn't really register. Three and a half million?"

Chanler nodded. "And yet he was so poor that Diana wouldn't marry him. Ironic."

Mattie smiled. "Maybe I ought to get in touch with the Zanskis then."

"Wasn't that your whole idea?" Chanler staggered slightly when he took back the tuxedo jacket she held out; he'd drunk more champagne than he was used to. "You knew you'd have to be a Rawlings to be a Zanski."

"Chanler, I don't know what you're talking about."

He smiled at her. "Sure you do. I'm not an idiot, Mattie, I just love you."

"You're drunk and very silly." She moved against him, pulled him against the glass door, kissed him. She said, "I'm going back to the casino. Don't wait up." He took her arm, feeling suddenly queasy and fell back into his seat. "Get some fresh air." Handing him the tuxedo jacket he'd dropped, she helped him tug the glass door open. But she didn't follow him onto the observation deck. She went to the casino where she was unusually lucky; a crowd gathered to watch her win.

• • •

Early the next morning, the storm was behind them. Soon after they docked in Santorini, a horrified Mattie frantically called the steward. She couldn't find her husband anywhere!

She said she'd left him the night before in the Perseus Lounge. She'd assumed he was still in the lounge when she'd returned from the casino. As she'd felt a little seasick, she'd taken a sedative and quickly fallen asleep. When she awoke in the morning and didn't see him, she assumed he'd already gone down for breakfast, perhaps even gone into Santorini for a walk. But he wasn't in the dining room and no tenders had yet left the disembarking station for shore. Besides, his boarding pass was on the bureau, and why would he leave without it? She told the steward that she was growing alarmed. There were no traces of her husband's having come back to their suite last night at all.

They paged Chanler. They searched everywhere through twelve decks and fifteen hundred passengers. They couldn't find him. They interviewed the morning bartender in the Perseus Lounge who said he had found an empty bottle of champagne overturned in an ice bucket and had noticed wet curtains caught in the starboard door to the observation deck. Perhaps Mr. Swaine had gone out on the deck in the storm. They sent out radio messages to all other ships in the vicinity. No one had rescued a passenger fallen overboard.

A solemn captain, accompanied by the ship's doctor, spoke with young Mrs. Swaine. It distressed the captain deeply to have to ask her whether there was any reason her husband might decide to take his own life. He said the steward had told him that last night Mrs. Swaine was talking with a stranger at their suite door when the steward had given her a fax sent to Mr. Swaine from the States. The captain wondered if perhaps the fax might have had something in it that upset Mr. Swaine enough to cause him to "do something rash." Mrs. Swaine said that wasn't possible. Yes, she had returned to their suite for casino chips that she'd left in their safe and, yes, a fellow passenger had been there asking her directions when the steward came by and gave her a fax. But the fax had been completely insignificant; an insurance matter about a lost bracelet. She'd given the fax to Channie in the bar. Stricken, indignant, she dismissed the possibility of suicide.

Other first-class passengers assured the honeymooning bride that their prayers were with her, that surely her husband would show up safe and sound. The ambassador's wife was particularly solicitous, recalling Chanler's romantic comment about how he'd been in love with his wife before he'd even met her.

• • •

At three that afternoon, one of the crew found Chanler's tuxedo jacket, still soaking wet, in a heap caught under a bulkhead, near the rail on the observation deck. They found blood stains on the cable housing. At dusk, the Santorini police arrived with a man's patent leather dress shoe that had washed ashore. Mattie identified it as Chanler's.

The captain felt he should prepare Mrs. Swaine for the probability that her husband—after drinking more than customary—had walked out on deck for a breath of fresh air, tripped, fell, and hit his head on the cable housing, disorienting himself. It appeared that he had recklessly climbed up on a railing (despite the posted warnings) and, losing his balance in the rough weather, had fallen overboard. His cries unheard, he had been swept away to his death. Mrs. Swaine began to shake violently; the ship's doctor offered her tranquilizers, but she declined them. The captain said the ship had to set sail for its next port. The Santorini police bowed and disembarked.

Chanler's mother took the next plane to Athens and a helicopter took Mattie from the ship to join her. She and Mattie were a comfort to each other; after a week, they were forced to accept the verdict of the Greek police that Chanler was dead. His mother's only consolation was that her son's wife was pregnant with his child. She was very solicitous of Mattie, terrified that she would miscarry in her grief.

Mattie phoned Chanler's best friend Tugger Whitelaw to tell him the news and to ask him to speak at Chanler's memorial service. As soon as she hung up, Tugger called a friend at his firm who specialized in criminal law. This friend gave him the name of a homicide detective.

•   •   •

Two months after Chanler's memorial service, a good-looking young man from Queens paid a call on the young widowed Mrs. Swaine at her townhouse in the East Fifties. Mattie found him waiting for her in the living room, looking at her portrait in the gold BGC gown. The picture hung over the marble mantel, where Chanler's mother had placed it as a surprise gift for Chanler on his return.

Detective Eisenberg said the painting was a good likeness of Mattie. He was sorry to bother her—she didn't look well—but would she mind a few questions? She asked what the questions would be about?

The detective felt it only fair to tell her that certain accusations had been made by a Mr. Timothy Whitelaw.

Mattie looked at him calmly. About what?

Accusations that Chanler's death was not an accident, the detective answered. And that Mattie was involved in that death.

Mattie confessed that she was surprised to hear this. She knew that Tugger had never particularly liked her, perhaps resented her taking Chanler away from him. He'd made no secret of his opposition to the marriage. But as Mr. Whitelaw had been three thousand miles away from the site of her husband's drowning, she hardly thought he could have anything relevant to say about it.

Probably not, Detective Eisenberg agreed. But he guessed Mrs. Swaine knew how it was, how the system made them check things out, even things that probably weren't useful.

Mattie understood the detective's problem. How could she help?

First, the policeman wondered if Mrs. Swaine could tell him a little about her background, for example, where she and her father DeWitt Rawlings IV had lived in New Orleans, where she'd gone to school, when had she first come to New York?

Mattie noted that she couldn't see the point in these questions, but she answered pleasantly, if briefly and perhaps a little vaguely. Then she said she was still under an emotional strain and not feeling well (she was pregnant) and she hoped Mr. Eisenberg would excuse her.

"No problem," he said blandly. "I just got a couple more things here."

Mattie politely sat back down.

He looked at her a long while. Then he said, "Tell me about your relationship with Mark Toral."

She looked back at him for as long a time. Then she shrugged. "Mark and I dated casually, years ago. Nothing serious."

"I meant, since your marriage?"

She stood up. "I don't care for the insinuation, Mr. Eisenberg."

He cocked his head, studied her. "What insinuation?"

"Don't be coy. I assume you heard this from Tugger Whitelaw. I haven't seen Mark Toral since my wedding day."

Eisenberg looked from her to the painting over the mantel. "You sure?"

"Of course I'm sure."

"Hmmm. See, Mr. Toral is kinda telling us something different. He's in custody, I guess I didn't mention that."

Mrs. Swaine blinked just once. Then she said that she didn't care what Mr. Toral might or might not be telling them.

"Why not?" asked Eisenberg. "I sure would be curious in your shoes." He stood, rummaging through his jacket pockets until he found a plastic baggie with a police seal on it. Mattie's face stayed perfectly still as he carefully pulled out the bracelet of rubies twisted in gold and showed it to her. "Mr. Whitelaw found this bracelet of yours at your wedding reception." Eisenberg pointed at the BGC portrait of Mattie over the mantel, where the same bracelet circled her perfect white wrist.

Mattie reached for the jewelry. "Found it? He stole it. If he'd found it, why didn't he return it to me."

Detective Eisenberg shrugged. "You got a point. He admits he wanted it real bad. He had an idea about it. Maybe," he said, "you could help me out with that idea. Mr. Whitelaw says—"

She interrupted him. "That the bracelet is a fake." She looked directly at him, poised, waiting. "Is that the idea? Yes, it's a fake."

Detective Eisenberg seemed to lose his bearings for a moment, not expecting her admission. He said, "You told folks this was a bracelet your dad had inherited from some turn-of-the-century lady named Diana Rawlings? Right?"

"Yes."

"But that wasn't true?"

"No, it wasn't." She waited calmly.

Eisenberg took back the bracelet. "Mr. Whitelaw's appraiser at Tiffany's claims it's only a couple of years old. And it's paste."

"Quite possibly." Mattie looked at the young policeman coolly. Finally she said, "So?"

"So," he smiled. "Well, then you know my problem."

"No, I don't. What has this got to do with Chanler's drowning?"

"I've had lot of talks with your friend Mark and he says he was on that honeymoon ship with you and your husband, and far as he was concerned, three was a crowd."

"Are you accusing me of something specific, Mr. Eisenberg?"

"How 'bout telling me what's your real name?"

"My real name is Mrs. Chanler Swaine," she replied.

"Yeah." He nodded at her slowly. "I guess that's true."

Mattie walked to the door. "I think I'll call my attorney. Would you excuse me a minute?"

"Take your time." He sat back down, facing the portrait. "I'm not going anyplace."

•   •   •

In the end, only the murder of Chanler was a crime and Mark Toral confessed to that before his lawyer could stop him. Afterwards, visiting him in prison, Tugger told Mark that he should have known from his love of film noir that he didn't have anywhere near the nerves of Mattie Rawlings Swaine—born Madeline Gart—and that she would throw him over to save herself.

Mark swore that Mattie was innocent and she agreed with him. She confessed to a number of things that weren't crimes, but she denied having the slightest knowledge of Chanler's murder, either before or after the fact. When they charged her with homicide anyhow, her lawyer arranged for her to be tried separately.

Throughout her ordeal, the BGC crowd of Chanler's many friends stood by Mattie. She asked them to forgive Tugger's animosity to her; after all, he'd lost his best friend and was irrational from grief. She could understand it; she was grief-stricken herself.

During the trial—Mattie's preceded Mark's—the elderly Mrs. Swaine never left her daughter-in-law's side; all her resources, both financial and social, were at Mattie's disposal. What else had Mrs. Swaine to live for? She had lost her only child. Mattie carried her only grandchild. By the time that opening arguments began, Mattie was seven month's pregnant. She wore sedate black maternity clothes and sat like a Madonna in the courtroom. "You look fantastic," her lawyer told her.

"The Honeymoon Murder Trial," the papers called it. Tugger sat in court day after day, taking notes. He was in the front row when Mattie was called to the stand. According to the State, Madeline Gart was a con artist, not so pure and never simple. Her plan to bilk the Jacob Zanski estate had been set up for over a year when she replaced it with an even more daring plan to seduce the wealthy Mr. Swaine. The prosecutor said that's the thing about the most successful hustlers; they have qualities not often combined in the same personality—both a ruthless patience and an imperturbable spontaneity. The way he put it was, "Wait like a snake, strike like a snake."

According to the prosecution, Mattie had met Mark at a cigar and martini club in New Orleans and had started an affair with him. Mark had just been let go from his job in his uncle's brokerage firm for urging clients to buy a great deal of stock in a friend's IPO that he was sure was going to double. It didn't.

Mattie worked at a shop in the French Quarter, selling to naïve millionaires in search of heritage overpriced antiquarian prints and autographs, many of them forged, some of them forged by her. She had a knack for such things.

A lonely alcoholic in his late sixties, DeWitt Rawlings IV, came into Mattie's store one day to sell off little bits of his past, just enough to allow him to finish drinking himself to death. It was from this last of the Rawlings that Mattie learned how amazingly she resembled the portrait of his grandmother Diana. He said the painting was hanging on the wall of a place called the Parnassus Club in New York City and she should go look at it someday. Rawlings asked Mattie out for a drink and, sensing something big yet undefined in this connection, she said yes.

The broken man developed a crush on her. It was in part infatuation with a younger woman, in part dependency on the strong, and in part the lonely desire for a daughter. Mark was jealous of the time Mattie was spending with Rawlings. His jealousy was such a problem that she broke up with him. He didn't take it well. He came banging late at night on the door of her apartment until finally she had a neighbor threaten him with the police. She refused to answer his calls when he tried to apologize. Mark started drinking and lost his job. He begged Mattie to move to New York with him. She said no.

Mattie had another plan. She was listening for hours to all the stories DeWitt could tell her about his formerly grand family, including the old rumors about Diana's affair with the famous painter Jacob Zanski. One day DeWitt brought Mattie his grandfather's "Mediterranean journal." She had read it carefully, not for any clues implicating Mrs. Rawlings in a murder; that hadn't interested her. What interested her was the fact that Mrs. Rawlings had slept with Jacob Zanski.

Mattie devised a beautiful con game: if she could "prove" that Diana's son DeWitt Rawlings II was really the only son of Jacob Zanski and if she could "prove" that she, Mattie, was the only child of DeWitt Rawlings IV, then Mattie would be the only direct descendant of Jacob Zanski, in line to inherit, not Rawlings money (there wasn't any), but Zanski money (there was a lot). The irony appealed to her: while the great Rawlings family had dwindled into pathetic shabbiness, the heirs of the poor Jewish immigrant Zanski were millionaires. There were dozens of Zanski portraits still in the family's hands and those paintings were worth a fortune.

The alcoholic Rawlings grew more and more dependent on Mattie in his last months; she was very sweet to him, she was his only visitor and she had many pictures taken of them together. She made herself at home in his shabby rooms and as he slept she poured over his letters, photos, all his little mementos. The day he died, she took everything she wanted away with her. Why not? She was in a way his only heir.

According to the prosecution (and although they didn't know it, Chanler Swaine had come to the same conclusion the night he died), Mattie set out to become a Zanski by claiming to be the dead Rawlings' daughter; she worked on her plan patiently for over a year, forging all the necessary legal documents and personal letters that she needed to make her case.

And here—as the prosecutor said in his summation—here's the thing about brilliant con artists like Madeline Gart. After all that patient work to bring her suit as the true Zanski heir, she dropped the whole plan. Why?

Because something better came along, simpler and quicker, something much less risky than prolonged legal maneuvering. That something was Chanler Swaine.

By this time, Mark Toral was working in New York, but he hadn't forgotten Mattie. He telephoned her, he sent her roses, he told her things were going great: a Yale friend (Chanler) had helped him secure a position in one of the best banks in Manhattan. Mark wanted Mattie to leave New Orleans, come up North, and marry him. She didn't say yes, but she didn't hang up.

When Mark flew her to New York to visit him, he happened to mention his wealthy friend Chanler's peculiar obsession with the painting of Diana Rawlings in the Parnassus Club, which Mark was now joining. He mentioned it to Mattie because she'd once told him that she was supposed to resemble a picture in the club. Mark and Mattie went to study the painting. She certainly did resemble Diana. It was amazing.

The next day, to Mark's delight, she told him she had decided to move to New York and give their relationship a try. She found a job at Sotheby's. (Her recommendations—most of them forged—were impressive.) She and Mark resumed their affair. Although she refused to live with him, they went out nearly every night; they shared expensive tastes, including a reckless habit of betting extravagantly on long-shot horses. Soon, Mark was playing the market to try to cover his credit card debt. The debt grew.

It was when Mark's financial troubles were near crisis that Mattie announced to him that she had a plan. It was a simple one. It would be easy for Mark to introduce Chanler Swaine to Mattie "Rawlings." Chanler's bizarre infatuation with the portrait of Diana and Mattie's uncanny resemblance would do the rest. Mattie would seduce and marry Chanler, then divorce him. She would have half his assets and, after a decent interval, return to Mark.

Mark didn't like the part that involved her marrying Chanler, but by now he would do anything Mattie asked him.

She had Mark bring her back to the Parnassus Club where she studied the portrait of Diana Rawlings carefully and took a close-up photograph of the bracelet in order to have a cheap copy made. She wore the bracelet to meet Chanler Swaine. Chanler was smitten the moment he saw her. The rest, said the prosecutor, was as easy as Mattie had predicted: eventually Chanler proposed. Eventually she accepted. She rushed nothing. She thought of everything. At first she had only two small problems: Tugger's suspicions and Mark's jealousy. Then she ran into a very big problem. Chanler's mother explained to her at the wedding that Chanler didn't control his own money and that Mattie would get nothing if she divorced him, or if she was caught out in an affair and was divorced by him.

Now—claimed the prosecutor—Mattie needed to maneuver her lover Mark Toral into killing her husband for her. She began by telling Mark at the reception that she was going to try to make the marriage to Chanler work. That their affair was over. As she expected, Mark flew into a rage.

When Mattie left with Chanler on their honeymoon, a tormented Mark began calling their ship, and when Mattie wouldn't talk to him, he flew to Athens. According to his own confession, he began tracking the cruise, searching for Mattie at the ports of call. Finally, at Mykonos, Mattie agreed to meet him, which she did by taking a "shopping trip" without Chanler. At that meeting, she told Mark that he had to leave her alone. Chanler had grown suspicious; they couldn't risk being together again. Not ever. It was over. Then she kissed him. And she kissed him again. How, she whispered, could she ever give him up? She loved him. She gave Mark Chanler's boarding pass so he could slip onto the ship and they could meet secretly that night and they could get rid of Chanler.

According to the prosecutor, Mattie knew exactly what she was doing the night of the murder. With his jealousy heated to a boil, Mark waited in the corridor until she returned alone to the suite while Chanler was off playing bridge. (Both the steward who'd brought the fax and a woman passenger identified Mark from a photograph as a man they'd seen on the ship; he had always been so handsome that people noticed him.) Mark and Mattie made love and then Mattie went to the card room to get Chanler, telling him she'd just come from the casino.

The only question, of course, was whether Mattie knew that Mark was hiding out on the stern deck when she took Chanler to the deserted Perseus Lounge. Did she deliberately get Chanler drunk and lure him out onto the storm-swept deck? There was no question about the fact that Mark had struck Chanler on the head and shoved him over the railing, then had sneaked off the ship with the early morning crowd headed for the Santorini shops. There was no question because Mark had admitted the crime to Detective Eisenberg.

The prosecutor told the jury not to let Mattie con them the way she'd conned both Chanler and Mark and God knows how many other men.

Of course when their turn came, young Mrs. Swaine's defense team put a very different construction on the matter. They told the jury not to listen to the prosecutor's "sick and libelous fantasy." Poor Mrs. Swaine was the victim here, not the villain. The victim of her woman's loving heart. In their version, Mattie had been a simple hard-working young woman seduced by a good-looking sophisticate (Mark) into playing a prank, a practical joke, on Mark's friend Chanler Swaine. It was Mark who had talked her into pretending to be descended from Diana Rawlings. It was Mark who'd had the copy of the bracelet made out of paste. Wasn't it Mark's name on the Tiffany receipt Tugger Whitelaw had tracked down?

In the defense version, it was during the playing of this prank that Mattie had unexpectedly fallen in love with Chanler and so had broken off with Mark. But she'd been too ashamed to confess her original lie, and so had allowed Chanler to go on believing she was a Rawlings. Because of her guilt, she'd tried over and over to say no to his marriage proposals, feeling unworthy of him, but she'd loved him so much that finally she couldn't give up her chance at happiness. Mattie cried during cross-examination when she begged the prosecutor not to torture her with his accusations. She had loved Chanler with all her heart. Her defense attorney told her afterwards, "You're fantastic. Best I ever saw on the stand."

Mattie told the jury it wasn't her fault that Mark wouldn't give her up. It wasn't her fault that he'd caused such a scene at her wedding that she'd had to ask him to leave. It wasn't her fault, and it certainly wasn't her doing, that Mark had followed her to Greece and somehow sneaked aboard the ship in Santorini. How could she know that Mark's violent obsession with her would lead him to murder her husband? Mattie broke down weeping, left the stand, and was embraced by her mother-in-law who sat behind her.

The jury felt sorry for Mattie, just as the defense advised them to do. There the poor young widow sat, after all, so pregnant with her dead husband's baby. After some hours of deliberation, they found Mattie not guilty. Naturally it helped a great deal that Mark would not testify against her. Tugger had never been able to get him to see that Mattie had used him. Mark still seemed to think that he and Mattie were in love.

A free (and wealthy) woman, Mattie walked out of the courtroom. She paused to look at Tugger, who turned his back on her.

A few days later, in a separate trial, Mark was sentenced to ten years in prison for second-degree murder. It was a good deal for the state; there were, after all, no witnesses, no real evidence, no corpse. Mark's jury didn't believe he'd premeditated the murder. They thought he'd done it on the spur of the moment, driven to the act by his jealousy over Mattie. In fact, part of the reason nobody believed Mattie and Mark had plotted Chanler's murder was that nobody believed Mark would murder for money. He had the looks of a man who'd murder for love.

• • •

Mattie moved into the Swaine townhouse with her mother-in-law, and sold her own. Sadly, the elder Mrs. Swaine, broken by grief, died of a sudden stroke only a year after the birth of the grandchild she'd been living for. The baby was a boy, with very black hair and very blue eyes. The following Christmas, Tugger visited his old friend Mark at the prison. Mark hadn't heard about the birth of Mattie's baby. In fact, Mark admitted, Mattie hadn't kept in touch. But he guessed she had to stay away to avoid suspicion. He grew upset when Tugger told him how much the little boy looked like him.

Around that time, Tugger married the young woman he'd known back in his hometown and moved down to Charleston to work in his father's law firm. Occasionally they came to New York and he visited his Parnassus Club friends, but Nancy didn't really feel comfortable with the old group and slowly Tugger drifted away as well.

But one autumn when they came to New York, Tugger took his wife to eat at the Club and, on their way out, he ran into Mattie. She was now married to a man Tugger knew from college named Bradhook, one of the old group, one of the wealthiest. During the trial, this young man had been a staunch supporter of Mattie's innocence, absolutely sure that she had had nothing to do with Mark's "craziness." Indeed Bradhook had broken with Tugger over the latter's "attacks" on Mattie and they'd stopped seeing each other. She and Bradhook were in the club hosting the dinner to plan the upcoming Ball for a Good Cause.

Tugger, seeing Mattie, walked his wife past the BGC table without speaking to anyone. But to his surprise, Mattie called out, "Tugger Whitelaw!" and he had to stop. Everyone said hello to him as if nothing had happened, as if Chanler weren't dead and Mark weren't in prison. They said hello to Tugger's bride and began to tell her stories about him. While this was happening, Mattie asked Tugger to walk with her into the bar. "You're look-ing good," she said. "Marriage agrees with you."

"I've lost weight," Tugger said. "You look good too. All your marriages agree with you. How's little Chanler Junior?"

"Fine. Terrible twos."

"Probably has Mark's temper," Tugger said.

She looked at him coolly.

"You oughta go see Mark, Mattie. I mean, after all, he killed

Channie for you. It's the least you could do."

She smiled at him. "You ever going to give this up, Tugger?"

He shook his head at her. "No."

It was a diamond bracelet that Mattie now wore. It looked real, and no doubt (unlike the ruby bracelet), this one was. She pointed at the club's painting of Diana Rawlings, the painting that had started it all. "You remember that fax you sent Chanler on the ship, proving how I'd faked Diana Rawlings' bracelet? I'm just wondering, had you already told him about it before you sent the fax?"

Tugger looked at her, surprised she'd bring it up. "Yes. He called me that night."

"I thought so." She nodded. "He was acting funny."

Tugger shook his head. "Is that why you had him murdered? He'd found out the truth about you?"

She smiled again. "Don't be silly. You think 'the truth' about my 'wickedness' would have made any difference to Channie? That's *why* he loved me."

Tugger was taken aback, remembering suddenly Chanler's strange talk about pirates. Mattie pointed again at the painting above the green marble mantelpiece, Zanski's portrait of Mrs. Rawlings as Dido. Mrs. Vanderbilt's Ball, 1883. "That's why Channie loved Diana. That was the whole point, Tugger. You just didn't get it, honey." She leaned toward him, touched his cheek.

Tugger stepped back from her. "I don't think Mark got it either."

She nodded again. "Mark always had a terrible problem with impulse control. He had absolutely no patience. He wanted what he wanted and he could never wait."

Tugger smiled. "That's true. I think he's going to be just as impatient about getting his son back, too. I told him that the baby looked just like him, by the way. He got very upset. You remember that temper of his." Tugger left her standing there.

Tugger's wife had moved away from the group and was waiting for him to join her. "Mattie does look just like the painting," she said. "It's so weird seeing her after all the stories you told me, Tim. I can understand how she could use the Diana thing on poor Chanler. They could be the same woman."

He put his arm through his wife's as he led her back through the bar. "They were."

Tugger looked back at Mattie, who was still standing alone near the painting of Diana. He was convinced that he'd shaken her. Not much maybe, and maybe not for long, but it was something.